## MOONLIT ENCHANTMENT

As Tamara moved into the cool water, her long hair drifting in the current, the sound of hoofbeats sent alarm coursing through her. She whirled about and there on the bank, his legs straddling the sleek, muscled body of his stallion, sat Falcon, gazing steadily at her. She watched him slowly dismount.

Her arms opened invitingly to him. He carefully shed his clothing as Tamara continued to watch, a willing prisoner to her agonizingly erotic lover. Beneath the warm, swirling waters, her body burst with excitement and anticipation.

"Falcon," she whispered, "how did you know I was here?"

"I always know where you are," he whispered in reply . . .

# FALCON'S LADY

## CAROLINE BOURNE

**ZEBRA BOOKS**
**KENSINGTON PUBLISHING CORP.**

ZEBRA BOOKS

are published by

Kensington Publishing Corp.
475 Park Avenue South
New York, NY 10016

First printing: December 1987

Printed in the United States of America

*For my daughter, Kristen, with love.*

*Special thanks to a super lady,
my agent, Meg Ruley.*

Beloved . . .
So dear a heart it is
that beats within thy breast.

The bounty of the autumn;
Rebirth of spring—divine!
The warmth of summer's flowing brook
And winter's icy look when ire
reflects in amber pools
like wine.

O, beauty's flesh!
So silken, passion's fair.
Share Love's eternal nest with me
In our sweet Delaware.

*Part One*

# Chapter 1

London, December, 1752

A freezing mist veiled the gas lamps of London Square, creating soft circles of light scarcely visible from the third floor of Gray House. An unusual darkness had settled in with the late afternoon hour, impelling street beggars to hasten to dark alleys and niches along the Square. It was not a day for bawdy gatherings, though such was the habit of celebrating Londoners in these last few days of the Christmas season.

Earlier that afternoon, with the rain pelting London for the third straight day, Mason Gray had buried his son. Ryan, who'd jumped at every opportunity to embarrass his father, had instigated and been killed in a tavern brawl. But had it not been for Ryan's untimely death, Tamara Fleming might never have learned the shocking secret her guardian had kept for thirty years.

Mason and Tamara were sitting in the tea room of Gray House, quietly discussing Ryan's few virtues, when, without any warning at all, Mason confessed, "Ryan was not my only son, Tamara . . . I had an-

11

other son, before my marriage to Mary Rhee Portland."

Tamara was at first startled, then visibly shaken by the news. She had considered her guardian a staid, dignified old soldier who'd have taken a properly recorded marriage certificate to bed with him.

For a moment, Tamara said nothing, but merely sat beside him, her head lowered and her hands gently resting in the folds of her gown. She felt uneasy and rather awkward, wondering whether Mason expected a response or was merely unloading his mind. Was his purpose in bringing up another son his way of soothing sorrow and loss?

Mason himself seemed deep in thought, his fingers drawn to his clean-shaven chin. This latest tragedy had aged him ten years in the two days since it'd happened. Tamara continued to sit beside him, lifting her eyes occasionally to study him for a long, silent moment. His thin face was framed by wide, graying sideburns and sliced by a needle-thin nose, but he had sparkling blue eyes that were seldom dulled.

Momentarily, as it became evident Mason was withdrawing into a quiet world of his own, Tamara put her slim fingers gently over his arm. "Please, sir, tell me more. . . ."

"Hmmm?" Startled, Mason felt his muscles jump.

"About your other son—" A restrained curiosity was reflected in Tamara's soft brown eyes as she looked across the tea table at her aging guardian. "About . . . him." Mason needed her concern and support right now, and she would suppress her own deep feeling of loss to give it to him. Despite Ryan's frequent states of intoxication and belligerence, he had been kind to Tamara and had been a caring friend.

"Oh—oh, yes, my other son." Mason gazed at Tamara, still adorned in her black satin funeral dress, then glanced toward the wide entrance leading to the foyer. It was apparent that he did not want one of the servants to overhear.

Tamara quietly took his hand in hers. "If you do not wish to talk about him, sir. . . ."

"No . . . no, that is not it at all. . . ."

When he again hesitated, Tamara squeezed his hand. "Then do tell me about him, sir." Then she herself hesitated, ashamed to bring up a reprehensible deed thirty years in the past. Mason, however, saw that special look in her eyes and laughed gently.

"Ah, you believe it was an indiscretion, eh, child?"

Meeting the reflection of sad humor in Mason's tired blue eyes, Tamara nodded. She had always been open and honest in her feelings. In the move a thick, soft wave of golden hair spilled across her shoulder. "Wasn't it, sir?"

Mason gently patted her hand. "I will tell you the story . . . then you decide." Again he hesitated, as if a great emptiness had filled him. But he breathed deeply, then turned and took both of Tamara's hands and enveloped them fondly between his own. "My first son's mother was the most beautiful woman I had ever seen," he softly began. "She was a servant here at Gray House and I, a brash and arrogant young man, was brought to my knees by her first timid glance. I fell madly, head over heels in love with her. No one else in the world was important to me from that moment on."

Slowly, Mason's hands drew away from Tamara's. She then linked her fingers and let them rest in the thick folds of her gown. "What was her name, sir?"

"Fedora . . . Fedora Hartley."

Fedora . . . in the span of a few seconds, Tamara repeated it over and over in her mind. She could almost envision her. "What was she like?"

Mason smiled sadly. "A gentle girl, pure of heart and soul. I wanted to make her my wife at the very beginning of our relationship. I asked my father for permission, but he had chosen a proper mate for me, a woman of breeding suitable to the Gray name."

"Mary Rhee Portland?"

Mason hesitated for a moment. "Y—yes, child, Ryan's mother. But Mary was not my first wife."

"You . . . you married Fedora?" Tamara questioned, surprised.

"Indeed, I did!" Again, Mason gently laughed. "I went behind my father's back and married Fedora, and I kept it a secret for two years afterward. When she gave birth to my son, my joy was such that I confided in a good and, I thought, trustworthy friend." Mason's voice suddenly turned bitter. "Like a Judas goat, he related the news directly to my father. Confronted, unable to lie to my own father, and hoping beyond hope that he would understand, I admitted that Fedora was my wife. In my passion—oh, but I was a hothead in those days—I swore that no power on heaven and earth would part me from her, and that I could never love another woman as I loved Fedora, not even the mate he had chosen for me from our social circle." Mason looked guiltily at Tamara. "Forgive me, Tamara, I do not mean to speak ill of Ryan's mother. She was a kind woman and I had a world of respect for her."

Mason had always considered Tamara a wise and perceptive young woman. His judgment of her was again confirmed as she quietly answered, "I have been your ward, sir, for sixteen years now. I am not blind. Somehow, I could always see that your heart

14

was with another. But . . . you were a faithful husband to dear Mary," she continued endearingly. "When she died last year, she died knowing that you cared for her, and that is all that mattered." Tamara threw her shoulders deliberately back and favored Mason with a smile. "Please, do go on. I want to know all about them—Fedora and your son." She was held spellbound by the romance of yesterday as Mason continued to speak. Usually, Mason spoke in a tired, graveled tone, but his voice became youthful and vibrant as he spoke of Fedora.

"My father was very displeased with me, Tamara. He forbade me to see Fedora again and sent her away from Gray House, to the household of a friend in Northampton, where she was placed in the kitchens as a scullery maid. He immediately began proceedings to have our marriage annulled. Then he learned that I had made several trips to Northampton to visit Fedora and the child, that I was going to take them and run away to America, and . . . damn England. Thereafter, before I could employ my plan for happiness, he used his influence with the king to have me appointed a special emissary to Scotland. While I was gone, Fedora and my son were sent away . . . far away from our beloved England."

"Oh, Mason. . . ." A world of compassion reflected in Tamara's eyes as she gently took his hand. "Did you ever find them?"

"I tried with every resource that was mine. The years led me to your father, to whom Fedora had been indentured." When he saw the strange look Tamara gave him, he allowed himself to smile sadly. "Yes, child, indentured. The wife of a London Gray indentured to an American . . . along with the indigents of the London slums. Thieves and murderers of Newgate Prison! My good father" (Tamara took

15

note of his sarcasm) ''could have had the decency to pay her fare to America and at least given her enough money to make life easier for her.'' Mason once again hesitated, as if it were too painful to go on. ''When my search eventually led me to your father, I learned then that Fedora and the child had both died shortly after their arrival in Delaware.''

Telling the story drained Mason's strength. He sat for a moment, his moisture-sheened eyes turned toward the parted draperies, where rain slashed against the window pane. Then his gaze returned to Tamara. He started to give her a reassuring smile but her own chin had dropped and moisture sheened her soft brown eyes. ''Tamara?'' Mason's voice reflected concern. She sat motionless. The secrets of all the years rushed through Mason's head: not just his love for the servant girl, Fedora, but the terrible circumstances that had brought Tamara to England as his ward. Was this the time for total confession? To tell her that her own mother, crippled by the emotional strain of hard work in an untamed land, had been unable to care for her? Should she know all before her return to the Delaware wilderness where she had been born? Could he keep from her the terrible accident that had befallen her father, an accident that would, inevitably, result in his death? Could he deprive Jacob Fleming of these last few months with the daughter he had loved so deeply that he had sent her away to protect her from neglect by her own bedridden mother?

No . . . this was something he would leave to Jacob. Mason looked up. Tamara had cocked her head sweetly to the side and was looking at him with a strange mixture of concern and wonder. He saw in her soft doe-like eyes a wisdom far beyond her twenty-one years. She was a bright, happy young woman who had been a great joy to him these past sixteen years. He had watched her blossom into a flower of perfect grace. She was as beautiful as Fedora Hartley had been . . . with pale, windswept hair worn long and loose; brown, almond-shaped eyes; and a full, sensual mouth.

And now, loyalty to Jacob would part him from this beloved girl. He was honor-bound to send Tamara, who had been a daughter to him, to care for her father and spend these last months with him. Mason couldn't bear the thought of being trapped alone within the walls of his big old London house, surrounded by more wealth than he would ever be able to spend and with all the sad Gray ghosts lurking in the crevasses and shadows. He couldn't bear the thought of the emptiness he would feel in his heart when Tamara was departed from him.

"Mason?" That was Tamara, softly speaking. She had poured another cup of tea and was offering it to him. Hesitantly he took the cup, betraying to Tamara how violently his hands were shaking. "Please, sir, tell me more about your dear boy and Fedora. What did they look like? What did they like to do? Why have you kept them a secret for so long? Oh, I simply must know everything!"

Slowly Mason put down the cup and rose from the divan. He then put his hand out to Tamara. "Come, girl, I will show you my secret room. Martha! Martha!" he called to the parlor maid. "Will you bring a lamp?"

Silence. A few moments passed before the rather droll Martha appeared and handed Mason the lamp. Tamara walked slowly beside her guardian, up the wide, carpeted stairway, up three flights until presently they stood outside a large mahogany door that had long been a source of speculation on Tamara's part. She could hardly restrain her excitement as Mason fumbled with his keys—keys she had seen him use to enter and leave this room many times, always locking the door securely behind him.

"No one else has been in this room for many years, Tamara," he said as he turned the key in the lock. "Not even Ryan's mother."

The soft glow of the lamp dimly revealed to Tamara what had been hidden all these years. Presently, as the dark room came into focus, Tamara knew why he had made this his refuge—his sanctuary. Tears moistened her eyes as the glow of the lamp illuminated a haunting portrait of Mason and a lovely young woman holding a small, dark-haired boy.

Tamara was enraptured. "Oh, Mason." And then came revelation. Tamara had once heard in their social circle that Mason was an accomplished artist. She knew that the love evident in every angle of Fedora Hartley's features could only have been painted by one man: her own guardian. After a few spellbinding moments, Tamara looked around. Off in a corner, she saw the shadows of a dozen easels, a small table, and jars of paint and brushes in a wooden tray. Tamara flicked away the tears that touched her cheeks, then studied the portrait of a seated Fedora Hartley, her golden hair not as thick and wavy as her own, and her smiling eyes as green as springtime meadows. She seemed a proud, gentle woman. Tamara could easily see how she had won Mason's heart, for undying love was painted into every stroke of the brush. Then her eyes moved slowly to the robust child who appeared about a year old in the portrait.

"How old would he be now?" Tamara asked softly.

"The boy? Ummm . . . thirty, no, thirty-one, I believe."

"What was his name?"

"I had planned to have him christened Marcus Weatherford Gray. But Fedora, because of my father's opposition to our marriage, called him by another name. Marcus was my grandfather's name."

"Oh, Mason, he looks so like you!"

Mason chuckled softly and in his usual way, roughly patted Tamara's hand. "Aye, I was quite a handsome rogue in my younger day. Yes, dear girl—" Suddenly, Mason's voice trailed off into a whisper.

"What is wrong, Mason?" Rather than answer, Mason pointed out still another portrait, complete in every respect except for the face, a blank, oval void that was odd and frightening to Tamara. She felt her nerves jump as Mason unexpectedly dropped his hand to her shoulder.

"It is my son," he said after a moment. "Fedora's son. For many years I refused to believe he was dead. I began this portrait when he would have been about eighteen. I had foolishly hoped that one day I would be able to finish it." Mason's voice choked with emotion and he firmly pressed his fingers to his eyes.

Tamara took his hand and gave it a light, affectionate pat. "Come, Mason, walk to the portico and watch the rain with me."

Mason, however, did not budge. His trembling fingers rose and gently touched the painted features of his beloved Fedora. "This portrait, Tamara . . . it reminds me constantly of my darling wife and son . . . and awakens so many wonderful memories. I come here just to see the portrait and to remember." Suddenly, Mason's hand, which had dropped to a small, dusty table, closed over a small gold medallion on a chain. He picked it up, then handed it to Ta-

19

mara. "Here, child . . . I want you to have this. The last person to wear it was my beloved Fedora."

"Oh, Mason, I couldn't take it from you."

"I want you to have it, Tamara," he said firmly. "It is the most precious thing I own. Should something happen to me while you are gone, should my nephew plunder Gray House . . . I fear the contents of this room would end up on a pyre. . . ."

"Nothing will happen, Mason. When I return, you will be here awaiting me." Tamara gently eased the delicate chain over her head and adjusted it at her neckline. "I will wear this forever, Mason, and always be reminded of you."

Mason now allowed himself to be coaxed from his sanctuary. Before the door was closed and securely locked, Tamara gave the portraits a last lingering look. Moments later, she and Mason stood on the portico. With his arms crossed, Mason stared absently into the light drizzle of rain that covered the rooftops of London. Tamara noticed his age, the hair turned to silver-gray, the loose, wrinkled skin that made Mason seem older than his fifty-seven years. Dark, swollen pouches sagged beneath his blue eyes. For a moment, the silence, their shared thoughts, and the gentle rain held them prisoner. Neither spoke, but each enjoyed the comfort of the other. Then, gently, Tamara's arm slipped around Mason's waist and her head rested against his shoulder.

Tamara was troubled. She had no memories of her true father and was reluctant to leave the life she shared with Mason. She had no objection to a visit, if that was what Mason wanted, but she was frightened. It had, after all, been sixteen years, and she felt as if she were being sent to the household of a stranger. Mason was the only father she had ever truly known. He had never told her, and she had never asked, why her own father had sent her away at such a tender age. Tamara knew only that she had been happy in England with Mason as her guardian, and she did not want to leave. This was her home, just as surely as if she'd been born here, to Mason and Mary Gray. As Tamara stood there, feeling the comfort and warmth of Mason's arm around her shoulders, tears traced a gentle path down her smooth ivory cheeks.

# Chapter 2

*Asher Arms Estate, Delaware, seven months later*

An early morning breeze brushed the small branches of an oak tree gently against the window pane. Minutes before, the sun had risen on the far timberline, and soon activity would stir another day into life at Asher Arms. Then scrubboards would groan beneath the raw hands of the washerwomen, servants' children would play between rows of half-grown corn, and the brisk voices of young stablemen would call the estate mares to their feeding troughs.

The servant girl, Glynnie, had risen earlier than usual and now sat before her boudoir mirror with her pert chin resting lazily on linked fingers. She was quite pleased with herself this morning. Just last evening, Master Fleming had assured her that he cared for her as a daughter, and she needed only to make her wishes known to him to have them granted. She could not deny that he'd been openly attentive to her these past few months.

But her own mother had not been attentive to her at all this morning. She was still waiting to have her hair brushed and her bath drawn. Glynnie was quite annoyed.

Glynnie's pale complexion was heightened by the facial powder she absently dabbed on in her mother's absence. She had a rather sharp chin, which her mother usually touched a little darkened powder to—a gentle disguise for a small flaw. She smiled to herself in the mirror, then smoothed her long auburn hair up from her neckline, trying to decide if she should wear it loose or pulled back in ivory combs.

Momentarily Bridie McFarland's tall, thin form appeared at the open doorway. She entered and quickly swept her hand over the bed rail. "Ye haven't dusted the bedchamber this morning, girl. The master demands cleanliness."

"The master, poof!" Glynnie replied with feigned indignation, picking up a brass-and-ivory hairbrush and pulling quickly through her hair, "The master," she said with slow deliberation, "is tied either to his wheelchair or to his bed and will not see the dust in my chamber."

Bridie was taken aback by Glynnie's cold statement. "The master has been kind to you, girl. 'Twas you to whom he gave his attentions after his wife passed away, poor thing. I'd be more respectful, were I you."

Glynnie had been pleased with the master's attention to her of late. Still, she could not let this opportunity pass to argue with her mother. "Yes! The week after she died, he ordered Broggard to whip me! And you and Papa allowed it!"

"You spat on his wife's grave, you did, and trampled the head cross!"

Glynnie was not in a mood to banter insults back and forth. All she cared about at the moment was having her hair brushed and her bath drawn. It was a lovely day and she wanted to have time to enjoy it. Still, she could not allow her mother to have the last word. "Well, I hated her!" she continued crossly. "She made life miserable—for all of us! I defiled her grave then, and I've spat on it every day since she died! Master Fleming has just never again caught me doing it! Besides . . . Master Fleming has been kind to me ever since." Glynnie raised her hand, then flexed her little finger before the mirror. "I have him wrapped around my little finger. Now . . . here is the brush," Glynnie continued. "And be sure to pick up the fine hairs against my neckline so that they'll not get wet in the bath you will draw for me."

Bridie absently took the brush, wishing Glynnie had not brought up the punishment she had received. She was pained by the thought of it. In her mind, she could still hear her whimpering from the wood shed, still feel the raised, raw welts beneath her fingers as she'd applied a salve. Glynnie had been fourteen. . . . "Aye, girl, he's pampered and spoiled you like you were his own," she replied after a moment.

"But will he pamper and spoil me," Glynnie countered, the corners of her full mouth turning down into a pout, "when that English tart arrives? I doubt it!"

"That tart," Bridie answered chastisingly, "is the master's daughter. And you'd best be remembering that your mum's a servant here . . . as you are."

"Oh . . . why must you constantly remind me, Mother? You can be evil and mean at times!" Glynnie was tired of her mother's meek ways.

She met her pale reflection in the mirror. She wished she'd been born a princess rather than a servant. She hated her mother for reminding her that she wasn't, and for breeding her into this world of servitude.

Presently, Glynnie's eyes lifted. "Forgive me, Mother. I'm afraid I'm a bit of a tart today. Now will you please do my hair?" But her mother had put the brush aside and was absently dusting the bedchamber. If she'd heard anything Glynnie had said, she did not betray it. "My hair, Mother!" Bridie returned, picked up the brush, and was just about to begin brushing her daughter's hair when Glynnie asked, "Has Falcon returned yet?"

The mention of Falcon brought life to Bridie McFarland. "I'd be forgetting him!" she snapped. "Halfbreed, he is, with a heart black as the devil's own. Not to be trusted further than you could spit! And you'd best be remembering he's a servant to Jacob Fleming, the same as you are!" Surprised by a second scolding in so many minutes, Glynnie pressed her mouth into a thin, angry line, an expression which caught Bridie's attention. "Yes, child, I heard you moments ago, disrespecting your old mum. Reminders! Reminders is what you need! Here. . . ." Bridie handed Glynnie the brush. "Do your own hair, child, and act like the servant that you are!"

Glynnie was furious but resolute in maintaining her poise. She willed a strange calmness to come over her, then released a small cough to catch her mother's attention. "I was thinking . . ." Glynnie's gaze drifted from her mother's thin, pinched features to her own reflection in the mirror, "that it'd be to my advantage to be the wife of Master Fleming. . . ." Having captured her mother's full attention, and failing to notice how her features suddenly paled, Glynnie raised an impertinent eyebrow, ". . . and the mistress of Falcon. I'd have the best of both worlds, don't you think?"

Bridie's Scottish temper could scarcely be contained. Yet she knew that an outburst was what her daughter wanted from her—a punishment for saying the things that Glynnie did not want to hear. There were times when Bridie was sure Glynnie looked for ways to upset her. Thus Bridie became thoughtful for a moment, then responded, "Mayhaps you're right, girl. Such a pretty wife for the master. Ye'll be takin' money off a husband, an' liftin' the fancy skirts it bought to a paramour. There's names for girls like you propose to be." Bridie gathered up her broom and dust pan and moved slowly toward the door.

Glynnie gasped in surprise, and her long, slim fingers closed tightly over her vanity brush.

The door had scarcely closed when the brush slammed against it.


Falcon had been hunting along the shores of Cape Henlopen for two days now. He fell to one knee on the grassy knoll at the mouth of Delaware Bay and absently watched the vague outline of a full-masted ship move upon the far horizon of the Atlantic Ocean. His bare hands gripped the smooth bore of a flintlock musket that had earlier brought down pheasants; these were now held to his wide leather belt by bits of ragged twine. He had been away from Asher Arms for three days but had only the few pheasants to show for his labors. His employer, Jacob Fleming, would expect him to bring back many more. Too bad! he thought, shrugging. He had simply relished the time hunting alone and making camp in the woods beneath a cool midnight sky. Lately, the drudgeries and obligations of Asher Arms had grated on his nerves.

Falcon breathed deeply of the clean ocean air. Moments spent watching a ship disappear over the horizon would not, in Jacob Fleming's mind, be considered a useful endeavor. With the ocean wind gently tossing his dark hair, Falcon rose, then arched his back to relieve the tension and stiffness he felt there.

Falcon had spent last night in the woods, roasted one of the pheasants over a slow-burning fire; then, after a good night's sleep, he'd risen this morning to begin his journey afresh. He was well rested and anxious to return to the estate on the Indian River, his home for the past three years. He wondered if any news had been received of Jacob Fleming's daughter.

By twilight he stood on the far rise of the hill overlooking Asher Arms. Resting his arm lazily across the butt of his musket, Falcon studied the valley, the house, and the soft glow of windows lit in anticipation of the approaching darkness. The setting sun splashed the forest in rays of crimson and gold, and a warm breeze blew down from the woodline. The estate house, set in a large grove of pines, dominated the scene. A long wide porch ran the length of the two-story structure built of cedar that had long ago faded to a light, weathered gray.

Drawing the evening air deeply into his lungs, he threw the musket across his shoulder and descended along a narrow path into the valley.

As Falcon entered the estate between two outlying buildings, he heard the dull, rhythmic thud of an ax breaking the silence. Nodding politely to a serving woman, Falcon rounded the estate house. Instantly he caught sight of old Saul, his thin form bare to the waist as he chopped wood on the block. Falcon deliberately and loudly shuffled his boot, so that the ax-wielding Saul would not be startled by his approach.

"Saul."

The ax moved slowly to the ground. Saul stood with his feet slightly apart and his hands resting lightly on the ax handle. He tried not to let Falcon see his exhaustion. He was not one to admit that he was getting old. "Falcon—enjoy your days hunting?"

"Hunting!" Falcon laughed as he removed the pheasants and held them out for Saul to see. "Four damned birds! Hardly a hunting excursion worth mentioning!"

"You had time alone . . . that is worth the trip." Saul again raised the ax, but before he could continue, Falcon took it from him.

"If you wouldn't mind taking the birds in to Bridie, I'll finish this." Saul held back a mild protest. His years of working with Falcon had taught him not to argue. Thus he pulled on his shirt and slung the pheasants across his shoulder.

Falcon watched until saul was out of sight. Then he heard the rustle of skirts and saw the petite form of Glynnie McFarland half-hidden in the darkness. Smiling to himself, he noted that the aroma of her perfume alone would have betrayed her presence. He removed his shirt, turned his back to the place where she stood, and began chopping wood. He had become so accustomed to her pursuits that they no longer bothered him. She was a child, bored with life at Asher Arms, finding excitement in her attentions to him and hoping for them in return.

Glynnie knew that he had seen her and was content to watch him from this distance, the sweat of his hard, sinewy muscles glistening in the soft glow of the moonlight. He was a handsome man, tall, broad-shouldered, and bronzed by the sun, his blue eyes a startling contrast to his dark flesh, his clean

28

hair cut in ebony waves that did not quite touch the collar of his shirt . . . when he happened to be wearing one.

His was a mixed past. Glynnie could imagine him in a drawing room, in velvet coattails and silk ruffles, drinking heady liqueurs and charming a lovely lady out of her skirts. Yet he was rugged too, and skilled in the ways of the woods. He often visited the Lenape Indians, whose village was nearby and where, she had recently learned, his mother lived. And each night, after his day's duties were completed, he journeyed into the hills and did not return until the first light of dawn.

"Come on out of the bushes, Glynnie." Falcon's deep, resonant voice startled her. Glynnie stepped out of the shadows and, with her fingers linked together, slowly approached him.

She stood beside him for a moment, her petite form dwarfed by his size. Then before he could pull on his shirt, the bold Glynnie threw herself against him and her arms clasped him around his glistening waist.

"Oh, Falcon, why do you tease me so? Why do you let me watch you and want you? Don't you care at all for me? Am I not pretty?"

Falcon studied her for a moment, appraising her round face, her wide hazel eyes, and her lovely auburn hair, like the morning dawn upon a pre-winter horizon. She was wearing a low-cut blouse and her full breasts were scarcely hidden beneath the scant fabric. Boldly his eyes dropped and held the smooth roundness of her. Then he smiled and his strong hands slipped to her tiny waist.

"Glynnie, Glynnie—" he said softly, lifting his eyes, "yes, I think you are very pretty, but you are

29

like a little sister . . . not a lover.'' He stepped away, retrieved his shirt, and then turned back to her.

Instantly, Glynnie was back in his arms. "I would die for you, Falcon. I would . . . would—"

When she hesitated to continue, the humored Falcon coaxed, "Go on—you would what?"

"There is nothing I would not give you, Falcon. I would give you what no man has ever had before. No man!"

Falcon lifted his fingers. Thinking that they would slip beneath her chin and lift her waiting lips to his, Glynnie closed her eyes. But Falcon merely fastened the buttons of his shirt, and when he had finished, began stacking wood to be taken into the house.

"Oof!" Glynnie's hands balled into fists, and when they gently hit his back, he spun around, dropping the wood, and pulled her to him in a crushing embrace.

"Is this what you want, Glynnie?" he asked roughly. His blue eyes were ever so close to her own. "To be taken and ravaged by a man who does not love you the way you want to be loved? Do you not hold anything sacred? Damn. . . ." Tenderly, he put her away from him. "Be glad, Glynnie, that you have thrown yourself at a man who understands your childish ways. One day . . . one day, you will be hurt." Falcon began restacking the wood.

"You tease me, Falcon. You wait . . . you just wait. . . ." She was now talking to his retreating back. "One day, Falcon, you will hunger for me!"

But Falcon merely drifted off in the wake of his own gentle laughter. Hunger for her, indeed!


Falcon raised his eyes to the night sky and the quarter moon scarcely visible through the timber line.

It was a warm, humid night and far across the horizon he heard the low, haunting trill of a night bird and the mournful cry of a she-wolf calling her cubs.

Falcon felt a kinship with the Delaware wilderness. His spirit was one with the peace and serenity that slowly enveloped him and drew him into its captivating mystery. Cresting the hill, he stood for a moment and looked down on the dark shadow of Asher Arms. The soft, glowing lights of the windows flickered like an iridescent blur. Falcon pulled his buckskin boots up to his knees, unfastened the top buttons of his shirt, and disappeared over the hill. When no sounds could be heard except those of the forest, he set his musket against a fallen log in a small clearing. He then unrolled his woolen blanket and lay down beneath a million bright stars against a background of purple velvet.

He had scarcely closed his eyes when a twig snapped across the clearing and the moonlight betrayed the glint of a musket. Quickly Falcon was on his knees with his own musket pointed menacingly across the clearing.

But a low growl of laughter drifted toward him— a familiar sound that compelled him to lower his weapon. His Lenni Lenape blood brother, Flaming Bow, stepped into the clearing. He approached Falcon, then crossed his arms and assumed an arrogant stand, with his feet slightly apart.

"What the hell do you want?" Falcon asked, with more affection than ire.

"Your mother has many times mentioned your name," Flaming Bow explained, dropping to his knees. "You leave yourself vulnerable to your enemy, sleeping beneath the stars like this."

"I leave myself vulnerable," Falcon softly amended, fighting the hint of a smile, "to idiots like you. I could bloody well have blown a hole through your skull.'' Falcon returned the musket to its prone position against his leg. "What are you doing so far from the village?''

"Hunting. Kishke wishes that a deer be killed, to prepare for the feast in honor of your mother.'' Flaming Bow uttered a low laugh.

"You are unhappy that my mother has become Kishke's second wife, aren't you, Flaming Bow?'' When he did not answer, Falcon continued, "She is a good woman. You should be as proud as I am to call her Mother.''

Flaming Bow settled back against a fallen tree, and his eyes became black and unyielding. His dark hair was long and loose down his back, with sections on the sides plaited with lengths of rawhide; it was a custom of the men of his tribe. "Perhaps. . . .'' His gaze pierced the veil of darkness and fell on Falcon's clean-shaven features. "And to your mother, shall I take word of your good health?''

"Tell her that I am well. Tell her . . .'' Falcon had been about to say that he loved her, but this was a sentiment a brave would not pass on to a woman. "Tell her that I will see her soon,'' Falcon offered.

"Very well.'' Then Flaming Bow's hand went out, and Falcon took it in a hard grip, in the Indian fashion. "Does the white man know who you are?''

Falcon's eyes narrowed. He was not accustomed to lying to Flaming Bow and found himself, again, disguising an answer in a half-truth. "He knows that I am Falcon, son of the great chief, Kishke.''

"But you are not the son of Kishke,'' Flaming Bow reminded him. "I am.''

"Kishke accepts me as his son. Therefore I am his son, no less than you.''

Flaming Bow broke his hold on Falcon's arm, then

rested both hands on his bent knees. "I must depart now."

Flaming Bow was not one for amenities. He rose slowly to his feet, adjusted the strap of his musket across his shoulder, and disappeared into the dark timber line as silently as he had arrived. Soon, content beneath the midnight sky, Falcon drifted off into a pleasant sleep.

He rose at dawn and bathed in a clear stream. The water was soothing and Falcon found that he did not want to leave the forest. Yet duty at Asher Arms called to him, duty borne of the expected arrival of Jacob Fleming's daughter from England. Falcon had just started to climb out of the stream when the plod of unshod horses sounded from the wood line. Waist-deep in water, he looked up and saw Kishke and his youngest daughter mounted on Indian ponies. Instinctively, Falcon walked further into the water to cover himself.

"My son," Kishke's deep voice radiated serious intentions. The sun was rising behind the mounted forms of the chief and his daughter and the rays blinded Falcon. "Come, ride to the trading post with us."

Falcon crossed his arms on his bare chest. He felt awkward. "You are going in the wrong direction, Kishke."

The old Indian smiled broadly. "I have been to visit the white man . . . Fleming. These old eyes still know which direction is east. Falcon—will you ride with your father?"

"I cannot, Kishke. I must return to the service of Asher Arms. I have much work to do."

"Then journey part of the way with us. We shall talk."

"Ummm . . . the sun is up. I must return to Asher Arms, Kishke."

Only now, watching Falcon slowly sink into the rushing stream, did Kishke understand Falcon's reluctance. "My daughter knows that a man's body is different from a woman's. She will show no shame at your nakedness."

"That may well be," Falcon replied, feeling a blush rise in his bronze cheeks. "And I certainly do not wish to witness her lack of shame. I will visit you soon, Kishke."

Understandingly, the chief nudged his horse in the side and he and his daughter disappeared through the sunlit forest.


Saul was dusting shelves in the library when Falcon entered the house. Falcon started to speak, but catching sight of Jacob Fleming's wheelchair in the shadows, and the open book resting in his lap, he kept his silence. Broggard, Fleming's manservant, stood beside Jacob. Falcon nodded to Saul, then started to leave, but Jacob Fleming's voice echoed softly in the darkened room.

"Falcon, is that you?"

Falcon stood a few feet away. "Yes."

Jacob Fleming's thin, frail hand waved impatiently at Falcon. "Come . . . come closer." When Falcon approached, Jacob lightly ordered, "Sit a moment," but did not look up from the book he was reading. All around them, servants rushed to and fro, dusting, cleaning floors and carpets and windows, making ready for the arrival of Jacob's daughter. Through the parted draperies, Falcon saw the stableman washing down and grooming the horses, and his stableboys sweeping out the stalls. He hadn't seen so

34

much activity at Asher Arms since a pipe-smoking scullery servant had set fire to the outhouse two years ago. When Falcon said nothing, Jacob Fleming turned his gaze toward him, then favored him with a tight smile. "You slept in the woods last night, did you?"

"I did," Falcon replied, "as I do every night."

"Respectable quarters have been assigned here," Jacob reminded him. "Why do you not use them?"

"You've asked me this question every week for the past three years, Fleming." Falcon did not like explaining his actions and was irritated to find himself doing so yet again. "As I have said, I am more comfortable in the forest. There," he continued in a tightly controlled voice, "I do not have to worry about being ambushed." Falcon rose, then approached the door. "When you hired me on, Fleming, it was agreed that the nights were mine. I do my day's work, as far as I know, to your satisfaction." Having said his peace, he started to leave.

"Falcon. . . ." Only when Falcon met his steady gaze, did Jacob continue, "Will you ever forgive me?"

Falcon frowned. "There is nothing to forgive, Fleming."

"Oh, but there is . . . there is," Jacob mumbled. Then he straightened his stooping shoulders and met Falcon's narrowed gaze. "Robert Beckland has arrived from the Bain estate in Virginia with seventeen thoroughbred horses. I want you to take charge and fatten them up for the November auction. I want manageable, well-fed animals, broken to the saddle. But first, pick the best of the lot as a gift for my daughter."

"Of course . . . I am at your service."

# Chapter 3

The ride along waterlogged, deeply rutted roads had taken its toll on Tamara's nerves, and on her body. Because of the previous evening's storm, which had washed out a bridge, the public coach had taken a diversion, adding half a day to the trip. A man with grease-slicked hair furtively eyed Tamara from across the darkened coach. Tamara averted her glance, first to the profile of the young, well-dressed man sitting beside her, then to the silent woman across from her.

Tamara twisted her handkerchief, her mind in chaos. Would her father know her after all these years? What kind of man was he? Would she be happy at Asher Arms, her birthplace? Her departure from Mason and Gray House had been very emotional for them both. She wanted to be happy, to accept these unacceptable circumstances, yet she could not help thinking of her last day in England, of the sadness she had felt. Mason had stood on the docks long after all the other well-wishers had departed. As the ship had pulled away from the dock she had watched him slowly become a tiny speck against the London harbor.

Tamara sighed deeply, then watched the green of the Delaware countryside slowly pass by. Occasionally, a cabin could be seen sitting among the trees or on the high rise of a hill. This morning, she had enjoyed watching a great herd of deer move gracefully through the forest. It reminded her of the day she'd seen the ponies running wild in Sherwood Forest. She suspected she would rather be there this very moment.

Twilight ended another long, weary day of traveling, and the young man and woman departed the coach for private destinations. Tamara felt sure that every bone in her body had been displaced by the jarring journey. She was stiff and sore and scarcely able to maintain a look of dignity. Bored and exhausted, she lowered her eyes to conceal sudden tears of frustration beneath the rim of her pale-blue bonnet. Her ivory-and-blue traveling gown was wrinkled and soiled by the dust of two days' travel, and the tightness of her bodice made her stomach churn sickeningly.

The odor of the unwashed body across from her made it impossible to breathe, much less catch a moment's sleep. Tamara tucked her hands beneath her light cape and watched the long shadows of the countryside slowly passing by. How much further, she wondered. How much longer must I bear this punishment? By sheer force of will, she was able to close her eyes and enjoy light moments of sleep until the sun once again appeared on the horizon.

When she awakened it was with a start, and a sensation of falling. She released a small cry, then put her hand to her head to catch her falling bonnet. In the darkness, the coach had gone off the road and one of the wheels had slipped into a small ravine. The coach was teetering dangerously on the edge, threatening to fall on its side. The driver was hurriedly unfastening the harnesses of the team, which was slowly slipping into the ravine.

Alarmed, Tamara moved toward the door. But she was pushed back into her seat by the greasy passenger, who was intent on leaving the coach first. Tamara had just offered her hand to the driver and was feeling for the step, when the coach slid into the ravine, pulling her hand violently from him. Baggage and seat cushions fell on her as she was thrown against the coach as it came to rest in the mud.

Tamara looked upward, toward the coach door that had been ripped from its hinges in the fall. She tried to shift the heavy baggage from her, but her arms were pinned down. Then she heard the thunder of horse's hooves on the muddy roadway and the unfamiliar voice of another man. She felt a movement, as if someone jumped up to the coach, and presently, an unfamiliar face looked in. A strong, hard arm moved down into the coach and baggage was being lifted from her.

When she was able to move her head, she looked up and discerned a masculine face scarcely visible in the early morning darkness. When she hesitated to take the hand he offered to her, his iron-hard arm slipped gently to her back and pulled her upward, toward the open coach door.

Although she felt bruised and muddy and heavy, Falcon lifted her as if she were weightless. Tamara met blue eyes that were distinctly unfriendly, and she was suddenly anxious to be free of this man's grip. Scarcely had her feet touched the muddy roadway when he curtly said, "I assume you're Miss Tamara Fleming?"

Her flushed features were ever so close to his own and her senses reeled at the contempt in his tone.

"I—I am," she stammered nervously. Thinking of the chaos her arrival was causing at Asher Arms, he released her quite suddenly, and she nearly lost her footing on the slippery roadway. "Ohhh!" she protested vehemently.

"Sorry," he apologized. "I didn't mean to be so brutish."

Shocked, Tamara stood there, flicking mud from the shoulder of her jacket. The man had turned his back to her and was moving toward the timber line, where branches suitable to construct a lever had been felled by the storm. "Barbarian," she mumbled to herself, crossing her arms. But he was, she noticed, terribly handsome. Despite her assessment of him as a bully, Tamara watched her rescuer's every move . . . his muscles hard and straining as he freed suitable tree limbs, his startling blue eyes narrowed, like the line of his angrily pressed mouth. He had rugged, sun-bronzed features and raven-black hair that appeared to have been recently trimmed. His tight buckskin pants were tucked into leather boots, and his white shirt was gathered at the waistline by a fringed leather belt. There was a ruggedness about him that Tamara found appealing, and a masculinity that very nearly frightened her. She was accustomed to thin, proper Englishmen with clean, manicured hands. What would it be like to be touched by this rough-acting, handsome American?

Despite the circumstances that had put her out on the road, Tamara was glad to be free of the stuffy, odorous coach. Ignoring the men, as they were pretending to ignore her, she retied her bonnet, then smoothed down the disheveled skirts of her gown. Off in a small meadow, through a grove of trees where a small cabin stood, she saw a clearing and a felled tree that looked perfect for a short, comfortable rest. Thus, she left the muddy roadway, eased between the rails of a ragged fence, and started across the meadow.

Then everything happened at once. She heard a loud angry bellow, then a large black bull broke from the darkened timber line, its front hoof angrily pawing at the ground. Tamara froze in her tracks. As the beast thundered toward her, a painted horse cleared the fence and she was immediately swept up into powerful naked arms. The fence was barely cleared again before the bull crashed into it.

In complete shock, Tamara looked up at the dark, tanned body of an Indian, glistening in the early morning light, who held her across his saddle like a captured prize. The danger of the bull was forgotten in the face of this new peril, and she began flaying him with her wrists and crying in outrage. But Flaming Bow merely tightened his hold and trotted the stallion up to the group of men where he announced dryly, "I have rescued this foolish squaw. I claim her as my woman."

"No, you don't, you . . . you savage! You barbarian!" Tamara cried, continuing to flay with her fists. "Let me down! Let me down, do you hear?"

Her anger amused Flaming Bow, whose hand traveled the length of her arm, squeezing it, then her small, slim waist. Then he flipped Tamara over and discarded her into the waiting arms of his blood brother, Falcon. "You may have this squaw. She is too small to do a good day's work."

Tamara struggled against Falcon, fighting to free herself from him. When her feet eventually touched the ground, she thrashed out at him with her fists. "You're a brute and a lout!" she gasped, beating at his powerful chest with her fists, "You're all brutes! This country is brutish, and—and—"

Falcon had never seen such rage in so pretty a face. Tamara's cheeks were crimson and her tear-sheened eyes black with anger. She was gulping short, pained breaths and her traveling jacket had come unfastened, exposing her lace bodice and a womanly cleavage that was moments ago well-hidden. Falcon realized what a beauty she was . . . with full, firm breasts and a tiny waist pinched tight by the bodice of her gown, a slim ankle exposed beneath her torn skirt, and wheat-colored hair now free of its pins and falling in disheveled, silken waves down the length of her back. He had never seen such beauty: exquisite oval features, a straight, classic nose, full, moist lips, and almond-shaped brown eyes that were now turned on him, assessing him who assessed her so boldly.

"And what are you looking at, sir?" she demanded breathlessly. Then she could not continue. The accumulated terrors of the long journey rushed at her like a sudden storm, and tears flooded her eyes.

Falcon and the other men fell silent. Realizing the extent of her fright, he started to put his arm around her shoulder for comfort. But she pushed it away, then turned so that he could not witness her tears.

Then Falcon remembered who she was—Jacob Fleming's daughter. "Driver . . . I've been sent by Miss Fleming's father to fetch her. Which of these bags are hers?" The driver looked around, then slowly pointed out two blue canvas bags and a small brown trunk. "Flaming Bow, bring the other horse for Miss Fleming."

Tamara's eyes widened in surprise. "Wh—what are you doing? I am not going with you!"

Before Falcon could answer, the driver said, "You'd better, Miss Fleming. This is as far as we go.

Travelers to Asher Arms must journey a day's distance through the woods yonder."

"Haven't you brought a carriage?" Tamara inquired of Falcon.

"Do you see one?" Before she could answer, he continued with haste, "A good riding horse is more practical in this country, Miss Fleming. We'll make better time."

"But my bags—my trunk."

Falcon did not turn his eyes from her as he spoke to Flaming Bow, "Bring the pack horse for Miss Fleming's things." When he saw how worried she looked, he added with mild sarcasm, "Don't worry. I have brought a gentle horse for you." Falcon retrieved his hat from his saddle horn and now flipped it back from his forehead.

"I am an experienced rider!" she countered indignantly, annoyed by his merciless and persistent degradations. "I rode frequently in the park in London!"

"The park!" Falcon laughed. "Sure . . . an experienced rider! Only dandies ride in London parks!" A humorous twinkle lit his eyes as he pointed toward the timber line. "Well, that is untamed brush, dear lady, not some fancy English lane, and you'd best be prepared to use that pretty gloved hand to protect your face from the brambles."

As their horses disappeared into the shadows and sight of the coach was finally lost, Tamara suddenly felt cut off from the civilized world. The sorrel mare swayed lazily beneath her, and one of her canvas bags, which the Indian had tied to the back of her saddle, was pressing painfully against the small of her back. All she could see of the man, Falcon, was his broad back and the black hair that rested neatly on the collar of his shirt. The Indian was behind her, the movements of his own powerful stallion keeping the aging mare moving ahead of him.

Occasionally, the men would talk to each other across the top of her head. Tamara kept her face low and hidden beneath the rim of her bonnet. She felt emotionally undone and simply unable to suppress the tears that flowed from her eyes. Oh, why, why, Mason, did you have to send me here? Why am I not home with you, at Gray House where I belong?

But all her wishes would not change the fact that she rode in a strange land between two strange men who seemed intent on ignoring her. Thus, she made up her mind to accept the situation. There was little else to be done. They rode on in silence, through cool, shady dales and over sunlit green hills, hour after hour until the sun high in the sky indicated the noon hour had passed. Feeling the ache of hunger in her stomach, Tamara chose to remind the men of her presence.

"Will we not partake of a meal soon?" she asked.

"It's early," Falcon replied. "Perhaps later."

Tamara pulled her horse to a halt, causing Flaming Bow, too, to halt. Falcon stopped, then turned his horse so that he could face her. "Later simply will not do, sir!" she retorted. "I am hungry now."

"We are all hungry, Miss Fleming. But a man is obedient to the wilderness, not to his stomach. We will eat later."

Clumsily, pulling her gown free of the saddle horn, Tamara dismounted her horse. "I am not a man," she reminded him. "I am a woman. I am obedient to my stomach, not to the wilderness. And I will partake of lunch—this very minute—even if I must shoot it myself."

43

"The white woman is undisciplined, and not accustomed to our ways," Flaming Bow said. "Perhaps we should stop for a while."

"Very well . . . we'll stop long enough to eat. But not here." Falcon's eyes blazed with anger. It was quite evident that Tamara Fleming had been spoiled by her wealthy English guardian and was intent on having her own way, even here in the wilderness. "There's a clearing over there by a stream. We'll rest there for a while. Get back on your horse, Miss Fleming."

"I prefer to walk."

Falcon was in no mood for this. Wanting only to avoid an argument, he approached and took the reins of her horse, pulling it ahead so that she had to step out of its way. "We will be just over that hill, Miss Fleming." Flaming Bow pulled up beside Falcon and rode with him along the trail.

Tamara found it refreshing to be on foot rather than in the heavy American saddle. The woods were fragrant with honeysuckle and cedar, and a thick carpet of damp leaves was soft beneath her feet. She walked slowly, linking her fingers behind her, lifting her face to the sunlight filtering through the thick foliage of trees. By the time she reached the clearing where the men relaxed against the trunk of an ancient oak, she had removed both her bonnet and the pins from her hair. Her hair was like golden clouds upon her shoulders.

She approached, smiling, then tossed her bonnet off to the side against a large boulder. "I had such a pleasant walk, gentlemen," she said, dropping to the ground beside them. "What are we having for lunch?"

Silently, Falcon cut a piece of bread from the loaf Bridie had baked the morning before and handed it to her, along with a thick slice of beef. "Eat quickly," he said. "We've got a good piece left to travel."

"Oh. . . ." Tamara sighed deeply, then shrugged her shoulders. "Ladies don't eat quickly." Her eyes made a slow, fluid sweep of the clearing and the stream that babbled over smooth white rocks. She was determined to make these men suffer for having been so brutal to her that morning. "Before we move on, I think I'll bathe in that deep spot—" her hand lifted and a long, slim finger pointed beneath a tall bluff, "over there." Neither man spoke as Tamara turned her back to them and settled comfortably to enjoy her lunch. Then, in the same silence, she rose, took some clean clothing from one of the blue canvas bags, and moved toward the stream.

"That spot is infested with snakes," Falcon said dryly. "I wouldn't go in there."

"Harrumph!" Tamara continued to move, then paused just long enough to say over her shoulder, "You're just trying to frighten me. I won't be long."

She was scarcely out of hearing range when Falcon mumbled, "Damned spoiled wench, isn't she?"

"She needs a brave's firm hand," Flaming Bow answered.

"She needs something," Falcon replied with a wry smile. "A good spanking might do."


Tamara didn't care what they were thinking or saying to each other. She stood behind a thick cluster of bushes and removed her travel-stained clothing, relishing the thought of this bath. With her clothing deposited to a small, neat pile on the rocks, she moved into the cool, refreshing water until she stood shoulder deep. Her thick, wheat-colored hair spread out on the water's surface and she flung her head back to wet it thoroughly. Then she began massaging her shoulders and arms with the bar of lilac soap she had taken from her canvas bag.

Nothing else mattered but that she was enjoying the cool water; a two-day layer of dirt was drifting off with the current. Smooth white sand shifted beneath her feet, and she shuffled them, feeling the sand move between her toes. Then she again flung her head back to thoroughly wet her hair. She gave a small cry of surprise. There on the bank stood Falcon, a long hunting knife in his hand and his feet apart in an almost careless stand.

Tamara cried out in indignation, "How dare you spy on me! You're despicable and indecent! You have no respect for a lady!"

Silently, Falcon moved into the water. As he approached her, the wide-eyed Tamara crossed her hands at her chest and backed away from him.

"Be still," he warned in a steady, even voice.

But Tamara was furious. "Get away . . . get away, do you hear? Whatever your intentions are—"

Without warning, the knife Falcon clutched in his right hand sliced through the water beside her. Then he merely slung the weapon across her head and caught it in his left hand. When his other hand withdrew, it held the sleek, dead body of a copperhead, one of the deadliest snakes in the Americas.

Silently, Falcon returned to the bank and threw the snake into the bushes. Without turning back toward her, he ordered, "Get out of the water and dress. And from now on, when I tell you not to do something—damn it, don't do it!"

It was the second time today he had saved her from peril. Rather than thank him, she had abused and insulted him. And now he had moved out of hearing range and she could not humble herself before him.

When she had dressed in a long-sleeved white blouse and tan skirt, and pulled on comfortable riding boots, she returned to the waiting men. They had already mounted their horses. Falcon's blue eyes glared at her with contempt as he threw her the reins of her horse, even as she shamefully returned his gaze.

"Falcon, I am sorry. I won't disobey you again."

Falcon nudged his horse ahead on the trail. "See that you don't, Miss Fleming."

Silently, Flaming Bow dismounted his horse and assisted Tamara into the saddle.

When they reached a fork in the trail at evening twilight, Flaming Bow departed from them and headed toward his village on the Indian River. Falcon rode on in silence, only too aware of the feminine beauty who rode a few feet behind him, subdued into a silence of her own by the shame she felt.

They reached Asher Arms shortly before midnight. The only visible light shone from the parlor window. Falcon alit, then put his hands up to assist Tamara down. She willingly moved into his arms.

"Go on in to your father," Falcon said. "I will take care of your bags."

"Falcon." He halted at the sound of her voice softly calling his name. "First name or last?"

"Only name I answer to," he replied a bit dryly. "Excuse me, please. I have matters to attend to."

Suddenly, Tamara did not want him to leave. It had been a long trip from England. She was tired and afraid and not quite herself. And somehow, in all of this land, she felt that the man standing before her might be her only friend, if she would give him the chance.

"Falcon, I don't want to end the night like this. Forgive me for my behavior. I can be a pleasant person. You might . . ." Tamara's long fingers closed gently over his arm. "You might even learn to like me."

Only now did Falcon's eyes meet her own. He said nothing for a moment but studied her features in the half-light of the veranda. "You might be right, Miss Fleming. I am sure stranger things have happened."

When he had disappeared into the darkness, Tamara turned toward the unfamiliar house. She moved slowly, feeling once again that nagging, senseless dread that had stayed with her these past few days.

In the parlor waited a man who would expect her to call him Father . . . a man who was a stranger.

*Chapter 4*

When her knock at Asher Arms's massive front door went unanswered, Tamara stepped into a foyer dimly lit by candlelight. The loud creak of the door hinges brought a shiver to her spine. She stood with her back pressed against the door, then looked around the hall, where large potted plants flanked ornate Queen Anne chairs, similar to the ones in her bedchamber at Gray House. Again, she felt a painful longing for home.

Approaching the lighted parlor on tiptoe, she paused in the doorway. Massive wood furnishings sat against the walls, and an ivory-and-blue oriental carpet ran the length of the room. The fifteen-foot walls were mounted with the heads of wild animals, some of which she knew were not native to the Americas. Large cedar beams spaced at odd intervals cast strange, oblong shadows on the massive white ceiling.

Still, Tamara found not one living soul. She'd come to a strange country and a strange empty house with not so much as a welcome from her own father.

But Tamara did not dwell on the absence of a welcome. Although she was very tired, and sore from riding in the saddle, she strolled casually into the room, trying to convince herself that she was not disappointed, and absently began flicking her fingers over the heavy wooden furniture. Everything was clean. The large fringed pillows on the couch smelled of the outdoors and were comfortable when she dropped heavily against them. With her arms outstretched, Tamara closed her eyes.

Desperate for sleep, she fought to stay awake to meet her father. Her thoughts were not really with this strange house in this strange land, but with the man, Falcon. She'd been terrible to him today. If he chose to avoid her henceforth, she couldn't blame him. Perhaps the abruptness he had displayed was just his way. Perhaps he'd meant no insult. She hadn't really given him an opportunity to present a calm demeanor; rather, she had slung insults and abuses of her own and had, perhaps, alienated herself from her first human tie to Asher Arms.

There was something about him, though, that beckoned her thoughts, even now, when she was so tired she could scarcely keep her eyes open. She remembered the icy fire of his eyes when he'd stood beside her in the pool. Nevertheless, beneath the cool water she'd felt a warmth rising, washing over her flesh, as she'd held his mesmerizing gaze. Tamara wasn't sure why he so filled her thoughts. She'd attended balls and dances and society functions with many young men—suitors and admirers. But none had been as handsome and rugged and mysterious as this Falcon!

Catching sight of a large portrait that had not been visible from the doorway during her initial scrutiny of the room, Tamara studied a woman with unsmiling features, fair-haired like herself. She was wearing a rose-colored gown with a cluster of tiny white flowers tucked into the cleavage, and her clasped hands rested demurely in the thick folds of her gown. Then Tamara saw the tiny brass nameplate beneath the portrait. She arose and approached the portrait, and in the semidark of the room was able to make out the name, "Marian Fleming," followed by the date, "March 3, 1718." Tenderly, Tamara touched her fingers to the portrait. This was her mother.

"So! You have finally arrived!"

Tamara spun at the sound of a brisk, feminine voice. In the doorway stood a petite woman who might have been twenty, though it was hard to tell. She was wearing a faded blue robe and matching slippers. Her eyes were narrowed and her lips were pressed into a thin line.

"Y—yes, I have," she replied, drawing her hand to her throat.

"Well, come along then. I'll show you to your room."

"But Falcon . . ." Tamara pointed toward the foyer, ". . . said he would bring in my bags."

"Come," Glynnie insisted in a voice now sweet and quiet. "I'll bring your bags to you when he brings them in. You must be very tired. I will bring you some warm milk, to help you sleep."

"My father has retired for the evening?" Tamara inquired.

"He has," Glynnie answered briefly. "You weren't expected so soon." Tamara smiled at the girl, a smile that was not returned. Then she silently followed the girl to the end of a long narrow corridor, where a small unpainted door stood open. Glynnie stepped aside. "This is where you'll sleep."

Tamara's eyes widened as she assayed the small, windowless room with bare, unpainted walls, a tiny bed against the far wall, and, off in a corner, a ramshackle chest of drawers stacked with old cleaning rags. "This is where my father has lodged me?" Tamara asked in surprise.

"It's the best available for the time being," Glynnie replied with a note of apology. "Make yourself comfortable." When Tamara stepped in, Glynnie started to close the door, but Tamara put her hand out. "May I ask who you are?"

"Oh—" Glynnie feigned indifference. "I'm a servant. You needn't concern yourself with me."

"Everyone has a name."

Glynnie was surprised that the girl would even bother to inquire. Perhaps she had judged Jacob's daughter too hastily. Perhaps she should reconsider . . . but no! She was an interloper, an unwelcome visitor. "Glynnie," she replied eventually, smiling a smile that held no true feeling. "Before you arrived, Master Fleming treated me like a daughter. I have willingly been his dutiful girl . . ." Glynnie gazed directly into Tamara's eyes, a look that bordered on loathing, "because he has no other true family."

Despite her exhaustion, Tamara was revived by Glynnie's hateful words. She quickly closed the distance between them and her hand tightened over Glynnie's arm. "You were prepared to dislike me the moment I arrived, weren't you? That is why you have shown me to this—this storage room?"

Glynnie removed her arm with a strange gentleness. "I shall return momentarily, with warm milk." Then the door quietly closed.

"All right," Tamara said to herself. "If this is where you want me to sleep, this is where I'll sleep." Then she approached and threw herself heavily onto the small bed.

Tamara shrugged. She had already presented herself in an unfavorable light to the man Falcon.

Would creating a scene about her room only make matters worse? Possibly.

Thus Tamara dropped to the pillow, tucked her hands beneath her head, and wearily closed her eyes. She did not acknowledge Glynnie's return even as she heard the clink of a glass being set on a small table. When the door again closed, Tamara propped herself up on her elbow and quickly drank down the warm milk.

"Welcome to America, Tamara Fleming," she said quietly to herself.

Falcon had just unsaddled the horses, put away the saddles, and dropped Tamara's belongings by the stable door when Glynnie entered, carrying a lantern. The way she crept up on him, like a thief, made Falcon's nerves jump. He turned, preparing to scold her; but with her long hair loose and disheveled about her shoulders and her robe open just enough to betray a womanly cleavage, she presented herself in too pretty a light to scold.

"What are you doing here, Glynnie?"

"You've got . . . her bags?" Glynnie inquired.

Falcon nodded, motioning toward the door. "Over there."

"I'll take them in," Glynnie offered.

"The small trunk is heavy. I'll take it to her room."

"No!" Glynnie had not meant to speak so sharply, and she immediately softened her voice. "I—I mean merely that she has prepared for bed and it would not be proper for a man to enter her chamber."

"She has prepared for bed without—whatever a woman wears to bed?"

This required some quick thinking on Glynnie's

53

part. She remained silent for a moment, then replied "She—oh, Falcon! Why do you embarrass me? The wicked English tart sleeps in the altogethers. You should have known."

Falcon laughed gently. "Oh, I see." then he turned toward her with a humorous yet accusing eye. "Thought she'd be ugly as a toad, didn't you, Glynnie?"

"She is ugly as a toad! You should know!"

Falcon dropped the brush he'd been using on the horse and approached Glynnie. Angered by his smile, she bristled back and brought her clenched hands toward his chest, but he merely took her wrists and held them firmly. "Jealousy makes a woman ugly as a toad, Glynnie. You'd better be nice to her," Falcon threatened, without malice. "She is Master Fleming's daughter. For many years you were his substitute daughter. But the attentions he has given you in the past will now be given to her. You'd best get that through your pretty head." Falcon's voice changed to a more serious tone. "Don't make him hurt you, Glynnie. You must accept Miss Fleming and be nice to her." Falcon drew Glynnie's hands to his chest and massaged them very gently.

His gentleness was a strange deviation from character. He usually went out of his way to avoid her, to be brisk and businesslike whenever she materialized. Perhaps he understood how she felt right now.

"It isn't fair, Falcon," she replied quietly, resting her head against his chest, "I'm the one who has been attentive to him. I'm the one who has had to listen to his boring stories about him being a direct descendant of Captain Klas Fleming, the wealthy old Swede whose money aided in the colonization of Delaware. Can you realize how many times my head ached with boredom? And I've had to sit there and

listen, and listen, and listen—until I was sick of it!''
Glynnie's eyes lifted to Falcon's. "I don't want her
here, Falcon. She has no right to move in and take
over.''

Falcon gently held her chin. "If it's any consolation, she doesn't want to be here either.''

"How do you know? Did she tell you?''

"No . . . it's just a feeling.'' Suddenly, Falcon
turned her away from him and slapped her rump.
"Now get, Glynnie! Take those bags to Jacob's
daughter.''

Glynnie wanted to believe she'd heard contempt in
Falcon's voice. "You don't like her, do you?''

"I don't like or dislike her,'' Falcon replied indifferently. "I don't know her well enough.''

When Glynnie disappeared toward the house, Falcon returned to the task of grooming and stabling
the horses. He tried to think about Flaming Bow
and the village and his last visit with his mother, who
was the Lenape chief's wife. He tried to concentrate
on tomorrow's chores, to put them in some semblance of order according to their priorities. He tried
to tell himself that he was exhausted and eager to
retire, but he felt strong and alive inside. Sleep would
not come easily this night. "God,'' he mumbed,
"why couldn't she have been a toad.''


Jacob Fleming rose early and with the assistance
of Broggard bathed and shaved, then dressed in his
finest suit of clothing for his reunion with his daughter. He had heard voices the previous evening and
had thought perhaps Tamara had arrived. But if she
had, surely he'd have immediately been told.

Broggard adjusted the plaid blanket Jacob always
wore over his knees. Broggard was an ugly man with

thick, pocked skin and large hands, but he was strong, a quality the invalid Jacob needed in his manservant. But Broggard's duties were not only as his manservant. He was frequently called upon to pull the lever at local hangings and to wield the whip when that punishment was prescribed. He was, therefore, not warmly embraced by the staff of Asher Arms.

"Come, Broggard . . . we must prepare for my daughter's arrival."

"She has arrived," Broggard replied. "Bridie informed me this morning in the kitchens."

"Tamara is here?" Jacob was surprised. "Why was I not told?"

"The girl was very tired. Glynnie saw that she settled into her rooms last evening."

Jacob felt his heart leap inside his frail chest. His daughter—his dear, precious girl—was in this very house. She had been five years old when Mason Gray, at his insistence, had taken her back to England. And now she was a woman. "Is she still asleep?"

"She is, sir."

"Come . . . come . . . take me to her chamber. I merely wish to see her sleeping."

"But suppose she is not . . . respectable?"

"Bah!" Jacob flipped his wrist impatiently. "English-raised girls are always respectable!"

Broggard opened the door and waited while Jacob wheeled himself into the corridor. Then Broggard was behind him, pushing the creaking old chair toward Tamara's chamber. When he reached the door, he again flipped his wrist at Broggard. "Go on! Open it! I will see her from the doorway." Slowly, Broggard pushed the door open. But the room was vacant and the bed did not appear to have been slept in.

"Could she have arisen already?" But Jacob looked around. There were no bags, no discarded clothing lying across the satin daybed . . . there was no evidence that she had ever been here. Fear twisted inside him. "Find my daughter, Broggard! Ask Glynnie . . . didn't you say she received Tamara last evening?"

At the same time that Glynnie joined the rest of the staff in the parlor, Broggard entered with a limp Tamara lying across his arms. "She was sleeping in that old storage room near the kitchens . . . and she's been drugged," he announced somberly.

Immediately, Jacob's fiery gaze turned to Glynnie, who dropped to her knees and began sobbing frightfully.

"Is she all right?" Jacob asked, approaching, touching his thin fingers to Tamara's loose, wheat-colored hair.

"She'll have to sleep it off. But she'll be all right."

"Take her to her proper chamber and return here." Jacob immediately spun toward the weeping Glynnie, who was being comforted by her mother. "Glynnie, come here." Despite the rage twisting inside him, Jacob's voice was strangely gentle. When Glynnie hesitated, Jacob ordered more sternly, "Come here, Glynnie!" With Bridie's assistance, Glynnie rose unsteadily, then approached Jacob Fleming. "Did you lodge my daughter in that storage room?"

"Y—yes, Master Fleming."

"Did you drug her?"

Glynnie nodded, scarcely able to see the angry, pinched features of Jacob Fleming through her tears.

"What did you drug her with?"

"A bit of henbane, sir."

Jacob said nothing for a moment, but brought his

57

fingers up to rub his closed eyes. He was sick at heart. He'd had no idea how vehemently opposed to his daughter Glynnie really was. He cared very much for Glynnie—she had been like a daughter to him—but he could not allow this act to go unpunished. Presently, he lifted his eyes, which immediately settled on the pinched, worried features of his faithful servant Bridie.

"You understand, Bridie, that I must punish Glynnie."

Bridie tried to remain resolute, to understand and show no emotion. "Aye, Master Fleming, I understand. But—not Broggard. I beg of you, don't let him lay the strap to my girl."

Broggard returned in silence and stood at the doorway of the foyer. He had heard, and inside him there twisted a gloating satisfaction that was not betrayed by his somber gaze. Glynnie had often jeered at him and called him names behind his back . . . cruel, vicious names.

Jacob summoned him by raising his shaking hand. "Forgive me, Bridie. There is no other way." Then he motioned to the sobbing Glynnie, who had again dropped to her knees. "I've spared the rod and spoiled the child, Bridie. Broggard—Glynnie has earned her punishment. You know what you must do." Broggard approached and pulled Glynnie up by her tiny wrists. She fought to break away from him and, unable to do so, turned her pleading eyes first to Jacob Fleming, then to her mother, who was powerless to stop Broggard. She knew from past experience that a plea for leniency would go unheeded.

"Please . . . please . . . I'll be nice to her from this moment on. Please, don't punish me."

Only now, as Broggard dragged the protesting

58

Glynnie toward the back of the house, did Bridie drop into a nearby chair and quietly weep.

Tamara fought to awaken. She was vaguely aware of a cool cloth on her forehead and the presence of another person in her chamber. Her eyelids felt heavy and would not lift. Then she heard a feminine voice with a heavy Scottish accent, and very slowly her eyes crept open, eventually focusing on a kindly middle-aged face whose brows were pinched with concern.

Then her gaze slowly drifted off, taking in everything about her—a lace canopy over her massive bed, newly papered floral walls and pink carpets, a dressing table in a small boudoir for which a new brocade skirt had been sewn and on which sat bottles of expensive French perfume. Dainty chintz curtains hung at two bay windows, and on an upholstered window seat sat several well-worn porcelain dolls that stirred a long-past memory in her. The chamber was very large and expensively furnished, and even had its own bathing alcove and sitting room.

"Child, are you full awake?" The concern in Bridie's voice returned Tamara's attentions to her.

"Y—yes, I believe. I feel a bit groggy, though."

"Tainted milk, child. You've been asleep for thirty hours or so. Time to arise and meet your father."

"B—but," Tamara unsteadily arose, "it's dawn. I've only been asleep for a few hours."

"Nay child . . . it's dawn of the next day. Time to arise."

"Who's chamber is this?"

" 'Tis yours, child."

"Oh! That indecent girl! She had me sleep in a storage room!"

59

"Now. . . ." Bridie roughly patted her hand. "A warm bath has been drawn for you, an your clothes freshened and hung away. Dress and come for your breakfast."

Although Bridie's words seemed kind, Tamara took note of a certain coolness behind them. When Bridie had closed the door, Tamara rose, approached the bathing alcove, and began removing the gown that had been put on her. She felt unclean, her skin was clammy, and she still felt very dizzy. Tainted milk, indeed! She thought the milk tasted uncommonly bitter. She had been drugged! Just wait until she confronted that wicked servant girl. . . .

A myriad of thoughts rushed through Tamara's head as she bathed and dressed in a simple rose-colored gown, matching slippers, and an ivory lace blouse, with a scattering of tiny crocheted roses across the bodice. She started to pull her hair into a soft upsweep and pin it in place, but at the last moment decided to wear it loose. She usually did not wear rouge, but because of her pasty hue, she touched a little to her high cheekbones. Then she fluffed her hair out from her shoulders and left the bedchamber.

Unsure of which way to turn toward the kitchens, she followed the pleasant aroma of eggs and ham drifting toward her from below. When she entered the large room, she did not see the pleasant-faced woman she had met this morning; but the servant girl, Glynnie, sat at the long, narrow table, supporting her forehead on her raised palm and absently spooning honey into a cup of tea.

Anger rose within Tamara and she approached Glynnie. "Stand up!" she ordered brusquely, drawing her hands to her hips. Glynnie had not seen her enter, and the cold tone of Tamara's voice startled her. Hesitantly, she rose to her feet. "You led me to a storage room to sleep when I arrived here, and then you drugged me! Why?"

"I—I—"

"How dare you! How dare you make me feel so unwelcome in my own father's house!"

The strange look on Glynnie's face, which she misread as a look of satisfaction, compelled Tamara to take a step toward her. Suddenly Glynnie started to fall and Falcon, who had quietly entered, caught her in his arms. Without words, he carried the now weeping Glynnie toward the corridor leading to the servants' quarters.

Tamara was furious. She hadn't said anything to the girl that she hadn't deserved, and there was a lot more she had to say. Thus, she made a sharp about-face and stormed through the corridor after Falcon. Immediately, she heard a woman weeping and followed the sound to Glynnie's small chamber—a chamber that seemed overly furnished for a servant girl. Falcon sat on the bed beside Glynnie, gently patting her shoulder.

"Why do you protect her?" Tamara asked, her eyes shooting amber fire. "Don't you know what she did?"

Falcon rose, scarcely able to contain his own anger. "Yes, I know what she did . . . and it was wrong. But—" His hand went down and quickly pulled the robe down Glynnie's back, exposing a dozen or more raised welts. "She was punished, Miss Fleming." Falcon quickly untied his rawhide belt and pulled it from the waist of his trousers. "Here. Here, take it," he ordered with a strange calmness. "Beat her again, if you think she deserves it!"

Tamara was horrified. She had not been able to take her eyes from the girl and looked up only when

Falcon's hand firmly nudged her arm. "N—no, I won't take it."

"Take it!" he ordered again, his eyes narrowed and his mouth pressed into a thin, angry line. "Give her what she deserves!"

Tamara turned and fled from the room, down the corridor and through the foyer into the morning sun. She stood for a moment, sobbing bitterly, then gained her sense of direction and began running toward the woodline. She ran where her feet would take her and soon crumpled in a sobbing heap by a quiet little stream that babbled over smooth white rocks. She cushioned her forehead on her arm and wept bitterly.

She heard nothing, not even the sounds of morning, the haunting echo of a whipporwill, a rabbit scurrying among the fallen timber just down the hill from her. She did not hear approaching footsteps, but saw the tips of someone's boots through her tear-moistened eyes. She did not look up but quietly ceased her weeping.

Falcon knelt to one knee and gently took her arms above the elbows to pull her up. She did not want him to see her tears and tried to break free. But he held her firmly, almost painfully.

"I know you had nothing to do with Glynnie's mischief. I know you were the victim and that you may have been hurt. But why did you have to attack her like that?"

"I—I didn't know she'd been punished," Tamara stammered brokenly. "It's horrible . . . barbaric."

When tears again moistened her eyes, Falcon pulled her slim body against his own. "Then I apologize for my anger."

"I—I never wanted to come here," she finally admitted. "My guardian forced me to make this trip.

He said my—my father was dying and that I should spend what little time I could with him."

"Yes, I know."

Falcon seemed willing to listen, and Tamara desperately needed the strength of a man right now. She became aware of his half-nakedness, his shirt that was unbuttoned and pulled back from his powerful hirsute chest. She surrendered to his warm embrace, content to shed new tears against his shoulder. Then she became aware of the pleasant masculine smell of him. She became aware of strong hands moving gently up her arms and to her soft shoulders, pulling her crushingly to him. She had never been near such a man, yet she was not frightened. Rather, a strange, alien warmth flooded through her, bringing a tightness to her chest. Her breathing became laborious and she thought that she might smother against him. But it was wonderful, like nothing she had ever before experienced.

Falcon's anger had slowly drifted off with Tamara's tears. He held her gently, her soft, warm body against his own . . . a warmth that penetrated their clothing and touched him, warming the coldness he had felt just moments ago for her. She was vulnerable, shattered by an emotional need for a man's comfort. Thus, Falcon took advantage of the situation, and slowly, gently, his hand slipped beneath her chin to lift her warm parted mouth to his own.

Her mouth trembled, yet she responded willingly, desiring him as much as he desired her. The sweet nectar of her kiss allowed no opportunity for him to part from her and his mouth closed crushingly over hers.

Tamara's emotional state had blinded her to what was happening. This man, this handsome American she'd met just yesterday, was taking advantage of her momentary vulnerability. And that brought her senses rushing back at her. Thus, without warning, she broke away from him, then looked at him as if he had lost all reasoning. Yet she wanted to move back into his arms, as if it were where she belonged. She felt all aflutter inside, a warm, as if the sun, reflected through morning mist, encircled her within its golden rays. Yesterday, she had thought him a barbarian. Today, this very moment, he was gentle and strong . . . and commanding. And she wanted very much to remain here with him, like this.

Her eyes lifted to his blue ones, then gazed for a moment over his taut jawline. "Falcon. . . ." She whispered his name in an unreadable tone. Was she asking for him, or scolding him? Was she soliciting his affections, or preparing to bristle back and slap him very hard? Falcon had never seen such a charming crimson flush. Yet her silence confused him.

Tamara breathed deeply, her gaze fixed to his for a moment, then rose quickly to her feet and rushed back toward Asher Arms.

## Chapter 5

Tamara felt overcome with despair. Tears filled her eyes and a painful lump choked in her throat. She walked quickly along the narrow wooded path toward Asher Arms, even as her thoughts lingered back there . . . in the small, sunlit clearing where Falcon's lips had so boldly touched her own. Had he been able to feel the warm, inviting tremble of her mouth as it was covered by his? Was it this land that gave him his outrageous boldness? Perhaps so. Even she, raised in a wealthy, reserved English society, had felt the difference the moment she had set foot in America. Seven months ago, the anticipation of a strange, new life had dwelled strongly within her. She had confessed to the man Falcon that she hadn't wanted to come here. Yet, when Mason had told her of the trip she would make, although she had protested, she had also felt the thrill of it all. Had she outgrown England and the high-society circles where a woman's only recourse was domesticity? Had she grown tired of the handsome young suitors hand-picked by her guardian who had placed her on a pedestal, like a cold marble statue?

Perhaps she had indeed. While her lips had pleaded

with Mason Gray not to send her on this trip, her heart had pounded with the anticipation of it. Her sense of adventure and her rebellious heart had never truly accepted the quiet, predictable life she'd had in England. There had always been a painful longing deep within her, begging for something new and exciting and dangerous to pursue.

Yet, in the two days she had been here, she had managed only to make enemies. The girl, Glynnie, she could handle. But Falcon . . . here was a tough one: a soul as rebellious and aloof, as her own.

Tamara sighed deeply, dismayed by her preoccupation with Falcon. Why had she allowed him to affect her so deeply? Why had she given him the opportunity to scold her and make her feel ashamed? Why had she conducted herself as a wanton woman when she'd found herself in his strong, possessive embrace? She had been responsive, as surely as if they were lovers and this a practiced tryst.

She had acted impulsively and shamelessly and there was no excuse for her behavior, she thought as she slowed her pace and allowed her gaze to drift along the narrow trail cushioned by damp, fallen leaves. Ancient cedars formed a ceiling above and around her, scarcely allowing the wind to trickle through the thick foliage and gently sweep her loose hair. The early morning light became thin golden rays that touched her ivory skin, warming her just as Falcon's embrace had warmed her moments before. She breathed deeply of the delicate aroma of honeysuckle entwined among the thick forest, fresh pine straw and the gentle, faint away aroma of the roses trailing along the stone walls beyond Asher Arms. The activities of the estate scarcely penetrated the hills and the thick green foliage that held her prisoner to the narrow path.

But as she closed the distance between herself and Asher Arms, the sounds of morning gained clarity. The large house came into view and she stopped for a moment to study it from the distance. It was a pleasant house, though plain and rustic—the type of house one might expect to find in this wilderness. Along the stone wall that enclosed a small garden to the right of the house the roses grew in profuse, colorful bloom, well-tended by the gardener who now pruned the bushes and lazily threw the discarded branches to a small pile.

An old wagon sat just off the trail. From its condition, and the weeds that had grown high beneath and around it, it had long since seen its better days. Several rotting canvas sacks were strewn about it. Tamara made a seat of them and continued to study the pleasant view before her. Then her eyes lifted. Beyond Asher Arms, thunderclouds gathered upon the far horizon.

Tamara knew that her father awaited her, yet she dreaded their first meeting. She was afraid of being too distant to him, or too affectionate. She didn't want to appear cold; yet she did not want to appear too anxious to resume a father–daughter relationship that had long since been forgotten. She considered Mason Gray her father, not Jacob Fleming. She was curious about Jacob and she had many questions to ask—about her mother, her early childhood, those short, vague years before her life with Mason Gray; about Fedora Hartley and the young boy who had lived at Asher Arms many, many years ago. She wanted to know so much. Most of all, she wanted to know why she had been sent away.

As she sat in the shadows of a sweet gum tree, her ankles crossed beneath her satin skirts, the man, Falcon, exited the trail and passed a short distance from her. He appeared dark and foreboding, as if one of the far thunderclouds had settled about him, and his penetrating blue eyes looked straight ahead. Tamara had never before met such a man.

And no man had ever before kissed her as he had. She'd received polite puckers to her cheek, but until this morning, a man's lips had never touched her own. Yet it had seemed a natural thing, almost a magical thing . . . she'd felt dizzy and scarcely able to open her eyelids so that she might see his closeness, rather than feel it in a gentle, masculine whisper against her cheek.

Oh, was she mad? Had she lost every degree of reasoning she had once possessed?

Falcon moved just a scant few feet away from her, his broad back turned full to her, unaware of her presence and the almost painful pounding of her heart. His hands were clenched into fists as he began moving quickly toward the estate.

"Falcon. . . ."

Tamara had not realized she'd spoken his name until he paused, then turned and met her gaze. She had hopped down from the wagon bed and her fingers were linked at her back. She watched him, silent and brooding and still, his blue eyes suddenly magical black wells that refused to betray their hidden secrets. He was a mysterious one! Everything she'd heard indicated his was an Indian heritage . . . yet there were those penetrating blue eyes . . . so blue, at times, that they were like a clear mountain stream. Suddenly, she wanted to be near him . . . to feel the sweet, warm breath of this ruggedly handsome man against her cheek . . . as she had a few moments ago, back by the forest stream.

Falcon threw his shoulders back, as if he were proud to display his tall stature. "Haven't you gone to see your father yet?" he asked with the same gentleness that was reflected in his eyes.

"I—I—" Oh, why couldn't she find the words? Why did he reduce her to this state of stumbling idiocy? Her hands moved to her front to straighten her lace collar. "I was just on my way. I—I wanted to apologize. I shouldn't have run away like that. I just don't know what came over me." Tamara approached and stood just within touching distance of him. "If you kissed me again, Falcon, I wouldn't run away." Oh, what invisible demon had made her say such a thing?

Silence. Did he intend to make her feel more uncomfortable than she already felt? Tamara wished that she'd said nothing, but had allowed him to pass on his way. "Are you saying," he began after a moment, "that you want me to kiss you again?" Before she could reply, or even protest the ever-so-slight hint of humor in his voice, his hands darted out, circled her arms just above the elbows, and pulled her close. Those penetrating blue eyes hovered menacingly above her. "You say you shouldn't have run away, but—I disagree. You had every right to flee . . . since I forced myself upon you. Next time—" Falcon deliberately paused over his words, "you should not conduct yourself as a wanton woman." Then he released her and stepped just outside her perimeter.

He expected an angry retort . . . or more appropriately, a display of rage. Rather, she favored him with a slight smile. "Of course, you're right, Falcon. I'll be more careful . . . and present myself as a lady from this moment forward."

As Tamara boldly held his penetrating gaze, thunder unexpectedly resounded. Her body convulsed. Falcon's hand moved toward her but did not touch her again. She had fallen silent, and tears filled her eyes.

At first, Falcon was confused by the silence that had suddenly come upon her. It had been only a moment or two since she'd spoken, yet it seemed like hours. And now, since she'd calmly and reasonably delivered her reply to his insult, he wondered why she felt this emotion. Had he overestimated her fire and spunk from the day before? Still, she stood there with an appealing vulnerability in the slight stoop of her shoulders and in the way her tear-moistened eyes dropped. And he imagined the flesh of her long, lithe body to be like the smooth, flawless ivory skin exposed through the lace bodice of her blouse. He could feel it in his mind, silken thighs, soft round breasts tingling beneath his fingers, his mouth. . . . But in view of her unexplained and unexpected tears, he quickly thrust the pleasant vision of her nearness from his mind, before his body betrayed its aching hunger for her. Tears or no, she was the most sensual creature he had ever encountered. His fingers lifted and gently brushed away her tears.

"When you have met with your father and have been dismissed," Falcon said after a moment, "come to the stables." When her look became puzzled, he continued with haste, "Don't look so worried. I have something that belongs to you."

Without awaiting her reply, Falcon turned and walked slowly toward the stables. Tamara watched until he disappeared into the dark interior. Quietly she linked her fingers behind her and walked toward Asher Arms. A door opened as she approached the wide veranda, and Bridie McFarland, her bony fingers wrapped around the handle of a broom, stood in the doorway.

"Your father's up and asking for you," she announced somberly, " 'twas for him you came here from England. Best be attendin' to your duty."

"Visiting my own father," Tamara replied, stepping past her, "is not a duty, but a pleasure." When she had entered the foyer, she turned, and lifting her chin somewhat haughtily, she continued, "Yesterday you were kind. Why today do you insult me?"

Bridie McFarland eyed her sternly. Her mouth pressed into a thin line, and unconsciously her grip tightened on the broom handle. "Didn't mean to insult you, Miss Fleming. Your father . . . he's awaitin' you in the parlor. Anxious to see you, I'd imagine," she added in departing.

If it had been possible to linger indefinitely between the foyer and the parlor, where the dark outline of Jacob Fleming's wheelchair could be seen, Tamara might have attempted to do so. She was quite at odds with her emotions and unsure of what she should say in greeting. Should she call him "Father" or "Mr. Fleming?" Should she hug him or merely offer her hand? She felt the warmth of the room rush upon her, as if the walls were closing in to eventually crush her between their massive, immobile structures. A tightness in her throat made it impossible to speak, yet her feet carried her slowly toward his dark, silent figure, to stand behind and just out of touching distance of him.

She would have stood there lost to words or sensible thought if he had not suddenly spun the chair toward her. Startled, she stepped back and brought her fingers to her slim throat to force down the painful lump that had settled there.

"F—Father," she stammered, "I'm your daughter, Tamara." Oh, how foolish she sounded! Of course he knew who she was.

Jacob Fleming said nothing, but narrowed his eyes

and studied her for a moment. Tamara watched them lower, silently appraising her, then quickly rise to meet her own, which cowered from his bold assessment. Then his thin dry face cracked into a smile. His arms left the folds of the plaid blanket across his knees and opened in greeting to her.

"Tamara . . . Tamara, my daughter. How lovely you are."

Suddenly, as Tamara was drawn into his frail arms, there was no longer a gap between them. He spoke to her as easily as if he'd seen her just yesterday and they had shared an intimate talk. "It has been a long, long time. There is much catching up to do."

"Y—yes, there's so much to talk about, Father. I almost don't know where to begin."

In the moments that passed, as she sat on the edge of the divan and allowed him to hold her hands, he spoke not of the time that had gone by these past sixteen years, but of the years before she was sent to England. Tamara heard love in his voice, which made it all the more confusing as to why she had been sent to England. She wanted to ask, but she felt that it was his place to offer explanations, and in his own time.

As the moments became hours that rushed quickly toward their noonday meal, Tamara was drawn into the magnetic warmth of his love and adoration. Enraptured by his kindness and gentle manners, it no longer mattered that she had been sent away.

They laughed over the amusing stories he had to tell of her childhood . . . stories that only a parent would cherish. By the time dinner was announced, Tamara no longer sat with a stranger, but with a warm man she was proud to call Father.

She didn't know why; perhaps it was the lightness

of the mood that existed between them, but Tamara found herself asking the one question that, unbeknownst to her, could turn her father's happy face solemn and brooding.

"Father, tell me about Fedora Hartley."

Silence. Jacob's hand covered his mouth momentarily. His brows knit together beneath shaggy white hair. "Fedora Hartley. . . ." he whispered hoarsely. "Well . . . that's a long time ago. There are other things more important," he continued, forcing a smile, "that a father and daughter can talk about."

The fact that he chose not to talk about Fedora served only to deepen her curiosity and he need to know. "But—" Any protest was lost to the darkening of Jacob's eyes as they held her puzzled features. She was more determined than ever to know about Fedora Hartley. But for the moment she relented. "Very well, Father."

Jacob had planned to take the noonday meal with his daughter, but now clapped his hands, summoning Broggard. "I must retire to my chamber, Tamara. I tire very easily. Bridie will see to your meal."

It was only when Bridie approached her a few moments later that Tamara was snapped from her momentary trance. "I—I must have said something to upset him," Tamara said quietly.

"What did you say, miss?" Bridie was rubbing her hands on an oversized apron.

Concern was now reflected in Bridie's graveled voice, compelling Tamara to turn her eyes fully to her before this rare emotion was lost. "I asked about a woman who was a servant here—a long time ago."

Bridie's graying eyebrow shot up. " 'Twasn't the Hartley woman you asked about, eh, girl?"

"It was."

"It's no wonder the master retired from you. A

73

bad one, she was—brewed trouble between the master an' his wife. Deserved to die, she did. Aye, deserved it sure as if she were the devil himself."

Tamara was suddenly very angry. Bridie's words were, obviously, the result of servants' wagging tongues. "And her child, too?" Tamara questioned. "He deserved to die?"

"Don't know about a child, miss . . . come, your meal is awaitin' you." Only when Tamara had seated herself at the dining table and Bridie was preparing to depart did she ask, "What's your interest in the Hartley woman, miss? Ye couldn't have known her."

"She was my guardian's first wife. I was merely curious."

"Curiosity killed the cat," Bridie mumbled without malice. "Stay to that what's your own business, miss, and you won't be gettin' hurt."

"Bridie?" The elderly woman turned back. "I'm sorry about Glynnie. I—I don't approve of brutality—"

"It isn't your place to approve or disapprove. Things are done differently here than they are in England," Bridie answered, cutting her off, "Glynnie done you wrong. It won't happen again."

"You don't like me, do you?" Tamara had lain her napkin in her lap and now fumbled with the edges.

"Like you fine, Miss," Bridie answered matter-of-factly. "Anything else you be wantin' to know?"

"Yes . . . I would like to know what malady is killing my father."

"You didn't ask him?"

"No . . . I'm asking you."

"A bullet, miss . . . took away the feelin' in his legs and now is restin' against his heart. Every move-

74

ment inches that bullet an' death closer to your father."

"How did it happen?"

"A huntin' accident, miss."

"He—he shot himself?"

Bridie pondered the latest of Tamara's questions for a moment. Then she removed her hands from the panniers of her apron where she'd tucked them and began absently rearranging the serving bowls on the table. "Your father was sittin' in the saddle an' firin' at a deer between the ears of his horse. Startled the poor, untrained beast and your father was thrown. He was bloody angry, miss, an' reloaded the gun to shoot the horse. 'Twas a struggle over the gun, an' your father was shot."

"Oh . . . I see."

"That's the story your father told. Me . . . since your father was shot in the back, I'm not so sure."

Puzzled, Tamara looked up. "You don't think it was an accident? Why? Who was with my father when it happened?"

" 'Twas Falcon, miss. The gun was fired from his hands. Now . . . I'll bring your dinner."

"Never mind," Tamara leaned back in her chair. "I—I'm really not hungry."

"As you please, miss."

Tamara felt a sick feeling in the pit of her stomach. She rose, placed the napkin beside her untouched plate, and started toward the foyer. "I think I'll have a talk with Falcon."

"Falcon's gone."

Tamara spun back, surprised. Just this morning, he had asked her to come to the stable after the meeting with her father. "What do you mean, gone. For good?"

"Nay, miss . . . for a few days, a few weeks, a

few months. None of us ever knows how long he'll stay away. I overheard him tell Saul he'd journey to his village, to visit his mother . . . do a little hunting—"

"He does work for my father, doesn't he? Did he ask permission to leave?"

"Sometimes it seems your father works for Falcon. It's his word that controls. Your father indulges Falcon . . . only God knows why . . . perhaps—" Bridie hesitated over her words, "he's afraid of him, and the Indian blood thick in this veins."

"If he's so Indian," Tamara shot back, crossing her arms, "why does he have blue eyes?" Why were they bantering cross words back and forth? Tamara suddenly wondered. It had turned into a degrading, immature contest to see who could make who feel more uncomfortable. Mentally shrugging, Tamara approached Bridie and her hand fell gently to her arm. "Please, Bridie, I don't want things to continue like this. I'm sorry about what happened to Glynnie. If I could snap my fingers so it never would had happened, I would." Tamara gave her arm a gentle squeeze. "Let's try to get along. I feel very alien to this land . . . and this house, Bridie. My father is almost a stranger to me. We can all continue to make one another miserable, or we can be friends. I prefer to be friends."

Bridie roughly patted Tamara's hand. "You're right, miss. For your father's sake—"

"No!" Tamara had not meant to speak so harshly, and she immediately softened her voice. "Not for my father's sake, Bridie . . . for our sakes, you and me and Glynnie. We've gotten off on the wrong foot, but sensible people can right a wrong. I'm willing to try if you are."

"Sure, miss." Bridie managed a sincere smile.

"Find Saul. Your father's bought you a fine mare. Saul will show you right away, if you wish." Bridie shuffled toward the entrance to the kitchens, but immediately turned back and added, "Falcon left afoot. Saul will saddle the mare, if you wish to catch up to him."

"But—I wouldn't know which way he went."

"Follow the path, girl . . . Saul will show you."

Yes, that was what she would do. There were no advantages to allowing this thing to fester and grow during an absence that could become days or weeks or months.

Bridie's insinuation that Falcon had been responsible for her father's injury would have to be cleared between them, since they would live in such close proximity to each other. He was her father's employee, yet she did not know how she planned to bring it up. Logically, she should be able to speak easily to him, yet she could not. His very nearness had intimidated her . . . excited her. She saw him more than as an employee . . . she saw him as a man. The spellbinding magic of his prowess could quiet her tongue when it might otherwise have lashed out at his sarcasm. She had initially thought this visit could become boring after a while, but with Falcon nearby, how could it be? His moods were as unpredictable as her own, a challenge she faced enthusiastically. He had character and appeal, and rugged yet gentle ways she had recognized even through tears of anger. And the way he looked at her . . . as no man had before.

She needed to know the truth about her father's accident. Yet she also did not want Falcon to leave. In all the land, she felt safest with him. Perhaps if she caught up to him, she could persuade him to remain, just for a little while, until she felt more comfortable.

The way she turned and fled through the kitchens startled Bridie, but Tamara cared only about catching up to Falcon. Even though she was in a hurry when she reached the stables and informed Saul of her wishes, she could not help her surprised look when she saw the sorrel mare—the gift from her father—as it was taken from its stall. The mare was as handsome as any she'd seen sitting beneath the saddles of English royalty. She admiringly stroked the firm muscles of the animal as Saul saddled her and warned Tamara to slowly accustom herself to the mare. Rather than heed his advice, she inquired of the direction in which he'd seen Falcon departing, hastily mounted, and nudged the well-gaited mare into a comfortable lope toward the Indian River.

The late summer season had cooled the air. The mare sped along the trail toward the hills, obeying its new mistress's commands. Tamara halted at the top of a hill and adjusted her skirts, which had become disheveled in her ride, and her eyes moved over the descending trail and the valley below her. She soon spied Falcon, carrying a backpack and musket across his shoulder, slowly ascending still another hill. She wanted to race with the wind toward him, yet something held her back for a moment.

Did there exist within her a nagging little voice warning her to be careful of this man? If she asked him to remain at Asher Arms, would he think her foolish, or worse, afraid to remain without him? Tamara heard the turmoil in her mind washing away sensible thought and forcing her to nudge her toe gently against the mare's powerful body. Before she could answer any of her questions, she was once again moving along the trail toward Falcon.

78

Falcon turned when he heard the thunder of horse's hooves fast approaching him. He caught a glimpse of Tamara's hair, like finely-spun gold glistening in the sunlight, of her ivory features and flushed cheeks. She was a vision of loveliness, a goddess, almost illusive against the midday sun. He felt that violent pounding inside him, the same that had compelled him to take this journey before he was caught in the web of the fiery beauty now quickly closing the distance between them. She was like no woman he had ever met before, and he was frightened of this thing inside him, destroying the firm countenance that had accompanied him all these years.

Tamara halted and dismounted without awaiting his assistance. Then she again straightened her skirts, brushed the disheveled strands of her hair back from her face, and turned to him. He did not return her smile, but narrowed his eyes and watched her slow approach.

Tamara suddenly felt at a loss for words. What explanation was she to give for pursuing him? Surely he would expect one. Still, Tamara was not one to be intimidated, and clasping the reins between her palms, she halted just out of his reach.

"When Bridie said you'd gone," she began after a moment, "I thought. . . ." Would he be receptive to the truth? His look told her that he would. "I thought how lonely it would be without you," she began afresh. "I really wish you'd stay at Asher Arms a bit longer."

"You have met your father," he replied. "I thought you'd be more comfortable now."

"A father is a father." Again, Tamara smiled. "But a friend is a friend. Stay, Falcon." Before he could reply, she continued with haste, "I know I've

79

left a nasty impression with you, and I've said and done things that don't meet with your approval. But I can be pleasant." Suddenly, Tamara realized she was rambling. Falcon was probably tired of her self-assessments. She unclasped her hands and, turning slightly away, began swinging the bridle reins back and forth. "Don't make me humble myself, Falcon."

Falcon became intimidatingly silent. Slowly he set his musket against a tree, shifted the weight of the backpack to the ground, then made a seat of it. He was about to say that he would stay, if that was what she wanted, but when his eyes lifted they met a strange gaze. He knew then that she had already heard stories.

"Something on your mind, Tamara?"

She turned slightly away, then linked her fingers nervously together. She was indeed thinking about what Bridie had told her this morning. "I understand you were with my father when he was injured."

"Yes, I was." Falcon approached from behind and his hands fell gently to her arms, to tenderly caress them. "But you must believe that I had nothing to do with his injuries. It was an accident."

"I was told he had trouble with a nervous horse." Tamara leaned her head back against his shoulder. The tender move surprised him, even as he touched his cheek to her freshly washed hair. Tamara enjoyed his nearness and his hands gently massaging her arms. "I was told that you tried to stop him from killing the horse. Is that true?"

"No."

Tamara spun rapidly toward him, and her eyes were wide with astonishment. "If it's not true, Falcon . . . then how . . . did it happen?" Her words came in short, pained gasps.

But Falcon's hands again circled her arms and drew her close. "I was reared always to tell the truth, Tamara. I will tell you that your father's injuries were the result of an accident, and that is all you need to know. If you believe that I am a truthful man, then you will need no further explanation."

A thousand hours of thought condensed into a few silent moments as she held his gaze. Why did she feel so content just to be with him, to trust him so inexplicably? He seemed such a gentle man; she could not imagine him being responsible for her father's accident. Tamara did not know where her strength came from as she quietly replied, "I do believe you, Falcon. And I trust you as I have never trusted anyone before. Now," she continued, favoring him with a shy smile, "will you remain at Asher Arms, at least until I've adjusted to my new life?" The smile faded as her eyes gazed over his features in a sincere plea. "Please, Falcon . . . as my friend, help me through this trial."

Unsmiling, Falcon took her hand and gave it a gentle squeeze. "Very well, Tamara, I will remain. But should you find me gone in the not-too-distant future, please understand that I have another life beside this one at Asher Arms . . . and my departures are never for long. I will always be close by," and only now did Falcon smile, "whenever you really feel that you need me." His arm circled Tamara's slender shoulders. "Come, daughter of Jacob Fleming, allow me to retrieve my musket and pack, and then I will show you a lovely place in the bend of the river, where the sun shimmers like amber wine. . . ."

# Chapter 6

With an accompanying lazy groan, Tamara sat forward and widely stretched her arms. These past few weeks the weather had been pleasant, with only a slight chill lacing the early days of October. Despite her fears to the contrary, her visit had been anything but boring. There had been new adventures daily and new people to meet—frequently, wagonloads of families heading toward the American interior in hopes of establishing homesteads.

This was a time when she saw another side of Asher Arms—not just an estate now building its wealth in the buying, selling, and trading of thoroughbred horses, but a generous host willing to feed families of struggling parents and solemn-faced children searching for new destinies. She saw, also, a pleasant side to the servant girl, Glynnie, who often spent many hours with these visiting children, engaging them in games and playing with them as if she were a child herself.

Tamara still thought often of England, but the pain of her memories diminished each day. Her visit to Delaware was a new and wonderful experience—wonderful because of the silent, thoughtful man who daily placed a single red rose on her window sill. Tamara threw none away when they withered, but pressed them in a book. Thereafter, she tied a satin ribbon around each and placed the faded remains in a small drawer in her vanity.

With this thought in mind and anticipating the continuance of this sweet sentiment, Tamara rose, pulled on her robe, and slowly approached the window sill. She smiled. There sat the loveliest rosebud from the garden, just beginning to open, moist with the morning dew and waiting patiently for her fingers to lift its fragrance to her. She did not realize, as she drew it caressingly to her cheek, that Falcon stood in the shadows of the garden wall, watching the golden cascades of her hair spill across a milk-white shoulder bared by her slipping robe.

It was the first Wednesday of the month, the day that Falcon traveled to the Packard Trading Post on Cape Henlopen for necessary supplies. He had promised her that she could accompany him on the two-day trip, if Jacob had no objection. Yesterday, begrudgingly, her father had given his approval.

Tamara hastily bathed and dressed, then chose a simple, loose blouse and a skirt that could easily be worn over her comfortable lace-up boots. She brushed her thick hair back and tied it at her nape with a satin ribbon. She then started to touch a little color to her face but there was no need. A pretty pink had risen in her cheeks. Could it be her thoughts of Falcon that had produced this flattering state?

She packed a few changes of clothing in a small canvas bag, then spoke briefly with her father in the parlor. "You won't worry about me, will you?" she asked.

Jacob gently squeezed her fingers. "You're a sensible girl, Tamara. You'll take care." Jacob's hand withdrew and he turned toward a small desk. He took several coins from a drawer and handed them to her. "Bring your father half a pound of the most expensive tobacco Packard has in stock, will you?"

Smiling, Anna took the coins. "Is that all you need, Father?"

"And your safe return."

Tamara's fingers reassuringly tightened on his thin shoulder. "Look for me two afternoons hence." Her lips touched his cheek in a light kiss. "You take care, Father, and don't overdo."

Tamara soon left the house and watched Falcon approach with the pack horses. He had a mountain of furs tied to one of the horses and had thrown a saddle blanket over the other. Falcon smiled when he saw her standing against the railing, lightly supporting herself. But before she could return the smile, Bridie approached from behind, startling her. She released a small gasp.

"Didn't mean to frighten you, miss." Falcon approached and drew his booted foot to the first step. "Falcon, I've got a list for you," Bridie explained. "If there's any explanations you need. . . ."

Falcon took the paper and his eyes darted quickly down the list. "It's in good order," he said shortly. "But Packard may have to order the window glass from the east." He folded the list and tucked it into the pocket of his shirt. Silence. Only when Bridie had reentered the house did Falcon's eyes return to the waiting Tamara. "Are you prepared for our journey?"

"Yes—oh, my bag, allow me time to retrieve my bag." Before she could pick it up, Falcon had traversed the steps and soon returned to the pack horse with it. He mumbled something beneath his breath; his eyebrows met in a frown. Suddenly, Tamara wondered if he really wanted her to go with him. "What did you say, Falcon?"

Falcon cocked a dark eyebrow. "Hmmm?"

"You said something that I did not hear—"

Having secured the bag, Falcon turned and his hands went out, inviting her to them. "Come, let me help you up . . . what did I say?" He looked puzzled, trying to remember. She moved into his strong arms and he easily lifted her to the saddle blanket. "I just thought of something I needed to add to Bridie's list."

"I've a bit of writing charcoal in my bag," she answered, "if you wish to write it down."

"Perhaps later . . . when we stop for a meal."

Before he moved out of her reach, Tamara's hand fell to his shoulder. She enjoyed the feel of iron-hard muscles beneath her fingers. "Thank you . . . for the roses."

He said nothing in reply, but merely moved away and took the reins of both horses.

Tamara watched as Asher Arms was lost over the crest of the hill. She wished she were walking beside Falcon, rather than riding the pack horse. Falcon seemed unusually quiet, as if he were deep in thought, and moved slowly along the trail. The furs on the pack horse beside her had a rather musky smell which rose above the clean, fresh aroma of the October wilderness. Soon they were moving out of the perimeters of Asher Arms with which Tamara, in her many rides, had familiarized herself. They were entering territory she had never seen before, deep sunlit valleys and fir-crested hills; they crossed many creeks babbling over smooth white rocks and passed small cabins where children played and women worked at scrubboards. She saw half-naked men furrowing dying fields back into the earth and chopping wood for the approaching winter. By mid-morning they had reached the trail along the shore of the Indian River and moved steadily toward the east and the Packard Trading Post at Cape Henlopen.

There had settled over Falcon a cloud of thoughtful silence which Tamara accepted without question. She was so enjoying the scenery and the foam-capped Indian River moving on its perpetual journey. But as the noon hour approached and she realized they'd been traveling for more than five hours, Tamara began to feel the ache of the pack horse's lazy gait. She arched her back to relieve the stiffness and suddenly felt herself slipping. She had scarcely called out "Falcon!" before he turned sharply and she slipped into his waiting arms. She half stumbled; his grip tightened. Flustered by her clumsiness, she looked up, at a half-cocked smile and narrowed eyes firmly fixed to hers. "I—I slipped," she said with some embarrassment. "And don't laugh!" While her words were sharp, she was not angry. Rather, she returned his smile. Although she had maintained her footing, his hands continued to firmly hold her tiny waist. "You—you can let me go now, Falcon."

He did not. Rather, he replied humorously, "Fair lady, must I?" But the humor instantly faded and his features were masked by another emotion, one Tamara could not readily identify. It took her off her guard. Her gaze held his, even as her hands moved and gently fell to his arms. Tamara had seen this look before . . . the time his lips had so gently touched hers. And she certainly did not find that distinct possibility—his tender kiss—repulsive now. She welcomed it, in fact, even hoped for it. But rather than the reaction she wished for, he released her and turned again to take the reins of the horses. "Come . . . we will share a meal."

A little disappointed in his reluctance, Tamara replied, "Good! I am famished," then straightened the folds of her gown.

Falcon laughed. "You are always famished!"

They found a shady spot beside the Indian River and ate a cold meal of biscuits, boiled potatoes, and pork. Falcon seemed deliberately to keep her at bay, even to favor her with his outrageous aloofness. Yet she couldn't help but notice the occasional glances, when he thought she wasn't looking, glances that spoke eloquently of his admiration. He picked at the tin plate of cold food as if he really didn't want it, yet she knew that he seldom ate breakfast and had every reason to be hungry. It pleased Tamara that she might have this effect on the quiet, strong-willed Falcon.

"Falcon," He glanced up briefly when she spoke his name. "Do you wish that you'd never invited me along?"

Falcon set his tin plate on the ground beside his outstretched leg. "Why would I? You've been no trouble . . . and I did invite you," he reminded her in a light, scolding tone.

Tamara gently shrugged her shoulders. "You've been so quiet. I—I know how you enjoy being alone."

Unhesitatingly, Falcon drew himself to his knees, then eased the foot or two toward her. "You should become accustomed to my silence, Tamara. It is part of me. Few people know me . . . really know me." Falcon removed the tin plate from her lap and absently tossed it atop his own. Then he took Tamara's hands and enveloped them fondly between his.

"How do I explain to you . . ." he began afresh,

his narrowed eyes holding her fixed gaze, "I have faced many dangers, Tamara. But you . . ." he continued, tenderly caressing her hand, "you are a different kind of danger. Everything I am and have been, you threaten to destroy."

'But—" Puzzled by his words, Tamara sat forward and quickly withdrew her hand, "I would never do anything to hurt you, Falcon."

He held her gaze, yet still saw her brows pinched in a worried frown, her cheeks suddenly flushed, her full, moist lips slightly apart, as if she had something further to say but could not find the words. A few strands of her wheat-colored hair had come loose from the ribbon. Instinctively, wanting only to feel its softness, his fingers rose and brushed it back. "It is my solitude you threaten to destroy, Tamara. These past few weeks, seeing you, being with you, enjoying you—I want more. I want. . . ."

Tamara eased toward him until only a breath of space separated their bodies. She knew how he felt because she felt the same way. She hoped he would say that he wanted her for his wife, his woman. But again the cloud of silence had fallen over him. They were divided by different cultures and standards. Would their feelings for each other bridge the gap created by their separate and distinct ways of life? Tamara prayed that it would.

She could not allow the confession he was about to make dangle in this aftermath of silence. She wanted to know once and for all how he really, truly felt about her. "Do you love me, Falcon?" She felt the question rush from her lips in a breathless whisper.

"Love," he echoed softly. "The elusive emotion without solid form . . . a feeling here. . . ." Falcon's balled hand rested for a moment against his chest, then he again took her hand. "A man needs a woman . . . it is not natural that he wake to each sun without the warmth of your gentle breed. . . ."

A black cloud suddenly enveloped her heart. She felt disappointment fill a suddenly empty space within her. "Oh, I see. You have been silent and thoughtful because you did not know how to ask me to warm your bed." A flush of hurt, of pride, rose in her cheeks. Before Falcon could reply, Tamara quickly withdrew her hands from his, spun to her knees and picked up the plates that needed to be washed. Before she could rise, though, Falcon took her free hand in a firm grip.

"You listen, but you do not hear, Tamara. I will not deny that I want you . . . that way. But a relationship between a man and a woman is much deeper than the flesh. That is the relationship I want. I will be good to you, Tamara. I am not a rich man, but I can provide well for you."

Tamara pulled her hand free. She felt a painful lump in her throat. She had heard and seen more than he knew. She had heard him confess to wanting her, but not to loving her. She wanted to be angry, but logic began to surface from deep inside her. He was an uneducated American accustomed to the hardships of the wilderness. His life had been rough and without frills. He had not been schooled in good graces and courtship. He had presented his feelings the only way he knew how. That he had chosen her of all the women he had met was a great compliment. He had not meant to insult her.

Thus, Tamara replied quietly, "I am flattered, Falcon. I—" She tried to prevent it, but the hurt she felt shattered into pieces within her throat. Her voice trembled with emotion. "I must wash the dishes," she said quietly.

She moved hastily among the smooth white rocks toward the shore, then knelt and cleaned the dishes in the river. She did not look around, but she knew he had settled back against the trunk of a tree and watched her every movement. She kept her back to him as she took her time with the dishes. She did not want him to see the tears that burned rivers down her wind-reddened cheeks.

They arrived at the Packard Trading Post at dawn the following day. She found the hustle and bustle of the trading post a pleasant diversion from the silence she had gotten from Falcon ever since their talk yesterday. They had spent the night in the wilderness, she beneath blankets and warm furs and a tent he had constructed for her between two pine saplings, and he in the clearing, bare-chested, with his fingers linked behind his head, staring thoughtfully into the clear black sky. She had watched him, wanting to be beside him and to feel the strength of his arms around her. Desire had coursed through her veins; it had been all she could do to keep from easing across the ground to snuggle against him. But she had fought her impulses, even when the wood line had stirred with animal movements and grunts that seemed a mere few feet away. She had forced herself to sleep but had awakened several times to see Falcon lying in the same position. He'd probably not gotten any sleep at all. Yet he had risen early this morning with the energy and vitality of a thousand men.

Tamara was troubled by thoughts of her own. She had expected her visit at Asher Arms to be of short duration. She had expected to fulfill her familial obligations, then return to England and fall into the patterns of domesticity and social engagement arranged for her by her guardian. But that was not what she wanted now. A powerful force rose within her, compelling her to rebel against undesired arrangements. She wanted to love a man of her own choosing. She had known a long time ago, even before the sweet sentiment of roses, that the man she wanted to love was Falcon. She was willing to give love. Was he?

"Miss?"

Startled, Tamara spun rapidly away from the racks of yard goods she'd been absently caressing. A young woman, great with child, gazed at her. "Oh, I do apologize. I was a thousand miles away."

The woman smiled. "Yes, I could see. You arrived with Falcon, did you not?"

"Yes, I . . . I did.'

"He has asked me to assist you in your purchases."

Tamara smiled a smile that was returned by the pleasant woman. "I have no purchases for myself, but I would like a half pound of your best tobacco for my father."

"We have nothing imported at the moment. But we have Virginia-grown tobacco. Will that do?"

Tamara purchased the tobacco for her father, placed it with Falcon's mounting purchases, then accepted Alice Packard's invitation to tea in the living quarters of the trading post. She showed Tamara the embroidered and tatted articles of clothing she was making for the baby she expected. It was a lovely visit, and Tamara and Alice talked, about England and Alice's home in Virginia, and about the baby she would soon deliver. But through the curtains parting the living quarters from the trading post area, Tamara saw Falcon pace back and forth, occasionally glancing at Bridie's list of supplies. Their eyes met once, but Tamara quickly averted her gaze back to Alice. Soon, Falcon announced that the horses were packed and that it was time to begin the return journey. Tamara said farewell to her new friend and promised to visit again.

On the return journey, Falcon was pleasant and quickly answered her many questions about the wilderness. She walked beside him on the trail, since both horses were heavily packed with supplies. She did not grow weary of walking, but rather seemed to be revitalized by it. Falcon admired her stamina. He admired many things about the tall, willowy woman walking beside him.

They may have continued with polite small talk had Tamara not tripped and almost reeled headfirst down a steep incline. Again she found herself swooped into Falcon's strong arms. It was as if he anticipated her every move. Actually, he'd seen the extended root, but before he could warn her, her foot had been caught. Her cry of surprise startled the horses, but Falcon managed to calm them even as he held Tamara against him.

Only when he saw her coy smile did he say, "I believe these little accidents are . . . how shall I say? Deliberate?"

"If they were, would you be angry with me?"

"I might . . . you're wasting valuable travel time." Although his words were sharp, there was an underlying softness in the way he looked at her, in the way his hands gently held her arms just above the elbows, absently caressing them.

Tamara bathed in the warmth of his look, the caresses of his fingers. She wanted to remain in his embrace forever. She didn't care if they never returned to Asher Arms. She would share the wilderness with him, if that was what he wanted. His eyes were like dark wells, gazing into her own, intimidating her, yet not intending to, warming her even though a coolness hazed them.

But to break this silent spell that existed between them, the unsmiling Tamara replied, "You've been aloof of late. Perhaps I did deliberately trip, to make my presence known."

Falcon's grip tightened. His blue eyes became even darker as they held her gaze. "I am very aware of you, Tamara . . . how can I not be?"

She said nothing but stood against him, mesmerized by the blankness of his features and the tightness of his jaw. She could almost feel the caresses of his gaze as it moved over her flushed features. A lock of his dark hair fell to his forehead, but he made no effort to sweep it back. Suddenly, she felt compelled to touch his taut features, to feel the softness of the dark wave of hair. She wanted to feel the softness of his mouth against hers. Waves of desire rushed through her as his body became iron-hard against her own. His embrace crushed the breath from her lungs.

Then, in the same moment that her eyes closed, his mouth captured hers in a gentle kiss. She savored its warmth, the caresses of his breath against her cheek, the firm, possessive embrace that she hoped would never end. This was what she wanted.

"Tamara, Tamara," he whispered against her hairline. "Be my woman, Tamara. I want only to please you. . . ."

"To love me, Falcon, as I love you. . . ."

She felt his body stiffen against her own, his breathing become shallow, almost undetectable. Rather than answer, he drew her to him and his arms slipped around her shoulders. She did not understand; why, if he was willing to make her his woman

93

and surely must care for her, was he so hesitant to confess his love?

Perhaps he was not capable of love.

No . . . no, that could not be. The single red rose each morning had spoken of his love. A deep-rooted inhibition forbade him to speak of this emotion so natural between man and woman, even as it tore from his heart. With the same gentleness, the same regret, Falcon stood away from her, fondly enveloped her hands between his own for a moment, then took the reins of the horses and coaxed them ahead.

What terrible emotion restrained him, when all he wanted to do was to love and hold her?

Upon their return to Asher Arms, Tamara stood against the porch rail and watched Falcon unload the supplies. Then, as the sun began to set on another day, he took up his musket and powder bags and left Asher Arms without again looking her way.

There was trouble in his heart. Tamara prayed that time might help him sort things out.

She prayed that he would return.


Falcon shifted the weight of the freshly dressed deer across his shoulders and entered the trail from the wood line. He moved quietly into the valley where Kishke's tribe lived, down the face of the steep hill. As he descended toward the rounded adobes, the gentle swirl of smoke from the cooking fires drifted toward him. There were few Lenni–Lenape Indians left in the Delaware wilderness. Most had migrated to the west and blended in with other tribes when the white man had landed on the shores of the Atlantic. But this small tribe had lived in harmony with its white brothers for hundreds of years. They were peaceful, at war with no one, not even the savage Iroquois to the North who gloried in making war.

The village children had seen Falcon appear from the woodline and rushed to the foot of the trail to await him, their dark, happy faces a pleasant welcome for the exhausted man. He spoke to the tribe elders in their native tongue, deposited the deer at the community cooking fire in the center of the village, and slowly made his way toward the adobe of Kishke, the great Lenape chief.

The chief exited his adobe and stood with his arms crossed, waiting for Falcon to approach. He thought how well his adopted son looked, even though during these past three years he had gradually taken on the appearance, manner, and dress of the white man. Although he wore fringed buckskin trousers made by one of the village women, he had tucked them into highly-polished boots such as those seen in the Packard Trading Post.

Falcon approached and respectfully extended his hand to Kishke. "My Father, I am happy to see you."

"And I you, Son," Kishke replied. "Why have you journeyed to the village so late in the summer season?"

"I have spent many days hunting. Before my return to the estate of Jacob Fleming, I wished to visit my father, Kishke, and his wife."

Flaming Bow approached, crossed his arms, and stood silently beside his father. Across his back he was wearing a quiver containing many arrows, and his right hand held his tightly-strung bow.

"Your mother," Kishke replied, "journeyed at sunrise to the trading post of Packard to deliver his woman's child. She will not return for many suns."

Falcon knew that the silent Flaming Bow had not

spoken because it was disrespectful to interrupt the words of a chief. But now, Kishke withdrew his hand from Falcon's and, sharing a last look between Falcon and Flaming Bow, a look that gave Flaming Bow permission to speak, he quietly entered his adobe.

"Come, Falcon," Flaming Bow said, "it has been many suns since we have hunted together." His powerful bronze arm went across Falcon's shoulder in a rare display of affection. "Now, you will tell me if you have tamed the fiery white woman who would walk in the path of a mad bull."

Falcon replied, "Give me time . . . it has been but a few weeks. The fire is still there, burning bright and hot."

But Falcon did not return his friend's laughter. The very thought of Tamara Fleming sent an icy fire through Falcon's veins. He had left Asher Arms to escape those spellbinding golden-brown eyes and the sensual mouth too willing to share its softness with his own. He had told her that he wanted her for his woman . . . but she wanted love, something he wanted to give but was afraid to. Thus he had come to the village so that he would not have to think about her, but Flaming Bow, himself enamored of Tamara's rare and exquisite beauty, was determined, it seemed, to keep her constantly in his memories.

In the days to follow, he hunted and fished with Flaming Bow and other braves of the village. He whittled wooden toys for the children and enchanted them with tales of the white man's way of life. The days became weeks, and the weeks dragged into a month. finally, news reached the Lenape village that Packard's wife had died, and that Falcon's mother would remain at the Trading Post to care for the newborn child until Packard's sister arrived from Virginia.

The late September night was as cool as a pre-winter eve. Falcon gathered his belongings and weapons together, preparing to return to Asher Arms. These last few weeks, Tamara had filled his heart and his soul. How many early mornings, as he'd stared into the haunting ground mists of the forest, had he seen her exquisite features taking shape, coaxing his return to Asher Arms?

Time and distance had not—would not—quell his thirst for her.

## Chapter 7

A cool wind swept along the Indian River, created lulling, lapping waves that moved slowly toward the shore. Tamara sat quietly, watching the early morning dawn filter glittering rays of light through the dew-dampened oaks. Their leaves were just beginning that gentle transition from green to autumn brown and gold.

Sundays were bittersweet to Tamara, carrying her thoughts back to her beloved England. Sunday was the one day of the week that Mason Gray had put aside his duties to Parliament, King, Country, and business, and had devoted his time exclusively to her. First, there had been church services at Westminster Cathedral, then long walks and picnic lunches in Kensington Park; ofttimes there was a bold excursion through Covent Garden, or a tranquil carriage ride along the lovely wooded lanes southeast of London toward the picturesque village of Maidstone, where they frequently visited Tamara's first beloved nanny.

But England was so far away that it made Tamara ill just to think about it. These past few weeks in the Delaware wilderness had been pleasant, though, and she had gotten to know her father better. Yet there was something macabre and frightening behind his narrow, unblinking stares. When unpredictable moods came over him, he seemed to be not a man but a hard, impenetrable shell. Those were the times that she could silently rise and leave him, and he would never realize she was gone.

Tamara was wearing a Sunday dress, a tight-bodiced, bouffant-sleeved emerald gown with a matching jacket trimmed in darker green embroidery. It had been one of Mason's favorites and he . . . oh, why couldn't she forget that which was past? Why couldn't she put aside Mason and England and Maidstone and picnic lunches in the park?

But she was lonely, more lonely than she had been in all her life. True, she was surrounded by people . . . her father, his house servants, many workers in the stables and fields, and occasional passers-by who were offered the hospitality of Asher Arms. But Falcon had been gone for four weeks. It pained her to think that he had left because of her.

Although the gently sloping Delaware hills had parted him from her, he remained close in thought and spirit. He was ever on her mind, even as she deeply engaged herself in the domesticity of the household. She enjoyed baking the daily bread and assisting Saul when he weeded the vegetable gardens. She was slowly befriending the indifferent Bridie, but Glynnie still remained at arm's distance from her. Her enterprising habits and enthusiasm had brought her closer to the other servants as well.

Tamara pulled her legs up, straightened her voluminous skirts and wrapped her arms around her knees. She felt a different kind of sadness as she thought about young Alice Packard, who had died following the birth of her child. She sat silently on the grassy knoll above the Indian River and the gently lapping waves that made her eyes drowsy on this lovely morning. There was a winter chill in the air which brought a shiver to Tamara's satin-clothed shoulders. She heard the morning sounds of Asher Arms gain clarity in the distance and the occasional snort of the bay thoroughbred mare that had been a gift from her father. The mare, which Tamara had named Ginger, stood just behind her, lazily nibbling at the last remnants of a patch of summer-sweetened clover.

Suddenly the sounds of morning drifted away, and Tamara detected movement in the woods just to her right. The mare pricked her ears toward the wood line and, alarmed, Tamara impulsively spun on her knees. She felt her heart quicken as a dark shadow appeared just beyond the timber line. Tamara rose and moved hastily toward her horse. But when she met the all-too-familiar blue eyes of Falcon, she felt a mountain of relief suddenly rush upon her. "I— I—" She stumbled over her words. She was so happy to see him. "You gave me a terrible fright."

Four weeks in the wilderness had more deeply bronzed his skin, and his hair had grown a trifle longer, just touching his broad shoulders. She thought it odd that he did not pull it back with a ribbon, as was fashionable. But he was Indian, and Indians did not conform to the white man's fashion. Tamara had almost forgotten how handsome he was.

"I apologize for startling you." She was quite lovely this morning, her loose, wheat-colored hair fluttered by the cool prewinter wind, her cheeks still flushed from her momentary fright, and her tall, slim body rigid, as if preparing itself for some defensive maneuver. He felt the warm rush of desire through his body as he continued to appraise her silent stand.

He knew that the long weeks of absence had not quelled his hunger for her. He met her eyes, sure that she knew what he was thinking. Then her horse snorted, and he looked across her slim shoulder toward it, a diversion from this thoughtful moment that existed between them. "You are enjoying the mare, Tamara?"

Tamara smiled, renewed by the lightness in Falcon's voice. "She's wonderful, Falcon. She has been my good, faithful friend."

A moment ago, standing in the woods watching her, he had wondered why she was alone in this isolated place. Now he had a good idea why: she was lonely. The very fact that she was English and educated and a lady of refinement had alienated her from the people of Asher Arms, and perhaps even her own father. She was lonely enough that she had found friendship in the horse her father had given her. Falcon wondered how many mornings she had come here to spend time alone and wish for that life she had loved and left three thousand miles across the ocean.

Before he realized it, he had opened his arms and invited Tamara into his embrace. He knew then how much he had missed her as he felt the softness of her windblown hair against his bronze cheek, her gentle form pressed close to his own. God! How he'd missed her! And now, again, she was in his arms, holding him as if there would be no tomorrow . . . and no Falcon to comfort her. He wondered if she felt about him as he felt about her. He had asked her to be his woman and she had asked for love. That alone answered his question.

"Lovely Tamara," he whispered against her hairline, "how lonely you must be for your other life."

Tamara shrugged. "Perhaps a bit, Falcon. I do

miss Mason and Gray House and the friends I'd made." She continued, lifting her eyes to meet his warm gaze, "But why did you leave Asher Arms? Why were you gone so long? You must have known how uncomfortable I was . . . am . . . and that I do so need you. I thought perhaps I had lost you as my friend and companion. I thought you had left because of me." Then she again dropped her head to his chest.

Falcon's fingers circled her arms and gently put her away from him, that his eyes might again meet her tear-moistened ones. "I did leave because of you," he confessed. "You frighten me, Tamara. I know that I am not good enough for you, yet I cannot bear the thought of another man ever possessing you. You know that I want you. You call me friend, but it is more than friendship that I feel for you. You were here only a few weeks when I journeyed to the village, yet I hungered for your nearness as if I had known and wanted you for a lifetime. I have held myself aloof for a long time and suddenly, without any warning at all, my heart has opened and welcomes you to it. I have been alone my entire life, and I had planned to remain alone until the day my last breath was drawn. But you have changed all this. I asked you not so long ago to be my woman. This is something I still want, yet I know that I did not give you time to—"

"Falcon," Tamara rushed back into his embrace. All her life she had hoped to be loved by a man she could love in return, and she felt that possibility distinctly in Falcon's arms. "I don't know why you are so hesitant to express love for me, but I can see that you do love me. Falcon. . . ." Again, she drew back and lifted her happy, smiling face. "You might think me mad, but I want to be yours until the end of time if you truly want me. I don't know what has come over me . . . certainly I was not raised to throw myself at a man I have known so short a while. A world of thought has rushed through my head in the weeks of your absence. I do want to be with you. But . . . I must know that you love me. Perhaps love means little to you, but it means so much to a woman. Oh, Falcon . . . I will try to understand your hesitation. I truly will. I can envision no happier life than with you, as your woman and your wife. Perhaps one day you will journey with me to England, to the home of the man who is truly my father.''

Slowly he released her, then stepped just out of her touching distance. ''I don't know about that, Tamara. I have never felt a desire to leave this land.''

''Falcon, I didn't mean forever . . . just a visit. England is wonderful.'' Tamara did not understand his hesitation. She knew only that the very mention of England pinched his brows into a worried frown. She had seen it before.

''We'll see,'' he replied after a moment.

Tamara rushed back into his arms. When he failed to respond to her closeness, her trembling hands rose to gently rub his strong shoulders. ''I feel that I have known you forever, Falcon, and I will be proud to show you off to my guardian. We could visit with him, then return to the land of the Delaware . . . and your people, the Lenapes.''

Fighting her nearness and her words, Falcon turned away. ''You scarcely know me, Tamara. You don't know what I am, or who I am.''

''You are Falcon . . . son of the great chief, Kishke.''

''Do you see what I mean?'' he countered, turning back, ''You know nothing about me. I am not Kishke's true son. The man who called himself my father was a drunken trapper who died bound hand and foot to a wagon bed, bitten by a rabid wolverine, raving and foaming at the mouth. For years I saw him treat my mother like dirt and no one was happier than I to see him dead. Even my mother wept with relief when the earth covered his rotting, putrid body."

"I—I'm sorry, Falcon," Tamara replied, shuddering. She had never heard such bitterness in her life. "I thought you were truly the son of Kishke. Your father, then, was a white man?"

Falcon hesitated for a moment. "He was."

"I—I do believe you, Falcon. And I trust you, as I have never trusted before."

"Do you believe me . . . trust me . . . because you now know that I am a white man?"

The question was almost an accusation. Tamara was a bit taken aback. She became silent as she carefully composed her reply. "Ofttimes, Falcon, things I say don't come out quite right. I believe you, and trust you, be you Indian or white. I did not mean to imply otherwise."

Her soft words and nearness managed to soften his voice. "Then your trust means the world to me, Tamara. I shall never lie to you, I swear this."

He felt the warmth of her penetrating her clothing and his and flaming his body with the fire of her innocent beauty. With her golden brown eyes trustingly, enticingly holding his, his mouth captured hers in a deep, probing kiss. Tamara's arms slipped around his strong, sinewy shoulders and held him possessively. She felt his strong hands firmly at her back, touching, caressing, stroking the sensual length of her, slipping beneath the jacket to gain a more intimate closeness, only to meet the satin threads of still another barrier.

104

Then she felt herself being eased to her back on the grassy knoll and the weight of his body covering her own. She did not protest, but enjoyed his mouth, which trailed caresses across her cheek, her pert nose, the silken softness of her eyelids, that gentle, throbbing pulse in her throat, then returned to recapture her parted mouth in a fierce, bruising kiss that took the very breath from her body.

Tamara quivered as his mouth provoked tantalizing sensations such as she had never before experienced. His fingers moved confidently over her passion-warmed flesh, causing tremors and warm waves of desire to wash over her body. Then his hands moved to her firm, round breasts and gently kneaded them beneath the silken bodice before moving to unfasten the stays at the front of her gown. His body was hard and firm against hers, and his breath was sweet and warm and enticing against her flushed cheek.

Suddenly, the blissful, wonderful torture ceased. Falcon's hands slid to her back to gently hold her, then rose to cup her smooth, ivory face. Tamara's soft brown eyes were glazed with the fire of passion and want, and yet confusion settled behind their silent gaze. She had never before tasted of the pleasures of man, and she wanted Falcon with a fierce desperation.

But Falcon controlled the moment and it was obvious by the narrowing of his eyes that something was on his mind, something powerful enough to silence his own craving hunger for her.

Tamara didn't care that she was lying on a grassy knoll beside the Indian River, her silent gaze begging this proud, strong half-breed to make love to her. She didn't care if the whole world were looking down. She wanted him and that was all that mattered. He had brought her this far; would he leave her cold, unspoiled, and perplexingly frustrated?

But that was precisely what he intended to do. He pushed away from her and rose quickly to his feet. He offered no explanation as he moved slowly toward the woodline, retrieved his weapons where he had set them against a tree, and moved up the knoll toward Asher Arms.

Tamara sat up, then straightened her satin skirts. "Falcon." He looked back. "I may never forgive you for this."

Only now did life spring back to his bronze features. "Forgive me for what, Tamara? For not taking you like a common whore? I care for you—I left Asher Arms to try to convince myself that I didn't. But a lifetime away from you would not be long enough." He suddenly felt the determination rushing from him. "I—I can't forget the fact that you're a lady, as well as Jacob Fleming's daughter, while I am . . . who I am."

"Jacob's daughter or not, you have asked me to be your woman." Tamara was not sure where her calmness came from. With a demure sigh, she rose and began smoothing the wrinkles of her skirts. She approached Falcon, then deftly began refastening the buttons of his shirt. Her eyes lifted to meet his narrow, unblinking stare. "I believe my horse has picked up a stone?" she said quietly, changing the subject. "Will you take a look at it before you return to Asher Arms?"

Her cool delivery surprised him. It was as if the past few moments had not existed between them. But he did not want her to see that her indifference bothered him. "Which hoof?"

"The front . . . right, I believe."

Silently, Falcon approached the mare, picked up

the hoof, and held it firmly between his knees. Then he removed his knife from its scabbard and dug out the stone, which he then skipped across the waves of the Indian River. "The mare has an ill-fitting shoe. Before you ride her again, she should be reshod. I'll take her back for you," he added, taking the reins.

"Falcon?" He turned back. "May I walk with you?"

He bowed slightly. "I would be honored."

Only God knew why he'd ever denied himself the pleasure of her. She was a sensual, desirable woman and a prize such as he had never before enjoyed. She had wanted him; there was no doubt about that.

Thinking about it now, and how close he'd come to possessing the grandest treasure of all—the hidden treasures of the beauty walking silently beside him— he could have kicked himself in the britches.


In the weeks to follow, neither Tamara nor Falcon mentioned the incident beside the Indian River. Tamara frequently sought him out in the stables or the running pens where he worked the new horses on long leads. He often laughed at her as she momentarily forgot that she was a lady and joined the servants' children in their games. Daily he walked with her along the wooded trails where hues of gold and bronze and brown were replaced by bare trees and gusts of December snows. He enticed smiles from her with his own, now more frequently and easily offered than in the past. Watching him, Tamara learned so much . . . from his gentle, yet firm hand with the horses . . . his tendency to overlook the vices and idiosyncrasies of the people he worked with . . . his quiet admiration of the changing season, as if he'd never witnessed this gentle transition before . . .

his tenderness when he drew her to him and was content simply to hold her. Tamara looked forward to the warm moments and the affectionate embraces of this man. She learned to look to him with pride and promise and patience. Every day she fell more deeply in love with the tall, proud half-breed who had come so close to making her his woman.

But something often threw a veil over the light, carefree moments they spent with each other, something that very much confused Tamara. She couldn't help but notice the tension—almost a hatred—that existed between Falcon and her father. She had never heard disrespect in Falcon's voice—only a dry indifference when he and her father spoke together; but her father's tongue was like a lethal venom—scarcely typical of an invalid, dying man—he could somehow summon the strength to castigate Falcon's every move, his every action, virtually every breath he drew. Tamara had often seen Falcon's jaw tighten as he tried not to respond to her father's degradations, and all the while her respect and admiration for Falcon grew, while for her father it deteriorated.

Tamara had pulled a rabbit fur cape about her shoulders this brisk December evening. Night had fallen early and she stood on the long porch of her father's house, hugging her cape to her and staring up at an ominous black sky threatening rain. Thunder shook the far horizon, casting an eerie golden glow upon the clearing where Asher Arms nestled sleepily. It was a quiet night; she could vaguely hear the rushing waves of the Indian River far beyond the hills and the mournful cry of a nightbird, far, far away in the Delaware wilderness that surrounded her.

Tamara felt thoughtful this evening. She'd been at Asher Arms almost four months, and had spent another two months before that aboard ship. She was thinking of Mason Gray, whom she hadn't seen in so long. What would he be doing now . . . reading in the library of Gray House, listening to the perfect, melodic notes of John Parkervale's daughter, who had spent her hours playing the pianoforte while her father and Mason visited? Would he be thinking of her and wondering what she was doing?

Oh, how she missed Mason. She could almost hear his pleasant voice calling to her, soliciting her affections and wanting to hear how she'd spent every minute of the day. He had never grown bored of her.

"Tamara?"

Tamara felt her nerves jump as Falcon quietly spoke her name. She turned, slipped her hands beneath her fur cape, and smiled. "Falcon, you did startle me. I—I was deep in thought."

"You're lonely again, aren't you?" he asked, his hands rising to touch the fur cape covering her shoulders. "And cold."

Why did Falcon always read her mind? "A little," she replied, "on both accounts. I hadn't expected it to be this cold."

"It will be many months before it is warm again."

Tamara enjoyed the tenderness of his hands absently caressing her shoulders through the fur cape. She enjoyed the pleasant, masculine aroma of him and the gentleness of his voice as he spoke. Just a few short weeks ago, they'd come close to making love. And right now, she couldn't imagine anything more pleasant. The long Delaware nights had afforded little relief in her thoughts of him. He had filled her dreams. But he had held himself deliberately aloof, almost coldly, at times, although they had spent long hours alone, walking in the woods and sharing occasional undemanding embraces.

"Falcon, what do you want?" Tamara asked, nestling against him.

He wanted to reiterate his proposal to make her his woman, but instead, he replied in a soft whisper against her hairline, "I really haven't thought about it, Tamara."

"Do you ever want a wife and a family?"

Falcon turned slightly, so that she could not see his features in the twilight shadows. "A wife and a family," he echoed softly. "Both a treasure, Tamara . . . perhaps one day."

Tamara regained the nearness to him, and her hands darted out from beneath her cape and slid gently around his waist, beneath his buckskin jacket. "You must decide, Falcon, before it is too late. You will want to enjoy both while you are still a young man."

"I have told you that I want you," he replied, returning her embrace, ". . . enough so that I will wait until your stubbornness is gone. Besides, I have seen only thirty-one years." Falcon laughed gently, "Or am I an old man in your eyes, Tamara, my friend?"

Silence. Tamara closed her eyes against his powerful, hirsute chest. How casually he had called her his friend. Did he not realize that she wanted more from him than friendship, that she was on the brink of accepting his proposal to be his woman, rather than his wife? He had been the one bright spark in her life these past few months. His very nearness gave her enthusiasm and vitality and a reason to wake up in the morning. Always, when she climbed lazily from her bed she would amble to the window, pull back the drapery, and see him in the running pens, working with the horses. Sometimes she would look at her window sill and remember the days of summer slowly drifting into autumn, and a rose carefully placed there for her to find.

Suddenly, echoing from the direction of the gardens, Tamara heard her name called. It was Bridie, impatiently reminding her of the late hour. Fearful that Bridie might approach the garden gate and see her in Falcon's arms, she pulled quickly away.

"I—I must go in," she said, dropping her eyes.

"I will see you tomorrow then?" Falcon's hand darted out and took her own to give it a gentle squeeze. "I will show you a lovely place where the deer come to quench their thirst. Would you like that?"

Tamara smiled as she lifted her golden eyes to meet his thoughtful ones. "Yes . . . yes, I would like that."


Tamara spoke briefly with Bridie in the kitchens, tasted a small morsel of venison and dressing being prepared for tomorrow's dinner, said goodnight to her father, who was reading in the library, then sauntered slowly toward her bedchamber in the north corridor. She felt spry and happy and not at all tired. She was thinking only of tomorrow, and seeing Falcon again.

Seven months ago Tamara had begun a quest for the answers to puzzling questions, partly as a diversion to the loneliness she had anticipated in this wild land of the Delaware. Since the afternoon Mason had confessed that he'd had another son before Ryan, Tamara had decided to come to America and find out as much as she could about Fedora and the child. Somehow, though, in the past three months, these two tragic people had flown from her thoughts. They had been replaced by something alive and wonderful,

111

something that made her happy to have been born a woman.

Mason Gray's first love, and his son, had been dead these many years and were part of the past. Now, the only thing that filled Tamara's thoughts was the proud half-breed who had become her constant companion and who wanted her to become his woman. Falcon . . . she enjoyed speaking his name, over and over again.

By winter, she no longer yearned constantly for the life she had left in her beloved England. She no longer brooded in the morning hours, sitting alone beside the Indian River and throwing stones into the water. The machinations and dramas of Asher Arms, even Glynnie's polite, yet aloof, behavior, could not penetrate this warm, wonderful, invisible shield she had thrown up around herself and Falcon. She had once considered herself a sensible woman, but would such a woman allow the affections of a man like Falcon into her life? Oh, yes . . . yes, my sweet, wonderful Falcon . . . my love.

Tamara hadn't realized she'd been standing at her chamber door for quite a few minutes, daydreaming, her fingers resting lightly on the door handle, until she heard a noise from within. Deftly, she opened the door, then stood for a moment, watching the petite, auburnn-haired Glynnie, wearing one of Tamara's dresses and admiring herself in the cheval mirror.

Tamara was surprised to find Glynnie in her private bedchamber, though she knew the seventeen-year-old servant girl could be a precocious child. Now, here she was, wearing one of Tamara's gowns, a lavender day gown with a low bodice and wide, puffed sleeves that became narrow and clinging just below the elbows. And Tamara could not help but notice how lovely she looked in it.

Glynnie did not see Tamara step into the chamber and quietly close the door. She was still admiring her own reflection and positioning the columinous skirts over the hoops and petticoats she must also have taken from Tamara's chifforobe.

"You look lovely, Glynnie."

Glynnie spun rapidly, very nearly losing her balance, shock sweeping over her features. Then she drew her hand to her mouth and looked at Tamara as if she'd seen a ghost. "I—I saw you with Falcon—I—didn't think you would be—back so soon."

Tamara approached, linked her fingers at her back, and slowly circled Glynnie. "It looks much better on you than on me." It didn't, really, but Tamara had to say something to ease this tense moment.

Glynnie's mouth pressed into a thin line. "Why don't you say what you mean, instead of giving me this false flattery? You're angry . . . you're just trying to make me feel terrible about being here."

"Well . . ." Tamara raised an impertinent eyebrow, "we both know you *shouldn't* be here, don't we?" Tamara turned slightly away from the intruding servant girl. "What were you doing here, by the way?"

Glynnie looked quickly toward Tamara's bed. "I—I was making sure your fire was still burning warmly," she replied, averting her glance toward the fireplace. "And I saw your chifforobe open . . . and your lovely dresses." Then she lifted her chin in a stubborn gesture. "And I suppose you'll tell my mother about the intrusion?"

"I really hadn't planned to. . . ." Tamara approached the fireplace and began jabbing at the logs

113

with a poker. "Why don't you tell me why I shouldn't, Glynnie?"

"I—I don't think I can, Miss." Her look elicited sympathy and understanding. "I've treated you awfully."

"Yes, you have, Glynnie." Tamara casually replaced the poker at its resting place against the fireplace. "And it is time you and I ceased this childish quibble and tried to be friends."

"Hrumph!" Again, Glynnie looked surprised. "I have given you no reason to want to be my friend. Besides . . . I am your father's servant. It isn't proper that we be friends."

"Will you try, at least?"

Glynnie had begun removing the dress and now stepped out of it and the petticoats as if they were one garment. Then she picked up her own plain muslin dress and pulled it over her head. She was relieved that Tamara had not pounced on her like an angry cat for invading her private sanctuary, but she was not willing to concede to a friendship with the woman who had caught Falcon's eye. "I think we can be cordial to each other . . . because the master expects it, Miss Fleming."

"You are saying then that we cannot be friends?"

"I'm not saying one way or the other." Glynnie's voice was not rude but was, rather, a dull monotone. "And, Miss—I know it's none of my business, but you and Falcon—"

"You're right," Tamara hastily replied. "It is none of your business. But, to clear the air, we care for each other."

"Hrumph!" she said again. "Just as well, miss. Mother said—" Glynnie's smile was laced with sarcasm. "Mother said that I am much too good for Falcon!"

114

Tamara said nothing, but once again engaged her patience. Glynnie moved toward the door and Tamara toward the satin gown she had discarded to the floor. She picked it up, then approached and laid it across Glynnie's arm. "We shan't bicker, Glynnie, and cast insults back and forth. We shall agree to be cordial to each other, and I'll agree not to tell your mother about this. Please, won't you accept the dress as a gift from me?"

Glynnie's eyes widened as if she'd been physically struck. "The dress, miss . . . you're giving it to me . . . for my very own?"

"For your very own, if you'll take it."

"Yes—yes—thank you, miss. . . ." For the first time in three months, she favored Tamara with a smile. But the smile instantly faded as she again looked toward the bed. Tamara, too, looked, confused by the unreadable expression, akin to regret, in Glynnie's eyes. Then Glynnie turned and fled toward the door and the corridor with her new treasure.

Tamara looked around the bright bedchamber, feeling quite pleased with herself.

## Chapter 8

As a sudden, early darkness erased the gentle ray of light filtering in through the slightly parted draperies, Tamara sat on the edge of her bed and absently stroked the soft wool of the coverlet folded the length of it. Then she felt something hard and rectangular tucked just beneath the top layer of the coverlet. She turned back the edge, exposing a dark blue velvet-covered book with the initials M.E.F. scrolled in the center of an oval brass plate in the lower right corner. The initials were her mother's—Marian Elsa Fleming—and only Glynnie could have left the book there. Was this why Glynnie's gaze had wandered and a tinge of regret had replaced her pleasure in receiving the dress as a gift?

Tamara opened the book, finding that the pages were worn and browned by age. The twilight darkness made it impossible to see and Tamara rose with the book in her hand, walked over to the white mantel, and turned up the flame of the lantern. Then she leaned back in an elaborately carved walnut daybed, pulled he short riding boots off, and drapped them to the floor with a dull thud. The lantern cast an eerie glow that encircled her and cast a purple sheen across the small book she slowly opened. Inside the cover was inscribed, "To Marian . . . From your mother, April 10, 1719." Tamara smiled to herself; her mother had been twenty-one, the same age as Tamara, when this small gift had been given to her. But how did it come to be in the precocious Glynnie's possession? Tamara wondered.

Still, she felt the excitement of having something of her mother's as she tucked her bare feet beneath the skirts of her dress, then turned a page, excited to see the first entry, dated April 11, 1719, written in her mother's firm, youthful hand. She eased back on her bed, then fluffed a pillow behind her. She was about to begin reading from the front of the diary when her fingers caught and lifted a thin red ribbon marking a place halfway through the pages. Instinctively, she flipped to the marked page and began to read:

December, 1732,
I have dwelte upon this land for twelve years with my husband, Jacob. He has built a fine house, and hired more servants through indenture. Life has been faire to the Flemings. But today, I feel upon my hearte a desolation, a despair that pryckes my conscious minde and leaves a painful void. A letter from home announces the death of my deare father of the blacke vomit. I remember his kinde face and jolly laugh. Yet, I, too, remember his berating voice when I wept, not wishing to be parted from him and mum and brother Sam, and our warme parlor on Beacon Hill. My beloved Boston is a dream now, tucked far into the recesses of my minde. I cannot dwelle upon the unhappiness that settles upon my soul, for I suspect

that Jacob and I shall soone be blest with God's gentle song. I feele within my wombe, which I had feared to be stricke barren, the tiny stirrings of a new life. And I weep for the poor little one's future in this savage lande of the Delaware.

The next entry, on the right side of the page, was dated June 16, 1733, and the handwriting, although it bore vague similarities to that of the preceding page, was not written in the same careful, flamboyant style.

A fortnight ago, in a great agony, I birthed a female child whom I have called Tamara. Jacob despairs, that it is not a male child, who might grow and helpe him worke this fertile land that he has called Asher Arms. In a fitte of rage, Jacob swore that we should have been blest with no child at all, than to be burdened with a worthless female child . . . but I pray he spake his disappointment, and not his heart.

Tamara felt a sick, sinking feeling in her heart. Was this how her father had welcomed her into the world? And was this the passage, boldly underlined in thick, dark ink, that Glynnie wanted especially to bring to her attention? Yet . . . Tamara stopped to think about it. Perhaps that had been Glynnie's initial intention, but she probably felt as bad about it as Tamara now felt. Although tears moistened her eyes, Tamara forced herself to read on:

. . . dear, dear little girl, my Tamara . . . how shall she fare? Like my poor mother, my hands become gradually weake and palsied. My minde

118

drifts and I cannot remember the important things. Tho I try, I cannot care for my sweet girl. If not for my deare Fedora . . .

Fedora! Tamara felt a sudden silencing of her heart as a winter coldness crawled across her flesh. Instantly, her hand searched among the folds of her gown for the medallion Mason had given her before her departure from England, a medallion that had been worn by the tragic Fedora. Was the Fedora mentioned in her mother's passages Mason's Fedora? The woman who had flamed his youthful passions and resulted in the vehement disapproval of his own father? But it could not be! Fedora and the child were supposed to have died soon after reaching this land. The child could scarcely have been two years of age. But if Fedora and the child were still here when Tamara was born . . . my God! A discrepancy? The child would have been ten years old, or older. Why did her father lie to Mason Gray so many, many years ago? Tamara read on:

If not for my deare Fedora, I could not fare. She is my strength and my hands . . . this dear hearte. If only she were content, and might cease to grieve after these many years for the loss of her beloved husbande, and the father of her handsome boy.

Oh, yes! Yes, it had to be! This was the first tangible evidence she'd had that Fedora had ever been here. Fascinated, forgetting the cruel, stinging passages she had read just moments before, she read page after page, noting both the dates of the entries, over a three-year span, and the deterioration of her mother's handwriting. One thing was evident—her mother

119

had loved her very much. There were many, many references to her. But Fedora's name was mentioned only once more, in a scrawled, barely legible, and broken hand, which read:

Confined to bed . . . Jacob had brought me news, Fedora and her son dead . . . I try to weepe for my sad friend, but no strength. I feare time passes quickly for me. What shall happen to my deare girl . . .

Tamara dropped the diary to her lap. She realized only now that tears traced gentle paths down her cheeks. Her poor, tragic mother. It saddened Tamara to know that from the time of this entry, in 1735, her mother had lived and suffered another ten years, most of those years spent knowing that the daughter she had so dearly loved had been sent away from her. And the child and Fedora . . . Mason's son and his one and only true love. What had killed them? What terrible fate—disease or tragedy—had taken their lives? Instinctively, Tamara touched the gold medallion that had belonged to Fedora, this gentle tie to that forgotten face. Why, God, she wondered, had her father lied about the time of their deaths? They could have been gone only a few short months when Mason's quest eventually brought him to the home of her father.

Suddenly, Tamara's hunger and exhaustion were forgotten. She heard the distant, gentle roll of thunder upon the horizon. She looked around, at a strange mixture of walnut furnishings . . . delicate Queen Anne chairs and the elaborately carved and gilded harpsichord and stool that had belonged to her mother. She did not want to be here, within these four walls, surrounded by these strange furnishings with their sad, lonely past. She did not want to believe that her father had not wanted his newborn daughter. She did not want to think about her mother's palsied hands and failing memory . . . and the heartache that filled her every moment. She did not want to think about Fedora and her young son . . . and their mysterious deaths.

Tamara quickly rose, unaware that her mother's diary had fallen to the floor, and fled from her bedchamber, down the wide, unlit corridor, toward the parlor and the cloisonné table in the corner that was cluttered with her father's liquor decanters. She carefully chose a decanter of red wine and a goblet from the breakfront and turned slowly toward the rear entrance of the house.

"Where you going with that, miss?"

Tamara had not seen Bridie enter and was visibly startled. "Oh, I—I thought I'd walk out of doors, Bridie."

"With your father's spirits, miss?"

Hesitantly, Tamara held the decanter up. "My father . . ." she replied quietly, "won't miss this one."

" 'Tis evil, miss . . . the drink . . . and foul as the devil's breath."

"Then I hope . . ." Tamara rolled in her same soft tone, walking slowly past Bridie, "that a handsome rogue does not take it upon himself to kiss me."

Tamara felt that all the world's hurts were shut out when the rear door slammed behind her and she felt the soft grassy cushion beneath her slippers, reminding her that she had left her bedchamber without changing into her shoes. Thank goodness Bridie had not seen her slippered feet! Servant or no, she'd have taken the opportunity to remind Tamara that it wasn't proper. Dark, rumbling clouds hid the night

121

sky and a stormy breeze whistled through the tree-tops. But Tamara saw and heard none of it. She saw only the lonely forest path, and felt only the damp, rotting leaves beneath her slippers. She wanted only to be alone, and to hear no other sounds but those of the night, and her pounding heart. As she left the lights of Asher Arms far, far behind her and walked quickly along the dark trail that tunneled through the forest, she felt the hot flames of tears burning her ivory cheeks. She cared not how far she'd wandered from Asher Arms. She cared only that she was away from every tangible reminder of the day's pains.

She really didn't know why this melancholy had settled upon her. Her father's dispassion of twenty-one years ago had developed into a deep, undying love for her. Every living being, at one time or another, had felt an emotion he or she was ashamed of. Surely he was ashamed of his. Oh, that girl! That meddling Glynnie! Why did she persist in following this vindictive course? Would Tamara's kindness to-day end the vindictiveness? She prayed that it would.

As for her mother's suffering, it had ended with her death. She knew no more pain and sorrow. She was at peace in God's hands, and somehow, Tamara felt her gentle presence, guiding her and keeping her safe.

Then why had she dropped to her knees beside the night-darkened waterfall, whose eternal rumble drifted across the few feet of space toward her? She did not even feel the evening cold as she carefully set the decanter on a smooth bit of ground, settled the skirts of her gown about her, then poured the spar-kling red wine into the goblet she held gently between her fingers. The moonlight, sifting in through the ceiling of mast-high trees, caught the crimson liquid in a glow of light. She lifted it to her eyes and swirled it in a delicate, hypnotic motion, then touched its sweetness to her lips. It was like a warm river in her throat, tingling, settling in an intoxicating pool in the pit of her stomach. She quickly emptied the glass and poured another.

Yes, yes, this was the peace she wanted . . . this warm, numbing thing within her, robbing her of sensible thought . . . filling her lungs with a heady pre-storm breeze that whipped her hair around her relaxed features and her closed eyes. Nothing mattered but that she was alone, with only the haunting sounds of night for company: the far-away hoot of an owl . . . nocturnal creatures prowling for food . . . the lazy, melancholic water falling into a deep, clear forest pond.

Despite her wandering senses, Tamara suddenly felt that she was no longer alone; yet she felt no peril. Had the wine dulled that inner warning, the delicate, instinctive sense that kept her alert to danger? She looked toward the dark, forest trail and heard the long, even bootsteps of a man, the plod of horse's hooves on packed earth, and the clink of a powder horn against metal. Yet all she felt was the gentle pulse of her own heart and a foggy vortex created by the wine, lifting her senses far away from that mysterious, yet familiar stranger whose shadow suddenly darkened her expectant features.

The half-naked Falcon emerged from the shadows, the sleeves of his shirt tied carelessly around his narrow hips, his chest rippling with muscles. She wondered how he could bear this bitter cold wind that surely must sting his flesh. Tamara watched his slow approach: the long, confident strides, the reins of his horse dragged lazily across his bare shoulder, his tight buckskin pants tucked into black leather boots. Her golden brown eyes lifted to his blue ones, reflected in a soft beam of moonlight like a vast inland river, and his steady, narrow gaze held her mesmerized.

He stopped before her, his feet apart in a careless stand, his hands drawn to his narrow hips. Before he could speak, Tamara lifted her goblet, filled afresh with the crimson wine, and asked him quite boldly, "Have I ever told you, Falcon . . . that I am a virgin?"

He said nothing for a moment, but his penetrating gaze took in her soft, feminine features, accented by the sheen of moonlight that also caught and reflected the brilliance of her golden hair. He felt an ache in his groin . . . never had he seen her so lovely, and so seductively influenced by the wine she had been drinking. "You won't be for long, Tamara, if you continue that kind of common talk."

Tamara arose as quickly as the wine would allow her, then sauntered slowly and deliberately toward him. Then she turned and leaned against him for support. "Falcon, you're such a bore!" she teased, "My handsome rogue—wouldn't you like—" She turned, moistened her lips with the wine and lifted them closer, "to taste my wine?"

Falcon's jaw became taut. Her wine-sweetened mouth and smiling eyes were mere inches from his face. God . . . how he wanted to taste her willing lips, to take her in his arms and feel the warmth and passion of her. He had tried these many weeks to conduct himself as a gentleman, because she was Fleming's daughter. But a red-blooded male could maintain just so much control. Thus, Falcon's strong hands circled her arms with a strange gentleness and drew her close. And his mouth captured hers, sweet with wine and womanly passions.

"Tamara, Tamara," he whispered, his lips coursing a deliberate path over her delicate features, violet

124

eyelids, and her small earlobe exposed by her wind-tossed hair. "Why do you torture me? God, how I want you."

"Take me, Falcon . . . I am . . . yours." Her reply was broken, erratic, so softly whispered that he was not sure he'd heard her correctly. Was this truly her desire, or was the wine speaking for her? Was her body truly liquid hot against his own, her breasts passion-sensitive and aroused against his naked chest? Or did the wine surge through her veins, cruelly deceiving him?

As the heavens opened and a brutal rain suddenly and unexpectedly lashed against their enraptured bodies, Falcon picked her up in his arms, again claimed her mouth in a flaming kiss, then put her across the saddle of his horse. And, scarcely aware of the howling, screaming storm that slashed against them, he moved slowly and deliberately toward a small cabin a few hundred feet up from the waterfall.

"Where do we journey, Falcon?"

"We are far from your father's house, Tamara. There is an abandoned cabin where we can seek shelter from the storm. You will catch your death if you do not get out of those cold, wet clothes."

When they'd reached the cabin in the dale, Falcon helped Tamara down, then slapped the flank of his horse. He knew the animal would head for the dry stables of Asher Arms. Then, with a gentle laugh, Tamara broke away from him and, with her arms outstretched, twirled and twirled, until she was dizzy and laughing and scarcely able to feel the merciless pounding of the rain against her tender flesh. Then she stumbled, fell into Falcon's strong arms and, as the wine surging through her veins left her dizzy and powerless, she felt herself being lifted again into his embrace.

Falcon threw open the door of the cabin, which creaked on its ancient hinges, and entered with Tamara in his arms. He quickly pushed the door to with his foot, closing out the cold, whipping rain, and eased her to her unsteady feet. When he turned and saw that her normally full tresses were lying in limp, disheveled strands, her body swaying from the effects of the wine, he drew his hands to his hips and laughed gently. But his laughter did not linger as his eyes lowered to her pale silk blouse, its top stays unfastened . . . soaked, clinging to a lithe, womanly figure, the pink, peaked breasts revealed beneath the silk folds made transparent by its wetness. He felt again the ache in his groin . . . it was all he could do to keep from overpowering her that he might feel her soft, sensual curves against his hard body.

Tamara noticed the humor instantly melt from his strong, unshaven features. She was only too aware that his eyes had lowered, and that they admired her. His body shivered violently. She could almost see the pounding of his heart. She was pleased. She wanted this moment . . . this opportunity . . . there was a wild, uncontrolled thing within her that fought for his nearness, a desire that had not been nurtured by the sweet red wine that made her senses real, that made it impossible for her to feel the cold. She felt a gentle pulse through her body increase in intensity, its invisible fingers reaching out from her body, to draw him closer . . . closer. . . .

She had not seen him move. Suddenly, the distance closed between them and she felt his strong grip on her arms, drawing her closer, lighting a flame between their separate bodies and making them one. Tamara met the brilliant blue of his eyes, slightly narrowed, his lips parted, his jawline tight, his raven-black hair in thick wet strands against his forehead. And his mouth closed bruisingly over hers, caressing, possessing . . . tasting her wine-sweetened lips and taking away her breath so that she thought she might smother against him. And it was wonderful . . . a magical thing that erased all the world's noise, so that they were all that existed, she and Falcon, their bodies molded in a liquid hot river against each other's. There was no longer a violent storm, nor blackness upon the far Delaware horizon—there was only this warm, tender, obsessive thing that pulsated between them, a mutual desire to own and conquer.

Falcon's lips were like hot flames against her cheek, her closed eyelids, the small, throbbing pulse in her neck, her heaving chest . . . and then the pale pink buds of her breasts peaked against his mouth . . . his tongue. Then he dropped to his knees, taking the weight of her body with him, taking away that very small breath of space that had existed between their thirsting bodies.

"Tell me that you do not want this," he whispered hoarsely. "Tell me, Tamara . . . and I will stop."

Tamara took a small, deep breath. "I—I cannot. I . . . don't want you . . . to stop, Falcon," she whispered in reply. She wanted him so badly that tears touched her cheeks, even as her fingers closed tightly over his strong, rain-dampened shoulders. Then Falcon's fingers rose to brush away what he thought was the rain upon her cheeks, then gently entwined through her thick, loose hair. She saw the blur of him, of gentle, masculine features that could gain no depth and clarity, but seemed to look down on her from some distant place, like a dream from which she could not awaken. She felt the tenderness

127

of his hand stroking her neck, felt his hard, masculine body against her soft one, and slowly, his solid form penetrated her private sanctuary, the dream world she had built around herself, a world that, without him, was sterile and empty. The Falcon she thought she knew had been indifferent and demanding, not this man whose gentleness now, without spoken words, promised to enflame the very core of her stubborn heart. Tamara felt the gentleness of his hands massaging her now bare shoulders, then lower to firmly grip her arms just above the elbows and pull her close to him. Yes . . . yes, this was what she wanted! This wild, uncontrolled thing that moved swiftly through her body, coursing a desire into her veins that she had never felt before. And as full, masculine lips possessively captured her own, she knew that, for all time, she wanted nothing more than to be his prize . . . his lover . . . she wanted his hands to be the ones that awakened and quenched the thirst within her, exploding in wonderful rhapsody beneath skin that tingled from his very touch.

"Oh, Falcon . . . Falcon, what is it that I feel for you?" she whispered against his bronze cheek.

"It is a good thing," he whispered in reply, "a destined thing. Tamara . . . you and I, like this . . . from the moment I first saw you, I knew. . . ." Falcon's hands slipped to her back and eased her blouse down, exposing small, firm breasts, one of which he captured with his mouth while he gently massaged the other passion-sensitive peak until it hardened beneath his fingers. An unbearable ache crawled through his groin. He wanted nothing more than to feel her naked skin beneath his body, to bury himself deep within the sweet, moist depth of her . . . his hands lowered and slipped beneath the waist of her skirts to ease them down her slim hips.

Tamara's fingernails dug madly into his shoulders as his mouth, his lips . . . his tongue tasted the sweet nectar of her bare flesh, painfully arousing some deep, hidden place within her, beneath her smooth, ivory stomach that heaved under his caresses, and . . . lower. Instinctively, her thighs eased apart and his strong, steady hands tenderly, masterfully, massaged warm, soft flesh and smooth, perfectly-shaped legs, easing her to her back on the musty hay carpet of the cabin floor, and slowly, moving toward that warm, moist inner place that, when touched, drove the breath from her body.

Then she felt his black hair soft against her stomach as he stroked that golden red mound hiding her most intimate place, then gently coaxed her thighs farther apart, that his mouth, his hands, his tongue might probe the sweet, moist depths of her. And as the breath raced from Tamara's heaving lungs, Falcon quickly unfastened his belt and eased his tight buckskin pants down the length of his body, discarding them along with his black boots, exposing a well-endowed manhood that ached with hunger for her.

Tamara felt her senses soaring high . . . her mind was no longer in control; her body's desires commanded every moment, the fulfillment of every wish his caresses had stirred within her. And the wonderful moments, in which he possessed her very soul, moved quickly toward the first of a violent burst of spasms deep within her that wracked her body with sweet, delicious pain. And as his convulsing movements slowed to a series of gentle breaths, Falcon's naked body moved upward and covered her own. She felt the hardness of that commanding part of him against her parted thighs and her hand lowered, instinctively, as if it possessed a mind of its own, to touch what she had never touched before.

Falcon's lips gently nipped hers, playing, teasing, covering her flushed features with their gentle caresses. She saw his eyes . . . the magical wells of his heart, as if they were telling her not to worry. She was eager for him . . . eager for the fulfillment of their union. Her body wanted to feel the power of his strength and love. Nothing else mattered. Yet, she was aware of his hesitation, of his body gently covering hers, not betraying how much he wanted her. She knew that this reserve must be very difficult for him, and that he was thinking only of her. Unconsciously, her hips lifted, that she might feel the strength of him against her.

The movements of her body told him everything he wanted to know. The fire that filled him filled her also. And slowly, oh, so slowly, he began to ease himself into that soft, moist, throbbing place that ached for his fullness.

Tamara gasped, scarcely able to catch her breath. As she felt his movements against her tender thighs and his gentle, partial penetration, she closed her eyes and her fingers dug painfully into his shoulders. Her tightly drawn features paled with pain.

It was something that had to be done quickly. Without giving her warning, Falcon drove himself deeply into her. When she opened her mouth to cry out from this sudden, fiery pain, his mouth pressed bruisingly to hers. He felt her body convulse, then stiffen beneath him. And, choking back the lump that hung in his throat, he gently kissed away the tears—tears of pain and happiness—that traced paths down her cheeks.

But it was so momentary a pain to be nonexistent, and Tamara's hips slowly began to move and match his rhythm and pace. His strong hands held . . . caressed . . . explored every inch of her searing flesh.

She saw nothing but the blur of his features above her, felt nothing but the pleasant wave of fire consuming her and the strength of his manhood filling her. Each breath she took was filled with the musky aroma of him and her lips tasted only the sweetness of his, and of his tongue that probed and captured her willing mouth. He commanded her every sensible thought, and coaxed from her a low, kittenish moan that whispered against his damp hairline.

Tamara's hands explored the tight muscles of his body, his strong sun-bronzed back, his narrow hips that moved confidently against hers. Then her hands lifted to cup his proud, bronze features, to coax his parted mouth to her once more. She touched his clean, damp hair, and his powerful chest separated from her soft one by a mere breath of space.

Then his body filled with an almost superhuman strength and his movements increased in intensity, pounding, driving himself against her with the ferocity of a sudden storm. The sweet breath of a sudden groan filled her mouth, simultaneous to the explosion deep within her abdomen that drove his body bruisingly against her tender hips.

His damp cheek rested gently against hers and over the succeeding moments, his rapid breathing became soft and even. His hands lifted and tenderly cupped her face, then entwined through her loose hair. "What a woman you are, Tamara," he whispered.

"Your woman, Falcon," she whispered in reply. Tamara was content to lie here with him, like this, their bodies one with the other. It seemed so natural a thing, his body joined to hers . . . like this. And still, deep within that very intimate part of her . . . that hidden treasure he had captured for his own . . . the spasms of fulfillment . . . of their love, continued to pulsate against their joined bodies.

131

Presently, Falcon lifted his weight from her, then eased to his side, pulling her warm, damp body gently against his own. "Yes, you are my woman, Tamara," he whispered against her tousled hairline. How innocent she appeared, her ivory features relaxed, radiating youth and loveliness . . . and . . . love. If only she knew the torment that darkened his heart. Was this the moment, when they had loved one another to the fullest extent, to confess the secret that bound him, body and soul, to Asher Arms? No, he could not. He could not risk losing her . . . not now, when they had shared their most intimate moments. She was his now . . . her willing body was his for the taking from this moment forward. But . . . she would expect love in return. Was he capable of giving it? Falcon's eyes darted over her lovely features, her closed eyelids that appeared violet in the semidarkness of the small cabin parted from the storm outside by only a few rotting timbers. Tamara's eyelashes fluttered. He could see that she was fighting sleep. Instinctively, Falcon's arms tightened around her slim, bare shoulders and, as he closed his eyes against her crimson cheek, he whispered, "I will protect you, Tamara, from all the world's hurts."

"Yes . . . I know," she purred sleepily, snuggling against him. Outside the confines of the small cabin, the heavens again darkened and mercilessly pelted the earth with rain. Tamara fell asleep against Falcon—her warrior, her lover—content to be held prisoner by the storm and his strong, protective arms . . . to know that, no matter what, he would protect her from all the world's hurts. Nothing existed outside this private little world she shared with the man who had moments ago loved her, and made her a woman.

*Part Two*

## Chapter 9

*January, 1754*

It had been a long, dream-filled night for Tamara, who snuggled down into the soft, downy quilts of her bed, hesitant to touch her bare feet to the icy wooden floors. At half past the hour of seven, darkness still hovered over the far timber line which, yesterday, had been veiled as far as the eye could see in glimmering sheets of ice and snow. Scarcely awake, with that aura of innocence one might see in a waking child, Tamara looked across the semidark chamber toward the fireplace where there glowed no more than a few small embers, all that remained of the night's peaceful fire. Wishfully, she envisioned a warm, beckoning fire crackling in the hearth, rather than this sooty black nothingness that made it impossible for her to rise from her warm bed.

Still, she felt vibrant and alive and eager to meet this new day. She felt a crinkling beneath her hand which momentarily startled her, then remembered that she'd been reading her latest correspondence from Mason Gray when she'd fallen asleep last evening. The lengthy letter had accompanied a large trunk filled with a dozen fashionable items of clothing, lovely gowns and capes and jackets, something for any occasion from ballroom to a day on horseback, specially hand-sewn for Tamara by the Gray family's personal seamstress. But she had found much more joy in Mason's letter, which was happy and enlightening, assuring her of good health and happy dispositions, keeping her abreast of the happenings of friends and acquaintances, and assuring her how much he missed her.

Tamara thought of all the things she had to tell Mason in reply. Would he be happy for her when he learned that she was in love? Would warnings follow in future correspondence, and endearing fatherly lectures?

Oh, but she was in love . . . madly, passionately in love with Asher Arms's moody half-breed. These past few months they had been inseparable, sharing their laughter, their pleasures, and their intimacies. Her isolated bedchamber had frequently hosted their passion-filled bodies, and she cared not who knew of their trysts. She recalled the talk she'd overheard in the servants' quarters not too long ago, where she'd gone in search of Bridie. But she was a woman, no longer a child, and her body was her own, to do with as she pleased, and to give to whom she pleased, whenever she pleased. Only Falcon knew its secrets and enjoyed its passion. She was his woman, and she found nothing immoral in that. Small minds bred vicious gossip, she concluded with a sigh.

Tamara eased to her back, flipped her hair up from her neck, and smiling as she thought of her love, glanced dreamily over the clean white ceilings of her bedchamber. Winter-cold air touched her skin, but she felt only the warmth of Falcon, who filled her thoughts this morning.

"Where are you now, my love?" she whispered happily. "And why aren't you where you belong . . . with me, snuggled beneath my warm blankets?"

"He's tendin' his duties, miss . . . if you're speakin' of Falcon."

Startled into betraying a sudden crimson flush, Tamara sat upright in her bed. Bridie had quietly entered, carrying her ever-present straw broom and dustpan. In the corridor, Saul patiently held an armload of logs for the fireplace. "Oh . . . I—I must have been talking in my sleep," Tamara replied, stretching widely.

"Sure, miss." Bridie did not bother to disguise her doubt behind polite words. "If you're decent enough Saul will be startin' up a fire for you." She did not await Tamara's reply, but moved toward the fireplace to sweep the soot and embers into the large dustpan.

Tamara linked her fingers around her drawn-up legs. These past months she had been able to see tenderness behind Bridie's brisk tone, although Bridie spread her fair share of the gossip at Asher Arms. Bridie, however, seemed at times pleased that Falcon's attentions had been captured by the pretty daughter of Jacob Fleming. Tamara could not deny that she enjoyed the company of the older woman and had spent many long hours with her, helping to prepare the bread in the kitchens, and getting to know and understand Bridie better. Hers had been a tragic past. Indentured to a heartless tyrant at the age of fifteen, the young Scottish woman had fled Virginia with her husband and had given birth to their only child along the shores of the Savannah River in the Carolina colony. Months afterward, they had been forcefully brought back to Virginia by bounty hunters and just weeks later the sudden death of their master had ended the indenture. Then Jacob Fleming, whose ailing wife needed the constant attentions of a nurse, had purchased their indenture, which had been listed as part of the property tied up in probate proceedings. But the indenture had ended years ago, and Bridie and Saul, accustomed to the good life of Asher Arms, had stayed on as permanent employees.

"It's time you were arisin'," Bridie said dryly. "Your father'll be wantin' to talk to you, miss . . . about Falcon."

Tamara's head snapped up, scattering up disheveled golden tresses around her shoulders. "Falcon? What about . . . Falcon?" She had heard idle gossip lately that her father disapproved of him as her constant companion.

"Be mindin' my own business, Miss Tamara."

"Oh, Bridie!" Tamara could not keep the exasperation out of her voice. "What is everyone saying now?"

Only now did Bridie turn back, and the stony look left her face. "It's no denying, Miss Tamara, that Falcon comes often to your bed. Your father has said nothing, because you're a grown woman . . . and he was hopin' some sense would come to you. But now . . . it don't appear it ever will. An' your father's concerned."

A rush of anger filled Tamara. She scarcely felt the coldness of the floor as her feet swept from beneath the bedcovers. It did not matter that she was in her nightclothes and Saul was in the bedchamber, absently placing logs in the hearth.

"I am a grown woman," Tamara emphasized. "And I will be with Falcon whenever I please. He cares for me. He will always stand by me."

"You were raised to be a lady, miss. . . ." Suddenly, Bridie ceased her latest of many motherly lectures and, with the flames lapping at the newly cut logs, merely looked at the quiet Tamara, whose moment of anger was betrayed in her crimson cheeks. Then Saul moved slowly into the corridor and Bridie continued, "When I first noticed the blaggart was interested in you, miss, I encouraged it, because it took his eye away from my Glynnie."

"I believe Glynnie was the one with the interested eye, Bridie."

"Well, that may very well be. Nevertheless, miss, I once sent you in search of him, and I'm sorry for that now. You can do better, Miss Tamara,"—Bridie's voice had now softened—"than Falcon. An' should you feel the swell of life in your womb, put there by him, will he stand by you then?"

Surprised that this delicate subject should have been brought up by the elderly servant, Tamara merely looked at her for a moment. Then, she softly replied, "I think that he would, Bridie. He—he loves me. . . ." The words trailed off into a dismal whisper. Bridie silently moved toward the corridor and soon pulled the door to. Many confused thoughts filled Tamara's still sleepy head as she once again drew her feet under the warm quilts. Did Falcon love her? In all of their trysts and encounters, she could not recall any one occasion that he had whispered those special words . . . *I love you.* She had whispered them often to him, but now that she thought about it, she had never heard them in return. He had said many times that he cared for her, and wanted her, and even that he needed her, but he had never said that he loved her. And now, on this cold January morning, with a crackling fire burning in the hearth and radiating its warmth through her bedchamber, Tamara felt the icy coldness of those absent words. The vitality and jubilance she had felt just moments ago were suddenly gone. She became more aware of the shroud of fog just outside her window, and the irritating thump of bare branches against the window pane.

"Oh, Falcon, Falcon . . ." she whispered despairingly, "do you love me, indeed?" Then, for a long, long while, she placed her chin on her drawn-up knees and sat there, dreamily staring into the flames of the hearth. But she saw more than just the flames. She saw Falcon's pleasant, masculine features, his eyes so blue they were like a clear mountain stream. She saw his mouth, moist, softly parted, flaming her own with a kiss that spoke eloquently of love.

Love! Was it indeed love that his caresses betrayed to her? Or lust? A man's selfish, blinding lust! Oh, why, why did she have these doubts now? Why couldn't she be as happy as when she'd first opened her eyes to this cold winter day? Why couldn't Bridie have stayed away and left her alone in her fantasies?

With a weary sigh, Tamara again swung her feet to the floor. She could brood, miserably, all day, but that would not give her the answers she wanted. The only thing to do was to confront him openly about it. If he loved her he would tell her so, unhesitatingly. If he did not . . . oh, but she couldn't even harbor such a thought. He did love her; there were no doubts to be had. Their bodies had joined in love and passion, one synonymous with the other. That anything but love had brought them together was an unfathomable thought.

Absently, Tamara arose, chose one of the new dresses from her chifforobe, and slowly began to dress. Her long hair was disheveled from her sleep. She sat at the boudoir mirror and silently met her reflection—icy pale cheeks with only the slightest pink blush, her pale, copper-colored eyebrows and fawn-colored eyes tear-moistened, yet unrelenting in their gaze. She felt anger quicken the pace of her heart as she picked up the brass and ivory brush and began to pull it quickly through her thick hair. Then she touched enough rouge to her cheeks to take away her bland look, dabbed a little perfume behind her ears, and moved slowly toward the door.

Her father was in the study, his favorite room in the house. Broggard, as usual, stood off in a dark corner, waiting for the master's summons whenever he was needed. Tamara did not care for her father's manservant. He was macabre and intimidating, yet he had never spoken so much as a word to Tamara. But those icy, emotionless eyes were all the warning she needed to avoid him whenever possible.

"Father?" Jacob Fleming looked up and smiled. "You wished to see me this morning?"

"I wish to see you every morning," he greeted warmly. "How lovely you look in your new gown."

"Thank you, Father. . . ." But Tamara was not receptive to compliments, or to her father's appraising look. She wanted only to know what he especially wanted to say to her this morning about Falcon.

"Come . . . sit, Daughter," Jacob coaxed, motioning to a chair beside his own. "Broggard, please leave us alone. I shall summon you." Jacob watched Tamara's eyes follow the burly manservant. "Yes, he is frightening," he continued, startling Tamara. "And you shall do well to avoid him."

"But Broggard is not the reason you wish to speak to me, Father," Tamara reminded him, linking her fingers and gently laying them in the folds of her skirt. "It is Falcon, is it not?"

Jacob half-spun the wheelchair away from Tamara. "Falcon . . . yes, Daughter. It is indeed Falcon about whom I wish to speak."

"Before you say anything, Father. . . ." Tamara was not sure where her courage came from. Because of the tension that existed between Falcon and her father, she had avoided speaking of Falcon in his presence. But now, foremost in her mind was the need to defend the man she loved and, once and for all, to confess to her father her true feelings for Falcon. "I love him, father . . . I love him with all my heart." Jacob's lips parted, as if he were preparing to reply, but before he could, Tamara continued with haste, "I know I've only been here a few months, but in this time I have been more content than I would ever have imagined. Falcon has filled me with happiness. He is everything I have wanted in a man and in a husband. If he were to ask, I would be his wife and constant companion, to live as he wishes to live, be it a castle or a cabin."

"And Falcon . . . does he feel the same about you, Tamara?" Tamara threw her shoulders deliberately back, even as she inwardly slumped. "Has he confessed his love for you, and his desire to make you his wife? Or is it merely your bed and your willingness that beckons the primal instinct within him?" Anger suddenly laced Jacob's words, sharpening them into a truth that was to Tamara like a vicious slap across the cheek. She lowered her eyes, unable to meet her father's unblinking stare. "I do not mean to be cruel, Daughter," Jacob continued softly, "but you do not know Falcon . . . not as I know him."

"But why . . ." Tamara looked up as she spoke, "why do you employ him if you dislike him so?"

"I do not dislike him, Tamara. What is between Falcon and me—well! That is best left alone for the time being."

"Why do you not send him back to his people? Although he is an uneducated man, he has the good sense to leave a place where he is not wanted."

Despite his frailty, Jacob threw his head back and filled the dark study with sardonic laughter. "Uneducated, indeed, dear, dear Daughter. . . ." The laughter ceased and Jacob's solemn gaze again met hers. "Falcon has been taught at William and Mary College in Virginia. He is not the ignorant country bumpkin you believe him to be! Falcon is a highly educated man!"

This came as somewhat of a shock to Tamara. She had painted a picture of her love as a man raised in his mother's tribe, surviving the trials and tribulations and feats of prepubescent, dark-skinned boys who wanted to be braves like their fathers and their fathers' fathers, learning the ways and skills of the Lenni–Lenape Indians and living off the land as generations of those gentle people had lived before them. Suddenly, a picture of a highly educated man in coattails and stiff collars—a man who lived a lie— was thrust into her lovely image . . . a man who had allowed her to believe that the forest alone had been his tutor and his guide. She wondered now if everything he had told her had been a lie . . . and why he had felt the necessity.

Always . . . always, the mystery enshrouded him. She'd often felt that his silence alone spoke lies, especially when she questioned his past and he either did not answer or changed the subject. Behind his strong, caring facade ofttimes lurked the slyness of a fox. Was she merely a game to him and a pawn to be used in some silent, sinister intimidation of Jacob Fleming? Or was the animosity completely her father's in this jousting tourney that existed daily between them?

What part did she play in Falcon's life? Today the questions jumbled in confusion through her mind.

"Tamara?" Jacob softly spoke her name and her tear-moistened eyes returned slowly to him. "I must ask you to do something that will be very difficult for you. . . ."

"Difficult?" she responded quietly. "How so, father?"

"It is something that only you can do." Jacob hesitated for a moment and Tamara readily saw that his hands were shaking. "You must send him away, Tamara. Away from Asher Arms. . . ."

A sledge hammer driven into her chest could not have had more impact. Tamara's breathing suddenly ceased and she felt cold inside. It seemed that hours passed in the very few moments Tamara's mind whirled in the darkness of this terrible request, "You must send him away. . . ."

How had her day turned so topsy-turvy? She was torn between her father and her lover and forced to choose between them. Could she make such a decision and live comfortably with it? These past few months she had shared a warm, loving relationship with her father, spoiled only by his animosity toward Falcon. But to Falcon she had given her heart and her body. She dutifully attended the daily sessions with her father, but desire and passion drove her into Falcon's arms.

Tamara's hands were sweating. Absently, she rubbed them and did not lift her eyes to meet her father's, who waited expectantly for her answer. She was at a loss for words. Her father had asked her to tear her heart from her chest and cast it out, like so much rubbish, and she was neither able nor willing to do that. Falcon was her breath, her life, her very reason for existence. Without him she would surely die, like a tree cut off from the sun.

Thus Tamara lifted her eyes to her father's and steadily held his gaze. "I cannot send Falcon away, Father. I love him. I will do anything else you ask of me . . . anything at all, but I cannot send him away from me. If it is your wish that he leave Asher Arms, then my wish is to accompany him and live the life that he makes for me."

This was as Jacob had feared: Falcon owned her. He could see that Tamara would readily die for the man she loved. Jacob suddenly felt the loss of his daughter, as deeply and painfully as when she'd been a young girl, boarding ship in New York Harbor in the company of Mason Gray.

Jacob's hand covered his mouth, in an effort to regain the moment. "I lost you once, Tamara . . . I will not lose you again . . . not to a man like Falcon. If the only way I can keep you here is to also keep him here, then so be it."

Why, why did he despise Falcon so much? The question spun rapidly through her head. But should she be so bold as to ask him? Tamara met a fierce, unblinking gaze. Despite the infirmities that bound him to the wheelchair, Jacob Fleming was an unrelenting man, and one who instilled fear, even in his daughter. No . . . she could not ask him.

Absently, angrily, Jacob flipped his wrist at Tamara, dismissing her. Yet his actions did not match his softly spoken request, "Take lunch with me, Daughter," to which she responded with an imperceptible nod. Only when she had pulled the door to behind her did Jacob Fleming call hoarsely, "Broggard!" The faithful manservant was always within hearing range. He entered the study and stood a few feet from Jacob but did not speak. "I am very tired, Broggard. Please . . . take me to my bed."

Tamara returned to her bedchamber, donned her full-length hooded cape, and left the house through a back exit. She was in no mood for a lecture from Bridie this morning.

The air was bitter cold and the fog had lifted, leaving a clear, brilliant morning that yesterday Tamara might have enjoyed. But she felt only the gloom that had settled over her heart. If she could only understand the animosity that existed between Falcon and her father. Could it have been the end product of the hunting excursion that had left Jacob bound to a wheelchair? Was there any truth to the rumor that the shooting had been deliberate? Falcon had once told her that he did not shoot her father and she had believed him then. Was she a fool to continue believing in him?

Tamara suddenly found herself walking along the forest trail that tunneled beneath bare branches gleaming with ice and snow. How lovely winter could be, even as it nipped her nose and numbed her fingers and toes beneath the warm wool cape.

She did not know why, but her feet took her where they would, on a deliberate course toward the cabin in the dale where she and Falcon had first made love and where they had met many times in these past months. She could see it through the trees, scarcely visible amid mounds of freshly fallen snow. She knew only that she needed to be alone, and this was a place familiar to her . . . a place where she had known only happiness.

Snow was piled high against the door and Tamara pushed it open, finding scarcely enough space to climb between the snow and the top of the door. It was very dark inside, but she was able to find the rosin and brimstone in the corner where Falcon had put it months ago. He also kept a fresh supply of logs in the cabin at all times. Tamara put several in the hearth and soon had a fire burning. When the room had warmed, she removed her cape and laid it gently over the back of a small wooden chair.

She sat for a long, long while, her hands clasped lightly in her lap, staring into the flickering flames. For the first time in many months she felt lonely. How easy life had been before she'd fallen in love! How painless it had been. Today, she'd been forced to choose between Falcon and her father. She'd chosen Falcon, and now, sitting here alone, she wondered if she'd done the right thing. Had she severed the familial bonds by this betrayal of her father? And would her decision today change the feelings he had for her? But could she have sent Falcon away?

No . . . that was one thing she could never do. Falcon had filled her life with happiness. He needed only to cross her line of vision from a distance to stir the want within her. Nothing had ever had this effect on her before. Had she lost her mind? Had she bound her love to a man who might not even love her in return?

Her thoughts made moments of the hours that passed, hours that reduced the fire to glowing embers that cast dancing reflections across Tamara's ivory features. She became weary, her back stiff and sore, and she arose, picked up her cape and moved toward the small clean cot in the corner of the cabin. Soon, with the warmth of the one-room cabin making her eyelids heavy, and wanting only to put the day's worries in the back of her mind, she drifted off into a deep sleep.

But even in her sleep her mind revolved in a vast vortex of concerns and regrets. Perhaps her mind willed it, but in her dreams the small cabin in which she slept seem to float away, to break away from the snow-covered earth that held it prisoner. She saw it tumble back and forth on winds she could not see, and eventually come to rest on a wide, peaceful sea. Then her spirit became separate and distinct, arose from its materialistic bonds, and looked down at her own peacefully sleeping form. Then it moved toward the small window at the far side of the cabin to look out, longingly, at gently lapping waves and a blue horizon far, far into the distant mist.

It was peaceful. The worries crumbled into nothingness and floated away on the waves. A warmth filled her with inner peace. She heard no despairing words or disgruntled sighs, no sarcasm to bite at her and make her mean and defensive. She felt only peace.

Suddenly the gently lapping waves began to take on solid form, like earth and rolling hills. The horizon became snow-covered mountains and gloomy gray skies. Something, someone as small as an ant in the distance moved slowly toward her, gaining clarity, depth, dimension . . . She wanted him . . . his eyes . . . blue and penetrating, holding hers in a soul-searching gaze. Then he stood just outside touching distance of her and held out his hand. But she did not take it. Rather, she tried to speak, but her mouth felt numb and the words hung painfully in her throat. Then her words came, slowly and painfully, "Falcon, do you love me?"

But was it indeed Falcon who stood before her, his features blurred and unrecognizable? Did she dare offer her hand or repeat the words she had spoken and to which no answer seemed forthcoming? Did his cold, chiseled mouth smile a macabre and frightening smile?

Tamara knew she was dreaming, yet she could not force herself to awaken. She wanted to run away, but her legs were heavy and would not move. She looked back at herself on the small cot, struggling to regain consciousness. As she vainlessly searched for an escape route, Falcon's hand darted out and held her wrist in an icy grip.

She awakened with a start. With her awakening came sensible thought, and she heard men's voices far, far away in the forest. Her name echoed hauntingly on the brisk winter wind.

She suddenly realized she'd left Asher Arms without telling anyone where she was going. It was only logical that with darkness fallen, her father would have sent his men out to find her.

She swung her feet to the floor, which immediately produced a low, growling sound from the darkness of the cabin. Frightened, unable to see an arm's distance in front of her, she slowly began easing backward, coming to rest against the rough cabin wall. Then she saw the flash of red eyes with oblong pupils. As a sleek, screaming creature leaped across the cabin, she quickly pulled a table over, protecting herself behind it in the corner of the cabin.

She soon realized that the menacing creature was a wildcat pacing back and forth the length of the table, thrusting large, taloned paws into the narrow space on either side. Tamara was too frightened to scream and too sensible to cry. If she could only find her voice long enough to make her presence known to the men who searched for her. Then she realized that the cat could possibly get to her through the triangle of space above her, and she eased herself lower to the floor. Then she pulled her legs and arms beneath her fur cape.

The cat screamed and crashed its body against the table. Several times its probing paw caught in the strands of her hair. How foolish she'd been to leave the house, and to venture so far away!

Suddenly, the silence seemed as life-threatening as her madly beating heart. She knew the cat still lurked about, trying to figure out a way to get to her. She could hear the insane scratching of its claws against the cabin floor.

"Tamara!"

Her name spoken so clearly brought piercing cries from the angry cat. Tamara was filled with renewed fear for the man speaking her name. "Falcon . . . be careful . . . wildcat. . . ."

"Yes . . . I know. . . ." The moment she heard Falcon's boots touch the cabin floor, the cat pounced with a mighty growl, throwing him backward into the snow. She heard a different cry—Falcon's—as she realized he had deliberately used himself as bait to draw the danger away from her.

She forgot her own safety as she rushed from her hiding place. She quickly found Falcon's musket where it had fallen, then stumbled from the dark interior and collapsed in the snow. She saw only the black writhing form of her love and the attacking wildcat as her trembling hands raised the musket. Falcon cried out as the massive claws again dug into his flesh. Tamara ran frantically toward the writhing form.

"Tamara . . . Tamara, shoot . . ." Falcon pleaded weakly.

"I—I might hit you . . ." she screamed.

"Shoot, Tamara . . . for God's sake!"

Tamara raised the musket and eased her shaking

150

finger to the trigger. She didn't remember firing, but suddenly, the musket bucked back against her shoulder, bruising it. An animal's scream filled the winter sky. In its death throes, the cat managed to scramble a few yards away before collapsing, dead, in the clean white snow. Tamara sank to her knees, then slowly began moving toward Falcon. He quickly came to his feet and impatiently flicked snow from his coat and breeches. But Tamara saw that his hands were trembling and spattered with blood.

He spoke only when she was within touching distance. "Are you all right?" he asked, touching his fingers to her wind-cooled cheek.

Tamara drew near, then dropped the musket and slipped her arms around his waist. "I am . . . are you?"

"A scratch here or there . . . nothing serious."

"You are trembling," she responded quietly.

"Come . . ." he roughly put her away from him, yet retained the gentleness in his voice, "let us return to the cabin and see what damage this devil-cat has done."

Once inside, Tamara insisted on placing logs in the hearth and lighting the fire herself. Then she lit the oil lamp from a burning bit of ember and approached Falcon, who had already removed his jacket. There was a small amount of blood spreading through the white material of his shirt.

He watched her intently, her eyes deliberately refusing to meet his own, the crimson flush of her face against the glow of the hearth. He saw her grimace when the wound across his shoulder was revealed. The talons of the cat had been razor-sharp, though the wound appeared to have scarcely scratched the surface. Quickly, Tamara tore a bit of cloth from

151

her petticoat and, dampening it with melted snow, gently cleaned Falcon's wound.

But Falcon cared not about the throbbing wound. He saw before him the glowing features of love and passion . . . his pride . . . his woman. The warmth of her penetrated the space between them and enveloped him, his body, branding him with the want and desire he shared with her.

His hand rose and held hers, causing its movements to cease. Then he brought her trembling fingers to his mouth to gently kiss them.

"Do not fuss over this small wound, Tamara," he said quietly, his mouth trailing kisses over her flushed cheek, her warm, willing mouth . . . her eyelids that closed, waiting for the gentleness of his mouth. "It is you I want . . . now . . . this very moment."

## Chapter 10

*Gray House, London*

Mason Gray had spent a very restless day. He'd been unable to concentrate on the duties demanded of him or to coax himself, with half a bottle of his favorite brandy, into a more subtle temperament. As night approached, a dense London fog shrouded the city outside his bedchamber. For an hour or so he'd stood there, deep in thought, unable to see the tall, archaic landmarks and the fog lights of the boats moving upon the Thames. He felt weary, defeated, an annoying nervousness crawling through his shoulders. Presently, hoping yet for a miracle cure for his moment of depression, he summoned Pipps, his manservant, and ordered a healthy dose of warm milk and rum, a favorite bedtime drink.

Silently, he berated himself for his lack of self-discipline. But he felt he'd been dealt a stunning blow. He looked again at the portfolio of documents delivered to him that morning. Although no correspondence had been included, he was sure it must have been sent by Tamara. While her intentions had been good, he had been deeply affected by the contents of the package. He was to have entertained dinner guests this evening, but at the last moment had sent a messenger with apologies.

Pipps returned, quietly placed the milk on a side table, then left Mason alone. Mason selected a book from the many he kept in his chamber and sat down to engage in a few moments of reading. He needed a diversion, and it was so seldom he had time to enjoy this favorite pastime.

But the words would not hold his attention and he found himself gazing over the top of his spectacles toward the portfolio. Then, like a powerful magnet, it drew him toward it. Clutching the portfolio, he returned to his chair.

Although he recognized the sentiment with which the package had been sent, it nevertheless opened many painful wounds. The leather bindings guarded memories precious only to Mason Gray . . . an array of faded hair ribbons, a well-worn Bible, a bundle of letters . . . a gold barrette with the initials of its owner engraved within a wreath of roses. Mason's trembling hand fondly caressed the bundle of letters. A flood of memories rushed upon him and he remembered how, as a young man, he sat at his desk beside this same window, gazing dreamily across the rooftops of London and composing the letters to his true love—the quiet-spoken wife he had been forbidden to see.

Whatever had possessed Tamara to send these things on to him? She had made no mention of a discovery of the small treasures in her latest correspondence, nor had a note accompanied them. Where had they lain within the walls of Asher Arms these many years, collecting dust, touched last by the hands that had placed them there? What dark corner had harbored these secrets of a day long past? The letters he had written to Fedora were tied with faded rose-colored ribbon, and he could almost detect the faintest aroma of the rose she had placed just beneath the bow. He touched it and felt the stiffness of the ribbon, once as soft and silky as the ivory skin that had, many yesterdays past, eagerly responded to his gentle touch.

"Tamara, Tamara, my child . . ." Mason whispered quietly, "your sweet sentiment has poured salt in an old wound."

Yet he could not be angry with his young ward for this gentle hurt, these wrenching memories that flooded his thoughts. She had wanted only to return these long-lost treasures to him, to give him some small reminder of the past and the woman he had loved. Tamara was a dear, devoted daughter to him whose only wish was to please him. She would never have deliberately hurt him.

Oh, how he missed Tamara! The house had been empty without the timeless treasure of her smiles and happy moods. She'd possessed the uncanny ability to materialize when things seemed dark and somber, to bring happiness when he'd felt anything but. She had been happy at Gray House. He prayed that she had found happiness in her new Delaware home.

Thinking of Tamara brought a sad smile to Mason's tired, drawn features. "Dear girl," he spoke aloud, resting his head wearily against the chair back, "I do not need these small treasures to remind me of my wife and son. But bless you, child, for your sweet sentiment. May the happiness of the world be yours tonight."

Tamara could not have been any happier than she was this very moment. Falcon's body gently covered her own, his fingers gently entwined among the silken strands of her hair, caressing, soothing away the pain and fright that had, moments ago, reflected across the barrel of the musket she'd held in her hands.

Tamara's fear was a thing of the past. She was safe and secure with Falcon beside her. He had built a new fire to warm the small cabin, then had returned to her, a silent comfort who had stilled her trembling fear. She wanted only to feel the caresses of his strong hands and his powerful body covering and claiming her own. She wanted everything he had given her in the past, the ultimate fulfillment of timeless love, possessing no boundaries and inhibitions when their bodies met.

Yet for a moment, Falcon seemed content to lie beside her, his now naked chest covering her own, his hands gently massaging her disheveled tresses. He occasionally brushed his cheek against hers in a tender caress. He said nothing, yet many thoughts reflected in his eyes, which were narrowed, glimmering in the flames licking at the hearth. He paid no attention to the wound left across his shoulder by the wildcat. He cared only about her, and being with her.

Within moments, the small cabin was bathed in warmth. Falcon studied his quiet Tamara, the ties of her wool blouse loosened, exposing smooth white flesh that curved gently into firm breasts just below the fabric. Her lovely oval features were framed by disarrayed golden tresses that were like the last scatterings of clouds upon a gold horizon. He touched them, then brought their softness to his cheeks. He wanted her; she could tell by the hardening of his body against her soft one. Yet he held back as if this were their first meeting and he wanted to explore every inch of the smooth curves and supple flesh that seemed to rise to meet his caress.

Tamara's movements spoke eloquently of her desire, aroused by the very nearness of the man she loved. The musky aroma of him drifted into her senses and, like a powerful drug, made them soar to heights far above the physical plane she shared with him. His hands, gentle just moments ago, became almost rough and demanding as they moved beneath the thick wool of her blouse, tearing apart the ties that held it to her ivory skin and her hardened breasts, one of which he captured with his mouth. Her heart pounded fiercely. She lifted her fingers to his thick dark hair, entwining them, then traced a path with her fingertips down his firm jawline. Her breathing became rapid, and only when her fingers firmly gripped his shoulders did his mouth ease upward and cover her own in fierce, demanding kisses. All the while, his hands worked miracles on her waiting, willing body, uncovering, stroking, warming the flesh that tingled beneath his masterly explorations. The stays of her skirt were pulled apart, and she lifted her buttocks to assist him in removing this thick, tangled garment that kept their most intimate flesh apart from each other. Momentarily, his buckskin trousers and boots, along with her skirt, were dropped to the floor beside the cot.

"Tamara . . . Tamara . . ." he whispered against her tousled hairline, "my angel . . . my woman . . . we shall possess each other, here, in this secluded place where we have so frequently sought comfort. You and I, as it should be."

"I—I love you, Falcon," she whispered in reply, "With all my heart and all my—" His mouth covered hers, breathing in the words she would have spoken, taking her breath and commingling it with his own. Tamara's hands moved fluidly to his bare back, to muscles firmed as he supported himself above her, then pulled him close to her willing body. She felt the hardness of him throbbing in anticipation of their union. Unconsciously her thighs eased apart. Her fingers lifted to his dark hair to guide his mouth again to her passion-sensitive breasts. Their bodies molded together in liquid fire, his hard one against her slim one. For the moment, it did not matter that Falcon had not returned her confession of love. His passion for her was persuasive; that he did not love her was something that simply could not be. He merely found it hard to express in words what his body and his gentleness so often confessed to her.

After a moment, his mouth caressed a path across her breasts, the small throbbing place in her neck, her earlobe, taking it gently between his teeth and kneading it until she moaned with pleasant pain. He kissed each closed eyelid, tasting the salt of a tear of ecstasy, then again captured her mouth in a probing, possessive kiss. She felt his tongue between her teeth and playfully nipped it, all the while her hands moving the length of his firm, narrow hips and his buttocks. Her knees lifted, squeezed his thighs between them, and arched to feel the throbbing length of him against her body.

"Now, Falcon . . . now," she whispered deliriously. With a moan, she coaxed his mouth again to her own.

"My little wildcat," he laughed, gently breaking the kiss. "Your flesh is like fire. It burns through me."

"Then make it yours, Falcon . . . as only you have. As only you ever will. . . ."

Suddenly Tamara was seized by the fervor of her passion. He had aroused a whirlwind, a fury within her, and she wanted only to be filled with him, to have this terrible thirst quelled by his love. Trembling, her hand lowered, touching him, guiding him into the warm, dark cavern that was immediately filled with the fullness of him. She was impatient for him, heaving in wild, abandoned rapture against his body. She wanted the thrill of him, of his well-endowed manhood driving with the full wrath of passion into her moist intimate place, a place only he had possessed.

And Falcon, his eyes lovingly, teasingly, holding her tear-sheened ones, began to move within her, filling her with the erotic pain of his own desire. She was like a wild woman beneath him, her fingernails digging painfully into his shoulders, traveling the length of him, her lips pounding against his, matching his rhythm and pace as if their bodies were made to be together, like pieces of a puzzle snugly fit together. It pleased him that he could make her feel this way.

Their bodies melted into a world of their own, lifting them to ethereal heights and a vortex of swirling mists that made their senses reel in ecstasy. They were ensnared within the sweet, warm, wonderful arms of each other, melting quickly into a passion-heated river of fire that crawled through their entwined bodies. Intoxicated by rapture, blinded by passion, their bodies rocked in a turbulent storm, thrashing against each other's until the winter-cold gush of wind through the partially open door was not felt by either. Tamara felt the tremors deep within her pulsating against his throbbing member. She groaned as her arms darted around his broad shoulders, drawing herself firm against him. She scarcely felt the sweet liquid of love and satisfaction burst within her as Falcon drove himself deeply into her.

In the moments that followed, their breathing slowed in gentle harmony. Falcon's dark hair rested on the small pillow beside her flushed features. His body remained one with hers, as if he could not bear to be parted from her. Then, as he slowly withdrew, she moaned in disappointment and understanding, knowing that he would regain the closeness by pulling her into his strong, welcome arms.

Momentarily, Falcon covered their naked bodies with the blanket, then playfully drew her across his own body.

"You are quite a woman," he said softly, cupping her chin so that he might meet her sensual gaze. "Where did you learn to please a man?"

"I shall say what you wish me to say . . . you taught me, Falcon. Only you. I wish no other tutor."

"And you shall have no other, my Tamara," he whispered, touching his lips briefly to her own. Then he became silent, and for a long while was content to hold her close to him. The fire in the hearth crackled when the logs shifted, and the sudden movement made Falcon's muscles jump.

Tamara could imagine no place she would rather be. With Falcon beside her, even this dreary old cabin was a castle, erected for the moment—their moment—in the snowy valley just across the hills from Asher Arms.

"Oh, Falcon . . . Falcon, I do so love you," she whispered, nestling her head into the curve of his neck. "Whatever would I do without you?" When he did not answer her, she continued quietly, "Falcon, why do you not speak of love to me? Surely . . ." she drew even more closely to him, "you do love me."

Silence. Tamara did not see Falcon's dark eyebrows knit together in a thoughtful frown. She was aware only of that all-too-familiar silence when she spoke of love, as if it pained him. Perhaps she should listen to what both Bridie and her father had said to her. Perhaps she should harbor some suspicion, rather than total trust. Again, she looked at Falcon's firm profile outlined against the glow of the hearth. What was he thinking? What terrible thing had destroyed his capacity, or desire, to express love?

Tamara sighed. He could be so outrageously perplexing. She would have to follow the whims of her heart rather than listen to those mortal fools who would cast shadows across a glowing love. Falcon's feelings for her were obvious; their moments together were a true confession of their love.

"Falcon?"

"Hmmm?"

Tamara brushed a lock of hair back from his forehead, then tenderly caressed it between her fingers. "Jacob told me this morning that you have been formally educated . . . at William and Mary College in Virginia. Is this so?"

"It is," he replied.

She shrugged delicately against him. "But . . . I believed you were educated in the wilderness, that it and the trapper and the village of Kishke were your only tutors."

Only now did Falcon's eyes open. "Did I tell you this?"

"You did not. I—I assumed—"

Immediately, Falcon turned, then supported his head in the palm of his hand. "Yes, you assumed, Tamara, something you should never do. If you wish to know something about me, ask. If you hear some

161

derogatory thing said of me, ask me if it is so. Never assume, Tamara.''

"But—" Tamara, too, turned, and her eyes met his sharp blue ones. "You never volunteer anything, Falcon. You were raised in the wilderness; therefore I had no reason to believe it was not your tutor. You are Indian . . . half Indian," she quietly amended. "I did not know your ties to this proud people would allow you to be educated in a white man's society. Frankly—" Again Tamara shrugged, "I am disappointed, Falcon. I love you for what I thought you were—"

"An ignorant peasant?" he responded with a sudden sharpness. "Someone to control, Tamara? Is that what you want? A man to whimper at your feet like a puppy, and be so enamored of your attentions that he knows no better?"

He seemed to physically withdraw from her. Immediately Tamara's hand touched his chest, caressing a path to his strong, tense shoulder. "Not a peasant, Falcon . . . not ignorant. Unspoiled, perhaps . . . unspoiled by the selfish demands, the lust for power, that has for centuries plagued the white man. The wilderness has been your home. I—I want it to be mine, too."

"And what of your merry old England? Do you not long for its sterile society and domesticity? Its easy life?"

Tamara eased to her back, forcing her gaze to leave his narrowed one. She felt a pain, fed by his cruel accusation, wrench in her chest. "You are being sarcastic, Falcon . . . you know very well that I don't want to return to England, except to visit my guardian. I want the life Delaware, and you, will offer me. I want to know everything there is to know about you, yet you take pleasure in harboring your secrets.

162

You allow me to assume; therefore you should not criticize me for doing so."

"Forgive me, Tamara." Stung by her truthful voice, his tenderness returned. "Anything you wish to know about me I shall tell you. But you must ask, Tamara. Believe me," Falcon's hand touched her cheek in a gentle caress, "I shall tell you anything you wish to know. And I swear by all that is sacred, I shall never lie to you. I have spoken more to you, Tamara, these past months than I have spoken in the entirety of my life before you. My heart is yours, if you want it."

"And your love?"

"I have given it to no other."

"No other," she quietly echoed. "Is this a confession of love, Falcon? Have I elicited it, finally?"

Falcon gently laughed. "You are an assumer, Tamara. Assume now, and cease this childish interrogation."

"You cannot say it, Falcon . . . will you ever? Why do you find it so difficult to say 'I love you'?"

Without warning, Falcon swung his feet to the floor. He rose, allowing the blanket to fall from his nakedness, and began redressing. "Come—" He did not again face her. "We must return you to Asher Arms before the men find us here . . . like this . . . and tarnish your reputation with vicious gossip."

The hurt returned. Silently, Tamara rose, then slowly began pulling on her garments. She kept her back to him and did not see him turn toward her, his eyes tracing the gentle curves of her naked form, his heart wishing to God he could be open and honest with her.

There were things about him she would not want to know.

* * *

For the following week, Falcon seemed to deliberately evade Tamara. Even Drew, the stableboy who frequently assisted Falcon with the horses, shrugged his shoulders when she inquired of him. Bridie began to eye Tamara with a rather contemptible 'I told you so' look, and Glynnie merely flitted around the estate with an equally contemptible frivolity. Her father, however, knew what troubled her and frequently brought up the subject of Falcon. He found the moment to do so now, with Bridie returned to the kitchens after serving their noonday meal.

"You haven't been the same happy girl, Tamara," he said, "the one you were before, that night the men had to go in search of you."

He spoke of it as if he knew what had happened, knew of the tension that now existed between Tamara and Falcon. She felt crimson rise in her cheeks. "I'm fine, Father. You mustn't worry for me. I'm a big girl now."

Silence. Jacob Fleming quietly laid his fork to the side of his plate and leaned back in the wheelchair. "Yes, you are, Tamara. As a father I feel obligated to see that you are well-settled for the future. It is time you were thinking of marriage."

Tamara, picking at her plate just moments ago, now quickly looked up. "Marriage? There is plenty of time for that. Besides—Asher Arms shall sustain me."

"I am ill, Tamara . . . not long, I fear, for this earth. It will greatly please me—relieve me—to know that your future is secure."

"Please don't speak with such imminence and doom," she responded. "It distresses me greatly."

"The truth distresses you, Tamara." Jacob Fleming carefully chose his words, "I have invited an old

164

friend up from Virginia, a horse breeder by the name of McKenzie Bain.''

''I've heard you speak his name,'' Tamara absently replied, again picking at her plate.

''He will be accompanied by Sterling, his son.''

''I shall be a pleasant hostess, father.''

''No!''

Tamara looked up, startled by the sharpness in her father's voice. ''You shall not be a hostess, Tamara. The Bain estate is in serious financial distress. McKenzie and I have discussed it at length through correspondence . . . it is arranged that you and Sterling shall be married, and I, as your father, shall offer the dowry appropriate to your station—''

Tamara quickly stood, upsetting the cup of tea beside her plate. Trembling, she began dabbing at it with her linen napkin. ''No—no—I won't marry a man I have never met!'' Suddenly, tears filled Tamara's eyes. She could see nothing of her father but a blur. ''It is Falcon!'' she shot back, unthinking. ''You hate him! You hate him even more because you know how much I love him. You will marry me off to some whimpering Virginia breeder because I am . . . frequently with Falcon!''

Jacob gritted his teeth. Only when Tamara turned to flee from him did he harshly order, ''Do not leave, Daughter, until I grant you grace!'' She halted, her hands clenched into fists, but did not turn back to him. There had never before existed such tension between them. ''Do you not think I would give you my blessing if I thought Falcon truly loved you? God forbid, girl, that you should be so ignorant . . . a daughter of mine!''

Tamara was sick with grief. Is this why Mason had sent her back to Delaware? To be forced into a loveless marriage? She became irrational, unaware of the degradations about to spew from her lips. "Daughter! How easily you call me Daughter! But I have read my mother's diary. I know you never wanted me, that you cursed me for not being the son you desired. Did you drive my mother to her death as just punishment for disappointing you?" Suddenly faced by the grave look in her father's face, Tamara only now heard the words she had spoken. They echoed cruelly through her head, over and over and over. She was moved into action only by the silent retreat of Jacob's wheelchair, powered by his own weak, trembling hands. Tamara rushed toward him, then fell to her knees and cradled her head in the folds of the blanket across his knees. "Forgive me. Forgive me, Father . . . I know you love me. I—I don't know what overcame me to speak such evil words."

Jacob said nothing, but gently dropped his frail hand to Tamara's head to stroke her silken hair. "Perhaps," he said after a moment, "It is my fault you have been roused to anger. I should have prepared you with more grace and patience. But—you shall marry Sterling Bain, Tamara. And Falcon be damned!" With a strength she scarcely thought he possessed, he gripped her shoulders and put her away from him. Then he called, "Broggard!" and the ugly man-giant appeared from the shadows.

It was almost impossible to summon her own strength. Tamara quietly returned to her chamber, donned her hooded cape, and slipped out-of-doors through the kitchen entrance. She prayed to God Falcon had not left Asher Arms on one of his frequent visits to the village on the Indian River.

She trod gingerly through the melting snow, en-

166

tered the dimly lit stable where the boy, Drew, was cleaning out stalls. Startled by her silent approach, he turned, then lightly bowed to the mistress of Asher Arms.

"Where is Falcon?"

Before, she had been tolerant when she'd inquired of Falcon, even knowing the stable hands would evade answering. The boy noticed the difference. It was not just a question, but an order. "In—in his quarters—back there," he replied, pointing toward a rear door.

Tamara turned, hugging her cape to her, and soon entered the corridor that led to a partially open door. With the same quietness she pushed open the door, which revealed a solemn Saul sitting beside Falcon. He was in bed; she found that odd.

Saul, aware of her approach only when she stood beside him, immediately came to his feet. "Miss . . . what are you doing here?"

He tried to take her arm and lead her away, but beyond Saul, covered to his shoulders by a brown woolen blanket, lay a gravely ill, unconscious Falcon.

"My God!" Tamara uttered in disbelief, falling to her knees beside him. "What—what has happened?"

"He wouldn't allow me to summon you, miss . . . it's the wound left by the cat . . . badly infected, miss. He's been delirious for three days now."

"Oh, Saul. . . ." Tamara looked accusingly at the aging servant. "How could you not summon me, knowing how much he means to me?" She picked up a cool cloth from the bowl beside the cot and began to dab at Falcon's sweating forehead. "We must take him to the estate-house, where I shall care for him."

167

"He won't like it, miss."

"I don't care what he likes or dislikes!" she shot back, her voice trembling with emotion. "I will have my way this once, Saul."

She arose, unable to fight back the tears as her gaze met Saul's guilty one. "You know how much I love him, Saul. I may never forgive you for this."

## Chapter 11

Endless snowfalls imprisoned Asher Arms within the quiet little Delaware valley, with no foreseeable leniency in the weather. Moods were solemn. The children stood forlornly with their noses pressed to windowpanes, feeling themselves imprisoned, their childlike mischief and enthusiasm subdued by the harsh winter weather. The young ones missed the tall, dark-haired Falcon, whom they'd watched many hours while he'd worked with the untamed horses newly arrived from Virginia. They'd stood in awe of him, admiring, yet wary of the quiet man who'd been with Asher Arms these past four years and who'd attained a phenomenal popularity. They knew some tragic thing had taken place, something that had taken Falcon away . . . something that had made their parents silent and solemn. The tragedy hung over Asher Arms as surely as the gray-black winter sky, a cruel, ugly, depressing thing.

Tamara sat quietly beside the gravely injured Falcon, watching his ashen features. Bridie had mixed a poultice of chewed Alder bark and plaintain mixed with witch hazel to reduce the swelling. Occasionally a nerve would twitch or his body would grow rigid as his unconscious mind fought the pain. These past twenty-four hours she'd nursed him through bouts of high fever and delirium. The closest doctor was in Dover, and even if summoned, he would be unable to reach Asher Arms in this weather. Thus Tamara had cleaned the wound and had bathed his fevered skin. He had risked his life to save her from a peril, and for his heroism, death might be his sole reward.

If only the hours of nagging regret could bring life back to her love! Tamara had berated her foolishness many, many times this past week. She should not have left Asher Arms. If something had bothered her, she should have confronted Falcon rather than flee alone into the ice-laden forest. True, she'd never heard him speak of love, but his actions and his tenderness had eloquently spoken it many times. She remembered that night after the attack, when they had been together. Without a thought to the throbbing, painful wound, he had gently smoothed away her fears with love.

She could blame this terrible tragedy on Bridie, for questioning Falcon's love for her . . . she could blame the wind for its cold, merciless journey through the forest, draping it in its icy tentacles . . . but all these thoughts were senseless and time-consuming. Nothing would undo what had already been done. Falcon was her love; the absence of those words, *I love you,* could not shatter the special bond that had grown between them. Tamara prayed that death, as vicious and lethal as the wildcat that had attacked him, would not end the special, wonderful thing that had grown between them, nurtured by the undying devotion and love—yes, love—that set them on a deliberate course of eternal togetherness.

Tamara looked around the large, masculine bedchamber where she cared for Falcon. It had occasionally been used by men who'd had business dealings with her father. But it had not been used in more than a year. The room reeked of musky odors; Tamara could not understand why, of all the available rooms in the house, her father had insisted Falcon be brought to this one. But Tamara had managed to keep him warm despite a leaking ceiling. She had managed to keep a fire burning in the hearth, despite the water-soaked logs Broggard had brought to her. Saul kept her supplied, behind Broggard's back, with everything she needed, including medical supplies and dry logs for the hearth. Behind Saul's sad, silent eyes she saw an understanding and a courage that helped her get through these trying hours. She had apologized for her cruel words, and he had said he'd forgiven her. She didn't think, though, that he'd ever forget.

Tamara's thoughts flew back to one brief, lucid moment this morning, when Falcon's hand had gently closed over hers, refusing to surrender it so that she might care for his wounds. She remembered the only sensible words he had spoken, "My sweetheart, my Tamara . . . .do not worry for me." Then he had closed his eyes and the long hours of pain and agony had thrust him into a darkness that her words and assurances could not reach. His journey into that dark netherworld seemed endless, and each passing hour reduced his chances of survival.

"Please, please, my love," she whispered exhaustively, holding his deathly-white fingers to her cheek. "There are so many years ahead. Without you, I do not wish to face them." A light rap at the door startled Tamara. Her back stiffened and simultaneously she turned in the chair. Glynnie stood there, her silent gaze transfixed to Tamara. "Yes, Glynnie, what is it?"

171

"It is Falcon's friend . . . the son of Kishke. He demands that you speak with him."

"He demands, indeed!" Tamara shot back, angered by the implication of it. "He may be able to order around the women of his village like his slaves and washerwomen, but not me!" But the subservient position of women was the Indian way. Tamara had to remember that her refusal to see him would not change hundreds of years of custom. Falcon had told her much of the life he had known before, and the respect and servitude a woman was expected to bestow on a brave. Like her gentle-hearted Falcon, she did not always agree, but she respected their ways. She also knew that Falcon would be angry with her if she shamed and dishonored his blood brother. Thus, she rose to her feet, then completed her statement as she smoothed back her disheveled hair. "I shall see him, Glynnie."

She did not want to leave Falcon, but just this once she would not deliberately challenge the fierce pride she had witnessed in the tall, handsome Indian who waited outside. "I should be grateful, Glynnie, if you'd sit with him until I come back." Then she leaned over and touched her lips gently to Falcon's forehead. "I shall return soon, my love."

Flaming Bow, adorned in fox furs, had not alit his horse, which drew a travois stacked with thick woolen blankets. Tamara had pulled a shawl across her shoulders to meet him in this blistering cold wind. She said nothing when their eyes met, but waited for him to explain the reason for his visit.

Wild horses could not have forced Flaming Bow to admit that the beauty of this white woman took his breath away. His eyes narrowed, studying her,

172

catching each shiver of her body beneath the thin shawl. Her wheat-colored hair was long and loose, catching the glimmer of the morning rays through the ice-laden trees. He could see that she was exhausted.

Presently, Flaming Bow announced the reason for his visit. A deep, resonant voice echoed in the quiet valley where Asher Arms stood. "The mother of my blood brother, Falcon," he began, "wishes that he be brought to our village, to the adobe of my father, where she herself can tend his wound."

Had Flaming Bow asked that her heart be torn from her body, it could not have had more impact. She would rather die than see Falcon parted from her. "This is unreasonable, Flaming Bow. You would move a critically ill man in this weather?" Tamara asked quietly.

"She is his mother," Flaming Bow immediately retorted, "while you are—" He had been about to say, "nothing to him," but that was not true. A grimace deepened the lines in Flaming Bow's bronze features. Unaccustomed to being questioned by a woman, he was forced to take a moment to collect his thoughts. "It is his mother's wish," he said after a moment. He did not feel compelled to give any further explanation. Though he saw in Tamara great beauty, he saw her also as a mere woman.

"Please. . . ." Tamara carefully descended the icy steps, then lifted her eyes to Flaming Bow's. "Take word to his mother that Falcon is in good hands . . . that he is being cared for by a woman who loves him as much as she." The fire of indomitable courage reflected in her soft brown eyes.

Though her argument stung a little, Flaming Bow couldn't help but admire her forthrightness. He could not help but envy Falcon the treasure he had captured. These past few months Falcon had been happier than he'd ever been. Though he had spoken very little of Tamara, Flaming Bow knew she was the reason for his newfound joy.

Thus Flaming Bow slowly turned his horse.

"Flaming Bow—" It was Tamara, quietly calling his name. He halted, but did not turn back. "Do you wish to see him?"

"A man whose strength has washed away does not wish to be seen by a blood brother. I shall see him when the Great Spirit again smiles on him." Then he nudged his horse in the side and began the journey back toward the village on the Indian River. He would pass along to Falcon's mother the words of Tamara Fleming that echoed softly in his head.

As Tamara stood hugging her shawl to her arms, Saul approached and dropped his hand lightly to her shoulder. " 'Tis a brave thing you did, miss, standing up to him that way. You have smote down his arrogance a bit."

"It isn't arrogance, Saul," Tamara quietly answered, favoring him with a small smile. "It's . . ." She'd been about to say "love," but rather said, ". . . more than that. Falcon is his blood brother. It wasn't my intention to smite him," she continued, employing Saul's choice of words. "I wanted only to keep Falcon here, and to let Flaming Bow, and his mother, know exactly where things stood. Falcon belongs here with me."

Together they walked back into the foyer of Asher Arms. "I'll not argue, miss," Saul's thin, veined hand lightly patted Tamara's. "But Flaming Bow, on the other hand, might argue that Falcon belongs with them. I pray he doesn't cause trouble."

"He won't," Tamara replied reassuredly.

Saul stepped back, then turned and slowly walked toward the kitchens.

In the storm a trip that normally took four hours now took eight. Flaming Bow's horse, grunting with exhaustion, struggled through the snow. Several times Flaming Bow, in respect of his faithful mount, alit and led the animal through knee-deep snow, clearing the way with his own body. He'd abandoned the travois once he'd gotten clear of Asher Arms and did not have the added burden of it on the return trip.

Darkness had just fallen when he was greeted by the swirling smoke of the village adobes. His hands and feet were numb with cold. On foot, with the reins of his horse resting across his shoulder, he descended the trail toward the village. Only the posted sentry was aware of his return to the village, though the movement of his horse brought several of the braves from their adobes. He had approached Kishke's hut when Falcon's mother appeared.

He absently adjusted the straps of the white man's saddle Falcon had given him and did not at first meet the silent gaze of the woman called Gentle Doe in the village. She was not a Lenape and had reluctantly accepted the unspoken law of the village. Flaming Bow knew she would not speak first but would, in respect of his position, allow him to commence the conversation. The women of the village spoke only when spoken to, although Flaming Bow knew Falcon's mother and the chief did not abide by this age-old custom. Falcon's mother spoke her mind freely to the chief, a disrespect that the aging Kishke allowed. The disapproving Flaming Bow had many times been forced to grit his teeth and say nothing.

Flaming Bow saw her slim form from the corner of his eyes. Bundled in blankets, the only exposed part of her was her face. Her eyes were lovely, expectant—eyes surrounded by smooth, unlined, winter-pale skin hardly appearing to be that of a woman who had lived fifty winters. He did not have to see her fear to be aware of it. Her son meant everything in the world to her and the lack of a travois at the back of Flaming Bow's horse made her fears almost catastrophic. Unlike some of the other women in the village, Kishke's wife was an eloquent example of strength and grace and dignity. She would employ these virtues in accepting the news of her son, even if it was news of his death, and would keep the grief where it belonged . . . inside herself.

Momentarily, Kishke, too, exited the adobe and stood silently beside his wife. Then Flaming Bow turned full toward them and in the moment that followed noticed many things. He noticed how old his father appeared. He noticed that Kishke's wife had braided her hair and had intertwined lengths of brightly dyed rawhide strips among the thick strands. He noticed the exhaustion in her features, as if she hadn't slept for many nights. And he saw the anxiety there in her upturned eyes.

Then he quietly said, "The daughter of Jacob Fleming spoke these words: 'Take word to Falcon's mother that he is in good hands, that he is being cared for by a woman who loves him as much as she.' " Flaming Bow saw the relief flood the eyes of Falcon's mother.

"You saw him?" she quietly asked.

"I did not set foot in the white man's big cabin. Wife of Kishke—" Flaming Bow had always addressed her as such, and never by her given name, "the love you have for your son and my blood

176

brother is a ray of sun in your heart. My own heart feels the warmth, and my admiration for you is deep. . . ."

Falcon's mother could not contain her small smile, nor the pleasure she felt in these first kind words spoken by her husband's true son. With an almost imperceptible nod, she turned and reentered her hut. The weight of the world was lifted from her shoulders . . . and her heart.

Tamara watched Falcon's sweating features for each slowly unfolding sign of consciousness. She watched his eyelashes flutter, his jaw tighten, his fingers tightly clutch the downy quilt beneath them. Unconsciously she eased her fingers beneath his own. How cold his skin felt. It broke her heart to see him like this, weak and ill and lost to a darkness that had thrown a barrier between them.

Tamara couldn't imagine life without him. His very being had become the staple of her own existence. Without him she was an empty shell. Without him, tomorrow was a ceaseless storm rather than a rainbow. Without him . . . Dear God! Tamara thought desperately, Why must I feel this emptiness within? I have asked so little of you. Please, please, give life back to my hopes . . . my dreams . . . my love—

She had not realized her thoughts had become softly spoken words. Suddenly, through her tear-moistened eyes, she saw his fingers close weakly over her own. Then her gaze shifted, met his and froze. Falcon managed a very weak smile. "You weren't worried about me, were you?"

Relief flooded her. She felt the weight of a thousand worlds lift from her shoulders. "Oh . . . just a little." She wanted to jump for joy, proclaim her love for him for all to hear, weep in happiness for his recovery, yet a strength from within kept her dignity intact. "You gave us quite a fright, my love. We, that is to say, I—"

She didn't feel them coming on, but suddenly, tears flooded her downcast eyes and traced gentle paths down her cheeks. Whatever she was about to say was lost in her throat, like a painful, choking thing. A quiet strength filled Falcon's eyes as he held her gaze. Then his hand lifted to her cheek in a light caress, and she moved to meet its touch.

"Tamara . . ." She loved the sound of her name whispered on his lips. "The strength you have assessed in me has been a facade . . . a disguise for a hatred I have never betrayed to any man, or woman. It is a thing I wish . . . I must . . . keep within myself for now. If you are willing to accept these things about me, without question—these things I cannot change and which must remain in the vault of my own soul—then your love and trust will help to crumble this barrier I have unwittingly built around my heart. . . ."

She said nothing, but brought his hand to her cheek in a tender caress. She felt the wild beating of her heart, as if it knew her wait was at long last over. She envisioned the words forming on his lips, heard their tenderness, their sincerity. The noises of the world suddenly ceased, as if they had been snatched from the face of the earth and placed in a silent, eternal vortex.

And still, as she heard him say, "Tamara, I love you with all my heart and all my soul," she could not believe these coveted words had actually been spoken. "Yes, Tamara . . ." he continued, weakly sitting forward to pull her into his embrace. "I love you. You are my light and my life."

Tenderly, unable to suppress tears of happiness, Tamara moved into his warm embrace.


Tamara did not want to leave her beloved, not even to answer a summons from her father. The moment she entered the parlor, where he absently swirled a goblet of Bridie's homemade dandelion wine, she was aware of the gloom that permeated the darkened chamber. She had passed Broggard in the corridor and was glad of his absence. She was frequently intimidated by both his size and unpopularity.

"Father, you summoned me?" Tamara stood just out of his touching distance.

"Hmmm?" Jacob looked up. "Tamara . . . yes . . . I—" He impatiently flicked his wrist, dropping a book that had laid open in his lap. "Please . . . pull a chair beside your father."

"Would you mind . . ." Tamara approached and gently rested her fingers on his arm, "if I stand? I'm terribly tired of sitting."

"I'm sure that you are," Jacob reflected, nodding his head. "Tamara—" Jacob slightly turned the chair from her. "Falcon's wound heals?"

"Yes, it does," she quietly replied, "despite the cold, drafty room you condemned him to."

Jacob said nothing for a moment, but merely looked at her. Confusion narrowed his gaze. "The room, Tamara? I instructed that the large room in the east corridor be prepared for him."

"It was not, Father . . . the small room to the north, with the broken windowpanes."

Jacob drew his hand to his mouth to recover the moment. He muttered something beneath his breath,

179

but Tamara caught only the word "Broggard." Then Jacob again meet her gaze. "A misunderstanding, daughter. Instruct Saul to have Falcon moved to the chamber I personally designated." He immediately dismissed the subject by asking, "Have you given any consideration to our last talk?"

Tamara had avoided her father since learning of his plans to wed her to the Virginian. "I—I've been much too busy to think about it. With Falcon needing me—"

"I don't wish to hear this right now, Daughter—" he replied patiently.

Tamara, aware of the gentle chastisement in Jacob's voice, stepped back and linked her trembling fingers. "Forgive me—"

Again, Jacob flipped his wrist. "I don't mean to be unkind, Daughter," he apologized. "I've had much on my mind of late." Turning toward her, he forced a brief, insincere smile. "Give my proposal some thought, Tamara. It will be to your own good. I pray for a much more secure future for you than you would have with a man like Falcon."

Tamara could not just sit back like this, aware of her father's immense, unspoken dislike of Falcon. Without thinking, she threw herself to her knees before him and drew his frail hands between her own. "Father, can't you understand what Falcon did? He risked his life to save mine. If he had not appeared at the precise moment he did, I'd have been torn apart by the wildcat. He did not just happen upon the scene. Without a thought for his own life, he drew the she-cat away from me. Oh, Father, you must be able to see that Falcon's love for me is as great as yours!" Tamara's eyes touched his features with a pleading, searching gaze. "We love each other, Father. I could never give my love to another; just

Falcon. I would be his woman in a rough-hewn cabin furnished with straw mats and clay bowls before I'd be the Virginian's wife in a mansion furnished with oriental carpets and English china.''

Silence. Jacob tenderly withdrew one of his hands and lifted his frail fingers to his chin. His gaze did not leave Tamara's. "You love him this much, daughter?''

"I would die for him a hundred times over.''

"A pity . . .'' he muttered sadly. "Broggard!'' Jacob called crossly to his manservant before dismissing Tamara with the brief order, "Dine with me this evening, Daughter.'' Assenting, surprised that he had made no reply to her confession, she turned to leave and had just entered the corridor when Broggard appeared.

Jacob drew his fingers to his clean-shaven chin in a moment of silence. A frown touched his shaggy eyebrows and drew deep furrows into his forehead. He was hardly aware of Broggard's approach and looked up only when the large man's shadow fell across him. "Broggard, you did not follow my instructions.''

"In what regard, sir?''

"I instructed the large, comfortable room in the east corridor to be prepared for Falcon—''

Broggard's crooked smile was not detected by Jacob Fleming. "A misunderstanding, sir, I assure you.''

"A misunderstanding, indeed!'' Jacob became silent. His frail fingers twisted among the folds of the blanket covering his legs, then rose to firmly grip the arms of the wheelchair. "What am I to do with my daughter?'' Jacob did not actually expect an answer, rather, the verbal display of his grief helped to relieve his mind.

181

"I have a suggestion, sir."

Jacob quickly looked up. "A suggestion, Broggard? What might that be."

"Falcon is the root of your problem . . . get rid of him."

"Bah!" Averting his gaze to a dark, empty corner of the parlor, Jacob continued, "I have tried that, to no avail."

"There are other ways . . . permanent ways."

Again, Jacob looked toward his burly manservant, attempting to disguise his shock behind a somewhat passive look. He remembered suddenly that Broggard had condemned Falcon to a dank, cold chamber that could kill even a strong man in weather like this. "What do you suggest, Broggard?"

Broggard smiled a toothless smile. "I shall kill him for you."

For a moment, Jacob said nothing, but held Broggard's unblinking gaze. He had always suspected that Broggard's murderous acts had not been confined to the scaffolds and hanging trees. He had heard tales that could not be dismissed as idle gossip. Now the man stood before Jacob proposing the vilest of sins.

"Broggard, you have been a valuable aide to me. I appreciate your loyalty . . . and your discretion in certain matters. But you have greatly underestimated me. I do not want Falcon to marry my daughter . . . but I shall willingly give her to him before I'll see him dead at your hand, or at the hand of any man."

"Master Fleming, should you change your mind—"

"I shall not change my mind!" The anger drained Jacob's strength. He tried to confine it within himself, but it was like a caged animal, with Broggard the merciless trapper hovering just above him. "Get out, Broggard! I shall remain here for a while."

"But, Master Fleming—"

"Get out!"

Broggard bowed somewhat sarcastically as he backed away and drew the door shut.

Jacob sat for a long, silent moment, encircled within the impenetrable gray-black fog that was his mood. His body trembled. He felt a lump choking his throat, and his breath escape his lungs in short, pained gasps. Murder Falcon, indeed! He had considered it, once, but just for a moment, and only in the blackest rage. If he had only been rational that morning on the cape . . . if he had only listened to what Falcon had had to say . . . he would not be bound to his wheelchair today. But Falcon's confession had shocked him. He had raised his rifle to Falcon's chest by instinct, a caged animal himself fighting for survival. Falcon had every right in this world to hate him, yet he had overlooked the vicious slurs and degradations of the past three years and had been patient and tolerant of his black moods.

Jacob felt the hot flood of tears fill his eyes. How could he ever make up for what he'd done so many, many years ago?

He looked around at the expensive furnishings of Asher Arms, the shelves and shelves of books he could see through the study doors that stood open, awaiting his daily visit. He looked across the snow-laden hills, now barely visible through the parted draperies, lands comprising the estate of Asher Arms as far as the eye could see. At that moment, Drew, the stable boy, crossed his line of vision, leading one of the blooded thoroughbreds that passed frequently through Asher Arms on their way to new markets to the north. He had built an empire in this quiet valley of the Delaware. The lands fed hundreds of mouths, and over the years had been a burial place for loyal servants. Jacob felt that his own time had passed quickly. In his heart, he knew he would not see the snows of another winter.

Asher Arms yielded more wealth than Tamara would ever need in her lifetime. She would be safe and secure as the Virginian's wife.

In his heart, Jacob knew what he had to do.

## Chapter 12

*May, 1754*

It was the first truly warm day Asher Arms had enjoyed this spring. Tamara had been awakened at dawn by one of the stableboys gleefully announcing that her sorrel mare had birthed twin foals. After hurriedly dressing, Tamara had rushed out of doors to see this wonderful sight.

Everyone had gathered around the stall where the mare, confused by all the fuss, busily licked the healthy foals that glistened in the early morning light. Several of the children hung over the edge of the stall and were nipped at by the protective mare. Soon, with eyes watching every move, the foals rose on wobbly legs and began the search for mother's milk. At that moment, with the encouragement of the groomsman, the children and servants returned to play and other duties.

Tamara lingered a moment, spoke with the groomsman, and was about to leave when Falcon stealthily approached her from behind. At first startled, she soon turned into his arms, then favored him with a happy smile.

"My love," Tamara looked past him, toward the saddled horses and pack mule. "You remembered?"

Falcon's hands eased to her slim waist. "God forbid that I should forget, considering half a dozen reminders in the past week!" he laughed. "This trip to Lewes is all I've heard for two months, from both you and Glynnie."

"Glynnie?"

Again, Falcon laughed. "Glynnie has been well rewarded for the sewing she did for Ora Macy. She has asked that yard goods be purchased for her in Lewes so that she might now sew for herself."

Tamara felt a small twist of jealousy. "She asked you?" she questioned, dropping her eyes. "What do you know of choosing yard goods for women's garments, or of Glynnie's taste in clothing?"

"Nothing," Falcon whispered against her hairline. "But Glynnie need not be made aware who does the actual choosing."

Tamara bit her lip to keep from snapping some waspish reply. Glynnie was being her usual inconsistent self. One moment she and Tamara were the best of friends, with Glynnie eager to learn social graces under Tamara's tutelage, and at other times she was that familiar rebellious child Tamara had first met upon her arrival at Asher Arms. Tamara also suspected that she still harbored a warm place in her heart for Falcon and had not quite gotten over the loss of him to another woman. Still, Glynnie's good moods outweighed the bad, and Tamara had learned tolerance since her arrival in the Delaware wilderness.

"Very well," Tamara conceded after a moment. "I'll assist you in this very delicate matter. Now," Tamara managed a smile as she dropped her hands,

"I shall require an hour to prepare for the trip—and to meet with my father."

Moments later, Tamara relaxed in a warm, perfumed bath prepared by Bridie, contemplating the two-week trip to Lewes and back. She'd been so long in the wilderness that she could hardly imagine herself surrounded by brick buildings and the hustle and bustle of city life. Civilization! Did she truly long for it?

After her bath, Tamara hurriedly dressed, packed a few necessities for the trip, then went in search of her father for last-minute instructions. She found him in the parlor, enjoying the morning light spilling into the usually dark chamber. Approaching him from behind, she wrapped her arms around his neck and kissed him lightly on the cheek.

"You're looking chipper this morning," she greeted.

He smiled. "I am feeling chipper, Tamara." Taking her hand, he pulled her around to assess her appearance. She was dressed in a tan riding skirt and white long-sleeved blouse, and her wheat-colored hair had been pulled back in yellow ribbons. Her face was clean and fresh and pretty, and the light of happiness shone in her eyes as she returned his look. "How lovely you are," he reflected softly.

"Oh, Father—" Tamara dropped to her knees before him. "I feel lovely! It's a warm, wonderful day, and I'm so happy to see winter behind us. I thought it'd never end!"

"You'll get used to the winters, Tamara."

"Perhaps. Have you heard about the twin foals?"

"Yes," he replied. "That has never before happened at Asher Arms."

Tamara rose, then clasped her hands in front of

her. "Now! What luxuries shall I bring you from Lewes? Imported tobacco, perhaps?"

"I've given Falcon a list of things, Tamara. But . . ." and here Jacob held out a small leather pouch, "there is enough gold here to make a necessary spring purchase for yourself."

Confused, Tamara did not take the pouch. "There is nothing I need, Father. Besides, I have money of my own."

"You have Mason's money!" he retorted bitterly, physically taking her hand to place the pouch in it. "Take this to a Mrs. McFurder on the village common. Falcon sees her on every visit to Lewes. She shall take the appropriate measurements for your wedding gown. Sterling Bain and his father should arrive within a fortnight."

Tamara felt her smile fade and her fingers close firmly over the purse. She wanted to argue, but she knew he would not listen. She wanted to scream her indignation, but she'd vowed months ago not to allow her father to anger her again. Thus, she replied indulgently, "Very well, Father."

"By the way, Tamara . . . this came for you last evening by courier." Jacob handed her the leather portfolio that had been exchanged between him and Mason since her arrival in Delaware. "You might wish to read its contents before you leave."

Tamara took the portfolio from him. "I shall read it later." She felt argumentative, seething inside that her father insisted on making her life miserable with these constant threats of forced marriage. She had never met Sterling Bain of Virginia, and yet she loathed him. She loathed the very sound of his name. She passed Bridie in the foyer, unaware of her until the elderly woman spoke in a sarcastic tone. "For-

give me, Bridie. I—I am so excited about the trip,"
she lied, "that I did not see you."

"Passed right by me, miss?"

"I—I know." Tamara smiled apologetically.

"I'd be pleased if you'd add baking powder to the
kitchen list when Falcon stops at the trading post on
the way back home."

"I'll see to it, Bridie." Tamara turned toward the
porch. "An' miss?" Tamara turned back at the
sound of Bridie's voice. "Keep alert. The Frenchies
are all about these days."

"Falcon will take care of me."

Bridie turned toward the kitchens, mumbling,
"Falcon will take care of himself first." She had
meant for Tamara to hear the insult. She was long
past the point of being delicate in the presence of
Fleming's daughter.

Just the mention of Falcon's name revived Tamara's spirit. She exited the house humming a happy
tune, quickly traversed the steps, and did not waste
time as she moved toward the stables. The horses
were where Falcon had left them, but Falcon was
nowhere to be seen. Then she heard voices coming
from the stables—one of them she recognized as Falcon's. She moved in their direction but halted just
outside when she heard argumentative voices.

"She doesn't know, nor does she need to know,
damn it!" Falcon's voice was a hushed, angry whisper.

"This is also what her father said, Falcon." Tamara recognized Broggard's graveled voice. "The
master wishes you to leave Asher Arms and is not
pleased that you remain. It would be different if you
truly cared for his daughter. But you do not, Falcon.
You merely use her to hurt the master. And when he
is unhappy, he makes everyone unhappy. I am telling

you. . . ." In the semidarkness of the stables, Tamara saw Broggard's long, thick finger jab repeatedly into Falcon's shoulder. "End this thing between you and Fleming. I don't want to have to . . . well! There is no need to say what I might have to do."

Only now did Falcon's hand come up, to hit Broggard's arm away from him. "Don't threaten me, Broggard!" Tamara took several steps back, then turned and moved quickly toward the horses. She did not hear Falcon's departing words, "And, damn it, Broggard, don't you underestimate my feelings for Tamara Fleming!"

All Tamara really remembered of the conversation was *If you truly cared for her.* . . . Momentarily, Falcon, his face flushed with anger, exited the stables, saw her, and started toward her.

The look in her eyes hinted that she had overheard. He saw the hurt as she met his gaze. He saw tears, which she sniffed back as she tossed her loose, silken tresses and said in a quick, high-pitched voice, "We'd best get under way, Falcon, if we wish to enjoy the morning."

He said nothing as he tied her bag and assisted her into the saddle. She did not meet his gaze, but clicked her horse ahead before Falcon mounted.


They rode along the familiar trails toward the Indian River for an hour before Falcon said anything, and then it was only to warn her of overhanging branches. She rode ahead of him in silence, her eyes picking at the ground. She had intended to be so happy and had wanted only to enjoy being alone with Falcon once again. But try as she may, she could feel only gloom.

It seemed that fate and mortal man were determined to cast the shadows of doubt upon her relationship with Falcon. His every look, touch, caress, and kiss spoke eloquently of his love for her. Her heart told her that he loved her, yet always there was the doubt. Was this the way it would always be between them? A life of doubt and suspicion and mistrust? Of wondering from one day to the next if his every action was a vicious lie?

He knew she had heard the exchange of words between the two men, yet he did not volunteer an explanation. Did he think she would forget it, and not question him? Did he think her a fool?

The more Tamara thought about it, the angrier she became. She felt more strongly the heat of her anger as the day wore on. Suddenly, she realized her horse was the only one moving and, alerted to the silence, halted and turned in the saddle. Falcon sat atop his horse back on the trail, his wrists crossed and resting lightly on the gelding's mane. His eyes narrowed as they met her gaze.

A crimson flush rose in Tamara's cheek. "For what reason have you halted, Falcon?"

"To wonder . . ." he began in a slow, patient tone, "how far south you will travel when it is due east we wish to go."

A little embarrassed, Tamara broke eye contact. "You might have said something, Falcon!"

Slowly, Falcon nudged his mount, closing the distance between them. "Say something?" he echoed with mild sarcasm. "You ride along at your own merry pace, wallowing in that woman's anger of yours, caring not in what direction you go." Falcon hastily dismounted, then approached and put his hands out to her. She held it to the saddle steadfastly. "Get down!" When she refused to meet his gaze but rather pressed her mouth into a thin, angry line, he physically took her waist and dragged her down from the saddle. "I won't spend two damned weeks with you in this mood, Tamara!"

She struggled to break away. "Let me go, you . . . you scoundrel! I should let you go to Lewes alone and pick out the yard goods for Glynnie's dresses. See if you can manage that by yourself!" She made a feeble attempt to hit his chest with her fist, but it became a gentle caress instead. "Oh, Falcon . . . you do so frustrate me with your secrets. Whatever am I going to do with you?"

His voice became firm and serious. "I have never lied to you, Tamara. When you have asked me something, I have told you, haven't I? You overheard my conversation with Broggard," he directly accused. "If something was said that disturbed you, confront me with it! Damn it, you've never been delicate before! Don't be now!"

Tamara's fist unfolded and rested gently on his chest. She felt his firm muscles through the thin muslin shirt. "Broggard accused you of trying to get to my father through me. Why would he say such a thing?"

Falcon's fingers came firmly under her chin to lift it, to force her eyes to meet his own. "Ask me, rather, if I love you, Tamara. You know the answer to that question. Whatever vicious slur is made by any man . . . or woman . . . at Asher Arms, it cannot dampen this thing I feel for you. You are the one, Tamara, who has the problem. Every time you hear something, you nurture your doubts rather than your heart." Ashamed, she tried to lower her eyes, but he would not allow it. "Look at me! Do I not speak the truth? Listen to no man but me, Tamara. I shall never lie to you. Listen to no man but me, and you will never be hurt."

Tamara gently shrugged against him. "Then . . . what did Broggard mean?"

"Don't be naive, Tamara. I am quite aware that your father has promised you in marriage to the Virginian. We both know that he does not want me at Asher Arms."

"But why, Falcon? I don't understand why."

Falcon's eyes narrowed. He wanted so much to tell her why. He wanted to unload this terrible thing that had been buried in his heart for so long. He wanted to tell her, but he knew he could not. Not now.

"Always, Tamara, I have asked you to trust me. When the time is right, you shall know everything there is to know about me. But . . . not yet. Trust me a little while longer."

"Oh, Falcon. . . ." Tamara's head rested gently against his chest. "There's just so much I want to know. I'm sorry I have doubts. I cannot help it. I love you so much that I worry constantly that I'll lose you. Now, with my father and this . . . this Sterling Bain . . . and he—my father—has ordered me to purchase a wedding gown in Lewes."

Falcon laughed and his hands rose to her slim shoulders. "And so you shall buy a wedding dress, Tamara. But the Virginia dandy shall not stand beside you where you wear it. That pleasure I reserve to myself, even if I must kidnap you and flee into the wilderness. And . . . your father be damned!"

Tamara looked at him with shock and disbelief. Never before had marriage been mentioned between them. "Falcon, you are . . . asking me to be your wife?"

A thousand hours of thought existed in the short span of seconds that followed. Falcon's eyes caressed her features, and his fingers rose, to gently, briefly, touch her warm, moist lips. "Yes," he whispered against her crimson cheek.

"Not just your woman?"

"My wife," he said softly. "Mrs. Falcon. . . ."

The silence fell like a dying breath. He'd been about to say something that he deliberately held back. Her eyes lifted and met a look of indecision. He had a last name . . . one that he had never told her. She could still feel the unspoken whisper of it against her flushed cheek.

"My God, Falcon . . . who are you? Will I ever know?"

He said nothing for a moment, but lowered his hands to her small waist. He held her tenderly, a world of thought rushing through his head. "Yes, you shall know, Tamara . . . come . . . we are just a few miles from Kishke's village. Everything shall be revealed to you there."

But Tamara did not like the look in his eyes; it was like nothing she had ever seen before. Her fingers, entwined among his own, suddenly broke out in a cold sweat. Instinctively, her hand closed around his and, unmoving, her eyes lifted to meet his steady, unblinking gaze. "No . . . Falcon. . . ." She heard her words, yet could not believe they were actually her own. Her entire being seemed to be swept along helplessly in the rapid river of another life, as if she viewed herself from some far distance, like an unwary onlooker. Suddenly, she did not want to know everything there was to know about him. The mystery of him kept her constantly on her toes, always reaching for him . . . always wanting him. He was like the pages of a book, closed under lock and key, suddenly sprung open by fate to reveal all there was to know.

Tamara was frightened. This man who caressed

194

her hand with his own was the Falcon she wanted and loved . . . not another Falcon who might be revealed . . . a Falcon who had constantly been required to soothe doubt and to assure her of his deepest love. Now . . . with the two of them standing alone on the narrow trail, enveloped within the sweet sounds and aromas of spring . . . this was the time to cast all doubt aside and assure him of her love.

Tamara's voice was a breathless whisper as she continued, "You are my love, Falcon. Whatever you wish me to know, you will reveal in your own way and at a time of your choosing. I shall never again back you against a wall. I shall never again challenge our love."

Suddenly, there was no more need for words. Falcon's arms slipped to her back and gently pulled her against his iron-hard body. The musky aroma of him made her senses real. His breath was cool and sweet against her temple, his mouth moist and warm, caressing a trail of kisses across her forehead and down the bridge of her nose to her waiting mouth. Something wonderful sprang to life between them . . . a mutual understanding that would never again breed interrogation or require answer. Doubt was a despoiling pestilence of the past, and only a warm, aching, savage beauty—manifested in their love for each other—walked the path of destiny, hand in hand . . . the only man and woman in a world that existed only for them.

A clear forest pond and its perpetual waterfall beckoned to them. Falcon picked her up in his arms and moved slowly over the soft, cool carpet of leaves beneath his boots. But Tamara cared not where they were going; she cared only that she was with the man she loved, and he had that special look in his eyes.

They emerged from the forest into a small clearing. A doe and her fawn, drinking from the pond, quickly scurried away. Tamara had caught only a fleeting glance of the white flagged tail of the doe disappearing into the forest. She had eyes only for Falcon.

How strong and handsome he was! His skin was bronzed by the early spring sun, his dark hair was pulled back and held by a strand of rawhide, the dark hair of his chest was exposed by his unbuttoned shirt. Holding her gaze, Falcon eased her to her feet and again took her firmly by the shoulders to pull her against him in a timeless embrace.

But Tamara wanted the commanding power of him. She wanted the look in his eyes to become a seduction in itself, like the powerful body that firmly held hers. She felt the aching hunger rush through her, binding them in a fiery embrace. "The . . . the horses, Falcon. They'll . . . run away." His mouth, capturing hers in brief, teasing kisses, broke her words into fragments.

"Well trained," he mumbled. "Forget them." Falcon dropped to his knees on the soft mat of clover beneath them, taking the weight of her body with him. "God, Tamara . . . what is this power you have over me? I cannot resist you."

Tamara's lungs burst with excitement and anticipation. She felt the sun against her back, radiant and warm. Then, laughing, she eased to her back on the blanket of clover, and her arms opened to the man she loved.

Falcon wasted no time filling them, feeling them slip around his shoulders and hold him tightly. For a moment, he was content to cup her lovely ivory features between the palm of his hands and study them as if he'd never seen them before this moment.

Her beauty was like an awakening innocence, her

smile a seductive nymph, her body an alluring siren. Then her hands slipped from her shoulders and slowly began to unfasten the stays holding together the thick, gathered ruffles of her white blouse. Her silence and her look spoke eloquently of her desires.

"You are a wild thing," he laughed gently. "My wild little doe . . . and this . . ." He looked around him, but his gaze returned immediately to her, "This shall be our nest. . . ."

The tips of Tamara's fingers touched his lips. He kissed them, nipped them playfully, then brought them to his cheek to feel their softness. Tamara said nothing, but held his loving gaze, then gently swept the locks of dark hair back from his forehead. At times Falcon could be an impenetrable shell, like a rugged wilderness man unaccustomed to human contact, but at others—like now—he was the little boy wanting to be loved. He was like two men, both of whom she adored with all her heart and soul.

Supporting himself above her, Falcon's lips captured hers in a tender kiss that soon became a series of alluring caresses that drew a path over her exquisite oval features. Then, annoyed by the garments that separated their bodies, Falcon swiftly removed her blouse and skirt, and just as swiftly discarded his own clothing to a pile in the sweet clover forming a circle around their bodies. He knelt naked beside her, and for a long, silent moment his eyes alone tormented her body, probing deeply below its surface to awaken the wild passion he knew to be waiting there, willing to be seduced and conquered, unfettered by puritanical convictions. Tamara enjoyed that look; she reveled in the well-muscled physique that loomed possessively above her, his moisture-sheened skin bronzed and healthy, his throbbing shaft standing firm against his tight belly, inviting her tender touch.

Falcon moaned in exquisite agony as her fingers closed over his passion-sensitive flesh. He could no longer bear that merciless breath of space separating their bodies and he fell gently upon her to capture one of the pink buds of her breasts between his lips, to knead it until she could no longer stifle a cry of her own. His hands explored the soft curves of her naked form, clearing the way for his mouth that trailed tantalizing kisses across the small throbbing pulse in her neck, her sensitive breasts that rose to meet his caress, her tight, flat stomach, and lower . . . to the inviting mound hiding her most intimate place. She groaned in delight beneath his masterful explorations and instinctively, her thighs fell apart, inviting his mouth to her. Sweet agony filled her abdomen, now become a passion-sensitive cavern begging to be filled. Then, as his mouth continued to sweetly torment her, his tongue to probe the throbbing depths of her, her fingers dug into his thick, dark hair, guiding him away from this sweet agony.

Falcon was in an agony of his own and quickly thrust his manhood deep into her waiting, willing cavern. He felt her muscles contract around him, eliciting an intoxicating moan from him, coursing a wonderful pain through him that drove him deeply into her. His mouth hungrily found the tempting peak of her breast, captured it, kneaded it gently between his lips, then left a trail of tormenting kisses back to her moist, parted mouth. Her hips rose to meet his rhythm and pace, to drive that throbbing part of him deeply into her.

Then, pressing his manly chest to her soft breasts, his groin pounded against her hips, coursing a river of no return through their entwined, passion-filled bodies. And their spasms blended together in a wonderful explosion, like fireworks, like cannon exploding all around them, yet not touching them at all. For an instant, they became one with the clouds that refused to return them back to earth.

Their bodies remaining joined; they held each other until their staggering, ragged breaths slowed in gentle unison.


The village of Lewes was nestled against the ragged jut of Cape Henlopen. Snug, sea-weathered houses, many built of the spars and innards of shipwrecked vessels, stood along the shores at the mouth of the windswept Delaware Bay. In years past the tiny village had been a mecca for pirates who had preyed on ships, looted wrecks, and plundered houses. Captain Kidd himself had once put in at the port for supplies and waters and, despite his notoriety as a pirate, had proved quite a gentleman, trading and bartering with the citizens, rather than plundering them as was his usual custom.

This morning, a gang of young boys stood on the commons and threw tomatoes at two unfortunate fellows confined in the stocks. The dock barters were setting up their wares, and the milliner had set displays of the latest ladies' hats on the wooden walkway outside her shop.

Bethel McFurder had risen late this morning. She'd scarcely had time to pull on her newly powdered Paris wig before the bell above her door rang, announcing the arrival of her first customer.

Bethel was a rather portly woman, required to turn sideways to pass through the door at the back of her shop and through the displays of newly sewn gowns placed at intervals around the wide, spacious, well-furnished waiting chamber. In a rather untidy corner sat many bolts of the latest yard goods from England and France, sewing notions, and laces and ribbons in every shade and color imaginable.

Mrs. McFurder's plump, crimson features broke into a smile when she saw the tall, slim lady sitting by the window, her gloved hands resting rather humbly in the folds of her gray gown. Bethel did not know the name of this woman who was spoken so highly of by the street vendors and shopkeepers. But Bethel, notorious for making a point to know everyone's business, knew very little of this infrequent visitor to Lewes.

"Madame, how may I serve you?"

The slim woman arose, then graciously offered her hand to the shopkeeper. "For many months," she replied, "I have intended to stop in and meet you. The man, Falcon, speaks so highly of you."

"You know Falcon, do you?"

"Yes . . . I know him."

"Aye, young Master Falcon . . . I understand he is expected in Lewes this week, with Master Fleming's daughter." The shopkeeper withdrew her hand, then motioned to the rear living area of her shop. "Please, madame, honor me . . . I have prepared a pot of cinnamon tea and blueberry posset. Breakfast with me and we shall talk."

She returned the woman's smile. "Tea would be nice. And I must announce the reason for my visit, so that I may soon return to my home."

"Which is where, madame?" Silence. Bethel McFurder pulled a chair out from the neat table where a basket of freshly baked bread emitted swirls of heat into air thick with the aroma of the posset baking in the oven. "You said, mum?"

"I live with my husband beside the Indian River,"

she replied, taking the chair offered her. "The reason I've come, Mrs. McFurder. . . ." She withdrew a letter folded in thirds, with a length of rawhide tied round it. "Falcon advised that should I find a need to get a message to him, you will see that he gets it."

"Indeed, I shall, mum."

Bethel's curiosity was alive and her questions were still there in the slight rise of her voice. There was so much she wanted to know about this woman of mystery. The slim woman raised her eyes to that plump, friendly face, then watched as she slowly poured cinnamon tea into delicate china cups.

A moment of indecision reflected in her gaze. She felt suddenly pale, her throat dry and parched. She wanted so much to voice her pride and tell this woman who she was. But she did not want questions asked. She wanted to carry on as she had all these years, keeping intact the shroud of mystery that had everyone wondering who she was and where she had come from. In her quiet way, she enjoyed being the center of attention.

She had heard, too, of Bethel McFurder's reputation. The woman was known to peer quietly from behind doorways and keep her ears open for the latest gossip . . . gossip she always kept to herself. She derived her pleasure from hearing it, not from passing it on. She knew also that she accepted a person for who that person was, no questions asked.

Thus, the tall, slim visitor quietly replied, "I am Falcon's mother."

"Nay, mum, cannot be." Bethel argued matter-of-factly. "Falcon's mother is Indian."

The slim woman smiled. "Then Falcon is a fortunate man."

"Why is that, mum?"

"Because if that is so, Falcon has two mothers."

## Chapter 13

*Williamsburg, Virginia*

Sterling Bain sat back in the comfortable terrace chair and allowed the aroma of newly bloomed roses to fill his senses. He was still nursing the leg wound he had received at Laurel Ridge in his regiment's encounter with French troops some weeks back and had enjoyed being pampered by his mother and sisters. He suffered occasional nightmares stemming from that encounter, when his regiment had dozed to the calls of whippoorwills, wolf howls, and musket shots. He remembered Major Washington's orders, brisk in the evening air, as he'd spaced them behind the ramparts. He remembered seeing nothing, hearing only the wolves and whippoorwills and the wind whistling through the trees.

Yet, with the arrival of dawn there had been no corpses, although six of Washington's men were later found to be missing. Christopher Gist had arrived later in the day with a report that fifty Frenchmen had passed his house the day before, coming the way of Washington's troops.

Washington had then dispatched half his troops

and with Lieutenant Sterling Bain second in command had sought out and engaged French troops. It had proved to be a rather disastrous engagement, as the French shouldered their firelocks and concentrated fire at Washington's exposed company. Immediately, one man had fallen dead and three others sank with wounds, among them, Sterling Bain.

Although the encounter had terminated in victory for Major Washington, known among his men as the "Tenderfoot Commander," Sterling had been too busy writhing in agony to enjoy the sweet nectar of their victory.

"Sterling?"

He felt his nerves jump. Regina, his youngest sister, set a tray beside him containing a bowl of potato-and-watercress soup, soda crackers, and steamed periwinkles. She'd garnished the tray with a bud vase containing green fronds and a single yellow rose. Regina was the favorite of his three sisters. She never missed the opportunity to spoil and pamper him.

"How good you are to me, Regina," he said, adjusting his napkin in his preparations to enjoy the meal.

Regina was quite pretty this morning, with a delicate pink hue glistening in her cheeks and her auburn hair pulled back in ivory combs. While his two eldest sisters were stout, like the women on his father's side, Regina was slim and graceful and very much favored her mother.

"I worry about you, Sterling. Major Washington sent a message two days ago that he would visit you today, yet you have made no effort to dress for the occasion. Look at you!" Regina flipped the lapel of his lounging robe, then clicked her tongue. "Mind you, Brother, that Major Washington is your superior and expects some degree of dignity. He does not expect to be greeted by an officer dressed for bed!''

"George," Sterling replied patiently, sipping at his soup, "merely wishes to see if I am well enough to return to the fields. He's had a taste of blood, and—I've heard mere rumors, mind you—hopes the Virginia Assembly will grant him a promotion.''

"George is a nice man. Why . . .'' Regina laughed delicately, "if he weren't so enamored of Betsy Fauntleroy, I'd have a mind to go after him myself!''

"Regina, you wouldn't want him," Sterling answered distractedly. "He's actually a very boring man.''

"You would say so!'' she laughed. "You have a betrothed, Sterling.''

His eyes narrowed, betraying tiny lines of resistance. The soup spoon clattered noisily to the tray. "I once thought being the only son was an advantage," he declared bitterly. "But no more. I'm being forced into a loveless marriage with a rich man's daughter—a toad, I'd imagine—and I am entrapped by my own cage of rebellion! It makes me want to flee into parts unknown, and to hell with our Virginia!'' Sterling swung his feet to the floor, being careful of his still-bandaged right leg. His appetite gone, he set the tray of food on the comfortable chair. "By God, if I have to marry the toad, I'll make her life miserable and beat her daily!''

Regina threw her head back and laughed. "Oh, Sterling! You are so full of tomfoolery! You, beat a woman? I'd sooner see mother flop in the hay with the excise collector!''

Sterling, too, laughed at the thought. He and Regina frequently shared these intimate moments, making jokes about members of the family, loving them nonetheless. But how precious to him was this dear little sister who would soon celebrate her sixteenth birthday. He would make it special for her.

"Thank you, Regina."

"Whatever for?" she replied coyly.

"For making me smile when I weep inside."

Regina took her brother's hand and held it fondly. He was a hero to her. She took great pride in the way her young friends admired and looked up to him and blushed girlishly when he was in their presence. For a moment she studied her brother's youthful features, with scarcely a wisp of hair on his chin. He did not look his twenty-three years, which might be to his advantage as he grew older. He was not a tall man, just under six feet, but he was slim and graceful in his movements, and he carried himself with an air of dignity. She knew how gravely opposed he was to their father's plans for his future.

Soon, he would make a trip to Delaware—a trip that had stirred mixed emotions in him and had made him rebellious and bitter. He was well apprised of the financial situation of the Bain estate, and his father's pride that would go before the fall. Sterling was the only hope of salvation for Bain House. The daughter of Jacob Fleming would bring a wealthy dowry to their Williamsburg estate—a dowry that would lift the Bains from the gorges of bankruptcy. Fleming's written promise was all that kept the creditors away from their front door.

Presently, Sterling rose, took his cane from its resting place beside the chair, and rested his arm across Regina's shoulder. "I shall appropriately dress to meet our Mister Washington."

"Is he aware of your journey to Delaware?"

"If he isn't, I'll apprise him of it. After all, half his regiment will attend Captain Paget's annual festivities in Lewes. It seems only appropriate that I, too, attend. After all—'' Sterling squeezed his sister's shoulders, ''It is there that I shall meet my betrothed. Oh, be still, my beating heart!'' he ended on a sarcastic note, placing his hand lightly upon his chest.

If Major Washington sent word that he would arrive at three in the afternoon, he could be counted on not to arrive a minute too early or a minute too late. He stood in the foyer, straight as an arrow and measuring six feet two, the only evidence that he was an officer the gilt, crescent-shaped gorget suspended around his neck. His red-and-blue uniform was clean and crisp, and he held his tricornered hat firmly beneath his left arm. He awaited, informally, the appearance of the bouncing Regina, whom he also regarded as a sister and who had never failed to be the first of the family to greet him.

Regina, however, stood at the top of the stairwell, out of his sight, and was content to stare at him with girlish admiration. His auburn hair was neatly pulled back, his red waistcoat a little tight across his well-developed muscles. He had a rather prominent nose and a long face with high, round cheekbones. His was a pleasing and benevolent, though commanding, countenance. Regina found him an engaging man, and one who looked you full in the face, deliberately and deferentially, when he spoke. His demeanor at all times was composed and dignified.

With a small sigh, Regina traversed the stairs and was soon dwarfed by the towering Washington.

Regina's gaze touched his and slid away politely. ''Why, Major Washington, what a pleasure that you could visit Bain House today.''

Washington smiled, keeping his lips firmly closed

to hide defective teeth. "Miss Bain, how lovely you look today. And the family? All fare with health and happiness?"

"Indeed, yes," she replied. "And Sterling—Lieutenant Bain—grows stronger each day. The leg remains stiff, but I suppose it will be so for a while."

Washington often indulged Regina with painful attention. She was a pleasant girl, mature for her young years, and ofttimes a bit perplexing to the staid colonel. Logic warned him to treat Regina as the blossoming girl she was, but his heart viewed her well-developed frame as that of a woman. If she weren't of such a tender age, she might easily distract him from the fair Betsy Fauntleroy.

Sterling, who had given the doting Regina a moment alone with his commanding officer, now entered the foyer from the parlor. "Colonel . . ." He outstretched his hand in greeting, which Washington took. "So good to see you. Regina . . ." Sterling smiled, "run along and instruct Maidie to bring a bottle of wine." Regina held back a mild protest, then bowed perfunctorily and disappeared toward the kitchens. "You do lift the girl's spirits," Sterling said to Major Washington. "She says frequently that you shall aspire to great heights."

Washington laughed. "I shall aspire, perhaps; and one hopes, to heights rather than ravines. She's a charming girl. Now!" Washington clasped his hands. "Shall we discuss the heights to which *you* shall aspire? I understand that . . . matrimony shall soon be among your aspirations. Sterling, have I the pleasure of knowing the fortunate lady?"

The fortunate lady had spent two agonizing days on horseback. She was stiff and sore and scarcely able to get down from the pack horse without Falcon's assistance. Only the nights had afforded consolation on the hot, sticky trip, as she had lain in Falcon's arms and enjoyed the cool wilderness breeze with him.

She smoothed down the crumpled folds of her skirt and flicked dust from her cheeks and forehead. She then reached into her pocket for the handkerchief she had dampened in a stream just an hour ago and wrapped in rawhide and felt, also, the letter that had arrived from Mason Gray. She was still a little confused by its contents. Mason had mentioned a package he had received and had thanked her for it. Yet she had sent nothing to him. She had mentioned it to Falcon, but his only response had been, "The gentlemen is getting on in years."

Falcon's first stop in the quiet little village beside the Delaware Bay was Bethel McFurder's shop. Falcon and Tamara found themselves coaxed to the living quarters in the rear for mulled cider and freshly baked lemon pound cake. While Bethel and Tamara sat and chatted, Falcon, sitting at a small desk off in a corner, went through various correspondence and messages that had been left with Bethel over the past few months. He was especially attentive to the short message delivered only a few days ago.

Falcon,
Among my possessions was a portfolio containing letters from Mason Gray written many years ago to his wife. I am aggrieved to find this portfolio missing. We had both agreed to allow Fedora and her child to rest in peace. I pray you have not seen fit to destroy these few remaining possessions of Fedora Gray.
Knowing you so well, my son, I hasten to add

that no worldly good shall come of opening old wounds for Mason Gray.

I beg of you to leave well enough alone.

Yours with love and faith,

Mother

A cat jumped up to the desk, startling Falcon. He quickly folded the letter and tucked it into the pocket of his shirt, then took a moment to scratch the head of the friendly old cat. The other items of correspondence and bills he tucked into the pocket of his saddle case.

"Come, lad," Bethel ordered, "there shan't be a morsel of cake left to fill an empty belly."

Falcon rose. "I'm afraid I'm not much of one for sweets," he said a trifle sullenly. He sat at the table but did not so much as taste the large slice of cake Bethel slid under his nose. His thoughts were far away.

"Falcon?" Tamara's hand gently touched his arm. "Are you troubled?"

His hooded eyes narrowed slightly. He masked his desolation behind a brittle smile. "No . . . just tired. It's been a long journey, and it's time to reach our lodgings."

Bethel McFurder released a haughty "Harrumph! This girl's going nowhere with you, Falcon!" she said endearingly. "I've orders from her father to see that she's lodged at Paget's house, in the care of proper servants. You, lad, may sleep in the woods if you've a mind to . . . but not this girl."

"But—" Tamara could not stifle a mild protest. "I had no idea arrangements had already been made. I—I wish to enjoy whatever lodgings Falcon finds for me."

Falcon spoke in an inconsequential tone of voice.

"Take whatever lodgings your father has arranged, Tamara. I shall have no trouble finding lodgings for myself."

"Falcon, you have—"

Immediately, Falcon's finger came up to his lips, to silence Bethel McFurder. Tamara did not like the secretive looks that were exchanged between them. Her long-lashed eyes turned to Falcon with a certain defiance. "Did you know about this, Falcon? Were you merely my escort, your intentions all the while to dump me into someone else's care?"

"I did not know arrangements had been made," he offered. "I shall fetch your bags for you."

She gave him a stern, implacable look. "Just like that, Falcon?" Then her eyes dropped in spite of herself. "Very well. If you wish to treat me like this. . . ."

"I shall get your bags," he repeated without emotion.

Only when Falcon had left did Tamara drop to the chair beside the table. "I knew nothing of this," she said softly. "I feel that I've . . . betrayed Falcon. I want only to stay with him."

" 'Tis better to obey the wishes of your father," Bethel reasoned, "than the wishes of your heart. If Falcon cares for you, he won't be far away."

"And what other plans have been made for me?"

" 'Tis a grand ball—an annual festivity here in Lewes—to be held at Captain Paget's home. This year, you and Master Sterling Bain of Virginia are his special guests. At your father's direction, I have made a gown for you. We shall fit you properly, and I'll make the necessary alterations."

Falcon entered silently, dropped the bags to the floor, then turned to leave. Tamara quickly rose, and her hand on his arm delayed his departure. "I had no idea, Falcon. Will you be very far away?"

Falcon suppressed his frustration, even though an emotional storm fell over him. "Your father, Tamara, is a very determined man. But it will take more than some stupid dance and that Virginia dandy. . . ."

"You heard?"

"How could I not?" he replied. "Nothing shall keep us apart, if you want us to be together. You need only assure me that is what you want." His voice had lowered so that Bethel McFurder would not overhear. But she was busy at the table, wiping cake crumbs into a linen towel. Then she went to the rear door and ordered a young boy to take a message to the Paget house to have a carriage sent around for Miss Fleming.

Tamara walked to the front of the shop with Falcon and out of doors, where the heat shimmered in visible waves. "We shan't let my father's thoughtlessness dampen our feelings for each other, Falcon, shall we?" Tamara's voice was softly persuasive. "Oh, please, let's not ruin this journey with hostile feelings toward my father."

Falcon's fingers closed gently over her wrists. "Attend the dance and meet the Virginian, Tamara, to please your father. But I don't like it."

Frustrated, he released her wrists, then reached into his pocket and handed her a small linen purse. "Choose some comely yard goods for Glynnie and . . ." he permitted himself a strained smile, "you might have your wedding gown fitted. Your father need not know it is for your marriage to me."

Tamara did not care that people walked to and fro. She cared only that Falcon stood there, hurt and bewildered by this strange turn of events. She threw herself against him and hugged him tightly. "I don't want to be parted from you, Falcon. But . . . promise me you won't be far away."

Falcon felt a burning sense of outrage. He despised Jacob Fleming and his persistence. "Tonight, when the clock strikes eleven, I shall await you at the stables behind the Paget house. Do you think you can get away?"

"Oh, yes . . . yes," she replied, closing her eyes against his powerful chest. "I shall be there, even if I must climb the thorniest rose trellis!"

Falcon stepped back and they stared at each other with mute understanding. His lips formed the words, "I love you," a sentiment she returned. Then he mounted his horse, took the lead of the pack horse, and disappeared toward the bay.


The following three days were like a thousand years for Tamara. She looked forward only to the late evening trysts with Falcon, none of which had been detected by the Paget household, although she expected that Mrs. Tweed, the head housekeeper, suspected.

The days had been very busy. She'd been fitted for the wedding gown that was now being sewn, she'd stood through readjustments on the gown to be worn to the dance on Friday evening, and she'd made various house calls at her father's direction. He seemed to have left callous little notes for her throughout the village of Lewes, and all were designed to keep her busy . . . and out of Falcon's company. But she took great pleasure in defying him through the late night meetings with her beloved—meetings that always culminated in lovemaking.

She had chosen to enjoy life and snatch at its transitory pleasures. She had chosen to overlook her father's idiosyncrasies and unwelcomed plans for her future, and to follow the path she had chosen for herself. She was Falcon's woman . . . and the whole of Delaware could know it for all she cared.

Thus she drifted through the days in a pleasant stupor and came alive only when the hour neared eleven. Her mind saw smiling blue eyes and Falcon's attractive, confident stance. Her body felt his hands awakening her flesh, and she savored the warm glow she felt inside. She felt fierce and independent and belligerent, and she welcomed the signs of inefficiency in the Paget household that allowed her nightly escapes. She suspected Mrs. Tweed had been ordered to keep close tabs on her, but by nine the elderly servant was usually nodding away in her rocking chair. Tamara would allow nothing, not even the portly Captain Paget, who seemed to have eyes in the back of his head, to subdue her into resignation where this untidy state of affairs of her private life was concerned. The only resolve she had made was to be with Falcon.

As she had the previous two nights, Tamara slipped out of the house by the rear entrance of the servants' quarters. She was wearing a lavender gown that Falcon especially favored and had adorned her hair with a spray of silk violets that was immediately caught up in the rose vines covering the trellis by the rear entrance. She gasped in surprise, then immediately covered her mouth, fearing that she'd been heard by one of the Paget servants. She stood for a moment in the semidarkness, then when she was sure her movements had not been detected, she untangled the spray of violets, lifted her skirts, and half-ran across the lawns toward the stables.

Just as she was about to enter the stables, someone

approached from behind and her mouth was immediately covered by a firm hand. Unable to scream, she flayed her arms, but the humored Falcon merely turned her into his arms.

"Falcon . . . you frightened me to death!" she whispered harshly, regaining her momentarily lost composure.

He was unable to subdue the faint tremor of laughter. "Sorry, love, I couldn't resist the temptation."

Looking up, she caught every detail of his humor, his narrowed blue eyes, the tiny laugh lines, his half-cocked smile that made her also want to smile. How could she be angry with him, her noble warrior who had brooked every opposition to be with her? She could not love him any more than she did at this moment, feeling his hands tenderly caress her shoulders.

"You look lovely tonight," he said after a moment. "For me?"

"Always for you, Falcon. Only for you."

Then, together, they turned toward the meadow east of Paget house, where they had walked the previous nights. They moved slowly toward the place where they had made love in the sweet clover, surrounded by the iris and day lilies and a bed of roses in wild, fragrant bloom.

The meadow had been their secret meeting place, where they had defied those who would keep them apart . . . those who would scheme to deny them the only thing in the world they wanted. . . .

Outlined against the purple pre-midnight sky, they turned into each other's arms and sank slowly to the velvet blanket nature had provided for them.

## Chapter 14

Most of the guests began arriving in the early afternoon, well behind the officers of Washington's Virginia Regiment, who had arrived that morning. Captain Paget's annual ball was, indeed, a well-advertised affair which attracted guests from the far corners of the colonies.

The facade of Captain Paget's large house displayed six-over-six windows flanking a four-paneled door. Gingerbread arches from a dismantled veranda festooned a screened porch, which extended across the rear of the house. That is where Tamara sat, watching the carriages arrive and the grooms stable well-nurtured carriage horses that flung magnificent manes into the breeze sweeping across the bay.

The house stood like a massive fortress against the cloudless skies, which were speckled by gulls flying inland from the sea. Twilight approached and presently the Japanese lanterns were lit along the circular drive leading to the front of the house.

But Tamara was unhappy. She had intended to enjoy this trip with Falcon as her escort and would not have accompanied him had she known her father had made other plans for her. She had always found gatherings of this sort boring and uninteresting, requiring smiles when they were not easily given.

Soon, she returned to her assigned bedchamber with its gaudily stenciled wicker furniture and calico draperies. The only pretty thing about the room was the 17th-century Kermanshah rug that was similar to the one in her own bedchamber at Gray House. She returned to the chiffon-and-satin gown her father had arranged to have made for her to wear. This evening would provide the setting for her first meeting with the Virginian her father had ordered her to marry. She touched the gown and felt its newness beneath her fingers. Hating it, she picked it up and tossed it across the room to an untidy daybed where she'd unpacked her canvas bag. Then, for the second time today, she threw herself across the small bed and wept.

"Oh, Falcon . . . Falcon, why didn't you just. . . ." There was a gentle rap at the door. Surprised, Tamara sat forward and quickly dabbed at her cheeks with the hem of her dress.

The door opened and Captain Paget's spy, his head housekeeper, looked in. "I'm instructed, miss, to assist you in preparing for the ball."

Tamara's bold defiance returned. "I've no desire to attend the dance," she shot back. "Advise Captain Paget that I shan't attend, and that I wish Falcon to be summoned."

The servant had apparently been forewarned of her obstinance. She stepped in and closed the door. "I shall do nothing of the sort, miss. Now. . . ." She brought her hands to her hips and rested them there for a moment. "I see you've laid your gown out. Shall I help you undress for your bath?"

* * *

Tamara tried pouting for an hour after she'd dressed and pinned up her hair. The servant, Mrs. Tweed, had adorned it with a circle of entwined bridal veil and miniature roses "so that you'll look your very best for your man, miss," she'd informed her. Tamara had patiently indulged this whim.

Tamara lingered in her bedchamber as long as possible. She knew she would have to make an appearance, even if briefly. Thus, she quietly left her bedchamber and slowly moved down the long corridor toward the circular stairs.

Women's laughter filled the hallways. On the stairway a young woman boldly flirted with a red-coated lieutenant of the Virginia Regiment. He made a rather grand bow as Tamara passed, but, ignoring him, she moved on her way toward the ballroom where handsome, velvet-coated gentleman danced with ladies in silks and satins and expensive brocades in a multitude of pastel colors. She hoped to blend into the mixture without being noticed.

Her host, Captain James Paget, a man enormous in his proportions, was ofttimes taken to spells of irrational behavior. Tonight he succumbed to the heat somewhat haughtily, his voice shrill and nervous. He had a deep-rooted fear that his female guest of honor would not make an appearance tonight.

The music swelled in volume, then ended abruptly, and its rhythm was replaced by the laughter and chatter of small groups filling the ballroom.

Then Captain Paget spied Tamara Fleming slowly walking among the guests. Proud and erect, she seemed to carefully evade the captain whose party she attended. She was still a little angry that he had gone into league with her father to arrange this meeting with the Virginian, and that he had so obviously excluded Falcon, her escort, from the guest list.

At the same moment, Sterling Bain entered from the west veranda. Tall and blond and clean-shaven, the uniformed lieutenant was a distraction to the ladies, two of whom entered the ballroom with their arms linked through his. Needless to say, he was very much on the defensive and had not yet accepted his father's arrangements for his future. He enjoyed flirting with the ladies and knew his antics would be relayed by Captain Paget to his father on their next visit. In a renewed act of defiance, Sterling Bain's arms went around the shoulders of the pretty girls and he moved with confidence toward Captain Paget.

"So, old boy," he greeted, "where is my beloved?" Even as he spoke, he spied the tall, golden-haired Tamara, who had stopped to chat with a young woman she had met the day before. She had also drawn a small gathering of young soldiers of his regiment with whom she exchanged small talk. She was quite fetching and certainly had caught the admiring Sterling Bain's eye. Presently his hands fell from the girls' shoulders and he said politely, "Excuse me, ladies. I have business to attend to." As he spoke to Paget, he could scarcely keep his eyes off Tamara. "You didn't answer me, Paget. Where is this toad my father has betrothed me to?" He could almost detect the aroma of the roses in Tamara's golden hair.

James Paget cleared his throat. "The toad," he laughed, "fills your eyes this very moment, young man."

"Indeed?" Sterling gave his host a dubious look. "She should have any number of suitors. Why would her father find it necessary to arrange a marriage?"

Should he be told? James Paget wondered. He liked Falcon very much and did not wish to say anything to this young man that would cast a shadow on Falcon. Still, if he did not tell him, he might find out from someone else, and the chance was that it wouldn't be presented in the proper manner. "Do you know the man called Falcon?"

"Everyone knows Falcon," Sterling answered dryly.

"The young lady considers herself to be Falcon's woman and has eyes for no other man but him."

"And Falcon? How does that vagabond treat such a woman?"

Very few people knew the real Falcon. Most knew only the man who trapped and hunted and lived with the Indians. Most knew the Falcon who could be rough and demanding and engage in a bloody good fight when the mood struck him. Very few knew the man who would gingerly lift a fallen fledgling back to its nest, or set the broken leg of an Indian child's pet rabbit.

"I—I don't know," Paget replied presently. "Shall we call the young lady over and ask her?"

"No." Sterling Bain moved into the crowd. "No need for formal introductions," he continued, halting for a moment. "I shall introduce myself."

Sterling Bain had haughtily approached the circle of people where she stood, yet he did not feel that same haughtiness now. The rebellion returned. No matter how lovely, this was the woman his father had arranged for him to marry . . . a woman not of his choosing, though she possibly could be. Needless to say, he had always hoped to find a woman as beautiful as she. But beautiful women were usually fickle and flighty, and Sterling could not envision himself spending the rest of his life with a woman who could not carry on an intelligent conversation.

The music began to play again. A young man

asked Tamara to dance, which prompted a round of competition, drawing offers from the other young officers. Then Sterling boldly stepped forward and announced, "I shall have this dance with the lady. She is, after all," he smiled as he extended his hand to Tamara, "my betrothed."

Tamara did not take his hand but gave him a look that held both surprise and rebellion. Then, lifting her chin impertinently, she reluctantly offered her hand, "I shan't dance, Lieutenant Bain, but I shall walk with you so that we may talk."

So! Sterling smiled to himself. She was as rebellious toward this arrangement as he was. Sterling took her slim hand and guided her through the crowd.

Soft, lazy moonlight shimmered onto the portico. They moved toward the steps, exchanging words along the way with guests, then proceeded into the garden, where the roses and hydrangea and bitter marigolds were subdued in the soft mist of night. The cobbled garden path echoed the click of Sterling Bain's boots. Then, when they were well out of sight of the house, Tamara withdrew her hand and turned sharply toward him.

"I do not wish to marry you, Lieutenant Bain. It is nothing personal, mind you, but I am in love with another. I am sorry about your father's financial dilemma, but I simply cannot agree to this arrangement." Only now did Tamara meet his gaze. His eyes were violet, stern, holding her look unblinkingly. She only now realized how handsome he was in his red military jacket, his clean white breeches tucked into black boots that were polished to a high gleam. His hair was the same color as her own, fashionably swept back and tied in a velvet ribbon. She thought it odd that he did not wear a powdered wig like the

220

other young officers of his regiment in attendance tonight.

"Go on . . . you were saying, Miss Fleming?"

She had been rude. It wasn't her nature. "I—I believe I've said all I wish to say, Lieutenant Bain."

"Then I shall add my sentiments. Neither do I wish to wed you, Miss Fleming . . . however, we should both try to be civil and, rather than exposing our feelings here and now, spend time at Asher Arms as our fathers have planned, and let them see, first-hand, that we are not suited to each other. As for my father's financial state, I do not wish to discuss this very delicate matter with you and ask that it not be brought up again. Now," Sterling Bain offered his hand, "shall we return to the ballroom and make the best of this evening?"


The darkness surrounded Falcon and enveloped him within the confines of his momentary solitude. He met no one on the garden path, though subdued laughter echoed and caught his attention. He had never before attended a function to which he had not been invited and felt somewhat uneasy doing so tonight. He stood for a moment near the dark coaches, where impatient teams stamped their hooves on the cobblestones and pulled nervously at their bits.

His mood was black with jealousy, as black as the foreboding storm clouds gathering on the far horizon. He had really intended to give Tamara some breathing room, but just the thought of her in another man's arms brought a seething rage to him. There were so many people in attendance tonight that he hoped to blend in without causing a stir. He wanted to see how Tamara got along away from his company. That she might enjoy the evening without him did not settle well in his heart. She had claimed to love him. Could she, then, enjoy the evening in another man's arms?

There was only one drawback to Falcon's unnoticed attendance. Too many people either knew him personally or by sight. Thus, he had not even entered the veranda before he was drawn into a boring clique of small talk. Falcon, as always, graciously excused himself.

When Captain James Paget spied Falcon's towering form across the room he was not surprised. Rather, he would have been surprised had he not attended. He had never before seen Falcon dressed in breeches and coattails, attire that suited him well.

On the other side of the ballroom, Tamara was entering with Sterling Bain. A new waltz had just begun and instantly Sterling took Tamara in his arms. She was swept along helplessly and her feet moved mechanically to the rhythm. Her heart, though, was far, far away, with the man she truly loved. She was like a puppet, manipulated by circumstance, and found herself unable to lift her eyes to her dance partner's, though she knew his gaze bored holes through her. Then, suddenly, she felt his hands being wrenched away, and her body moved into familiar arms. Surprised by the move, her eyes lifted to the sparkling blue ones before her. "Oh, Falcon . . . Falcon. . . ." She had never seen him so handsome. Indeed, she had never seen him in anything except rawhide trousers and a muslin shirt. The lapels of his black velvet coat were embroidered in silk threads and his jabot was tightly knotted at his neck. He had pulled his freshly washed hair back in a black ribbon.

He said nothing, but swept her along in the gentle, then almost violent rhythm of the waltz. Falcon's arms were like a dream world outside this materialistic thing existing around her—the high ceilings and walls adorned by magnificent chandeliers and European tapestries, the buffet tables that offered feasts of brown bread, mushrooms in wine, pheasants with apricots, and an array of dishes surrounding the remnants of a roast suckling pig. All day long she had been hungry and had refused to eat. And now, being in Falcon's arms was all the nourishment she needed or wanted.

Tamara never took her eyes from Falcon's, which appeared black in the sudden semidarkness of the ballroom. Then the waltz ended and the dancers began to disperse, returning to their select groups. Falcon, however, stood unmoving, gently holding Tamara's fingers between his own.

Sterling Bain approached. But before he could speak, Tamara hastily introduced them. "Falcon, this is the man my father has arranged for me to marry. Lieutenant Bain," Tamara's eyes held Falcon's expectant gaze, "this is Falcon, the man I love."

Sterling Bain was not surprised by her hastily tendered confession. He offered his hand to Falcon, but it was a moment before Falcon took it.

"Sir. . . ." Sterling could not prevent a smile. "I shall accompany you to Asher Arms when there you journey."

"Did you not hear what the lady said?" Falcon replied, withdrawing his hand.

"I did, indeed, sir. But there are more factors to consider than Miss Fleming's vow of love for you."

"And what is that?"

"Our fathers . . . and this arrangement between them."

* * *

It was well past midnight and Captain Paget's ball had gotten its second wind. The kindly old gentleman had made Falcon welcome, disregarding the lack of an invitation, and had enjoyed seeing the happy young couple defy forced prerequisites. Sterling had quickly found another young lady to reciprocate his attentions, the daughter of a close friend, and had not left her side all evening.

Hours later Tamara and Falcon walked slowly along the shore of Delaware Bay, glad to be away from the hustle and bustle of the crowd. Her arm was linked through his and they enjoyed the silence, the washing waves and each other's company.

Falcon had been quiet all evening. He had appeared solely to make his possession of her known and now brooded in the misery he had created for himself. Yet he knew Tamara loved him and they had made a vow only a few days ago never again to doubt each other's love. But seeing her beside Sterling Bain had done something to him and he could not get it out of his mind. He worried that Jacob Fleming might wield more power over his daughter than he had ever imagined. Tamara undoubtedly felt a certain loyalty to her father. But how far would she go to prove it to him? Would she go so far to marry this Virginia dandy?

The clean breeze sweeping across the bay relieved the stuffiness Tamara had felt in the confined interior of the ballroom. She enjoyed feeling Falcon's arm across her shoulder, enjoyed the possession it relayed to her. She was Falcon's Lady . . . she had no other goal, no other ambitions. Her only purpose in life was to be with him.

"Falcon?"

They had walked in silence until now and he was

visibly startled by his name spoken so softly. "Ummm?"

"Have you taken rooms?"

"I have."

"A far walk?"

Falcon halted, then pulled Tamara into his arms. "Why do you ask?"

Tamara shrugged lightly against him. "I—I'm so tired, Falcon. I cannot sleep in the gaudy little room at Captain Paget's house. The window cannot be opened and it is stuffy and hot, and I haven't slept for two days . . . not really slept." Her eyes lifted to meet Falcon's silent gaze. She smiled. "I wouldn't bother you, Falcon. I wish only a few hours' sleep before the morning . . . and to know you are close by."

Falcon tenderly drew her to him. "Then you shall have your sleep."

Falcon and Tamara turned back the way they had come, toward an overgrown, one-and-a-half-story fisherman's house several hundred yards down the bay. Then Falcon turned through a narrow covered gate and coaxed her ahead of him on the brick walkway.

"We will enter through the front foyer, Falcon?" she queried. "Your rooms have no private entrance?"

"We shall enter through the front," he said.

"But the landlord—"

"We have the landlord's permission. He is—" Falcon smiled a smile that she did not see. "Not presently at home."

"And where might he be?" They crossed to a long, open porch. Then Falcon took a key from the inside pocket of his jacket and opened the door to a darkened foyer, empty except for a brass spitoon in the corner.

Tamara was surprised at Falcon's familiarity with the parlor as he moved confidently among the furniture, eventually utilizing the rosin and brimstone to light a stick that he used, in turn, to light two lanterns. Tamara looked around at the furniture, masculine except for a delicately carved cherry backgammon table off in a far corner. In another corner sat a mahogany desk stacked high with dusty papers and documents. It appeared that the house had not been lived in for quite a while.

But the exhausted Tamara was suddenly very curious and strolled casually around the room, flicking her fingers over dusty objects, over the documents scattered about on the table. "This poor little house," she mused, "is in need of a woman's touch."

"This poor little house," Falcon echoed humorously, "hasn't been graced by your gentle breed in a long, long while."

"You seem familiar with its history, Falcon?"

"Because—" Falcon approached, then gently drew Tamara into his arms. "This house belongs to me, Tamara."

"Ohhh!" Tamara pulled quickly away, and her soft brown eyes shot daggers of renewed strength. "You and your little secrets, Falcon! You are such a . . ."—her annoyance could not remain and she smiled broadly, falling into his arms as she did so— "such a wonderful man," she added quietly. "And I love you." Again she pulled away. "Enough to clean this poor neglected house for you. How could you allow it to get to this state?"

"I said I owned it," he replied patiently. "I did not say I lived in it."

The gaiety of the evening was still with Tamara, pushing her exhaustion, for the moment, to the farthest corners of her mind. She closed her eyes and waltzed around the crowded parlor, laughing as she bumped into things. Then she merely threw herself down in the chair beside the desk, and her hand fell to the stack of papers that, like the house, had so long been neglected.

But she had eyes only for the humored Falcon, who had crossed his arms and was looking at her as if she had lost all her reasoning. She did not see the name on many of the documents . . . the true name of the man who now opened his arms and invited her into his embrace.

Falcon picked her up in his arms and took her to a small attic bedchamber that, in comparison to the rest of the house, was reasonably clean. A large spool bed was covered by a brightly covered quilt, and the only other furnishings were a walnut chest and a rocking chair where Falcon's rawhide trousers and shirt lay. Falcon placed the lantern he had brought with him on the chest.

"Rest," he ordered, easing Tamara to her back on the large, clean bed. "I have a few things to do." He kissed her lightly on the forehead. "You can catch that sleep you profess to need."

Tamara's hands went around his shoulders to draw him close. "You will leave me, Falcon? You do not . . . want to lie with me?"

Again, he kissed her. "I shall return later and awaken you, if that is what you want."

She smiled, even as her sleepy eyes closed. "I shall await you, Falcon . . . I will not fall asleep without you."

But Falcon could see that, even now, she was more asleep than awake.

Thus he gently pulled the quilt over her, to protect her from the midnight breeze drifting in from the bay, and turned down the flame of the lantern.

A turmoil of emotions turned over in Falcon's mind. He loved Tamara with every power that was his, but he wondered if he could truly give her the life she deserved. She had professed to love him and wished to spend eternity in the Delaware wilderness with him, but was this the life she truly wanted? She was accustomed to convenience, gaiety, having everything she wanted or needed delivered to her on a silver platter. But what could he offer her? Only a humble life in the Lenape village, or a humble life in this fisherman's cottage.

Could he truly expect her to follow him wherever he might go, without quarrel?

He knew that she would, but was he selfish to expect it?

Falcon returned to the parlor, sat at the untidy desk, and began sifting through the correspondence Bethel McFurder had accepted for him. Again, he read the letter from his mother, noticing that her hand was still firm and youthful, flowing in graceful curves over the linen writing paper that bore the watermark of her initials.

Then he picked up a lease contract affecting the fisherman's house that he had signed and then canceled. His eyes rested a moment on his legal signature . . . Marcus Weatherford Gray . . . a name he had changed at the age of eighteen to Falcon Gray.

After all, he had never known his true father, the Englishman whose wish had been to name him Marcus Weatherford. Thus, he had taken the name the Indians called him.

Falcon Gray . . . the son of Fedora, wife of Kishke, the great Lenape chief.

*Chapter 15*

Tamara sat next to Falcon on the grassy knoll beside the Indian River. He was in one of those silent, brooding moods and she'd spent the past day and a half trying to cheer him out of it. Lieutenant Bain had remained with the campfire in a clearing several hundred yards through the woods and Tamara suspected that he alone was the reason for Falcon's black mood. Falcon had been cordial and polite to the younger man, but every time Sterling had so much as glanced at Tamara, the black of jealousy had glazed Falcon's features.

This was a return journey Tamara hoped would soon end. They had made their stop at the Trading Post this morning and if they made good time should arrive at Asher Arms by tomorrow evening.

"I don't like him."

Falcon's deep, resonant voice startled Tamara from her deep thoughts. "Ummm? Oh, Lieutenant Bain, you mean?"

"No . . . Ivan the Terrible," Falcon mused in a moment of unfeeling humor. "Of course, Lieutenant Bain. I just—don't like this whole situation, Tamara. Damn your father for creating this tension between us."

Tamara shifted to her knees. "I am not tense, Falcon. Lieutenant Bain is not tense. "We—he and I—are confident that we can work this matter out. You are the one who is tense, because you are the one with doubts and apprehensions. Do I not speak the truth?" When Falcon continued picking at the ground with a twig, she took his hand and held it fondly between her own. "In light of what I have said, Falcon, what threat is Lieutenant Bain? He does not wish to marry me any more than I wish to marry him," she said reasonably. "But you must understand . . . both our fathers are convinced that, given time, we will grow accustomed to such a pairing. It is up to us—to Sterling and me—to convince them that we will not. Oh, Falcon. . . ." Her long, slim fingers lightly caressed his. "If there is anything in this world I have ever been sure of, it is the man I want to be with for the rest of my life . . . the man I want to love and to be loved by. If you don't know yet who that man is, you will never know."

The logic and direction of her thinking came to him as a sharp rebuke. Only now did Falcon's startling blue eyes lift to meet her soft brown ones. He permitted himself to smile. "A man is an angry, passionate creature, Tamara . . . women possess the logic. We could not survive without your delicate breed. You make up for the deficiencies in us. But . . . I still don't like him."

"Falcon, look at where he is now—this very minute," Tamara admonished quietly. "He's at the campfire, preparing a little supper for us, tending the pack horses and giving us this time alone. I think that's quite good of him, don't you?"

230

"Good of him, indeed." The sarcasm was still there, undeniable behind his quiet words.

Tamara gazed into his eyes, loving the way they returned her look, loving their gentle exploration of her features, their rebellion and jealousy. She felt the radiant glow of his strength and masculinity encompass her within his magic circle. Suddenly she knew if she did not make the first move to return to camp. . . .

When Tamara started to rise, Falcon gently captured her shoulders. "Do not go," he ordered lightly, pulling himself to his knees. His fingertips caressed her shoulders beneath the fabric of her blouse. Their eyes met, held, recognizing the mutual thing that existed between them, the desire that could not be quelled by earthly powers. His imperious hands moved lower on her arms, taking the fabric with him, exposing a soft, full breast which he imprisoned with his mouth. Tamara felt the familiar fire begin to burn within her, washing outward to encompass her flesh, his hands that were like a fire of their own . . . his mouth that masterly kneaded the erect, pink bud of her breasts.

She felt her breath escape her body in wild, sporadic waves. "Falcon . . . we can't . . . Bain . . . so close."

"To hell with Bain."

With noble resignation, Tamara pulled away from him. "Falcon . . . we can't!" Immediately, she caught every detail of his confusion . . . then the formidable darkening of his eyes. "We can't," she repeated more softly. "Not now." Rising to her feet, she valiantly composed herself and readjusted her clothing.

These past two days Falcon had tried so hard to be strong and patient. But now he felt a burning sense of outrage. "Return to the campfire," he said, settling against a fallen log. "You shouldn't be rude to Lieutenant Bain."

His sarcasm elicited a wince of pain. "Don't be like this, Falcon. Please—"

"Be like what, Tamara?" His eyes became lazy as they narrowed. But he could not be angry with her, and his tone assumed a note of pointless courtesy. "I do understand, love. We have tomorrow and a thousand tomorrows hence. I'll just sit here for a while."

Suddenly, Tamara was plagued by apprehension. Some dark, foreboding thing inside of her would not let her leave him alone. Thus she dropped to a seated position beside him and her tousled hair fell gently to his chest. She felt the rhythmic pace of his heart through his thin shirt and closed her eyes. Always, when things seemed to be going so well, some mortal presence, like young Sterling Bain who was as much a victim as she and Falcon, cast a shadow on their love for each other. She understood how Falcon felt. She understood her father's desire to secure her future, but she could not understand why he was so hostile to Falcon, the man she truly loved. Her father would rather see her bound in a loveless marriage to Sterling Bain than in a marriage of love and devotion to Falcon. She had never understood his hatred of Falcon and was sure the reason for it went far back into a past that preceded her return to Asher Arms.

It was a thing that plagued her daily and filled her thoughts. It was a thing she could speak of neither to Falcon nor her father. It was a dilemma without a solution, a paradox without an answer. Only time would answer the questions. Only time would heal the wounds that Falcon and her father inflicted daily on each other.

Even confined to a wheelchair, her father was a domineering man. She had seen him berate and humiliate Falcon in the presence of others. She had seen Falcon turn his cheek, even as his eyes shot daggers of hatred at his employer. Yet, Jacob kept him on at Asher Arms. That was the thing that baffled her the most.

What was it about Falcon he so despised, when she'd seen Falcon always cordial to her father? But she had often seen through the mask of deception.

And now she wondered why she'd allowed this to plague her once again. She was with Falcon, her beloved, in his favorite place—the Delaware wilderness. They were separated from her father, and Asher Arms, by time and distance. Yet just beyond the hill was a very real reminder of the power her father wielded over her. Beyond the hill was the man her father expected her to marry.

An anguished expression of misery and dread distorted Tamara's pale ivory features. Unconsciously, her arms around Falcon tightened, a gentle assurance that he was still with her, protecting her from all the world's pains.

Presently, in the silence of the forest, with the sky turning purple with evening, she fell asleep in Falcon's arms.

But he did not sleep. His thoughts had raged a burning anger within him. He had made Tamara his woman and was determined at all costs to confront her father and ask for her hand in marriage. He would offer Jacob that courtesy.

Lieutenant Bain had only a sense of direction, the morning sun, and the river to guide him toward Asher Arms. He had awakened at dawn, saddled his own horse, and left Falcon and Tamara Fleming somewhere back on the trail. They had made it only too evident last night when they had failed to return to camp that he was an unwelcome interloper. He almost wished he hadn't left the hastily scrawled note which he'd tied to Falcon's saddle, but had let them worry about him instead.

He knew that Asher Arms lay in a valley somewhere to the west, approximately a day's journey, then due northeast several miles from the Lenape village. Even if he became lost, he would have a good three days before his father arrived to find his way to Asher Arms.

Later in the evening, when he suddenly stumbled upon a large estate nestled in a quiet valley, he knew he had reached his destination. His father had described it to him many times in minute detail. He knew the large one-story buildings off to the right were the servants' quarters, the stables were to the rear of them, and centered among magnificent gardens that looked strangely out of place in this wilderness stood the main house, its long porch lit in anticipation of the approaching night. It was a hot evening and he dismounted his horse at the top of the hill and slowly began to descend to Asher Arms.

Suddenly from the dark outline of the estate he detected the clear ring of a woman's laughter commingled with the playful song she was signing. It was a lovely voice and he was drawn magnetically toward it . . . toward the small, enclosed garden between the servants' quarters and the main house.

He tied his horse, then stood behind a weathered fence and watched the pretty girl bathing in a large tin tub, splashing like a playful child and singing her happy tune. Her hair floated like an auburn cloud on the surface of the water. He wished, suddenly, that her back was not turned to him so that he could see her face . . . and her supple breasts. His delicate senses detected the fragrance of the rose water she splashed on her bare shoulders and her breasts, and he knew that he had never before chanced upon a more delightful scene. Who was this lovely, half-naked, auburn-haired doe who splashed in her late evening bath with no care in the world but making herself clean and pretty?

His foot slipped on a damp patch of ground and he ducked behind the fence just as she whirled, splashing water over the sides of the tub. He could vaguely see her dark, pretty features, her eyes that were round as saucers in her moment of alarm.

But the fence did not hide his slim frame and the red and blue uniform that stuck out like an eyesore. "Who are you?' she asked with indignation.

Sheepishly he stepped from behind the fence, then politely turned his back to her. "I'm afraid I'm the Virginian who is expected at Asher Arms."

Glynnie's eyes widened in disbelief. "You are the man who has been ordered to marry the . . . mistress?"

"Your mistress?" he questioned.

"In a way, yes, but . . ." Glynnie did not like admitting she was a servant and gingerly eased her robe from its resting place beside the tub, preparing to change the subject. "You really should be ashamed, sir, a gentleman such as yourself spying on a lady in my . . . state of undress."

"I do apologize." Sterling gently shrugged his shoulders. "Such a sweet voice I heard from the top of the hill . . . I was drawn to it."

Glynnie laughed. "Sir, you do jest with me!"

"No . . . really, your voice is lovely."

He could not continue to stare into the blackness

of the open garden when such a beauty sat just out of his touching distance. Momentarily, his narrowed eyes locked to her violet ones. His heart felt all aflutter. And for a moment, neither said a word, but looked at each other curiously.

Then his gaze slowly lowered to the supple, milkwhite flesh exposed above the bubbles of her bath. His imagination stirred like a mighty wind within him. Did she expose her breasts without inhibition? Did her fingers, gently holding the narrow lapels of her soaked robe together, now fall to the water's surface? Did her gaze avert to the well-endowed bulge at his groin? Did her robe slowly sink into the heaviness of her bath as she stood like a sensuous siren, and her moist, quivering mouth beckon him into her seductive, naked arms?

"Sir!" Glynnie had apparently been attempting to draw him from his dream world. "I said, sir, that if you'll turn away, I shall very much like to leave my bath and dress."

"Oh." Sterling felt crimson rising in his cheeks. "Yes . . . I do apologize." He walked just around the corner of the fence and sat in an iron garden chair. "Is it safe to bathe out in the fresh air like this?" he called to her.

Glynnie had hastily left her bath and in the same haste dried off. "On such a muggy night, all the women bathe here," she replied, pulling on her crumpled gown and lacing the stays. "Besides, what is there to fear? I have never been bothered, except, perhaps . . ." she allowed herself to smile, "by a Peeping Tom now and then. Will you be visiting long, sir?"

"A week or so, I'd imagine."

Presently, Glynnie, carrying her towel and bath items, approached and stood beside him. "Well, sir, shall I escort you to the main house and see to your lodgings? The master is expecting you." She looked around toward the stables. "Did you not travel with Falcon and the mistress."

"Part of the way," he admitted. "I chose to come on alone."

"Oh." Glynnie walked slowly beside him on the garden path, listening to the dull plod of his exhausted mount behind them.

Neither spoke, but occasionally they shared a polite glance. Sterling had never met such an exquisite creature as this petite girl who had confessed to be a servant.

Two hours later Tamara and Falcon dragged in from the forest. Her father had been too busy entertaining his young guest to worry about her. Although he didn't care much for Falcon, he knew she was in good hands.

Jacob was pleased with his choice of a husband for Tamara. He found Sterling Bain pleasant, intelligent, and witty. However, he was quick to take note of the young Virginian's interest in Glynnie and so ordered her to bed much earlier than usual.

Bridie had poured cool lemonades for Jacob and his guest when Falcon and Tamara entered the parlor. Sterling, in a mischievous mood produced, perhaps, by his pleasant meeting with Glynnie, quickly rose, grasped Tamara firmly by the shoulders, and touched his lips to her cheek in a rather obvious display of sarcasm. "I was worried about you, beloved. I'm so glad you've gotten home safely!"

Tamara merely drew back and looked at him with shock and disbelief. She did not meet Falcon's eyes, but she could feel his sudden urge to

237

spring and kill this scampish interloper. Tamara held her father's amused gaze and was too surprised by the past few moments to go in pursuit of the fleeing Falcon.

"That wasn't very amusing, Lieutenant Bain," she whispered harshly.

"You didn't think so?" he replied with feigned surprise. "Don't tell me the old boy is upset!"

Angered by the gentle laughter now erupting in the room, Tamara turned and fled into the darkness after Falcon. But she did not find him; she found, instead, Drew, the stable boy, unloading the pack horses. "Where is Falcon, Drew?"

"He picked up his musket and went across the hill," the boy replied sleepily. "He'll return on the morrow, methinks."

Tamara was sick at heart. The day had been wonderful for her. She and Falcon had ridden at a leisurely pace, enjoying the summer forest, stopping long enough to bathe together in a clear mountain stream. And now, he had fled, angry and hurt by Sterling Bain's cruel joke. But it would be useless to go in search of him. There were a thousand places he could be that she would not think to look.

Thus, she turned and walked slowly back and entered the house through a rear entrance. When she reached her bedchamber she found that her traveling bag had been put just inside the door. She unpacked it, then lay across her bed. Unable to sleep, she arose, gathered the letters that she'd received from Mason these past few months, and sat at the desk to answer his multitude of questions. It was just after midnight when Tamara pushed herself away from her desk. She stretched, then rose to fill her crystal goblet with cool, refreshing water.

Then, needing to get away from the stuffy atmosphere of her chamber, she pulled a shawl around her shoulders, took a blanket from her linen cupboard, and quietly left the house. In a matter of moments, she had topped the hill above Asher Arms and moved at a confident pace toward the bend in the stream, where she often went to bathe.

She reached the stream and stood for a moment in a patch of green clover. Slowly, savoring each balmy midnight breeze caressing her flesh, she removed her shawl, spread her blanket on the ground, and sat there to enjoy the time alone. But the night was warm and her flesh felt sticky and unclean. Thus, the stream inviting to her, she arose and began removing her clothing, which she deposited to a neat pile on the rocks. Moonlight shimmered across the creek as she moved toward it, catching her reflection there, tall and slim and blond.

As she moved into the cool water, her long hair caught in the current. She felt the soothing sand beneath her feet. The sweltering night heat soon warmed the water around her, which swept like a river of passion's oils over her body and between her thighs. Closing her eyes, she reeled almost drunkenly in the gently swirling waters. She was mesmerized by the velvet flow of the stream against her tingling tantalized flesh; in the foggy vortex behind her closed eyelids, she envisioned Falcon, her dream, her perfect lover, caressing her body until it exploded in a series of rhapsodic spasms.

The approach of a horse sent alarm coursing through her. She whirled and almost lost her footing on the shifting sand. The midnight darkness was a solid sheet before her; she could not see the timber line parting her from Asher Arms. As if on cue, the gray-black clouds drifted away, allowing moonlight to once again reflect in a brilliant silver path across the water. On the bank, his legs straddling the sleek, muscled body of his stallion, sat Falcon, gazing steadily at her. The shadows of the timber line cast macabre shadows on his face. She watched him slowly dismount.

Tamara's arms opened invitingly to him. He carefully shed his clothing, betraying his well-nurtured, hirsute chest. Tamara continued to watch, a willing prisoner to her agonizingly erotic lover. Beneath the warm, swirling waters, her body burst with excitement and anticipation.

Their gazes met and held passionately. When he approached her, mesmerizing her with his penetrating stare, she moved willingly into his outstretched arms. Then he took her hand and led her from the water. She wondered if he sensed the pleasure she felt in his embrace. She wondered if he could see the desire crawling across her silken flesh.

"Falcon . . ." she whispered, "how did you know I was here?"

"I always know where you are," he whispered in reply.

Tamara's vibrant, mysterious lover eased her to her back on the blanket she had left on the grassy knoll. Strong hands moved deftly, confidently, gently massaging her damp flesh. His mouth locked to hers and his tongue probed between her teeth, playing a wild game of tag with her own. As his hand lowered and two fingers gently entered her, her own trembling hands wandered over his strong, virile chest and shoulders to close the breath of space that existed between them.

With a husky groan, his mouth broke from hers, then traveled past the small pulsating hollow of her neck to capture one of the pink buds of her heaving breasts. His tongue drew circles around it, then caressed a trail to the other, taut for his attention. Wonderful, rhapsodic pain swelled beneath his fingers, which soon moved to the hungry, inviting place between her thighs. Again, his warm, exploring mouth left a trail of caresses over her heated flesh, over the flat mound of her stomach. She gasped with wonder and surprise as he gently coaxed her thighs apart and his tongue probed to depths she wouldn't have thought possible.

As exquisite sensations of pleasure shot through her veins, his hands rose to her heaving breasts. She was in rapture, her body a wild, uncontrolled thing.

She could bear it no longer. With a low, kittenish moan, her fingers buried into his silken black hair and coaxed his mouth back to her own. Instantly, he was buried within her, full and solid, molded to her as if they were one body. They rocked together in perfect unison, lust surging like an erupting volcano, breathless groans deep within their throats.

It was weightless magic, like nothing she had ever felt before. Then, on the verge of the ultimate explosion, Falcon withdrew and again turned and locked his mouth to hers while his hands savored the wonderful rhapsody of her flesh. But withdrawal was too painful and he again buried himself within her. Momentarily, they came together in an avalanche of pleasure. Exhausted and fulfilled, their breathing simultaneously slowed to a gentle rhythm. Then Falcon withdrew, and they clung to each other in exhilarated wonder.

Moments later, while their bodies lay entwined in the aftermath of sweet passion, Tamara said, "You are no longer angry with me?"

He laughed huskily. "I was not angry with you, my love . . . my goddess. You are the staff of my life."

His words held her in a vise of contentment and soon, beneath the midnight sky, in the arms of her lover, Tamara fell asleep. The first light of dawn jolted her sleepy eyes and she awoke to the faraway crowing of a rooster. Although she was immediately jarred by disappointment, she was not surprised to see Falcon dressed, standing alone beside a tree across the clearing, his thoughts in his own private little world. Last night had been a wonderful erotic experience and she bathed in the sweet memory of it. Dreamily, she sat up, pulled on her crumpled clothing, then rose and approached Falcon.

Her arms eased around his waist from behind him. "Falcon, will life always be like this for us?"

"Like this?" he echoed, momentarily bewildered.

"Wonderful . . . fulfilling. . . ."

He turned and took her in his arms. "Always, Tamara." In the morning twilight, Tamara saw him smile, but it really didn't register in her deliriously happy mind. Her gaze returned to his eyes, blue like the clear mountain stream, that seemed to say, "Tonight, my love, we shall meet again in the shimmering light of the moon."

## Chapter 16

Everything seemed to be going so well for Tamara. These past two weeks, Sterling had ignored the close scrutiny of his father and had been paying much more attention to Glynnie. Tamara and Sterling did manage to spend their required time together, and for the benefit of their fathers, who hung on their every word and action, bantered childish insults and abuses back and forth. Each day drew the concerned fathers more often into private conferences.

Sterling, however, was having second thoughts about the conspiracy he and Tamara had deliberately entered into. He was well aware that without Tamara's dowry the Bain estate in Virginia would crumble into bankruptcy. Thus he was at odds with himself. There was a certain loyalty a son should show to family, and he had not shown that loyalty. And his infatuation with the lovely auburn-haired Glynnie had not helped the situation. But she, in her alluring innocence and naiveté, was the most fascinating woman Sterling had ever met.

Tamara did not like having to sneak away in the night to be with Falcon; nor did she relish acting out the charade with Sterling in the company of their fathers. She did not like the conspiracy or the deceptions. It was all beginning to fray her nerves and set her on edge.

Still she would accept anything as long as she had her time with Falcon. He had been patient—much more patient than she'd have imagined these past few weeks. He had politely overlooked the time she was required to spend with Sterling and the time she could not spend with him. He kept himself busy, working with the new consignment of horses that the elder Master Bain and his servants had brought up from Virginia.

She did not realize that in a matter of hours her world would turn topsy-turvy. Last evening, she'd shared an unusually friendly hour with her father. They'd sat in the parlor sharing stories, enjoying each other's company, and had found a special joy in simply being together. But he had seemed sad behind the happy façade and his easily offered smiles. She'd been reluctant to part from him when Broggard had arrived to escort him to his bedchamber. Yet she had gone immediately to Falcon, following the silent call of her heart, and had spent the night in his warm, comforting arms. Then, in the predawn darkness, she had stealthily left his bed and returned to her own bedchamber before the servants arose.

She hurriedly dressed so that she could spend time with Falcon in the running pens before the Bains arose. She was just making her bed when Glynnie burst into her bedchamber.

"Miss—Miss—come quickly—" Glynnie was breathless, her face a sickly white.

"Glynnie? What is it?"

"Your father, Miss—your father—he's—"

"My God!" Tamara felt the strength leave her body. "Is he—?" Mutely, Glynnie nodded her head, answering the question that Tamara hesitated to ask. Immediately Tamara fled.

Tamara halted at the door of her father's bed-chamber. She stood there, shocked and bewildered, as Broggard gently pulled the covers over her father's lifeless body. He turned just as Tamara entered the room.

Stunned, she slowly approached the covered form, then looked at Broggard as if she could not quite believe this had happened. Still, she found the strength to request, "May I see him, Broggard . . . please?"

Broggard hesitated, then eased the sheet back from Jacob Fleming's still features. Tamara knelt, searched for, and found her father's hand lying across his chest. His skin was cold and firm; it was obvious he'd been dead for several hours. Guilt filled her. Even as she had lain with Falcon in the predawn hours, her father had lain here in his bed, drawing his last breath.

Gently, Tamara touched his forehead. "Oh, father, I really didn't get a chance to know you very well."

She could not cry, even when Falcon entered and she rose, mechanically, drawn to this familiar comfort. For some reason, her thoughts focused on all the times Jacob had made himself miserable, berating and humiliating Falcon, taking advantage of every opportunity to make him miserable as well. She remembered the time when she'd first arrived at Asher Arms that he'd had Glynnie so severely whipped. All those things stuck out in her mind.

Yet she knew her father had loved her. They had spent many warm, happy moments together. Now that he was gone, it no longer mattered that he had sent her away as a young girl. It no longer mattered that he'd shunned her at her birth simply because she had been born a girl. Nothing mattered but that he was her father, and he was dead. Then, quietly, she turned, and with Falcon's arm gently folded around her shoulder, she left her father's chamber.

Tamara went through the rest of the day in a silent stupor. She felt rather than heard the hustle and bustle of the household as everyone prepared for the funeral. She heard only the thoughts whirling through her mind in rapid succession.

Falcon was never far away, and the younger Bain was very helpful in making the formal funeral arrangements. The elder Bain, however, sat and brooded, looking very worried. He wondered if this unexpected turn of events would void the written agreement between him and Jacob Fleming. He needed the daughter's dowry to save his Virginia estate.

Very few outsiders attended the funeral at ten o'clock the following morning. Kishke, out of respect for the white man with whom he shared this Delaware wilderness, sent his son, Flaming Bow, and another brave to attend the funeral.

"My father sends to you his sorrows," Flaming Bow announced in his deep, resonant voice. Flaming Bow looked long at his blood brother's woman. Even the dowdy black dress she wore did not detract from her beauty. Her skin was translucent and white, her eyes filled with sorrow, yet he couldn't help noting the lack of tears.

At the funeral, Tamara stood silently alongside Falcon with her hands clasped while her father's simple pine casket was lowered into the ground just up the hill from Asher Arms.

Afterwards she retired to her bedchamber for some much-needed sleep. But she could not sleep. All the grief of the past two days suddenly built up, and she felt tears fill her eyes. She buried her face in her pillow and wept away all the hurt she felt.

But she knew she could not lose her composure now. There were too many problems to be solved and too many questions to be answered. She was troubled by the written agreement between her father and Master Bain and that, at the moment, took priority over every other duty facing her in this most tense moment of her life.

But since her father had just died, it would be inappropriate to discuss business so soon; so she spent the following week rearranging the household, assuring servants of their continued service, and generally setting up a proper atmosphere for her takeover of the estate. She also sent one of the men into Lewes to summon her father's solicitor and accountant to Asher Arms, and also to post an announcement of his death. Only when the servant returned to inform her of the haste with which her summons would be answered did Tamara decide to speak to McKenzie Bain about the marriage proposal.

That morning, she arose early, inquired of the groomsman whether Falcon had returned from his hunt with Flaming Bow, which he had not, then, to get this uneasy duty quickly set aside, sought out the elder Bain.

The portly gentleman with side whiskers was reclining in the parlor with a goblet of peach brandy clutched between his fingers. The exertion of rising when Tamara entered reddened his face and he stood there for a moment, puffing and wheezing like a man much older than his years.

"Master Bain, might I have a word with you?"

"Aye, Miss Fleming." McKenzie Bain returned to his chair and outstretched his hand to Tamara. For a moment, she found it amusing that he offered her one of her own chairs.

"Master Bain, I am well aware that you and my father have conspired to wed me to your son. . . ."

"Conspired?" he puffed, suddenly angry. "My son is a proper gentleman, aspiring to high service in our Virginia militia, and will be a responsible husband to you. Your choice of words leaves me cold, Miss Fleming."

"I apologize, sir. Perhaps conspiracy was a bit harsh. Agreed, then . . . does that suit your taste better?" An imperceptible nod answered her question. "As you may be aware—and if not, I shall make you aware of it—your son and I do not wish to marry. I have thought about it for the past few days, and I believe—in view of my father's death—that it is within my right to make an alternate proposal."

The elder Bain leaned back and brought his fingers to his clean-shaven chin. "Do go on, Miss Fleming."

"You have conducted business with my father, I understand, for many years. While I am aware that you may not wish to discuss your financial dilemma with me, I believe that in view of the circumstances I have the right to insist upon this discussion." Tamara lifted her eyes and met his narrowed gaze. "Master Bain, as my father's sole heir, I shall inherit all that was my father's. I propose to offer you a loan equal to the amount of my dowry, to be repaid over the next ten years, not in gold or silver, but in thoroughbreds. As you know, the horses are our sole commodity, a commodity you breed on your Virginia farm at a nominal expense and deliver to Asher Arms on a quarterly basis. I propose the loan, sir, in exchange for a ten-year delivery of thoroughbreds, without the quarterly payments, and for your cancellation of the marital agreement.''

"Excellent, old girl!'' Sterling Bain entered the study. "Sounds good to me, Father. What say you?''

The elder Bain was a little surprised that this young woman had the good sense to talk business. She seemed confident and sure of herself. And he admired her forthrightness. "Are you counting your chickens, Miss Fleming, before they hatch?''

"What do you mean?''

"You are so sure of your inheritance. . . .''

"Why should I not be?'' she replied indignantly. "My father advised me as to the contents of his will when I first arrived at Asher Arms.''

Silence. McKenzie Bain's gaze met that of his amused son. "This is what you want also, Sterling?''

"Want?'' Sterling drew his hands to his narrow hips. "Father, not only do I *not* wish to wed the fair Miss Fleming, who wants to marry another, but I, too, want to take another spouse.'' Tamara's head snapped up. She took note of Sterling Bain's humored look. "Would my father and my . . . ex-betrothed care to meet the woman I intend to take to the marriage bed?'' Immediately, Sterling returned to the foyer and Tamara heard muted words being exchanged. Then Sterling returned, dragging a very reluctant Glynnie beside him. "Father, Miss Fleming, this is the lady I wish to marry.''

Tamara could scarcely suppress a delighted cry. She rose, hastily approached Glynnie, and enveloped her hands with her own. "Oh, Glynnie, is this what you want also?''

She favored Tamara with a shy smile. "It is, miss.''

While Tamara hugged Glynnie tightly, the elder

249

Bain sank to the divan, mumbling something derogatory about his son "marrying a mere servant."

"I am so happy for you, Glynnie," Tamara replied. "You shall have a magnificent wedding!"

"At Bain House in Williamsburg," Sterling interjected. "We wish to be married at the end of August." He looked to his somewhat dejected father. "Do be happy for me, Father?"

"It isn't the proper time, miss . . ." Glynnie quietly offered in view of the elder Bain's silence, "to be discussing marriage plans . . . what with your poor father lain to his rest only last week."

Meeting Sterling Bain had done something pleasant and wonderful to Glynnie. She was no longer the spoiled little servant girl always wanting more from life than circumstance had given her. She had become a woman, with a woman's sense and dignity. Tamara liked to think that she herself was responsible for some of this change in Glynnie. "My father would be as happy for you, Glynnie, as I am. . . ." But she knew that wasn't true. She knew her father would be furious that his plan had gone awry, that he would be determined to put things back the way he had planned. "Soon . . . very soon, we shall begin discussing the arrangements." Tamara turned back to Master Bain. "And my proposal, sir?"

McKenzie Bain arose, then quietly poured another peach brandy, which he lifted in a toast. "To you, Miss Fleming. You have accomplished in a few moments what weeks of time and discussion could not." His voice grew quiet. "My son is happy, your servant girl is happy, and you are happy. I accept your compromise. We shall work out the particulars before my departure."

* * *

Tamara wished Falcon were with her so that she might give him the good news. He'd been gone for almost a week now, and time and distance could not quell her loneliness for him. She lay awake at night thinking about him and dutifully performed her chores during the daylight hours, hoping that by night the forest would again give him up to her.

This night she watched with a longing that wrenched inside her like a heartache. She felt that the whole of the world had been dropped to her slender shoulders, and that she would crumple under the weight without Falcon's strength and guidance. She remembered the last time they had made love . . . the night her father had died . . . she remembered his gentleness, his words of adoration and assurance, the gentle caress of his fingers among the strands of her golden hair. Oh, how she missed her tower of strength . . . her lover who was parted from her by the twilight forest of his beloved Delaware.

In just two short months she would attend the marriage of Glynnie and Sterling Bain. Glynnie had departed for Virginia this morning with the Bains and their servants and had wept openly in the arms of her parents. Tamara had never seen such emotion in the rebellious servant girl. Her heart had broken for Bridie, who'd tried so hard to remain staid and indifferent, and not display emotion as she'd watched her only child disappear into the forest.

Tamara sighed deeply. So much had happened in the past few weeks. She'd been betrothed against her wishes to the Virginian, her father had died, and now, in a strange turn of events, the same man to whom she'd been betrothed was going to marry their servant girl. Perhaps everything happened for the best.

For the following three days, while Asher Arms

251

was deluged with rain, Tamara continued with her reorganization, accepted the sudden and unexpected resignation of Broggard, whose services were no longer required anyway, and gave Bridie the title of head housekeeper. The lack of one before had seemed unjust to Tamara, considering Bridie's long service at Asher Arms. Saul, too, was promoted, to the position of estate manager, and other subordinate positions were assigned throughout Asher Arms. Tamara had employed the English method of boosting morale among the domestic servants and she found that it worked well to her advantage.

The Asher Arms solicitor, Mr. Inness, arrived on a Tuesday evening and, as Bridie advised was his usual custom, just in time for dinner. The thin, stooped man ate heartily, ignoring the fact that his rain-drenched clothing was making a puddle on the expensive carpeting.

"When shall you read the will?" Tamara asked, laying her own fork aside.

"Hmmm? Oh . . ." Mr. Inness looked across the top of his spectacles toward her. "No need for a reading, miss. The will has been filed in the probate courts. And I've a detailed outline of it in my attaché for your perusal."

"Oh? Then why have you ridden all this way from Lewes, if there will be no formal reading?"

"To pay my respects, miss," he replied reasonably. "And to inform you of the contents of the will."

"Which are?"

Inness now laid his fork aside and dabbed at the corners of his mouth with his linen napkin. "Provisions made for servants, of course, and for yourself. The bulk of the estate shall go to the young man, with you as secondary legatee. It's all outlined."

252

Tamara could not suppress a cry of shock. "Young man? Whatever are you saying, Mr. Inness?"

"Why . . . Master Marcus Gray."

"And who is—" Suddenly, Tamara's face drained a sickly white. She could scarcely believe the conclusion that formed in her mind . . . the conviction that her poor father, not only crippled of body, had also been crippled of mind. Marcus Gray . . . Mason's son . . . Fedora's son . . . had been dead these many years. What terrible guilt had made her father leave the bulk of his estate to a dead child who had been the son of his indentured servant?

Tamara quietly continued, "Mr. Inness, this may pose a problem in probate. . . ."

"Why is that, miss?"

"Marcus Gray died as an infant many, many years ago."

"This cannot be. . . ." Parle Inness settled back in his chair. "The codicil, voiding your unencumbered legitime and bequeathing the bulk of the estate to Marcus Gray, was made only last year. I assure you, Miss Fleming, when I met with your father at that time, his mental facilities were intact. He was very sensible . . . indeed, he pointed the man out to be from among your servants."

Tamara stood, feeling a weakness in her knees which compelled her immediately to return to her chair. "Marcus Gray died as a child," she reiterated. "Sir, you must advise what steps are to be taken to contest this part of my father's will and put the estate in my possession. I—I have obligated funds of the estate. I cannot have it encumbered by a bequest to a . . . a dead boy!"

Parle Inness saw the shock and concern in Tamara Fleming's eyes. She looked deathly white, and he worried that she might faint. "Miss Fleming, if this is indeed true—that the boy is dead—I must have proof. The location of a grave . . . a written confirmation . . . something tangible that can be produced to the courts.''

"I have my mother's diary. When she was told of the child's death, she made a written record. . . .''

"A diary, Miss. . . .'' Inness shook his head. "I am an old man who knew your mother very well. She was a gravely ill woman. I am sorry, but I cannot accept this proof.''

Tamara found the strength to rise. "I—I don't know what to do, Mr. Inness. I hadn't contemplated a problem of this magnitude. As I've said, I've obligated funds of the estate. I must utilize these funds now . . . not next year or the year after, while this matter is being settled in the courts.'' Tamara moved away, but immediately returned and gently supported herself with her fingers closed firmly over the back of the chair. "I shall begin going through my father's personal papers. I shall appreciate, sir, you remaining on at Asher Arms until the necessary proof has been found . . . there must be something!''

Inness nodded his assent. Then Tamara turned and walked quickly toward her bedchamber. She closed the door, then sat quietly at the desk. How could things have turned so topsy-turvy? All she needed now was the arrival of their accountant, and to learn that the estate was bankrupt. She shuddered at such an idea.

Oh, why, why did Falcon have to leave now? He had been selfish, leaving when she needed him the most. But hadn't she assured him she could manage well without him for a week or so? After all, he did have another life . . . the one he had shared with his blood brother, Flaming Bow. He had an Indian heritage that held him in bondage, that often divided him between Asher Arms and the Lenape Village on the Indian River. Tamara had accepted his loyalty; why now was she questioning it?

Because she needed Falcon now, more than she'd ever needed him before. He would know what to do.

It was daybreak. Falcon and Flaming Bow had spent the night in the woods a few miles from Asher Arms. Each had brought down a deer that would be divided, Flaming Bow's among the Lenape adobes, and Falcon's among the servants of Asher Arms. Their Indian companion, Black Arrow, had departed from them three days ago to return to the village and a wife who was due to deliver a child any day now.

At midday, Flaming Bow and Falcon went their separate ways. Falcon continued on alone, stopped along the trail to visit an old settler and his wife on the Indian River, then commenced his journey to Asher Arms by late afternoon.

He missed Tamara. But he had felt that his hunting trip with Flaming Bow was necessary. Falcon had not cared for Jacob Fleming. They had been at odds with each other for four years. It was not in his favor to be dispassionate, and he would not show false sympathy. Falcon had never fully understood why Jacob Fleming had allowed him to remain at Asher Arms. Before he'd learned Falcon's true identity, he had often remarked that he'd never met a man who worked so well with horses. Was that why he'd kept him on? Strictly good business?

Falcon had wanted to hurt Jacob Fleming for the injustice he'd inflicted on his mother so many years ago. He'd wanted to see him suffer, to ride a sea of guilt until the day he drew his last breath. At first, he had considered using Tamara as a tool against

Jacob Fleming. But Falcon hadn't contemplated falling in love with her. But even that had worked to his advantage; the fact that Jacob knew he and Tamara were lovers crawled under his flesh like a cancer. He had not sent Falcon away because he knew he would also lose Tamara.

So he had adopted a new strategy. He had pledged Tamara in marriage to the Virginian, knowing his daughter would be reluctant to disobey the loyalty of her dying father.

And now he was dead. What impact would that have on Tamara? They were both in a quandry, and they would have to work together to extract themselves from her father's final vengeance.

Falcon moved at a leisurely pace, enjoying the summer forest, unaware of the new dilemma facing the woman he loved.

*Chapter 17*

Tamara spent the afternoon in a dream state from which she could not awaken. Mr. Inness had made himself quite at home, and the accountant had arrived from Dover just before three o'clock. He was a pleasant gentleman who had brought his son with him, a lad who appeared to be about seventeen. Mr. Marland advised they would remain only overnight, since they were expected at the home of relatives in Virginia in four days. Bridie saw to their lodgings, while Tamara busied herself with her father's papers.

Every document she came upon in her search was dated subsequent to 1736. She was sure her father had kept thorough records dating back to the time Asher Arms had been built, yet she found nothing, not even a written record of her own birth. It was as if those years prior to 1736 had been erased from time itself. Only her mother's diary seemed to have survived this mysterious past. Exhausted by her vain search, Tamara eventually dropped her head to her father's cluttered desk and fell asleep.

But dreams troubled her. She found herself encased within an elusive, impenetrable mist. She felt her arms flailing, striking solid form, yet at the same moment, slicing through the cold mist that enveloped her. Then she saw the vague outline of Sterling Bain's features, blank and expressionless, suddenly smiling a macabre smile. His father stood behind him, his own features dark and foreboding, his lips forming words she could not understand. She tried to cry out, to turn and flee, but her legs were flaccid and weak.

Suddenly, Bridie's large hand dropped to her shoulder and she arose with a start. "Falcon's returned, miss. You wanted to be informed."

"What—what time is it, Bridie?"

"Past two in the mornin'."

Tamara gave Bridie a quizzical look. "Why are you still up?"

Bridie lightly shrugged her shoulders, then turned so that Tamara would not see the moisture sheening her eyes. "Thinkin', miss. Sittin' in the gardens thinkin' about . . . my girl."

Tamara smiled comfortingly. "I miss her, too, Bridie. We'd gotten to be good friends."

"Well. . . ." Bridie cleared away a lump in her throat, regaining her composure. "I'll be retirin' now, miss."

Bridie retired to her bedchamber and Tamara started toward the foyer. She was surprised to see a lamp lit in the parlor and stepped in, immediately facing Mr. Inness, who sat reading a book he'd taken from her father's shelves. It gave her a bit of a start, because he sat where her father always sat, beside the window facing to the east. "Mr. Inness, you're up late."

He gave her a long look over the rim of his spectacles. "I'm a late night reader, Miss Fleming. Require only two or three hours of sleep."

Tamara excused herself and walked out to the long porch. The night was warm, yet a refreshing breeze

258

blew across the forest. She saw the soft glow of a lantern at the stables and, picking up her skirts, moved quickly across the lawns.

Falcon had hung the deer up and was gutting it when she entered. Suddenly faced by the gruesome sight, Tamara turned away, unable to prevent a small cry of protest.

Falcon's hands were covered in blood. He immediately washed them in the pail hanging from the stable door and dried them on a bit of canvas hanging beside it.

"Sorry," he said softly, approaching her. "I didn't think you'd be up this late." Gently, his hands rose to her shoulders, and his lips briefly, lightly touched hers. Being so many days in the woods, he had missed the aroma of her clean, perfumed hair. "I'd have come to you after I'd cleaned up a bit."

Missing his strong, powerful arms holding her like this, Tamara momentarily forgot the problems she'd faced these past few days. She succumbed to his embrace, caring not about the musky aroma of the forest that permeated her delicate senses. But even though she wanted only to be with him, her thoughts stirred over the events of the past few days and eventually settled on priorities. "Falcon, we have problems," she said, almost too casually. "Mr. Inness has arrived from Lewes. Father's will. . . ." She looked up. "Father wrote a codicil last year that I didn't know about—a codicil that virtually disinherits me."

"What?" Falcon's voice trembled with surprise. "What do you mean, Tamara?"

"He left everything to a child." Tamara had dropped her gaze but again looked up, scarcely able to see Falcon's narrowed eyes in the semidarkness. "A child, Falcon, who died many, many years ago.

A child named Marcus Gray . . . my guardian's son." Even in the dusk, Tamara saw Falcon's face drain of color. His hands fell and he turned away. Tamara touched his shoulder, feeling his unexplained tremble. "What shall I do, Falcon?" she continued. "I've asked Mr. Inness to remain until this matter can be cleared up, but I've gone through father's papers. I can find no proof that Marcus Gray died. I can find no proof that he even lived. I don't know what to do."

"Mr. Inness, then, remains at Asher Arms?" he questioned grimly.

"He does, Falcon. I—"

"Then I shall talk to him in the morning," he replied, cutting her short.

"Talk to him now, Falcon, please."

"In the morning, Tamara. There is no reason to wake a man from his sleep."

"He is reading in the parlor."

Falcon's gaze met her soft brown one. "I believe I can get this matter straightened out," he replied after a moment. "I request only that I be allowed to speak to Mr. Inness alone."

"But—" Tamara instantly stifled her protest. "Of course."

"Come . . . ." His arm outstretched, inviting her into its protection and comfort. "Walk with me to the house. I'll see if the harm can be undone."

In the foyer, Falcon dismissed her with a loving gaze and a gentle touch on her shoulders. Then he entered the parlor and pulled the doors to. For an instant Tamara considered eavesdropping, but she could not do that with a good conscience. Slowly she walked back to her bedchamber. She was sure Falcon would come to her when he'd concluded his talk with Mr. Inness.

She hadn't realized how tired she was. She did not undress but pulled the covers of her bed back and lay there quietly, waiting for the sound of Falcon's familiar steps in the corridor. Minutes passed and became an hour, and the oil burned down in her lamp. She could scarcely keep her eyes open and kept imaging she heard strange voices and doors opening and closing. Then, far away, she heard the familiar sound of the parlor doors being opened and momentarily, Falcon's boots could be heard echoing on the hardwood floors. But they were retreating rather than approaching. Quickly, Tamara rose from her bed. She half-ran down the corridor toward the foyer and almost knocked Mr. Inness down in her haste to reach Falcon.

"Miss?"

"Beg your pardon, sir. Falcon—he was—" Suddenly, she could not find the words; "he was to report to me," she ended on a quiet note.

"He's had an emergency," Inness said more sharply than he'd intended. "An Indian—Black Arrow, I believe he called him—something about the chief's son being taken captive by the Iroquois."

"Flaming Bow?"

"I believe it was," he replied, nodding a head of thinning hair.

Tamara turned toward the foyer, then back to Inness, panicked by the fact that Falcon would loyally flee into the forest to help his blood brother before she could talk to him. There was so much they had to discuss. Confusion ran amok within her. Then, just as she'd gathered her senses together and rushed out to the long porch, she saw the shadows of two men on horseback being consumed by the black forest. She felt lost and alone and scarcely heard Inness approach and stand beside her.

"He asked me to give you a message, miss," Inness said.

"A message?" Tamara's gaze was torn between Parle Inness's aquiline profile and the trail where Falcon and the Indian had disappeared.

"He wishes you to be apprised that proof of the child's death has been confirmed, leaving you the sole legatee of Asher Arms."

Tamara gasped in surprise. "This cannot be! What proof could Falcon give you that you would so quickly accept?"

"I—" An awkward stammer stuck in Parle Inness's throat. Like it or not, he had been sworn to secrecy. He had given his word and would not break it, not even for the woman who would henceforth pay his legal fees for representing this wealthy estate. "I'm not at liberty to divulge to you, Miss Fleming, what the man, Falcon, and I discussed in privacy. I have been instructed only to advise that matters have been settled."

Silence. A moment later, Parle Inness turned and reentered the house.

Tamara could not take her eyes from the dark timber line. What manner of secrecy did Falcon share with her father's past? She felt the dilemma of confusion, the anger, the hurt . . . the loneliness.

Falcon was gone.

She wondered how long this mission of loyalty would keep him from her.

The Iroquois were a savage tribe, at war with all white men, and with the other tribes along the eastern seaboard. Every atrocity that could be done to man, they had done. It was no wonder they had gone into league with the French in their quest for land and power.

Suddenly, Tamara knew the loneliness would be with her a long, long while.

To take a chief's son captive was a noble feat, and the Iroquois would not give him up without a fight to the death.

Tamara suffered a sudden premonition of doom. She feared she would never see Falcon again.

And she wouldn't want to go on living without him.

Tamara rose early the following morning. She glanced out the window of her bedchamber where the anemones and marigolds were in bloom and where Saul seemed busy and preoccupied, weeding the gardens. She waved to him but she knew he could not see into the darkness of her chamber, where she silently sat, lacing up her riding boots and straightening the skirts of the gown she had just put on. Then she sat at her dressing table, absently dabbed a little rouge to her pallid cheeks, and brushed her long hair. She would wear it loose today, the way Falcon liked it. Doing things she knew he liked somehow closed the distance between them.

She was just about to leave the house when Mr. Marland called to her from the dining room. Tamara entered and favored both Mr. Marland and his rather dull-witted, blank-faced boy with a pleasant smile.

"Miss Fleming," Marland began in a droll voice. "I must commence my journey on to Virginia before long. May we go over the ledgers and conclude our business? Also—" Marland's eyes silently dismissed the boy, "In light of your father's death, may we discuss the dowry that was set aside for your marriage?"

Tamara took the chair just vacated by the boy.

263

"The dowry . . . yes. Where have the funds been deposited?"

"In the Bank of Williamsburg, as your father had directed."

"Good!" Tamara arose. "Then we have concluded our business, Mr. Marland. There will be no marriage."

"But, the dowry?"

"The dowry is now a business loan, Mr. Marland, being made by Asher Arms to McKenzie Bain. I shall appreciate you drawing up the proper notes for Mr. Bain's signature."

"Yes, but . . . I shall be required to confer first with Mr. Inness who is, after all, attorney for your father's . . . or rather, your estate."

"Confer with me?"

Frankly, Tamara was surprised to see the elderly Parle Inness up at such an early hour. He did, indeed, require only a couple hours' sleep, because that is all he got. Tamara rose, anxious to conclude business and depart to her morning walk. "I have explained to Mr. Marland," she began, "the fact that the funds comprising my dowry shall now be a loan to McKenzie Bain. Please explain to him that the estate will settle without problems, and that this transfer meets with your approval. Now . . . ." Tamara moved toward the foyer. "Excuse me. I have things that must be attended to."

"And . . . excuse me, Miss—" Marland's soft-spoken voice halted her retreat. She turned back. "An hour or so, to go over your ledgers?"

Tamara shrugged. "Very well, Mr. Marland."

The session actually took the better part of the morning. Tamara had not realized that such exact business records had been kept for Asher Arms. Mr. Marland opened ledger after ledger, explaining the profits and debits of the estate, and which expenses she would be required to pay from her domestic accounts. Finally the session ended, and Mr. Marland, gathering his books in a brown leather case, commenced the journey to Virginia with his son.

Alone at last, Tamara hastily left the house. When she was well out of sight of Asher Arms, she slowed her pace and enjoyed the warm summer morning. Several days' rain had left the forest clean, glistening like silver in sunlit patches.

Falcon had left so quickly in the early morning hours that they hadn't had the chance to discuss everything that had happened since he'd departed on his hunt. He still did not know about the approaching marriage of Sterling Bain and Glynnie and thought, perhaps, that this problem still hung over their heads.

Tamara was certainly at odds with Falcon's newest dilemma. How could Flaming Bow have gotten himself into trouble so quickly? Surely he and Falcon had parted on the trail just hours before Falcon arrived at Asher Arms. Had the Iroquois lain in ambush for Flaming Bow and had it been intended that Falcon, too, be among their victims?

She wondered how long Flaming Bow's captivity would keep Falcon away from her. Days, weeks, months?

Tamara did not know, as she walked peacefully along the trail, lingering reminiscently at the cabin in the dale and at other favorite places she had enjoyed with Falcon, that she would have weeks to wonder about it. Each day after her morning walk, she tended the duties manifested in her ownership of Asher Arms. Every little sound out of the ordinary brought her rushing out of doors, where she hoped to see Falcon appearing from the wood line. But as each week passed and he did not return, her hopes of seeing him again diminished just a little. But always, deep within herself, she kept a spark of hope. She and Falcon shared a special bond that neither time nor distance could disturb. If something happened to him, she would feel it in her heart. She kept her hopes alive on that assumption.

But, Tamara did not realize that her loneliness for him, together with the fact that she worked too long in the household and took very little nourishment, was taking its toll on her health. Just the thought of rising in the mornings and not seeing Falcon's sleeping face made her ill. But her sudden illness was a strange thing. Moments after becoming violently nauseated, she found that she could sit down to a big breakfast of eggs and ham and biscuits and feel wonderful. She mentioned it to Bridie.

"Ill, miss? How so?" the elderly servant questioned, clearing the dishes after Tamara's breakfast.

"Just . . . ill," Tamara replied. "I—I don't know." She'd been leaning back in her chair, but the front legs now hit the floor with an alarming thud. "Sometimes I feel nauseated, Bridie. It's—I'm worried about Falcon. You know that. You know how I allow things to fray my nerves. I guess I'm just not strong enough to face things out of the ordinary."

"This illness, miss . . . it comes on first thing in the morning?"

"It does," she replied absently, pouring another cup of tea and stirring a little molasses into it. "But as you can see, I feel wonderful now. I feel that I could eat four breakfasts, then go out onto the trail and run for miles and miles and miles. . . ."

"Any other peculiarities in your health, miss?"

Tamara began to butter another hot biscuit. "Nothing not caused by nerves, Bridie." Then she looked up and gave Bridie a quizzical look. She was surprised at the concern suddenly marring the older woman's thin features. "Why this interrogation, Bridie? I'm a human being, susceptible to the common maladies we all must suffer."

"You can't be so blind, miss, as to not recognize the signs—"

"The signs?" Absently, Tamara rested her fingers upon her slightly rounded abdomen. "Heavens, Bridie! Whatever are you getting at?"

"The seed of Falcon, miss . . . growing there beneath your hand."

Tamara felt as if she'd been struck a physical blow. "Dear God," she mumbled. She'd ignored all the telltale signs. Her body had been trying to tell her something these past few weeks, but she had played the part of the naive schoolgirl. How could she have been so blind? "A baby," she continued quietly. "Falcon's baby."

"Aye. . . ." Bridie set the plates down and, in a rare show of affection, gently squeezed Tamara's fingers between her own. "And are you prepared, miss, for the responsibility of raising a wee one?"

"I—I really don't know, Bridie." Suddenly, Tamara had to be alone. She rose and with a reassuring smile turned and walked quickly through the rear entrance. As she neared the trail leading into the forest, she broke into a run and could scarcely see through the tears sheening her eyes. She ran where her legs would take her and eventually crumpled in a sobbing heap in the patch of purple clover beside the stream.

This is where their child had been conceived . . . that night . . . the last night she and Falcon had made love. The night her father had died.

Again she placed her fingers over her abdomen. She really didn't know why she was crying. She could imagine no more wonderful blessing in the world that she could bestow upon her beloved Falcon. But would he consider their child a blessing . . . or a curse?

"Oh, God . . . God. . . ," she wept gently, "Why isn't Falcon here with me?"

But she heard only the morning breeze stirring among the forest, the wild chattering of martins high in the treetops, and the occasional scurry of a ground creature among the dry leaves that had fallen in seasons past. She heard only the waters trickling gently over smooth white rocks. She heard only the violent pounding of her own heart.

Suddenly she knew she could not face parenthood alone. Falcon had to be safe. He had to return to Asher Arms and share this wonderful blessing with her.

She closed her eyes and tried to imagine where he might be. She imagined him standing in a clear mountain pond, bathing and singing in his deep, melodic voice. She imagined his arms outstretched, inviting her into his embrace.

She imagined his mouth gently claiming hers.

"Oh, yes, yes," she whispered. "You are safe, Falcon. I know it in my heart."

## Chapter 18

For the time being Falcon was safe. He'd been following a trail of litter, cold campfires, and scalped bodies for the past six weeks. Three days ago, Falcon had come upon a burned wagon and empty jugs of whiskey beside the scalped, mutilated body of the wagon driver. He could tell by the deeper hoof indentations of the Indian ponies that many other whiskey jugs had been taken by the renegade war party. He had seen what the Iroquois could do. Worse yet, he had seen what they could do when they'd been drinking.

He wondered now if Flaming Bow were still alive. His blood brother, confident that Falcon would come in pursuit of him, had over the past few weeks left signs that he still lived. Falcon had found oak leaves with perfectly round circles cut by a fingernail, a sign they had brought with them from their boyhoods together in the Delaware forest. He had found Flaming Bow's half-buried pouch across a clearing from a cooking fire. He had found bloodstains on the low-lying limbs of trees where he had been tightly bound by rawhide straps.

Beside Wills Creek in the Allegheny Mountains,

the exhausted Falcon found the strength to continue on. Embers from the Iroquois campfire still glowed red, indicating that they couldn't be more than half a day ahead of him. It was the closest he had gotten in the six weeks since he'd left Asher Arms. They were plotting a deliberate course toward Shawnee lands in Pennsylvania.

Falcon set his musket against a tree. His stomach gnawed by hunger, he ate a strip of dried beef, then rested his head back against a fallen log to wait for the first light of dawn. But he could not sleep. In the darkness of his closed eyes, he saw Flaming Bow's features etched in agony, and in the same moment, he saw the soft ivory features of his beloved Tamara. Part of him urged him ahead, but another part of him beckoned him home. He had left Tamara at a time when she had needed him the most. He loved her deeply and wanted to return to her, but he could not abandon his blood brother.

He thought about his private meeting with Parle Inness the night of his departure. He loathed the secrecy, but it was not the right time to betray his true identity—that he was Marcus Gray—to Tamara. These past months that he had known her . . . loved her . . . he had shared many things with her. But he had always avoided a serious discussion of his past. He wanted more than anything for her to know who he really was, because he knew how deeply she loved her guardian—his true father. But her knowledge of his true identity would only lead to questions he did not wish to answer. Mason Gray had told her he'd died as an infant—a fact not substantiated by her mother's diary. How could he tell Tamara the circumstances that had thrust the young indentured servant and her ten-year-old son out into the Delaware forest, where they had fended for themselves for

270

months? How could he cast this black dye upon the name of her recently dead father?

Falcon gritted his teeth in outrage. Jacob Fleming, thinking Falcon wanted only the wealth of Asher Arms, believed he had finally succeeded in separating him from Tamara. He believed he had assured a more secure future for her as the wife of the Virginian. Had Jacob truly believed Falcon would turn his back on his love for Tamara in favor of the wealth of Asher Arms? Oh, how greatly he had underestimated him!

The meeting with Parle Inness had resulted in Falcon, recognized by Inness as the man identified as Marcus Gray, signing a renunciation of Jacob's succession. This he had done willingly. All he wanted of Jacob Fleming's estate was his daughter.

Falcon's thoughts were in turmoil. He knew that before he and Tamara could be happy—truly happy—she would have to know all the secrets. But would he be able to explain everything to her satisfaction, so that she would not think he had deceived and fooled her? She would want Mason Gray to know that his wife and son still lived. But could they—Mason, Fedora, and Falcon—pick up their life together where it had left off?

Slowly the curtain of dark withdrew from the forest. Even at this early hour the heat shimmered in visible waves. Falcon put his thoughts aside, washed his face in the cold stream, then picked up his musket and continued his journey. For the past few weeks, he had not shaved, had bathed very little, and had eaten just enough to maintain his strength.

Falcon moved across the mountains with the sun. Physically exhausted, only his determination to free the captured Flaming Bow gave him the strength to put one foot ahead of the other. Thunderclouds gathered overhead, compelling him to move at a faster speed. Rain, erasing the fresh hoofprints of the Indian ponies, could set him back several hours, necessitating a search of every gorge and ravine to pick up their tracks.

The sun high overhead indicated the approach of the noon hour. Falcon halted for a moment beside a creek and filled his cupped hands with cool water. He drank thirstily, then filled his pigskin canteen with fresh water. Birds, chattering in the treetops just moments ago, now became deathly silent. And in that silence Falcon heard them, the voices . . . the drunken laughter, muffled by a thousand yards of forests and ravines.

He rose stealthily, instinctively checked his musket and repositioned the flint, then began to move toward the smoke now swirling among the trees. As he moved closer, the voices gained in clarity, and he recognized the broken, slurred tongue of the Iroquois. He knew only a few words of their language but easily recognized their boasts of murder and rampage among both their own Indian brothers and the white men they drunkenly vowed to annihilate.

Falcon had learned the skill of stalking from his Lenape brothers. Once he had pinpointed the camp in a wide ravine, he silently approached, then crept low to the ground and scrutinized them from a large boulder. He counted them—eight in all. Then, in a darkened niche against the ravine wall, he saw Flaming Bow, his mouth gagged, his hands bound tightly with a strand of rawhide that also encircled his neck, pulling his hands high up his back. The wounds caused by the tight rawhide were encrusted with blood. From the appearance of Flaming Bow, he had been fed just enough to keep him alive.

Then Falcon remembered something from far back

in his past. He remembered a day that he and Flaming Bow—then two thirteen-year-old boys—had come across an Iroquois war party who had just taken seven of their Huron brothers captive. He remembered slits gashed through the tendons of their heels and cords drawn through to keep them together on their death march. In horror they had watched as the prisoners were tied to stakes and forced to sing death songs while the jubilant, screaming Iroquois burned them with torches, gouged out bits of their flesh with jagged pieces of seashell, and tore off pieces of their scalp to pour red-hot coals over bleeding skulls. Later, after they had fled in fear and shock, they learned from their Lenape elders that the Iroquois cunningly delayed such rituals of torture for days, until the last glint of life had died from the bodies of their victims.

Falcon knew that the notorious methods of torture utilized by the Iroquois awaited the captive Flaming Bow. They would begin their rituals once they had returned to their camp, where the women and children could also take part in the torture.

As if Flaming Bow had sensed him there, crouched above the enemy camp, Flaming Bow's gaze lifted and locked to Falcon's. He was not surprised to see him and his expression did not change. But his eyes, just moments ago dull and lifeless, now sparkled with what Falcon saw as rekindled hope and rebellion. Momentarily thrown off guard by the discovery of his friend, Falcon did not read the warning in Flaming Bow's dark eyes.

The Iroquois braves had let down their guard. They sat cross-legged around a fire where a freshly-killed rabbit had been skewered to a spit and drank heavily of the white man's stolen whiskey.

Falcon watched, waiting for the moment when his

enemy would become too drunk to realize what had hit him. Thus he did not hear the stealthily approaching footsteps behind him until a razor-sharp knife had been pressed to his jugular vein.

Under different circumstances, Tamara would have looked forward to attending the wedding of Sterling and Glynnie. Needless to say, she did not want to journey to Virginia but wanted only to remain at Asher Arms and to be there when Falcon returned. For three days, as she pointlessly argued with herself, she packed her canvas traveling bags and got together the peach-colored chiffon-and-satin gown and accessories she would wear as maid of honor, a distinction she would share with Regina Bain. She left an array of instructions for various Asher Arms servants, then left Mr. Potter, the head groom, in charge of the estate while she was away.

The trip to Williamsburg was expected to take five days, and Tamara especially enjoyed the ride by ferry across the Rappahannock River. Bridie, however, affected by the heat, was anxious to reach their destination. Saul accepted the whole experience indifferently, as usual.

They crossed the York River by ferry and hired a carriage for the last leg of the trip to Williamsburg. They were, however, given an undisciplined team that, frightened by a covey of quail suddenly taking flight, went off the road into a wide creek. The back wheels immediately sank into the mud and they were, for the time being, stuck.

"What shall we do now, miss?" Saul asked. As their only male companion and, unfortunately, down in his back, he envisioned the arduous task of getting them out left solely to him. Tamara, however, climbed spryly from the carriage. She did not heed Bridie's protests that she be careful "in her condition."

"Get behind the carriage, Saul . . . I shall get in front and try to sooth the mares."

This was the scene that Sterling Bain, journeying home from Jamestown, came upon. "Good thing I came along, eh?" he asked humorously.

Saul's legs had sunk into the thick mud and Tamara, the water up to her hips, continued to tug at the halter of the panic-stricken mare.

"Have you come in search of us?" Tamara asked, ignoring the chuckle of laughter that now drifted toward them.

Sterling dismounted his horse. "I have not," he replied after a moment. "I was on my way home from Jamestown and just happened upon you. I would say you're a lucky lady."

Sterling waded into the shallow stream. As he neared the carriage, he noticed how pretty Tamara was, her long hair fallen loose from its pins and dragging in the stream as she continued to pull on the mare's halter. She had put one hand to her face, leaving a smear of mud across her flushed cheek. Instinctively, Sterling took out his handkerchief, wet it in the stream, and handed it to her.

"Your cheek," he explained when her eyes met his amused gaze, "is not made prettier by mud."

Soon, with the joint efforts of the three of them, the nervous mares were coaxed from the stream.

The exhausted Tamara did not attempt to pull the heavy wetness of her skirts from her thighs and legs, and they clung, revealingly, to her perfect form. But Bridie, aware of Sterling Bain's unabandoned scrutiny, quickly ordered Saul to get the embroidered bedsheets she had made as a wedding gift for her daughter and hang them between trees to form some semblance of privacy for Tamara while she changed into dry clothing.

"No! No, Bridie," Tamara protested, "Not the sheets. Saul—" Tamara pointed her fingers toward the carriage, "Hand me my bag, will you? There's a nice, thick clump of bushes over here that will be adequate."

As Tamara changed her wet, tattered clothing, Sterling and Saul tethered and rubbed down the team. In view of the quickly approaching night, a decision had been reached that enough traveling had been done for the day.

Soon, the excitement settled down and a campfire was built. Tamara, aware of Bridie's exhaustion, offered to cook a rabbit Sterling had killed and tied to his saddle, and that had now been skinned and cleaned. Then she sat back, clasped her hands across her knees, and stared into the flickering flames. She scarcely heard the searing grease dripping from the meat into the burning logs. Her thoughts were far, far away from the lightly sleeping Bridie, and Sterling and Saul were deep in conversation on the other side of the campfire.

Falcon filled her thoughts. These past six weeks had been lonely without him and she existed, day after day, only for his return. She did not want him to return to Asher Arms and find her gone.

"Tamara!"

At the sound of her name, Tamara sat forward so quickly that a short pain came to her forehead. She realized only then that tears moistened her eyes, which she brushed away before Sterling detected them. "What? You . . . you startled me, Sterling."

276

Through the blur of her tear-sheened eyes she saw that the grease dripping from the meat had spattered away from the fire and was burning in small drop-lets. Sterling was on his knees, patting at the ground. Then he looked up at Tamara as if she had lost all reasoning. "You offered to cook the rabbit, Tamara," he said, grinning sheepishly, "not yourself. You could have been burned."

She shrugged weakly, once again clasping her hands. "I was deeply engaged. Sorry, Sterling."

He looked at her thoughtfully. Her state of repose and vulnerability made him see her in a different light. "You are worried, Tamara? About Falcon?"

Startled, Tamara looked into his perceptive eyes. She felt she could keep no secrets from this man against whom all her rebellion had been aimed just a few short weeks ago. Now she saw kindness in his eyes. He was on one knee, his fisted hand supporting his chin.

"He just hasn't returned to Asher Arms."

"After all this time?" Sterling looked visibly sur-prised. Falcon had been gone only a few days when he and his bride-to-be had departed Asher Arms.

"I fear I'll never see him again. I—" Tamara managed a small smile. "I want nothing more than to attend your wedding, but in all truth, Sterling, I did not want to leave Asher Arms. I—I don't want him to come home to an empty house."

"Well!" Sterling slapped his legs as he rose from his knees. "In the morning, we'll be on our way, get this blasted wedding over with, and send you packing for home. What do you say?"

Tamara returned his quickly offered smile. "Thank you . . . for trying to cheer me."

Sterling said nothing, but clapped his hands. "Saul—Miss Bridie—a bit of food and we'll retire

277

for the evening.'' Then he busied himself, preparing plates of food for everyone, fetching water from a cool stream, and cheering the somewhat somber traveling party.

Later, when Tamara and the parents of his future bride were sound asleep, Sterling sat against a tree trunk, deep in thought. There was one thing he was certain about . . . if Falcon had not returned to Asher Arms by now, the chance was slim that he would ever return.

The large, wealthy Williamsburg estate of McKenzie Bain reminded Tamara very much of Gray House in London. She and Glynnie's parents were shown into a large parlor filled with mahogany furnishings, where heavy blue velvet draperies hung in massive folds from twelve-foot windows. Tamara was awed by the wealth of an estate that had been so close to bankruptcy just a short while ago.

The upstairs maid had just arrived to show them to their assigned quarters when Glynnie burst into the room. Unlike the brooding, rebellious girl Tamara remembered so well, she seemed genuinely happy, hugging both her parents and Tamara.

"Oh, I am so happy to see you!'' She stood back and her eyes made a sweeping move over their faces. "All of you. Oh, Mother . . .'' Glynnie took both her mother's hands in hers, "I'll be married on Friday. I'm so glad you could be here. Come. . . .'' With a click of her fingers, Glynnie summoned a butler. He and the upstairs maid, carrying the traveling bags, fell in behind them as they slowly walked up the stairs of Bain House.

With renewed spirit, Tamara told her how they'd

met with Sterling fifteen miles from Williamsburg and how he'd traveled the rest of the way with them. They had half traversed the staircase when Sterling appeared from a lower corridor. "The carriage and team have been seen to, Tamara. Glynnie . . . I'm home."

"Oh, you silly boy!" Glynnie replied, laughing. "I can see that you are! Right now," she continued, "our guests are very tired. After all, they have traveled all the way from Asher Arms."

The mention of Asher Arms again forced thoughts of Falcon into Tamara's mind. How would he feel if he returned from his quest and found that she had chosen to attend the wedding rather than await him at home? Aware that Sterling Bain's gaze had moved to hers, Tamara quietly said, "Yes, we are exhausted, Sterling. We do thank you for accompanying us on the last leg of our journey . . . and for the assistance."

"Do go about your business, Sterling," Glynnie bubbled forth, "while I see to the accommodations of our guests."

"And where is your new mother-in-law?" Bridie asked her daughter.

"I'm afraid. . . ." Glynnie shrugged her shoulders apologetically, then looked to make sure Sterling was well out of hearing range. There was no sense in beating around the bush or avoiding the issue. "Mrs. Bain has not accustomed herself to the fact that Sterling takes a servant as a wife. She and her two eldest daughters have gone into league to boycott the wedding. But Regina . . . you will like Regina."

Bridie, too, shrugged. "So be it," she replied indifferently. "Be better off without the smug tarts at your happy occasion, girl."

279

Glynnie and Tamara both laughed. It was so seldom Bridie was heard to speak ill of another human being. The two younger women, walking ahead, overheard Saul say to his wife, "Here's to you, old girl!"

In comparison with Asher Arms, Bain House was a veritable mansion. With its stuccoed facade and Regency detailing, it very much reminded Tamara of the manor houses in England with their terraces and secluded gardens. Like many English mansions, Bain House had a billiard wing, and to the back of the house there was a permanent croquet lawn where Glynnie claimed to spend many afternoons with Regina.

Tamara was the first of the guests shown to her chamber. Glynnie, aware that her questions were only being half-answered by the exhausted Tamara, soon departed. Tamara removed her traveling jacket and bonnet and threw herself across the large tester bed. Alone, she felt the obligation of forced smiles and gaiety quickly drain away. Her chamber was comfortable and well-furnished, and the window had been opened to allow fresh air into the room. As promised by the departing Glynnie, the upstairs maid now rapped at the door.

"Come in," Tamara called weakly.

The pert maid looked in. "Shall I prepare a bath for you, miss?"

"That would be nice."

Later, when she again found herself alone, Tamara relaxed in a long, cool bath and tried not to think of Falcon. Glynnie's wedding was to be a festive occasion. She could not cloud that festivity with her morbid thoughts and fears.

But deep in her heart she knew . . . she had lost Falcon to the treacheries of the wilderness.

With the door to her chamber securely locked against unwanted intrusions, Tamara dropped her hand to her slightly rounded abdomen and quietly wept.

## Chapter 19

Waking with a start, Tamara was immediately disoriented by her strange surroundings. As she slowly regained her senses, she realized she had been dreaming of Falcon . . . a wonderful, erotic dream in which he had been lying next to her, enfolding her within the golden warmth of his embrace. She was suddenly very lonely for him, and it was a loneliness that brought tears to her eyes and a lump to her throat. Her fingers rose, absently, to soothe away the pain she felt there. Then, as if some strange metamorphosis had taken place, she bounced from the large tester bed and began hurrying about, intermittently attending to her dressing and her long, disheveled hair, which she brushed and left loose. Then, drawn to the lower floor of Bain House, where all hands were up in arms making last minute preparations for the wedding to take place on the morrow, she quickly traversed the spiral staircase.

Throughout the morning Tamara worked alongside family and servants, keeping herself busy so that she would have no time to think about Falcon. Sterling made several appearances but, unable to mask his humor as he watched the hustle and bustle of prewedding preparations, he was quickly whisked away by either Glynnie or one of the elderly servants. The doorways were decorated with arches of greenery to which fresh roses and bridal veil would be added tomorrow. Several cases of champagne arrived from New York, a week behind their scheduled arrival, and Glynnie tried on her wedding gown for last-minute tucks and alterations.

Throughout the day wedding guests arrived and were quartered throughout the Bain estate wherever room could be made.

Colonel Washington, in residence at his Williamsburg townhouse, made an afternoon appearance of both a social and business nature. Tamara learned only later that because Governor Dinwiddie planned to attend the wedding, Colonel Washington would not. They'd been at odds with each other since the Laurel Ridge affair some weeks ago.

Later in the evening, after a light supper had been eaten by all, Tamara and Glynnie were at last able to spend a little time alone engaged in sisterly conversation in Tamara's bedchamber.

"Are you happy?" Tamara asked in a moment of silence. "I mean to say, truly happy?"

Glynnie smiled, simultaneously dropping her eyes. "Happier than I have ever been, Tamara."

"You weren't happy at Asher Arms, were you?"

Silence. Glynnie fumbled with a gold bracelet at her wrist. "I never was, Tamara," she replied after a moment. "Not one single day in all my life was I truly happy. Tamara—" Glynnie looked up, then placed her hand over Tamara's. "A long time ago . . . when you first arrived at Asher Arms, I put your mother's diary in your bedchamber—"

Tamara gently withdrew her hand. "I know, Glynnie."

"I've wanted so long to apologize. I—I was so jealous of you and wanted to hurt you. I wanted you to think your father hated you. Will you ever forgive me?"

"Forgive you?" Tamara smiled a sincere smile. "I should thank you, Glynnie. I never knew my mother, and I had only vague recollections of my father when I returned to Asher Arms. I have learned much about both from my mother's diary. In a way—" Tamara took Glynnie's hand and gave it a gentle squeeze, "the diary has been a mirror to the past. Now, instead of being just a word, mother means gentleness and kindness to me. Did you—" Tamara hesitated to ask, "read my mother's diary?"

"Yes, I did, Tamara."

Tamara shrugged her shoulders. "Do you think, Glynnie, that my father . . . loved me?"

"Always, yes, always he loved you. He was like many men, of the conviction that producing a male seed son was a mark of true manhood. But . . . yes, he loved you. That is what so enraged me. When you returned, he ceased to treat me as a daughter and turned his affections to you instead."

"But you have your father, Glynnie."

"Yes, I know, and I haven't been a very good daughter to him, or Mother. But," gaiety returned to Glynnie, "I plan to change all that. No more spoiled, selfish Glynnie. I shall be a good, devoted daughter to my parents, and faithful wife to Sterling, just as you shall be to Falcon."

Falcon . . . oh, why did Glynnie have to mention his name? He was gone. Tamara's worst fear was that he would never return. The conversation had somehow drifted to a subject that pained Tamara and she quickly changed the subject. "Glynnie, do you remember reading the references in my mother's diary to a woman named Fedora?''

"Yes, Fedora Gray. She was an indentured servant to your father a long time ago."

"Have you ever heard her name mentioned?"

Glynnie thought for a moment. "Only once, Tamara."

"Can you recall what was said?"

"Of course . . . it was just a few days before your father died."

Tamara was visibly surprised. "What was said, and to whom?"

"Your father was talking to Falcon in the library. As usual, the master was short-tempered with Falcon. Falcon said something that I did not hear, and that is when Jacob mentioned Fedora's name."

"But . . . how was it mentioned? It's very important to me, Glynnie. What exactly was said?"

Glynnie drew her feet up, then rested back against the headboard of Tamara's bed. "Oh, Tamara . . . why do you want to know? The servant has been dead many years, and you know your father hasn't been right in the head since he tried to kill himself—"

"What?" Shocked, Tamara felt the color drain from her features. As she stood, she felt weakness in her knees but was still able to approach the window, where dusk had settled on the wide, spacious lawns of Bain House. "I—I knew nothing of this, Glynnie."

Glynnie, too, stood and approached Tamara. "You didn't know that he shot himself, Tamara?"

"Glynnie!" Neither woman had heard the door to Tamara's chamber slowly open, but both spun rapidly at the sharpness in Bridie's voice. "How dare you upset the miss with ugly gossip . . . how dare you be malicious on the eve of your wedding day!''

"Bridie, no, she didn't say anything malicious. I want to know. I knew nothing about this. Nothing of my father deliberately shooting himself. I must know! I'm tired of the secrets. I'm tired of everyone going out of their way to spare my feelings.''

Bridie gave Glynnie a stern, implacable look, a look that, without words, ordered Glynnie to leave. Soon, the door quietly closed and Bridie, holding her hand out to Tamara in a rare display of affection, motioned her to the edge of the bed, to sit beside her.

"Miss Tamara,'' she began quietly, "there's a lot we've kept from you, unfairly, perhaps. But, since you've been at Asher Arms, we've wanted only to spare you the hurt.'' Silence. Bridie choked back a painful lump.

"Go on, Bridie,'' Tamara urged. "I—I've always suspected there was something I should know. Falcon had told me the accident had not happened as you'd told me, but he did not elaborate. I wish to hear the truth.''

" 'Tis true, child. Your father turned the musket on himself. He and Falcon had gone hunting early in the morning. While I don't know what was discussed between them, your father became enraged. He turned the musket on himself and when Falcon tried to take it away from him, it discharged, striking your father in the chest.''

"How do you know this, Bridie?''

"Broggard came upon them in the woods. He witnessed it all.''

"Then why did you lie to me, Bridie? Why did you let me think that Falcon had shot him?'' Tamara gave the elderly servant an accusing look.

286

"To spare you, girl. I've been loyal to your father for many years. He wanted better for you than Falcon. He wanted to know you and love you before he died, but after that, he expected you to return to England and live the proper life of a lady. But you met Falcon, and he knew you would never leave Delaware. I thought—" Bridie dropped her head. "I thought if you believed Falcon had shot your father. . . ."

"Oh, Bridie . . . how could you?"

" 'Tis easy, girl. 'Tis easy for Bridie to deceive you for the sake of your father. You may have wondered. . . ." Bridie stood, then approached the window where Tamara had stood just moments ago. She looked out into the veil of darkness, across lawns gently swept by moonlight. "Twenty years ago, Tamara, I loved your father. I loved him enough to sacrifice all for him. And that is exactly what I did. I sacrificed my pride. Being Saul's wife, and he loving me the way he did—and still does—I took to bed with your father." Bridie turned, betraying to the shocked Tamara eyes that were tear-moistened and filled with regret. "Saul has always known, Tamara . . . Glynnie is your father's daughter, not Saul's. Jacob took to Glynnie as a daughter, yet prided himself in treating her as a servant. I don't mean to speak ill of the dead, but it wasn't right. No . . . it wasn't right what your father did to his own girl."

Tamara dropped her face to her hands and gently wept. She wept not for the deception but rather for Glynnie treated by her own father as a servant and ordered whipped for her infractions until the blood oozed from the welts left by the sadistic Broggard. "Does Glynnie know?"

"Nay, girl. I'd rather she didn't. It'd only hurt her."

Tamara gently flicked away her tears as the truth struck her like a physical blow. "Glynnie is my sister, Bridie . . . my half-sister."

"And you've been kind to her. You've treated her as a sister."

"If only I had known. I—"

"And what would you have done?" An unexpected sharpness came to Bridie's voice. "You couldn't have treated her any better than you did. Don't you think I saw how you took Glynnie to your care, her being cruel and impossible to you at times? You cared enough to give my girl patience and guidance and because of it, she has become every bit a lady, Miss Tamara. You did it for her. And I'll never forget you for it."

Tamara was too shocked to hear Bridie's kind words. She'd learned more these past few moments than she'd learned in all the months she had been at Asher Arms.

Momentarily, Bridie turned from Tamara, but immediately she turned back. "There's one more thing needs to be said, miss."

"What is it, Bridie?"

"Saul and I have been offered residence on the grounds of Bain House. We believe you'll understand that we wish to be near our—my daughter. We've discussed it, miss—Saul and I. It was agreed that we'd make our wishes known to you, but still offer to return to Asher Arms, if that is what you want."

This came as a very unpleasant surprise to Tamara. Since her father's death, she had relied heavily on the assistance of Saul and Bridie. Without them, she didn't know what she would do.

Yet she understood and was willing to make the sacrifice. Falcon would return and assist in the management of Asher Arms. Yes . . . oh, yes, he would return. Her hopes, dreams, and desires had never nurtured any conviction but that.

"I want you to be with Glynnie, Bridie," Tamara replied after a moment. "But, may I—" Tamara was not quite sure how to approach the proud Bridie on this very delicate matter. Nervously, she linked her fingers together, then let them drop to the folds of her gown. Her features paled for a moment. "May I offer financial assistance, Bridie?"

"No need, miss. Saul and I have saved funds over the years. We'll make do. The Bains—" Bridie approached and stood just out of touching distance of Tamara. "Master Bain has offered us a cottage for the remainder of our lives. If it be your will to release us from the obligations of Asher Arms, then we will spend our lives here, with Glynnie. And, miss . . ." Tamara looked up, "what we've discussed here is best left between us. Glynnie need never know about Jacob—"

"Of course . . . I'll abide by your wishes, Bridie. But—I will so miss you and Saul. You've been like family to me."

Bridie smiled, even as her voice trembled with emotion. "In a way, Miss Tamara, we are family. And now. . . ." She coughed, to regain her composure. "I'll bid you a pleasant evening."

Bridie turned toward the closed door, but at the sound of her name whispered by Tamara, slowly turned back. Tamara rose and approached Bridie, then took her hand to give it a gentle squeeze. "How can I ever thank you, Bridie?"

"For what, miss?"

"For giving me the most wonderful gift of all."

"Miss?" Bridie's thin gray brows pinched in confusion. "What is that, miss, that I've given you?"

289

Again Tamara gave her hand an affectionate squeeze. She met Bridie's almost blank gaze, then favored her with a smile. This evening, amidst the mad scurry of last-minute wedding preparations, Bridie had unloaded her conscience. Tamara had not known whether to appreciate her candor or silently scorn her father's past indiscretions. Only now, meeting the gaze of the aging servant, Tamara saw the beauty she must have been in her youth, the beauty her father had seen—tall and slender, with high cheekbones and arched eyebrows over expressive brown eyes.

"A sister," Tamara whispered, aware of the silence that had fallen between them. "A sister I shall love and adore for all time to come."


The hour or so she remained alone in her bedchamber gave Tamara time to think. So many things were beginning to come together. When she had first arrived at Asher Arms, she had been aware of the relationship between Glynnie and her father—a relationship that had veered from the gentleness her father showed toward Glynnie as a favored child to his unrelenting discipline following an infraction. She had often wondered why Bridie had allowed Jacob to wield so much authority over Glynnie, and why she had taken up for her father at times when he was obviously in the wrong. Tamara recalled many times that Bridie had quickly defended Jacob's actions. It was apparent now that Glynnie had received punishment not as a servant but as Jacob's spoiled, selfish younger daughter. Tamara had seen Saul quietly step back and allow this cruel punishment. She had never before understood why. She understood now.

But this development—Glynnie revealed as her

half-sister—had not startled her half so much as the admission that her father had tried to kill himself. It was human nature to bed a woman and conceive a child, but it was against every law of God and man to kill oneself. Tamara was hurt and shocked that her father could have been so unhappy that he would have chosen this alternative. And what could he and Falcon have discussed that would have affected him so deeply? There would always be questions; she wondered if she would ever learn the answers.

But foremost in her mind, taking precedence over every unanswered question, was her concern for Falcon's safety. It had been seven weeks since he'd left Asher Arms in the dead of night. She remembered her last glimpse of him—a dark shadow disappearing into the timber line of the Delaware forest. Where was he and when would he return?

Tamara shivered as if a winter chill had touched her spine. Would he indeed return? Would the man whose kindness and love had held her heart gently against his own ever again fill that empty void she felt inside? Would she ever again feel the pride and passion of this man who had professed to love her more than life itself?

Tamara dropped back to her pillow and let her hands fall to the downy softness beside her tousled hair. She closed her eyes, feeling the hot, salty tears of loneliness and fear and dread burning there in the darkness. The only light provided was a soft triangle of moonlight drifting in from the open window. She did not feel the warm breeze. She felt only the wild, panicked thumping of her own heart. She did not hear the whippoorwill far in the distance, the whinny of thoroughbreds at the Bain stables; she heard only the little voice inside her, luring her into a dream world where her brave-hearted Falcon traveled a deliberate path toward her.

Yet, she knew how slim the chances were that he would return. He was gone—swallowed up by the dark, alluring call of loyalty to Flaming Bow, his blood brother.

Tamara buried her head in her pillow and wept bitterly. She did not remember falling asleep, dreaming dreams she did not wish to dream, or sweltering in the early August heat. She did not remember cursing Flaming Bow for taking Falcon from her. She knew only that when she awoke the following morning, she felt as if she'd been dragged through the forest by a hundred screaming, maniacal horses. Bombs exploded in her head. She desperately wished, in a brief, lucid moment, that she could outgrow her tendency toward these sick headaches.

The upstairs maid immediately sent an order to the kitchens that a weak tea of heliotrope roots be made for Tamara. An hour later, when the tea had failed, Bridie brought her a dose of laudanum, just enough to relieve her pain without putting her to sleep. Tamara barely remembered Glynnie's midmorning visit, but she did remember overhearing her talking to another woman—possibly Regina—and whispers about "a doctor being called."

Thus Tamara had pushed herself to a sitting position on the edge of her bed, forced a smile without opening her eyes, and confessed to "feeling much better." With that assurance, Glynnie and Regina departed and Tamara again slumped to her waiting pillow.

A lunch tray was brought to her just before the noon hour. As her eyes opened slowly to allow their adjustment to the morning light, Tamara happily realized that the headache was gone. She yawned, then stretched widely, and quickly consumed the light lunch. Her only thought at the moment was of assisting Glynnie in her last-minute preparations before the five o'clock wedding ceremony.

Tamara approached the washstand and studied her appearance in the small oval mirror. Her eyes appeared weak and her skin was a pasty hue. She quickly bathed them both in cold water, brushed back her long, disheveled hair, and touched a little rouge to her cheeks. She chose a rose-pink gown, to give herself a little added color, and again assessing her final appearance, moved into the corridor and toward the stairwell.

Glynnie, the first to spy her, met her at the foot of the stairs and immediately dragged her into the hustle of last-minute preparations. The roses and bridal wreath had been cut from the Bain gardens and were being interwoven with the greenery in the doorways. Garden latticework, freshly whitewashed, was being set up along the long wall in the parlor that would serve as a pulpit, and mahogany pews, borrowed from the Episcopal church, were being set up on either side in straight, orderly rows. Each was being decorated with orchids tied with yellow satin ribbon.

Soon, coaxed by Tamara and Regina, Glynnie retired to her bedchamber to bathe and have her hair done by the Bain family hairdresser. Tamara chose this moment to present Glynnie with the gift she had brought for her—a cameo she had found among her father's possessions that had belonged to her— their—great-grandmother. The back of the ivory and gold cameo had been inscribed with the date 1663.

"For you," Tamara said, carefully removing it from the new velvet pouch she had placed it in, "Something old. . . ." Tamara laughed. "You do have something borrowed, something blue, and something new to go along with it, don't you?"

"It's too beautiful, Tamara." Even as she protested, Glynnie turned so that Tamara could place the fine gold chain around her neck. "And I do have everything I need to begin my marriage," she laughed. "Regina loaned me a blue garter, so that takes care of the borrowed and blue, and—" She quickly picked up a pair of ivory and diamond combs from her dressing table and showed them to Tamara, "and these are new . . . a gift from Sterling with which I shall pin my wedding veil."

"They're lovely, Glynnie. Now!" Tamara clapped her hands. "Your maid has drawn a warm bath. We can't have you late for your own wedding, can we?"

Glynnie hugged her tightly. "I never thought, Tamara, that you would become so dear to me."

Tamara could not prevent the tears that welled in her eyes as she hugged Glynnie in return. She remembered their first meeting, the glare of jealousy in the petite Glynnie's eyes, her haughty personality and sticky sweetness even as she'd drugged her with an innocent looking glass of milk. She recalled the many months she had been patient with Glynnie, befriending her with small gifts, assuring her that they could be friends, tutoring her in the graces of being a proper lady. Intermittently, Glynnie had rebelled, but not so much that she hadn't eventually been transformed into the lady of perfect grace who now stood before Tamara . . . a lady who was Tamara's sister.

How proud Tamara was! As she hugged Glynnie tightly, she looked up and saw Bridie standing in the doorway, her dark eyes smiling with approval.

\* \* \*

Tamara and Regina, in their perfectly matched gowns of peach taffeta and chiffon, stood quietly to the left and slightly behind the bride as the vows were being spoken. Tamara hadn't realized so many people would fit into the parlor of Bain House. Yet even with the attendance of two hundred guests, many holding small children in restraint, the room was silent except for the soft-spoken minister. The vows and prayers had been spoken and the half-hour ceremony was nearing its conclusion.

"Foreasmuch as Glynnie and Sterling have consented together in holy wedlock, and have witnessed the same before God and this company. . . ." Tamara, however, had allowed her mind to wander into her dream world. The words of the minister drifted into nothingness, along with his stern, mechanical features. She wanted only for tomorrow to come, so that she could return to Asher Arms and await her beloved. She had already packed her bags and stacked them by the door of her bedchamber, and with the first light of dawn—

Tamara was startled by a sudden burst of organ music. She looked up just as Sterling and Glynnie met in a tender kiss. As they turned to begin their retreat from the pulpit, they were immediately surrounded by the wedding guests. Tamara stood quietly beneath a latticed arch of roses and orchids and watched the newly married couple happily surround themselves with well-wishers. A little later, she assisted Glynnie in changing from the tight bindings of her wedding gown.

Tamara had been forewarned that the wedding celebration would last three days, after which Sterling and Glynnie would sail to Europe for a year-long honeymoon reluctantly agreed to by Major Washington. The reception began immediately, and the quiet

Tamara found herself drawn into a conversation with four missionaries of the Society for the Propagation of the Gospel who planned to take the Word of God to the Iroquois west of the Alleghenies, the same Iroquois, Tamara thought bitterly, who might have. . . .

She visibly shuddered. She couldn't think about Falcon now . . . not now, when she'd spent the last few weeks convincing herself that he would return to her. Politely, she excused herself from the company of the missionaries and made her way through the crowds of dancers, the tables of card players, and the small cliques of women engaged in idle gossip. She heard Glynnie's name spoken . . . and the label of "servant" that had been attached to her by her disapproving mother-in-law, who had done her best to poison the society of Williamsburg against her new daughter-in-law. Tamara knew, though, that the fiery Glynnie could take care of herself.

Tamara had not yet reached the staircase when she heard a loud, threatening voice echoing from the foyer. She froze at the familiar sound, then, regaining her senses, turned just in time to see Sterling Bain flying across the foyer. A crowd immediately gathered in the doorways, scarcely allowing room for Tamara to force her way through. Against the wall, spraddled like a weatherbeaten goose, lay Sterling, who patiently allowed his new wife to bathe his bloody lip with her clean white handkerchief. Immediately, two Bain servants closed in on the attacker, who was brought to his knees by their brute strength.

"Well, old boy," Sterling laughed, slowly rising to his feet. "Didn't you get your wedding invitation?" Then he turned to the crowd that had gathered and continued, "Do go on back to your enjoyment, friends. It's just a little misunderstanding." Slowly, Tamara's eyes averted to the man being held by the servants, scarcely recognizable beneath a ragged, unkempt growth of beard, and clothing that smelled of weeks in the forest. Tamara felt her breath rush from her body in slow, painful gasps. "Let him go," Sterling ordered of the servants. "Everything is well in hand here."

Tamara did not care how he looked or smelled. She did not care that several of the female guests, appalled at the unwashed appearance of the interloper, had covered their faces with handkerchiefs. She knew only that Falcon, her heart, her love and her joy, was here. As he slowly rose to his feet, she threw herself into his arms. But she did not expect the piercing daggers of his glare as their eyes met. He slowly removed her arms from his neck, stepped back, then turned and pushed his way through the guests in his haste to exit the house.

Tamara was shocked. She rushed out to the long porch after him. "Falcon . . . Falcon . . . what is wrong?"

He turned, and his eyes, taking in her beauty with a fluid sweep, again shot daggers at her. He was appalled that she betrayed her impurity by refusing to be married in white. "Nothing is wrong . . . Mrs. Bain!"

It took a moment to digest his words. Then Tamara laughed, throwing herself into his arms and linking her fingers at his back so that he could not possibly remove them again. "Oh, Falcon—you sweet, lovable man . . . my Falcon. I did not marry Sterling."

"But Drew said," his eyes narrowed as he spoke, "that you'd come to Virginia for the wedding."

Tamara kissed his lips, which were pressed into a

thin line. She did not care that ladies had gathered on the porch, like prattling old bitties, to disapprove of her public display of affection. "I did come to Virginia for the wedding, Falcon," she whispered, kissing him again solely for the sake of the women. "For Sterling and Glynnie's wedding . . . not mine."

"Then you . . . God! You—"

"Yes." Tamara and Falcon both looked in the direction of Sterling Bain, who stepped out to the veranda still nursing his broken lip. "Miss Tamara journeyed to Virginia to be maid of honor for Glynnie, Falcon. You should ask questions before you begin taking punches."

Again, Falcon's eyes narrowed. "I apologize, Mr. Bain, for being a hothead. I assumed—"

"It's forgotten, and your apology is accepted." Glynnie approached and Sterling rested his arm across her shoulder. "Now . . . if you'll accept my hospitality, I shall have quarters prepared for you. You are welcome to stay the night. It is good that you've arrived in time. I will not have to send one of my servants as an escort for Miss Tamara."

"I am glad you've returned safely, Falcon" Glynnie interjected, deliberately hiding her disapproval of Falcon's attack on her husband. "And Flaming Bow?"

Falcon bowed politely. "He has returned to the village."

Sterling and Glynnie turned back to the music that played indoors, beckoning the other guests to return to the celebration. Momentarily, Falcon and Tamara stood alone on the lawns of Bain House, save for a butler who stood silently at the entrance.

"I want to know what happened . . . why you were gone so long, Falcon. But for now," her gaze lovingly lifted to his, "remember for all time that I am your woman, Falcon. It hurts me that you would assume I had journeyed to Virginia to marry Sterling. We love each other. I thought you understood that when you were called away."

"Forgive me. It's just that I love you so much." Falcon's strong hands fell gently to her shoulders. That he was perplexed showed in his remarkable blue eyes . . . eyes that warmed as her gaze continued to hold his. "And you have some explaining to do, also," he fondly scolded. "About Glynnie and Sterling Bain."

"I'll explain after you've bathed. You do—" She could not prevent her gentle laugh. "You do smell a bit like a horse, Falcon." Then her cheek lifted to meet the roughness of his brindly beard and she whispered, "Shall I accompany you?"

## Chapter 20

On the fourth day, Tamara and Falcon stood on the rise overlooking Asher Arms. With his arm resting lightly across her shoulder, Tamara realized there was nowhere else on earth she would rather be than here, in the peaceful little valley where she had been born. They had enjoyed a leisurely trip from Virginia and had visited a Nanticoke village where Falcon had friends. Falcon had shown her lovely places the unskilled traveler would have missed, and they had enjoyed long, wonderful hours of togetherness and lovemaking beneath the full moon, surrounded by the forests and the shimmering night.

The morning of their departure from Bain House, they had announced their intentions to marry upon returning to Delaware. Sterling Bain had then presented them with a fine blooded mare and a stallion his father had planned to sell. Tamara recalled her private conversation with Sterling, in which she had told him of her affinity to Glynnie. She had also told him of her plan to cancel their loan contract and to present the funds to the Bain estate as Glynnie's dowry. Tamara did, however, discuss all aspects of their business arrangement with Falcon, who concurred in her plans to keep intact their ten-year contract for delivery of Virginia thoroughbreds to Asher Arms.

A few minutes later they dismounted at the stables. Tamara wanted only to take a long, cool bath, change into fresh clothing, and relax after the journey. Thereafter, the first priority of business would be to fill Saul's and Bridie's long-held domestic positions in the household.

As Tamara smoothed down her crumpled skirts, she felt Falcon's hands ease around her waist and pull her close. "Have I told you today that I love you," he whispered.

Tamara, resting her head back against his powerful chest, whispered in reply, "Not since this morning, Falcon." Then she turned, and her arms eased around his neck. "There's something we need to discuss before we take another step." He drew slightly back and his potent gaze held hers. "I want you to move into the main house. Will you mind?"

Falcon frowned, then drew away from her and began unsaddling the horses. "I really think we should wait, Tamara, until we are married. I will not have your character blackened by gossip."

Tamara drew her hands to her hips. "Gossip? For heaven's sake, Falcon, every man and woman here know that—that we are together frequently. I see no reason why we should hide our love for each other."

Falcon's gaze again met hers. How determined she looked, standing there, her mouth pressed into a thin line and her hands drawn rebelliously to her slim hips! Her golden hair was disheveled, and a long, loose ringlet lay softly across her left shoulder. He extended his hand, inviting her into his embrace.

"How about a compromise?" he offered. "Tomorrow morning, after we are well rested, we shall

301

journey to Kishke's village. There is a woman there you should meet—"

"Your mother?"

"Yes," he replied. "You will learn much from her. Thereafter, if you still want me, Tamara, we shall publish the required banns of our marriage and I shall move into Asher Arms—as your husband."

Tamara held him tightly, loving the manly aroma of him, loving the way his hand gently, confidently, caressed her back and shoulders. "Such a mystery you are, Falcon!" she laughed gently. "No power in heaven or earth could part us. I want no man but you."

Falcon frowned thoughtfully. He remembered a very lethal power just a few weeks ago that had almost separated them for all time. He had breathed a sigh of relief that Tamara had not asked for details of his search for the captured Flaming Bow. He did not think he would be able to admit that, when the fight had ended, he had killed seven Iroquois Indians who had been too drunk to stand upright and would have killed the others if they had not passed out from drink. But even blood diluted by the white man's evil spirits had not numbed the Indians's instinct for survival and war. Falcon still recalled the French knife held by the Iroquois guard pressed firmly against his throat. Shuddering, he recalled wrestling the knife from him and burying it deep in the startled guard's own throat.

Falcon shook away his grim thoughts when he realized that a small group of the servants' children had gathered. By the looks in their smiling faces, they had overheard his endearing words to Tamara. The embarrassed Falcon tenderly put Tamara away from him, then clapped his hands at the children. "Go on, the lot of you," he ordered affectionately.

"Or you won't get the treats the mistress brought you from Virginia!"

With delighted squeals, the children turned and began both running and skipping toward the servants' quarters, but Tamara quickly called them back. "Children . . . children . . . come. Falcon, hand me my canvas bag, will you?" After Falcon handed her the bag, she knelt to the ground, opened it, and took out a large brown package of candied rose petals, which she handed to the oldest of the children, a girl named Luba. "Take this package to your mother, and tell her to see that the treats are distributed equally."

"Oh, yes, yes, ma'am." Luba smiled widely. "Thank you, ma'am." They turned and hurried toward their parents' homes with their treasure and Tamara, still on her knees, watched until they were out of sight.

Then she became aware of Falcon's extended hand and took it, allowing him to pull her from her knees. "How good you are, Tamara," he said, drawing her again into his embrace.

The exhaustion of traveling was forgotten in her moment of happiness. "One day," she whispered, "we shall have little ones of our own." She had not yet told him of her suspicion; the right moment had not come.

Falcon said nothing, but held her for a long, long while.

Despite her protests and entreaties that he remain with her, Falcon journeyed into the woods that night to spend some time alone. Like a protective guardian with his musket propped against him, he sat on the rise above Asher Arms and watched the house throughout the long night. He had a thousand things on his mind that prevented him from seeking rest. This past year he had kept secrets from Tamara. He had avoided discussions of his past and had often changed the subject. He had made her feel like an unwelcome interloper in his private life, and she had loved him nonetheless. Now, with their vows of eternal togetherness, it was time to lift the shroud of mystery. She had a right to know who he really was. Their visit to the Indian village would answer all her questions. He only hoped that he didn't lose her.

As the timber line turned red with the approach of dawn, he returned to the house and attempted to rouse her from her sleep. As he sat on the bed beside her, watching her sleeping innocence, he felt the wrench of fear inside him. She thought she had fallen in love with Falcon, the half-breed. Since then she had learned many things about him that he had not told her himself, and she had openly confronted him. She was aware that he'd received the best education from the white man's universities, but not that her father had paid his tuition, nor why. She knew that her father had tried to kill himself, but, again, she did not know why. Would she feel fooled and deceived when she learned that Falcon was actually Marcus Gray, the son of her English guardian? Would she hate him when she learned the extent of his loathing for her father? She had spoken fondly of the man who was Falcon's true father—a man he had never known. He recalled the many times she had mentioned Fedora and her son and expressed sorrow at their "deaths." He remembered the many times she had spoken of Mason's love for them. And Falcon had always wondered why his mother had allowed Jacob Fleming to erect the "wall of death"

304

that had separated her from the man who had been her only true love.

There were many things Falcon had never understood but had accepted. His mother was a good woman and he would respect her motives. She had helped him through many trials and he hoped to God she could guide him through this latest trial. Falcon had once vowed to seek vengeance against Jacob Fleming for what he had done to his mother so many years ago. It had not mattered to Falcon that over the years Jacob had tried to redeem himself for the sin he had committed. When he had learned that Fedora was living with the trapper and that her son, well-tutored at his mother's knee, was approaching the age of higher learning, he had arranged to enroll him at William and Mary College in Virginia, an arrangement that Fedora had put aside her pride to accept. Falcon, however, had never forgotten the scene he had witnessed as a ten-year-old boy that last night before his mother had fled with him into the Delaware wilderness.

When Tamara had first arrived at Asher Arms, he had nurtured the idea of using her as a tool against her father. But that idea had been quickly extinguished. He hadn't planned on falling in love with her.

She was the woman he wanted, for all time . . . the woman who touched his heart with her warm longing and passion. She was the woman he had recklessly vowed to loathe and hurt, so that Jacob would regret what he'd done to Fedora. For the first time, Falcon admitted to himself that he had come to Asher Arms to make Jacob miserable, to be the constant reminder of his past mistakes. Jacob was now dead, and Falcon loved his daughter more than life itself. He couldn't bear the thought of losing her, yet his fear was that their separation was predestined by his own thirst for vengeance . . . a thirst that had died the night Jacob had died.

Falcon felt tears welling inside, but as Tamara's sleepy eyes slowly began to open, he smiled and choked back the painful lump in his throat.

"Awaken, sleepyhead," he coaxed fondly. "The early hours are best for traveling."

Tamara stretched her arms forward, and they softly embraced his shoulders. "How long have you been watching me?" she whispered, scarcely able to see his bronze features through the darkness of dawn. "Oh, I did so miss you last night, Falcon. One day . . ." she coaxed his mouth down to hers, to kiss him very gently, ". . . one day your place will be beside me. I will not allow you to journey into the forest, unless I go with you."

"And you shall go with me," he whispered in reply, his mouth trailing kisses over her warm, flushed cheeks and her partially closed eyelids. "Last night . . . I had many things on my mind. I would not have been good company for you."

His body physically responded to the sensual nearness of her. His eyes could not help but lower to the supple milk-white flesh exposed above her lacy bed gown. He loved the clouds of her golden hair spread upon the pillow, inviting his cheek to its softness. He adored the moist, pink lips which parted to invite his caress. He simply adored her . . . her slender, womanly frame emitting warmth, like the siren of ancient lore, hypnotizing him with her unconscious movements against his body. His hand lowered to her slender leg, then slowly eased up, taking her gown with it. His hooded eyes held her innocent, demure gaze.

"How lovely you are," he whispered against her

hairline. "But you must rise . . . so that we can prepare for our journey."

Tamara held him steadfastly. "Must we, Falcon? Couldn't we spend a little time . . . together?"

He gently laughed. "What a seductive wench you are!" he accused. "A man is not safe! Where is this proper English breeding you flung at me constantly when we first met?"

Tamara returned his smile. "I left it in England, Falcon—in the stuffy parlor of Gray House, where it belongs."

"We really must begin our journey, Tamara." But even as he spoke, his hands moved to her breasts to gently squeeze them, then lowered to explore the curves and hollows of her body through her thin bed gown. "We really must—" But his words were lost as his mouth captured hers in a long, searing caress, then moved slowly to the tiny earlobe exposed by her disheveled hair. Tenderly, still kissing her, Falcon eased her arms from around his neck; then, with a sudden impatience, he pulled the loose-fitting gown down to expose her ivory flesh. His fingers brushing against her skin were like fire and she groaned as his mouth gently captured her breasts, his lips and tongue teasing her nipples, giving each his equal attention.

Tamara could tell, as his movements quickened, that he wanted her, and that his own body pained with the wanting. He hungrily kissed her mouth, her closed eyelids, the tiny pulse that beat in her throat.

Suddenly, his hands skillfully, with the knowledge of her own needs and desires, moved to her thighs to stroke the soft inner flesh, then moved slowly upwards. His masterly caresses were like a river of fire burning through her, turning her inside out with desire. She felt her heart quicken its pace and her hips

307

lifted to meet the gentleness of his fingers, now exploring, caressing inside of her. Then, like a wild, untamed thing that had been mercilessly teased, Tamara's hands moved impatiently, pulling at his shirt, caressing the iron-hard muscles separated from her soft body by a mere breath of space. Holding his loving gaze, her hands boldly slid beneath the tightness of his trousers to his hard-muscled stomach, feeling him tense and catch his breath.

"What are you doing to me, little vixen?" he whispered, surprised by the intense boldness he had not experienced before. "We will reach a point," he spoke between quick, teasing kisses, "when we will be unable to turn back."

"That is my plan," she laughed gently, teasing him with kisses of her own, "to conquer, Falcon. To make myself irresistible. To seal my claim on you . . . as my man."

Falcon's body slid slowly upward to cover hers. He did not remove his trousers but merely shifted them to his knees as he covered her, then eased between her thighs. His body rested against hers and she lifted her hips and poised. Falcon, with a lusty groan, buried his length deep within her. For a moment, his body did not move, but remained embedded within her, as if he were a part of her. Tamara's hands slowly slipped to his back to feel the tenseness of his muscles, then slowly lowered to his firm buttocks, to rock back and forth with his intense, increasing, driving movements. She felt the erotic climax of his movements quickly approaching, felt, beneath her hands, the rhythm and pace of his hips thrust harder against her, driving himself so deeply inside her that she groaned from the exquisite pleasure of his fullness.

Tamara felt again the throbbing in her loins and

her body's writhing movements as she and Falcon soared together, high in the clouds and back in the same fulfilling, mind-numbing moment.

She felt deliriously weak as her fingers rose to his dark hair to entwine among the damp strands that hung on his forehead. Their breathing slowed in gentle unison and when his dark eyes met hers, she smiled lovingly.

"Now, my little vixen," he scolded, regaining his breath, "now that you have seduced me, we shall dress and begin our journey."

"Seduce you! Oof!" Tamara's hand closed over the pillow, with which she lightly hit him. "I seduced thee, my lord? Mayhaps it was the other way around?" Then they laughed together for a moment, before his body withdrew from hers.

Half an hour later, with a small bag packed with a few items of summer clothing and a tin box of freshly baked biscuits and smoked pork, Tamara met Falcon at the stables, where he had just saddled their horses. The Indian village was only a few hours to the southeast and they would arrive shortly after the noon hour. Tamara had made many trips to the trading post in the past year and had become familiar with the trails that would take them to the fork, where they would turn south toward the village. She had never seen the village, but she could close her eyes and picture it, the way Falcon had described it to her so many times.

Despite the morning's delay, they were well under way by seven o'clock. They rode in silence, through sunlit dales thick with fallen leaves of seasons past and across cool, babbling brooks where the deer came to drink. The sun slowly rose, signalling the end of another hour of traveling, and at midday they stopped beside a mountain stream to eat their light

309

meal. Unbeknownst to Tamara, Falcon had brought along a bottle of red wine he'd taken from the wine cellar, which they enjoyed with their meal.

Tamara felt a sudden pang of apprehension as they reached the fork in the trail. The Indian village was only an hour's ride to the south. She wondered what Falcon's mother would be like and tried to picture her in her mind. She imagined a tall, slim woman with distinctive bronze features gracefully touched by the lines of middle-age and dark hair gently swept by silver gray strands. She tried to imagine the bronze face with a smile, yet inside, she feared scorn and rejection. How much did Falcon's mother know of Tamara? How much had Falcon told her? Or Flaming Bow?

So deep in thought, Tamara was scarcely aware they had reached the village until Falcon's hand fell lightly to her arm. She sat atop the hill, looking down on the pole-and-wattle huts, the campfires emitting smoke into the clear blue sky, and dark-skinned, brown-clothed children in happy play. The village was as she had pictured it, a scene of contentment set against the Indian River.

"Come, Tamara." Falcon moved his horse a few feet ahead, but halted when Tamara did not follow. He turned, immediately caught off guard by the fear in her soft brown eyes. "What is wrong?" he asked, concerned.

"I—I'm afraid, Falcon. Suppose . . . suppose your mother doesn't like me."

Falcon laughed gently. "Preposterous! How could she not like you? Now . . . come."

Hesitantly, Tamara moved her horse up beside him, then ahead when she saw that the trail leading down the face of the hill was wide enough for only one horse. By the time they entered the village, chil-

310

dren had gathered around and were gleefully jumping up to touch Falcon. Tamara kept her head down and did not see the women who stopped their work to watch them enter the village. Falcon's gentle laughter as he responded to the children provided some security, but she still felt the fear inside.

Falcon soon dismounted, then put his hands up to assist Tamara down from the saddle. When Kishke exited his adobe, Tamara leaned close to Falcon and whispered, "Is it acceptable for a woman to look him in the eyes?"

Falcon laughed, for her benefit only. "I believe it'll be all right." Then he turned and extended his hand to Kishke, which was gripped in the Indian fashion. "Father, it is good to see you again."

Kishke smiled broadly. "My son." Then he averted his gaze to Tamara. "I see you have brought your woman to the village . . . finally."

"Yes, this is Tamara Fleming, Father . . . the woman I have taken to my heart."

Kishke's hand fell firmly to Tamara's shoulder. "You are welcome at the village of Kishke. My people will treat you as one of their own."

"Thank you," she replied, surprised at the meekness in her voice.

"My mother is here?" Falcon questioned.

"She is at the isolation hut."

"She is ill?" Falcon's brows pinched with concern.

"No . . . she has gone there . . . to think, she says."

"Is she alone?" Falcon asked.

"She is."

Falcon turned and pointed out the isolation hut out to Tamara, a long hut set against the backdrop

311

of a rocky cliff. "My mother is there, Tamara. You must go now to meet her."

"You will not come with me?" she asked worriedly.

Falcon took her hand for a moment and held it. "A man does not go into the women's isolation hut. It is their place only. And you must see her there without delay, Tamara."

The urgency in his voice took her aback for a moment. The fear returned. "Very well, Falcon."

"I will be here with my father. You will come to me when you have concluded your talk."

"She speaks English, Falcon? I don't speak—"

"She speaks English. Now . . . go." With his hand at her back, he gently prodded her into the first move.

Tamara felt her footsteps falter. She felt the eyes of the village women on her. And she felt very, very alone. Angry with Falcon that he would not accompany her, she did not look back, but was aware that he watched her. With a deep sigh and renewed determination, Tamara hastened her pace and soon stood at the lone door of the isolation hut. She hesitated, and immediately a woman's voice called, "Come to me, child."

Tamara stepped inside the hut and allowed a moment for her eyes to adjust to the diminished light. Then she saw the seated form of a woman with a shawl of some kind drawn over her head. Tamara could not see her face, which was lowered, as if she were deep in thought.

Tamara slowly approached, then dropped to her knees before the woman.

"I am Tamara Fleming," she said quietly. "You are Falcon's mother?"

The woman did not immediately look up. "I am," she replied.

"Falcon has sent me to you. . . . H—he said we must talk." Tamara felt herself foolishly stuttering. She was trying very hard to see the woman's features, but they were veiled by the shawl pulled low on her forehead.

A myriad of thoughts rushed through Tamara's head. Was something wrong? Was the woman disfigured? Was she blind? Tamara fought the urge to rise to her feet and flee, not only from the hut, but from the village as well.

Then, Falcon's mother looked up and her eyes met the younger woman's in a deep, penetrating gaze. Tamara was, indeed, horrified, as she looked into sea-green eyes. The woman slowly eased her shawl to her shoulders, betraying massive waves of golden hair untouched by the snows of time.

"My God," she whispered, "you're not an Indian at all." Then something clicked inside her, something she had seen a long, long time ago . . . a portrait of a golden-haired woman clutching a young boy—a portrait hidden away in a small dark room that had been locked for many years.

Tamara knew without a doubt that the woman sitting across from her was Fedora Gray. As the reality struck her, the trembling Tamara pulled Fedora into her arms. "Fedora . . . you're Fedora Gray," she said, unable to choke back the emotion, the tears that sheened her eyes. "You're Mason's wife. How can this be?" She felt Fedora's arms slip around her shoulders, returning her embrace. She felt Fedora's gentle breathing; her own had suddenly ceased in the excitement. "Oh, Falcon . . . Falcon, I hate you for this," she wept gently. "Why didn't you tell me. Dear God, why didn't you tell me?"

*Chapter 21*

Tamara's thoughts were a mass of confusion. She pulled away and looked at Fedora as if this could not possibly be happening. Instinctively, she touched Fedora's golden hair. It was as soft as it appeared in the portrait Mason had painted of her. Tamara looked deeply into Fedora's eyes, the same eyes that had looked back at her from the haunting portrait. Then, mesmerized by this pleasant feminine face from a far distant past, she very gently removed the medallion Mason had given her and slipped it over Fedora's head. "This was yours, Fedora . . . many, many years ago. Mason gave it to me the Christmas before I left England. Now I return it to its rightful owner."

"Mason . . ." she whispered softly, "dear Mason . . . how is he?"

"He was well last I saw him. And his letters—they hint only at his well-being and good health."

Fedora smiled. "Later we shall talk many hours and you shall tell me all about Mason, but for now, there are other matters to be settled between us. I am sure you are wondering why Falcon and I—"

"Yes—" Without thinking, Tamara cut her short.

314

She had not meant to be rude and immediately touched Fedora's hand in a gentle caress. "How can this be, Fedora? It was reported that you had died. And Falcon . . . my God! Mason's son!" Her words became a stunned whisper. "Why, Fedora . . . why the deception?"

"This is not important now," Fedora calmly replied. "What is important is your feeling for my son. He says that you do, but I must know . . . do you love him?"

"I—I thought I did," she replied. "But if he could deceive me like this . . . Fedora, I don't know if I could ever trust him again. What other skeletons will he drag forth in the years to come? Dear Lord," she continued, only now recovering from this stunning surprise. "Did my father know who he was? These past few years that Falcon has been at Asher Arms?"

"There is something you must understand about Falcon, Tamara—"

"Answer my question, please, Fedora."

"Yes, Jacob knew."

Her thoughts whirled nauseatingly. Her father and Falcon had been constantly at odds with each other. She had always wondered why, and she still wanted to know. It was imperative that she know now, so that she could plan her future accordingly. "I don't know what you are willing to tell me, Fedora. May I ask you a few questions? Are you willing to answer them?"

"Perhaps that is a better course, Tamara."

"Why, when Mason journeyed to America in search of you and his son, were your deaths reported to him?"

Fedora's brows met in a perplexed frown. She did not want to speak ill of Tamara's father, yet a sense of pride and honor within her compelled her to answer Tamara's question truthfully. "Tamara, when I was a young woman and was sent away from my husband, I was indentured to your Father."

"Yes, I know."

"His wife—your mother—was very ill, and I was employed as her nursemaid. We became very close friends as well. We shared our sorrows, our hopes and dreams. Your mother's hope was to get well and to be able to care for you, her precious little girl—a hope that was never to come to fruition—and my hope was one day to return to my dear husband. Your father was a proud, headstrong man who could not cope with the infirmities of his wife. As Marian took more often to her sickbed, your father learned to look elsewhere for. . . ." Ashamed, Fedora's eyes dropped.

"Please, do go on, Fedora. I am not a child."

"For his manly needs, Tamara," she replied softly.

"I see." Lines of disapproval touched Tamara's features.

"No, you do not see, Tamara. Your father was a gentle man—"

"My father was a vicious man!" she argued, unthinking. "I saw what he did to the servant girl—" Suddenly, Tamara realized what she was saying. "No, Fedora, not a servant girl. He ordered his own daughter to be whipped. Did you know that the daughter of Bridie, his servant, was also my father's daughter?"

"Yes, I knew."

Tamara's head fell abjectly. She pressed her lips into a thin, angry line. "It seems that everyone knows everything . . . except me."

Again, Fedora frowned. "There were times that Jacob wielded a strong hand of discipline. Nevertheless, he could be gentle."

316

"I am still waiting to hear, Fedora, why my father falsely reported your deaths."

Fedora picked up a small twig and dragged it absently across the dirt floor of the isolation hut. "Your father passionately claimed to be in love with me, Tamara, and I believe that he truly was. But my loyalties were strong to his sick wife—and to the memory of my dear husband. When I found that I was unable to cope with his amorous attentions to me, I fled Asher Arms with my son. I fled Asher Arms during one of the worst snowstorms ever to strike the forest there, and one in which no mortal could possibly survive. But we sought refuge in a cave and miraculously we did survive. When the snows had thawed and spring was well underway, the remains of a woman and child were found in the forest. Many seasons later they were suspected to have been the remains of an Iroquois woman and her son outcast by her tribe. You must believe, Tamara, that your father truthfully thought they were my son and me. He would not have deliberately lied to Mason."

"So, when Mason's search eventually brought him to Asher Arms, Jacob thought he was telling him the truth—that you were, indeed, dead. Only, he allowed Mason to believe you had died soon after your arrival."

"Yes," Fedora replied. "Jacob felt that our deaths after arrival would have produced fewer questions. He had no fear that Mason would learn otherwise. The servants had been sworn to secrecy, and your mother was so critically ill that she was not aware of anything around her. Ofttimes she did not even realize that she had a child of her own."

"She knew," Tamara argued softly. "She wrote in her diary that Jacob had sent me away. She also wrote of your 'deaths'."

Pain reflected in Fedora's eyes as her gaze lifted to Tamara's. "I—I didn't know this, Tamara. I was closest to her, and I thought she was not lucid most of the time?"

"My father sent me away." Tamara thought aloud.

"You must not feel anger toward your father. Guilt-ridden that Mason had lost his wife and son because of his own lust, Jacob gave Mason a substitute child. He gave him his own little girl. That is why you were sent away from Asher Arms—not because your father didn't love you, but because of guilt, and a terrible need to somehow make up for the wrong he had done."

"And Falcon? Why did he return to Asher Arms? Why did he torment my father?"

"It was not his intention, Tamara, to torment. He wanted only to know the man who had so dramatically changed our lives. Yes, he went to Asher Arms with a blackness in his heart, but he would never have hurt your father. Falcon has told me the truth about the hunting accident that paralyzed Jacob. That morning while they were hunting in the forest, Falcon admitted to Jacob that he was Marcus Gray. Many years ago, when Jacob learned that we were living with the trapper and that my son was approaching manhood, he offered to educate Falcon. I accepted his offer, Tamara. Your father spent a small fortune on his education, but he had never actually met him. When Falcon betrayed his identity that day in the woods, Jacob, emotional with shame, turned the gun on himself. Falcon wrestled it from him, and in the course of doing so, your father was wounded. Thereafter, your father grew to despise Falcon and to blame him for the accident that left him crippled."

318

Tamara rose unsteadily to her feet. She felt nauseated and weak, and momentarily disoriented. Only when Fedora's hand came out and lightly touched hers did Tamara regain her sense. "And how, Fedora, do you feel about Mason now? Shouldn't he know you and Falcon are alive?" When she did not answer, Tamara continued with haste, "Surely you want him to know. Didn't you send him a package of your personal possessions and papers?"

Fedora looked quickly up. "No . . . no, I didn't."

"Then who did? Who would have had access to your personal possessions?"

Silence. Fedora held Tamara's gaze for a moment. "Falcon," she eventually replied. "I confronted him by letter, and he has not denied it." When she saw the anger narrowing the younger woman's eyes, Fedora continued with haste, "Falcon has always wanted to contact his true father. He has not, because of me . . . because I felt that fate brought us where we are today, and that our lives are best left alone."

"And Mason, in the meantime, lives a lonely life, without any family. How cruel, Fedora, when he could have you and Falcon."

"I am Kishke's wife," she replied without shame. "Falcon, too, has chosen this way of life."

"Has he, indeed?" Tamara turned away, frustrated. "Games!" she muttered between clenched teeth. "Why do you and Falcon play these games with people's lives? Please . . . will you excuse me for a moment? It is imperative that I speak to Falcon."

"Remember all we have discussed, Tamara, when you talk to him."

Tamara left the hut, walked quickly across the village common to Kishke's adobe, and sharply called

319

Falcon's name. Momentarily, he pulled back the deerhide covering and stood beside her.

"May we speak in private?" She had not meant to sound brisk and rude, but her words came out that way.

He motioned her to a narrow path leading down to the shore of the Indian River. She heard the current breaking against the smooth white rocks and the cry of gulls that had flown inland from the bay. She heard the almost stalking footsteps of Falcon just behind her, yet all she really heard was the anger building inside her, threatening to explode into a million tiny fragments.

Then, when she was sure they were well away from the village and knew their conversation would be muffled by the Indian River, Tamara turned toward Falcon and her eyes met his. Caught off-guard by the anger and bitterness he saw there, he raised a dark eyebrow.

"You've deceived me and lied to me, Falcon. You brought me here to deliberately shock me. Are you pleased?"

"I brought you here," he answered quietly, "so that you would learn the truth. So that there would be no more secrets between us."

"All these months, Falcon . . ." she turned away, unable to face him, "all these months I have wondered why you and my father were at odds with each other. I wondered why he kept you on, disliking you so intensely. I wondered why you stayed on, when you were aware of his dislike. You could have told me who you were. You could have told me what happened between Fedora and my father and why she had fled in the dead of winter. Oh, Falcon. . . ." She dropped her head, feeling tears well in her eyes. "You could have told me you were Marcus Gray.

I've spoken so fondly of you and your mother, even thinking you were dead. You've had a thousand opportunities to tell me who you were. But—no!" She turned swiftly toward him, her eyes black with anger. "You had to tell me you were Falcon, the half-breed Indian!"

"I never said I was Indian, Tamara . . . you said I was Indian."

Frustrated, Tamara brought her palm to her forehead and pressed it there for a moment, He was right, of course, he had never actually said he was an Indian. "You let me assume as much, Falcon," she continued in a quieter tone. "That is as good as a lie. And you certainly didn't disagree with my assumption, did you? In my opinion, an omission is as black as a lie. And why?" Her voice softened as she turned away from him again. "All the times I spoke of Fedora and her child, Falcon, and spoke of them in the past tense, because I thought they were dead . . . you never once spoke up to tell me who you were . . . who your mother was. You made a fool of me. I—I don't understand why. You know how much I love Mason. You know that he was a father to me. You know that his hurt was my hurt. And all the while . . . all those many months that I knew you, and loved you—" She was now gently weeping, and when he approached her she angrily waved him away. "You could have relieved the hurt. You could have told me who you were at the very beginning. You could have told me you were Mason's son."

"And would you have told him—my father?"

"Yes! Of course, I would have!" she replied bitterly.

His mouth twisted. "And you would have loved me more, because I was Mason Gray's son?" he replied.

Tamara spun rapidly toward him, her hands clenched. "Don't be sarcastic with me, Falcon! I don't deserve that! I could never have loved you more! All these months you have played games with me . . . you have fooled and deceived me and laughed at me behind my back! I'll never forgive you, Falcon—or, or Marcus Gray—whoever you are! Never!"

Despite her protests, Falcon approached and his hands fell lightly to her shoulders. When she tried to pull violently away, his grip tightened and he held her steadfastly against him. "Why won't you let me explain, Tamara?" She heard the soft regret in his voice but refused to heed it. "I was afraid of losing you. I was afraid you'd think I had taken you as my woman because of some terrible thirst for vengeance I harbored against your father. Yes, I hated him at first, but dammit, I tried to stop him when he threatened to kill himself. That should account for something. God, Tamara! I admit that before you arrived at Asher Arms I nurtured the idea of using you against your father, but when I met you—"

"Don't lie anymore, Falcon." Her voice became cynical and bitter. "I can't take the lies. You'll never fool me again. Now let me go. What we were together is over. I—I never want to see you again."

This was as Falcon had feared. For so long, he had wanted to end the mysteries and reveal the secrets he had kept, which was why he had brought Tamara to his mother. He couldn't blame her for the way she felt. Surely Fedora had tried to explain in a way that she would accept, but he had never expected Tamara to react like this. Yes, he had expected anger and hurt and bitter accusations. He had expected her to feel fooled and deceived. But he had never expected her to turn her back so completely on their love.

"I can't let you go like this, Tamara. God! I love you! You are everything I want and need. You can't just walk out on us without so much as batting an eye."

"I can . . . and I will, Falcon!" she shot back. "And what can you do about it?"

Lines of disapproval were etched in his face. Tamara was acting childish and irrational. She struggled to free herself from him, her skin pale and almost translucent in her anger, and all she really accomplished by looking at him with such daggers in her eyes was to cause desire to surface in him.

Perhaps it was the heat of the afternoon, or the equally intense heat of her anger, but without any warning, Tamara's face paled and she went limp and lifeless in Falcon's arms. He picked up her up and held her close to him, then said gently against her hairline, "My precious Tamara, what have I done to you?"

He walked hastily back to the village, where he was immediately surrounded by the women who took her from him. Fedora ordered that she be taken to the isolation hut, but Falcon protested. He did not want to be parted from her. "You must leave her with us, Son. She is best taken care of by her own kind."

"I am her own kind!" he shot back.

His mother gave him a gentle look. "You are not a woman."

"But, Mother—" Falcon again started to protest, but Fedora's look quietened him. He turned and walked slowly toward the rocky cliff, leaned back, and stood there for a long while.

Meanwhile, Fedora bathed Tamara's face with

cool water as one of the women fanned her with a straw fan. When Tamara began to come around, Fedora's silent look asked the other women to leave.

Tamara could scarcely make out the ivory features above her, but she was only too aware of her worried look. She managed a feeble smile. "I—I'm all right, Fedora. I don't know what came over me. I feel so foolish."

Fedora's look saddened. She took Tamara's hand and gave it a gentle squeeze. Seeing the tears freely touch Tamara's pale cheek, she touched her fingertips to their wetness to flick them away. "What ails you, Tamara, is easily seen by another woman."

Tamara met her understanding gaze. "What do you mean?"

Fedora's smile faded with concern. "You are with child, aren't you?"

Tamara's eyes filled with tears. "Yes," she whispered. "How did you know?"

"A woman always has that special look at this time in her life. Does Falcon know?"

Bitterness came to Tamara's voice. She tried to rise, but Fedora's hand touched her shoulder, compelling her to remain still. "I don't want him to know. I'll have this baby and be a good mother to it. He—he doesn't care about me and he won't care about our baby either!"

Fedora gently held her hand. "How hurt he would be to hear you say that! I know you have been hurt, Tamara, but I am his mother . . . and I know he loves you very, very much. Give him a chance. He has been in such turmoil, wanting to tell you about us. The reason he did not was because I asked him not to." Tamara again gave her a disbelieving look. "It is true, Tamara. By the time Jacob learned that

324

we were alive, Mason had wed Mary Rhee Portland and had made a new life for himself.''

"But he always loved you, Fedora.''

"Yes, I know he did. But I, too, accepting finally the circumstances that had thrust me from Mason's life, had made a new life. Dear Tamara.'' Regret filled Fedora's voice. "Being near you, knowing you were raised by his gentle hand, makes me feel so close to him. But, my child, Mason and I are not what is at issue here. Don't make a mistake you will have to live with the rest of your life. You are too young to be unhappy. If you love Falcon—and I truly believe you do—you must not cast him aside because of my mistakes. My God, he has proven his love by bringing you to me. Don't you know how much he feared losing you?''

Tamara felt ashamed. She saw Fedora's features through her tear-sheened eyes, saw the wisdom of a thousand ages reflected in her silent gaze. "But— how many times will he lie to me, Fedora? Will the rest of our lives be based on lies and omissions? What else is there for me to learn? What secrets does he keep still, buried deep within himself?''

Fedora smiled a warm, sincere smile. "None that I know of, Tamara. And I—as his mother—know most of his secrets. You—as his true love—know the rest. Now, are you able to sit up?''

With Fedora's assistance, Tamara sat forward on the straw mat. "Fedora, I feel so ashamed. Will Falcon ever forgive the things I said to him?''

"He awaits word of your well-being. Go to him. There is no need for forgiveness. If you truly love him—''

"Oh, but I do!'' she immediately retorted, finding renewed strength.

325

"Then go to him, and tell him what is in your heart."

Slowly Tamara rose, then moved toward the entrance of the hut. She turned back to Fedora for a moment and her hand lightly fell to her abdomen. "And I will tell him about our blessing." Fedora nodded her assent. Tamara stepped into the mid-afternoon heat and looked around. She immediately saw Falcon sitting against the rocky cliff, his knees drawn up and his hands clasped lightly around them. He did not see her approach, but when she knelt before him, his eyes lifted and met her gentle gaze. She saw the strain of emotion in his bronze features, even as he tried to reflect impassiveness.

"Falcon . . . should I continue calling you by that name . . . or Marcus?"

"I am Falcon, Tamara, the man who has loved you."

Suddenly she was at a loss for words. She probed back into the past few moments and gained renewed strength from her conversation with Fedora. "Your mother said there is no need for explanations and forgiveness. She said that if I love you, I should simply tell you so."

"And do you?" he whispered.

Unhesitatingly, Tamara's arms slipped around his shoulders and her cheek gently touched his. "I love you so much, Falcon, that I don't ever want to be away from you again, not even for a moment."

Falcon's trembling arms slipped around her waist. He said nothing, but she felt the burning tears against his cheek commingling with her own.

"And you never will be," he replied, his voice trembling with emotion. "We shall seek our destiny together, Tamara—the two of us."

Tamara moved her cheek tenderly against his own.

She closed her tear-moistened eyes and whispered, "Not the two of us, Falcon . . . the three of us. You and me—and the seed that grows within me, the seed of our love."

Falcon's hug was as gentle as his expression of joy. "How much I love you, Tamara . . . my strength, my light, and my heart. For all time . . . yes, for all time."

## Chapter 22

In the days to follow, Tamara enjoyed the simple life of the village. The women showed her how to make round cakes of ground corn, and the children engaged her as the referee in games that often lasted well past twilight. Falcon and Flaming Bow, just now recovering his strength after his seven-week captivity, journeyed far into the forest to hunt wild boar.

Fedora's grace and beauty held Tamara in gentle awe. They spoke long hours about England and Mason and Gray House. Tamara could almost see Fedora take her words tenderly to heart. Fedora might have been Kishke's wife, but her love still belonged to Mason Gray, and it was a love that had thrived and grown over the past thirty years. The light of that gentle emotion shone in Fedora's eyes as Tamara spoke of Mason.

Tamara had many things on her mind. Yesterday morning, lying in a tender embrace with Falcon, they had talked at length. Even during the long hours she spent with Fedora, assisting her with her duties, her conversation with Falcon echoed in her mind. It was an echo that seemed to journey into a far valley and return in nerve-wracking repetition. She could still see Falcon's eyes in the morning twilight, dark and hooded, and his jaw, taut and angry as he spoke.

"Don't you ever want to see your father, Falcon?"

He hesitated for a moment. "No," he stated adamantly.

"But why?"

"Delaware is my home . . . I am an American. Kishke is my father now. What better reasons can I give for not wanting this previous life? I was an infant, Tamara. I never knew my true father. Besides—" As she cuddled against him, he gave her shoulder a tender squeeze. "What good could come of my father knowing about me . . . of knowing that I am alive?"

She had not brought this up before, although she had wanted to. Now, his question gave her no choice at the moment. "I believe you want him to know, Falcon."

"How do you reach this conclusion?"

"Remember several months ago when I received a letter from Mason, and he had mentioned some personal things of Fedora's that he thought I had sent him?"

He frowned thoughtfully. "Yes, I remember," he replied.

"I asked Fedora about it. She swears that she did not send those things to Mason and she was a bit upset by their loss. Only one other person would have been able—"

"Indeed?" He had cut her off too abruptly. Guilt reflected in the slight rise of his voice. "And who might that person have been?"

Tenderly, her fingertip touched his chin. "You sent

329

them, Falcon. And I believe you did so because in your own way you wanted to reestablish ties with your father. You used Fedora's things to break the ice, to force Mason to think of Fedora—and you—once more. Now, you are trying to find a way to make contact without going against the wishes of your mother. Tell me if I am wrong, Falcon."

"I cannot do so, Tamara," he hesitantly confessed. "I do want to know my father. For many years I have wanted to contact him, but—"

"Fedora was afraid of the questions that would be asked." Tamara finished the statement. "There are circumstances about her life since she left England that she does not want Mason to know." Tamara's eyes lifted to his firm profile, to his mouth pressed into a thin line. "Falcon, Mason lost you and Fedora so many years ago. He has lost both his second wife and his second son—your half-brother—in the past three years. What a joy it would be for him to know that you are alive . . . that Fedora is alive. It wouldn't matter that she was now another man's life. Mason would be so happy just to know that you are alive that he would not care to ask questions. He—he's such a wonderful man. You would learn to love him, as I do. It is ironic, Falcon." As she spoke, she nestled more closely to him, and her hand fell to his chest. "How parallel our lives have been! You have a half-brother and I have a half-sister. My father made you the sole heir of his estate. Your father has made me the sole heir of his estate. I can only conclude that in your private meeting with Mr. Inness, you renounced your right to Asher Arms in my favor. Isn't it only fair that I relinquish my claim to Gray House in yours?"

"There is a difference, Tamara—"

"What difference?" she hastily retorted.

330

"Your father's motives were selfish. He gave Asher Arms to me to keep us apart. My father truly loves you as a daughter. Therefore, as I see it, Tamara, you deserve to be Mason's sole heir. You have been his child, just as surely as if you had been born to him."

"But I wasn't born to him," she reminded him. *You* were born to him. I am sorry, Falcon . . . but I feel your mother is selfish in depriving Mason of his only son."

Falcon quickly sat forward on the soft mat. "Perhaps you are right, Tamara. My mother is not flawless. One day. . . ." He turned and supported himself on his elbow, then gazed into her eyes. There was no malice there. In light of the statement she had just made, she had reasonably expected it. "We shall not worry about my father now," he continued softly, dropping his hand to her abdomen. "That problem will, in time, work itself out. Right now, Tamara—" Tenderly, he caressed her mouth with brief kisses. "I care only about you and me and our small one. I care only about us being together . . . as man and wife, as it should be. Tomorrow, Flaming Bow and I shall go hunting. When I return in a few days, we shall journey to the cottage in Lewes, publish the required banns, and before the summer is over, you shall be my wife."

"How wonderful," she reflected thoughtfully, "if Mason could know that my new husband was . . . his long-lost son." His gaze provoked a tantalizing sensation, instantly taking away her gloomy thoughts. Tamara's hands rose and gently circled his shoulders to pull him close. "Oh Falcon, our marriage will be such a happy moment. I want nothing more than to be your wife. Mrs. Falcon Gray. . . ."

"I have never used my father's name," he replied.

"Do you object?"

Silence. He held her loving gaze for a moment, then smiled. "I do not object, Tamara. Indeed, I am proud to wear my father's name attached to my own. Besides—" he continued, gently laughing, "we cannot have you—my wife—going through life with the title of Mrs. Falcon Blank, can we?"

Tamara, too, laughed. "I would suppose it'd be a bit awkward and I might be forced to explain," she replied. "Falcon Gray . . . it—it'll be a little hard to get accustomed to. I have always known you simply as Falcon. But—it's a lovely name you share with me. And you—" Her lips puckered into a kiss that she instantly touched to his cheek. "You're a lovely man."

Again, Falcon lightly chuckled. "Men are not 'lovely,' Tamara. Just label me as I am . . . handsome . . . charming. . . ." He propped himself on his elbow and his dark eyes hovered over hers. "And a good lover," he teased affectionately.

Tamara's fingers slipped around his neck and linked together. "I can't argue with that, Falcon—you are." His mouth touched hers in a light kiss. She could tell by his movements, his hand moving confidently along the slender curves of her waist, exactly what was on his mind. "Falcon, we—you and I—we just—a moment ago—"

His mouth returned to hers, to tease it with brief kisses. "And why not again?" he whispered.

"I have no . . . objections . . . if that is what. . . ." Her reply was broken by his kisses gently caressing her warm, vibrant flesh, her flushed cheeks, that small throbbing pulse in her neck. His breath was warm and sweet, his hands masterly, yet gentle. She knew how soon their bodies would lift to the dream-state they often visited, the wide, vast plane of ecstasy where they often soared like eagles on the wind, to return to earth after spellbinding moments that could, if they would allow it, go on and on forever. . . .

"Tamara?"

That was Fedora, softly speaking her name. A slight crimson blush rose in Tamara's cheeks as she realized she'd been daydreaming. Falcon had been gone a day, yet it was as if she'd been with him just an hour ago. She wondered how long the hunting trip would keep him away from the village. She needed him now. She needed him now more than ever before.

"I—I apologize, Fedora," Tamara said after a moment. "I was thinking about—"

"Falcon," she replied, finishing Tamara's statement. "I can easily recognize the light in your eyes, Tamara. I see how deeply you care for my son. And I am very pleased."

Tamara smiled a gentle smile. "I love him very much, Fedora. I hope I can be a good wife to him."

"And you will, Tamara, just as he will be a good husband to you. I have made my mistakes in the past, but . . . I pride myself in the son I have raised. He is a good man. And I am confident that you will be happy with him."

"I am happy with him. I never knew before the happiness that a man like Falcon could bring to a woman."

Tamara saw the approval in the mother's gentle smile.

Soon they were joined by other women of the village. Throughout the afternoon, they talked and laughed as they did their work and kept out of the mens' way. At suppertime the women met at the cooking fire in the center of the camp, where Tamara learned to bake fish and molasses-sweetened maize cakes that would be enjoyed by the whole village.

In the days to follow, Tamara learned many of the Indian ways and customs. She watched the young braves breaking the wild horses they captured by riding them to exhaustion in the shallows of the Indian River. She watched small game traps being laid, and learned how to dress the meat for cooking. She watched the women curing the hides and softening them with animal fats. She especially enjoyed making pottery from the thick red mud of the Indian River; it was baked in stone kilns, then painted with dyes made of white oak bark, sumac berries mixed with copperas, and indigo.

Falcon and Flaming Bow returned three days later. They brought back both a wild boar and a seventeen-point stag. Later in the evening, in a gentle embrace within the confines of Falcon's private adobe, he and Tamara made the decision to travel on to Lewes the following morning. They would remain there at Falcon's cottage on the shores of Delaware Bay for three weeks, until the required banns had been published. Thereafter, they would return to Asher Arms and begin preparations for their wedding ceremony.

Although Tamara had affected a happy façade—and most of the time she had been very happy—a certain part of her wept inside. She loved Mason Gray as a father, and Fedora—the elusive love he had lost so many years ago—expected her to keep a very heartbreaking secret. Tamara envisioned the joy Mason would have if he were told about Fedora and Falcon. Yet she was bound by a promise to Fedora—and Falcon—to keep their secret. How could she correspond with Mason and not tell him? It would be the hardest thing she would ever have to do. Yet because she loved Falcon and his mother, she would go against the desires of her heart. Her letters had made Falcon as well known to Mason as if they'd been friends. Mason knew that one day she and Falcon would marry. Soon she would share with him her joyous news of the wedding and of their approaching parenthood. Yet she could not say the one thing she truly wanted to say: "Mason, I have wonderful news for you. Fedora and your son are alive." Rather, she would have to live with the guilt and pain. . . . She almost hated Falcon and his mother for putting her through this torment.

But all the dark powers in the world could not make her hate them. Falcon was her beloved, and his mother was a woman who had, perhaps sensibly, chosen to let the past die. She had made a new life for herself in the Delaware wilderness as Kishke's wife. The life she had shared with Mason had been destroyed many years ago by unfortunate circumstances. Mason had made a life for himself without her, and she without him. Tamara would have to understand Fedora's position and live with it. But she knew it would not be easy.

In his sleep, Falcon turned and embraced her within the confines of his powerful arms. She felt his breath, sweet and gentle, against her cheek. Oh, Falcon . . . Falcon, she thought, feeling tears moisten her eyes in the darkness of the adobe. What am I to do?

It troubled her all night, the problem of Mason and Fedora and Falcon. She heard every sound of the night, the far away howl of the wolves, the scurry of night creatures, the movements of the night guard upon the hill overlooking the village. Every sound magnified the bitterness she felt inside. And she knew, because of her tremendous love for Mason, that she had to make one last plea to Fedora before accepting her decision. Thus, the following morning, after they had dressed and Falcon was preparing the pack horses, Tamara went again to Fedora. "May we speak alone before my departure with Falcon?" Tamara asked.

Fedora was taken off-guard by the urgency in Tamara's voice. She motioned her to the trail that led down to the river. They walked together, then found a comfortable place among the rocks where they could sit. Fedora said nothing but waited for Tamara to speak.

"Fedora, I have a terrible pain in my heart."

Fedora smiled a brief, knowing smile. "Yes, I am aware of it, my child. You are thinking of your guardian. Your heart begs to tell him about us—Falcon and me—but your loyalty prevents you from doing so. You want my permission to tell him about us."

"Yes," she whispered, surprised at her perceptiveness. "That is what I want, Fedora."

Fedora stood, then turned away and linked her fingers. She thought how lovely the Indian River was this morning, breaking gently over the rocks. "Tamara, I shall never forget my first love . . . my only love. But something happened just before I left England . . . something that I have told no one . . . a terrible thing that I have had to live with all my life." She quickly turned back to Tamara, her eyes filmed with tears. "Even if I wanted to see Mason again, I could not, Tamara. I can never again return to England. To do so would be to endanger Mason's reputation. I thank God every day that your father believed we were dead when Mason journeyed to

336

Asher Arms so long ago. I cannot bear the thought of Mason being hurt.''

"Mason has been hurt ever since!" Tamara retorted bitterly. She quickly rose, then enfolded the emotional Fedora within the circle of her arms. "My God, Fedora . . . what on earth are you talking about? What could have happened—"

Fedora gently pulled away from Tamara, then returned to her seated position on the rock. "Sit, please, and I will tell you." Tamara returned to the rock and rested her fingers along the folds of her gown. Her expectant gaze met Fedora's transfixed. "Did Mason ever tell you of a man—Robert Pickford—who was supposed to have been a friend . . . a friend who betrayed Mason and told his father about our marriage and the conception of our child?"

"Yes, he mentioned him once, but not by name."

"He died several months after I was sent away from Gray House to the household of a family in Northampton."

"He died?" Tamara questioned.

"Yes . . . died. . . ." Fedora dropped her eyes. "He died several days after he'd fallen down a flight of stairs."

Tamara stood. "Why are you telling me this, Fedora? What could it possibly have to do with—"

Fedora, too, arose. "It has everything to do with it!" She had not meant to speak sharply, and she immediately softened her voice. "Mason had dissolved their friendship after Robert's betrayal. Robert refused to recognize his own fault and blamed me for it. While Mason was in Scotland, a very drunk and belligerent Robert, wanting only to mend his friendship with Mason, journeyed to Northampton and verbally attacked me, calling me vicious names,

337

threatening me, and saying that I had dragged Mason through the gutter. I asked him to leave and he became even more abusive. I fought him, Tamara, and he lost his footing at the top of the stairs in the servants' quarters and fell. I—I thought he was dead. I truly thought he was dead." She looked to Tamara and met eyes wide with shock. "I wrapped him in canvas, and one of the other servants, an elderly man who had been with the Hedgewick family for many years and who had seen Robert attack me, helped me get him into a wagon. We left him on the road just outside Northampton. Unfortunately, we had not checked his pockets, and he had Master Hedgewick's name and address in his coat pocket. The man who found Robert was a nefarious character—he had taken Robert to a doctor who asked no questions, then had approached Master Hedgewick, asking for gold in exchange for his silence. Master Hedgewick paid him, then conferred with Mason's father as to the course of action to take. Robert died without ever having regained consciousness, and the elderly servant, under pressure from Master Hedgewick, signed a statement that I had murdered Robert. With my young son, I was then placed aboard a ship as an indentured servant and told that if I ever again returned to England, my criminal act would see me hanged and would disgrace Mason and his family. I was forced to sign a renunciation of our marriage. So you see, Tamara, I can never return to England. I am, effectively, a murderess condemned to spend the rest of my life away from my beloved England. Not only would I endanger my own life, but I would disgrace Mason as well."

"But . . . thirty years, Fedora. Who is going to remember?"

"Master Hedgewick's son knows. He was entrusted with my confession and instructed to turn it over to the proper authorities if I so much as contacted Mason by letter. It is best, Tamara, that Mason continue to believe we are dead."

"Perhaps . . . but not Falcon. There is no reason to keep Falcon from his father." Ashamed, Fedora dropped her eyes and Tamara was immediately on her knees beside her. "Falcon was a baby when you left England. Oh, Fedora . . . I can understand the vicious circumstances that thrust you from England. I can understand the injustice that has been done to you—to both you and Mason—but Falcon was an innocent baby. Couldn't Mason know about him? Don't you think that Mason could—would—be able to get this injustice straightened out? He has powerful friends in London."

Silence. Fedora turned her eyes away from Tamara's pleading gaze. She did not know what to say. Was she being selfish? Had her silence done Mason a greater injustice? She had always been firm in her convictions before, but now she had doubts. Then, very quietly, Fedora said, "Fetch Falcon to me, child. I will await him—"

"You wish to see him alone?"

"No . . . the two of you, together. Quickly, child, before I—change my mind."

Tamara rose and walked quickly along the path toward the village. She did not look back at the gently weeping Fedora.

Fedora had lived many years in the Delaware wilderness. She had sometimes been happy—when she hadn't thought of Mason—and had worked very hard at putting the past behind her. Yet she had suspected, when Tamara had returned to Asher Arms and Falcon had confessed his love for her, that the past would catch up to her. There were so many things she hadn't wanted to remember that had now been forced upon her. As she sat quietly beside the Indian River, awaiting Falcon and Tamara's return, she saw the image of Robert Pickford's face clearly in her mind. She hadn't thought of him in years; now he was her nemesis—wrenching her heart into a painful knot. She remembered the shame of what she and the elderly servant had done . . . she remembered overhearing the conversation between Master Hedgewick and Mason's father, and their mutual decision to indenture Fedora and send her far away from England, where, they had thought, Mason would never be able to find her. And through the grace of God, he never had.

"Mother?"

Fedora looked up quickly, then smiled sadly at her son. "Falcon—I hadn't expected you to return so soon. Come . . . sit." He said nothing, but sat against a tree and brushed the ground with his hand when he saw that Tamara planned to sit beside him. He had never seen such despair in his mother's eyes; it alarmed him greatly. He wondered what she and Tamara had discussed, and was a little angry that Tamara had apparently upset her. "Falcon, Tamara and I have been talking—"

"I assumed that, Mother," he replied. "Whatever you have discussed has greatly distressed you."

"Not distressed, Falcon. Concerned, perhaps."

Falcon's fingers were linked through Tamara's; unconsciously they tightened, eliciting a wince of pain from her. "Forgive me," he said, loosening his grip. "Please, Mother, tell me what is on your mind."

"It is your father, Falcon."

"What about him?"

"I feel that it should be your decision whether to make your existence known to him. If you can do so without betraying my whereabouts, or the fact that I am alive, I have no objection to you contacting your father."

"What are you saying?" Falcon's dark, hooded eyes met Fedora's steady gaze. "Are you saying that I must . . . lie, if my father were to ask about you?"

Silence. Fedora thought for a moment, then softly replied, "Yes, Falcon, that is what I am saying. If you choose to contact your father when he asks about me, you must tell him that I am dead."

"I will not do that. I could not do that."

"You cannot ask this," Tamara interjected quietly. "It isn't fair, Fedora. Since I have known Falcon, I have never known him to lie deliberately. What you ask is against everything he believes in."

"What I ask, Tamara," Fedora quietly argued, "is to be allowed to rest in peace and to allow the past to die behind me. Kishke is my husband now. I do not believe Mason would be content to simply know that I am alive. We had been very much in love—I feel, to this day, a very strong tie to Mason—"

"And he for you," Tamara offered.

"He will want to see me. I know this. And—and it cannot be."

"This isn't fair, Mother," Falcon said. "You are giving me permission to contact my father, yet you are also telling me that I cannot. You know very well that I could not resume a relationship with my father only to tell him that you are dead. It isn't fair that you ask me to do this."

"These are my terms, Falcon. You have been a loyal son—a good son—and I ask you to meet my terms without quarrel."

"I decline," he replied, sitting forward. "I prefer

not to contact my father than to be forced to lie to him."

"Falcon . . . no!" Tamara was shocked at this turn of events. She turned her pleading eyes to Fedora. "I beg of you, don't do this to us. If it is what your mother wants . . . please, you must let Mason know! Meet your mother's terms, for God's sake!"

"I will not lie to Mason," he reiterated firmly.

"Then it is settled," Fedora replied.

"You have denied Mason his son!" Tamara argued flatly.

"I have not, Tamara. Here, in the presence of both of you, I have told Falcon that he has my permission to contact his father."

"But your terms—"

Falcon rose hastily to his feet. "We won't argue, Tamara. Mother, as always, I shall respect your wishes. But—may I say—I would prefer that you had made the decision for me than to have forced these unfair terms upon me—"

"The terms shall be moot, Falcon, after my death."

Falcon's narrowed eyes met his mother's in an unblinking gaze. Tamara saw the silent contempt behind his eyes. "You have placed me in a difficult position, Mother. Until you decide to lift the restrictions—" Silence. Unconsciously, Falcon's fingers tightened on Tamara's. "Until then, Mother, I prefer not to see you again."

"Falcon!" Tamara uttered his name, shocked and dismayed at the statement he had just made. Her eyes held his firm profile for a moment, then hastily looked over at Fedora's expressionless features.

Then Falcon turned and dragged the reluctant Tamara behind him on the narrow trail.

In a matter of moments, all they saw of the Indian village was the gently swirling smoke of the cooking fire drifting among the treetops of Falcon's Delaware forest.

*Chapter 23*

Tamara scarcely saw the trees gently swaying in the breeze, or the cumulus clouds easing lazily across the summer-blue skies. Her eyes were moist and blurred, her mind in a dilemma. Falcon had eased his horse into a half-trot, and he held firmly to the reins of the pack horse, which he dragged along behind him. She could scarcely keep pace with him. She kept trying to find words in her tightly-constricted throat, but they would not form on her tongue. She wanted to call him back, to talk sense into him, to plead with him to return to the village before this terrible situation between him and his mother became irreversible. He had completely severed his ties with her. He had forced her to accept his will, and Tamara suspected that she would be just as stubborn as the son she had raised.

Finally, after they had traveled about a mile from the village, Tamara was able to find her voice. She halted her horse and called weakly, "Falcon . . . Falcon . . . please, we must talk." When he continued as if he had not heard her, she called more briskly, "Falcon!"

He halted, repositioned the rein of the pack horse

across the pommel of his saddle, and turned toward her. "Are you all right?" he asked, narrowing his gaze.

"We must talk," she repeated.

"We have traveling to do. As I've told you before, the morning is best for it. The day will get hot in a little while—"

"I don't care!" she snapped, slinging her leg across the saddle and jumping down. "We must talk. We can't—we can't just leave the village like this. For heaven's sake, your mother. . . ." When Falcon did not reply, but continued to look at her, almost hatefully, she continued with haste, "She told me things, Falcon, that you may be unaware of—"

"I know everything about my mother and her past," he replied patiently. "Now, get back on your horse, Tamara, or I will be forced to put you on it."

He had so easily threatened her. Tamara was taken off-guard by the words hissed between his teeth. Nevertheless, she stood her ground, then drew her hands arrogantly to her hips. "To do so will require that you dismount," she replied briskly. "I believe you're too stiff with anger to be able to do so."

Falcon gracefully dismounted, then dropped the reins and turned toward her. "Stiff, am I?" he replied unsmiling, gently mocking her.

The look in his eyes frightened her. Instictively, Tamara took a step back, immediately finding her foot entangled among the ground roots of a large oak. She was kept from falling only by Falcon's firm hands circling her arms above the elbows. "Falcon—what—you are frightening me."

She saw the pain immediately glaze his blue eyes. "Frighten you, Tamara . . . for God's sake! I love you. I would never hurt you. If you don't know that

345

by now, you never will. Perhaps you and I . . . have been a mistake.''

Tamara felt a sudden stilling in her chest. "Never, Falcon. You are upset that ill words were exchanged between you and your mother."

Falcon tenderly drew her into his arms. "Yes, I feel the loss of a friend, Tamara. She and I were so close—"

"It isn't too late, Falcon, to return to the village—"

His grip tightened on her arms and he roughly put her away from him. "I will not retract my words, Tamara. My mother knows how I feel. She knows that I will not back down."

"She is your mother!" Tamara shot back. "She told me things about herself—about the past—"

"What things, Tamara?"

"About Robert Pickford . . ."

"Who?"

She met his steady, unblinking gaze. Her mouth opened, yet the words would not form. It occurred to her that what she and Fedora had discussed might be confidential, just between the two of them. She had not said so, but Tamara felt in her heart that Fedora would expect her to be discreet. How much did Falcon know of his mother? Did he know about the death of Robert Pickford? The glare of puzzlement that now met her indicated that the had not even heard of the man. Dear Lord, she thought, I can say nothing to Falcon . . . nothing about—

"I asked, what things, Tamara? And who is this Robert Pickford?"

Tamara suddenly heard herself saying, "Nothing, Falcon . . . no one at all." She knew in her heart how imperative it was that she talk again with Fedora, and that certain matters be cleared up between them. She would not relay any aspect of their discussion to Falcon without Fedora's permission. "May we please return to the village, Falcon?"

"No." Her lips parted to argue the matter further, but Falcon continued with haste, "We will not return to the village, Tamara! When my mother has a change of heart, then I too shall have a change of heart."

"And both of you are wrong!" she retorted. "Like mother, like son! As stubborn as mules . . . the two of you!"

"And it is between my mother and me," he replied indulgently. "I won't have you interfere again, Tamara. Now." His hands gently caressed her taut shoulders. "Let's not argue, but be on our way. We must make Lewes by tomorrow."

Tamara pulled away, then turned and dropped her forehead into her waiting palms. "We shall not journey on to Lewes, Falcon. I wish to return to Asher Arms."

"We must publish our banns."

She turned back, and her tear-moistened eyes lifted to his. "We will not publish our banns, Falcon, nor will we be married until this thing has been settled and you and your mother have resumed a cordial relationship. I am to blame for what has happened. I have caused all this unhappiness."

"That may well be," Falcon replied between clenched teeth. "But you are not justified in calling off our marriage. It isn't just you and me we must consider, Tamara . . . there is our child."

"Is that why you want to marry me . . . the child?"

"Don't be rash," he retorted.

"I—I apologize, Falcon. Please, take me to Asher Arms. We will have to see how matters settle for us in the future."

"This is blackmail, Tamara."

"Consider it what you will," she replied quietly. "I want only to see things the way they should be. I want you to apologize to your mother, and to assure her that you did not mean what you said."

"You cannot control our lives, Tamara. God knows you've tired."

Tamara spun toward him. "Controlled your lives, Falcon? I've done nothing of the sort. I've wanted only for everyone to be happy."

He was angry, and bitter that she could so easily call off their marriage plans. At the moment he wanted only to hurt her as deeply as she had hurt him. "Happy . . . bah! You've wanted only to control lives, Tamara, the way your father controlled lives. You just said 'Like mother, like son!' It seems to me that the shoe fits either way. 'Like father, like daughter!' Perhaps it's just as well," he turned toward the horses, "that we've called off our marriage. It is a farce anyway!"

Without warning, Tamara turned and fled afoot along the trail. Tears burned her eyes and her cheeks. She did not feel the sharp sting of switches against her tender flesh, but ran where her feet would take her. She did not hear Falcon desperately calling her name. She heard only the dull, rhythmic sound of his boots on hard earth fast approaching her. She felt only his hand briefly at her shoulder, attempting to halt her. Then, without warning, she felt it wrenched painfully away when she fell down the steep ravine and hit her head. She remembered nothing after that—only a dull, painless vortex of swirling fog as the life seemed to rush from her body. . . .

\* \* \*

When she came to she was lying on a blanket beside a summer-warmed creek. Falcon was bathing her face and a small wound on her forehead. Even in her foggy, half-conscious state, she felt the gentleness of his touch. Gradually, her eyes focused on a strong, tense face and eyes that were glazed with worry.

"Tamara, do you hear me?"

"Y—yes," she mumbled, attempting to rise, responding almost immediately to his hands at her shoulders holding her still. "What has happened?"

"You fell, and you're hurt."

"I don't feel—hurt." Instinctively, she put her hand to the small wound on her forehead. There was just a slight bump and it didn't hurt very much. Thus she again attempted to move—and instantly felt an excruciating pain in her right ankle. She cried out. "Oh, Falcon . . . what have I done? And the baby—do you think it is hurt? You must return me to the village."

"No . . . you seem to be a bit bruised and your ankle is strained. So far the baby is unharmed. I've constructed a litter so that I can return you to Asher Arms. It isn't far."

"Half a day's journey, Falcon. Dear Lord." Again she felt tears moisten her eyes. "Because of your stubborn pride, you will make me suffer through a long trip rather than return me to the village."

She was right, of course, he thought, his brows pinching into a frown. She was also right about his being stubborn. He could not argue with her assessment on that score, yet at the moment he was not willing to give an inch. Thus he gently picked her up, positioned her comfortably on the travois he had hastily constructed, and turned the horse on a deliberate course toward Asher Arms.

Throughout the long day she did not speak to him,

but when their eyes met, she gave him a pained look, a look that riddled him with guilt. Falcon had never before realized how truly stubborn he was, and it was a stubbornness that Tamara had thoughtlessly pointed out to him. In mid-afternoon he bathed her ankle in a cool stream, then wrapped it loosely in deerskin and a poultice of water lily roots to reduce the swelling. Even though she was angry with him, she couldn't help but admire his attention to her, as if nothing in the world were important to him except her well-being. He spoke softly to her, even when she did not answer him. And by nightfall, when Asher Arms came into view, their relationship had finally evolved to a state of pointless courtesy.

Falcon took her straight to her bedchamber, then summoned Mrs. Upwood from the servants' quarters to attend to her. Mrs. Upwood immediately made a tea of hops vine, which she forced her to drink, then rewrapped the slightly swollen ankle. Stubbornly, Tamara did not ask about Falcon, whom she had not seen for more than an hour, yet every shadow she spied across Mrs. Upwood's shoulder drew her eyes anticipatingly to the movement. But Falcon did not appear. All day long she had treated him badly, and she knew she would not be able to sleep if she did not apologize. But he did not appear, and, exhausted by the past few days, she did finally fall into a deep, peaceful sleep that lasted well past her usual waking hour the next morning.

While Mrs. Upwood busied herself in the kitchens preparing whatever concoctions were necessary to guarantee Tamara's health, Tamara hobbled about on a makeshift crutch that had been left in her chamber. Awkwardly, she dressed and brushed her hair, then went out to the running pens, expecting to find Falcon there. But he was not. She checked his quarters at the rear of the stables and when she did not find him there either, checked the stall for his horse. The gelding was gone, as was Falcon's pack horse. Tamara dropped heavily to an upturned half-barrel, and clutched madly at her temples.

"Falcon . . . Falcon . . . why must you always flee when there is trouble?"

But there was no Falcon to answer her. Thus she rose, repositioned the crutch, and hobbled back to the parlor of Asher Arms. She knew Falcon well enough to know that he could be gone days, weeks, or months. It all depended on his mood. And right now, it all depended on how badly he was hurting inside.

Three days later Falcon still had not returned. Depressed, ashamed, feeling a bit sorry for herself, Tamara spent many long hours alone, weeping into the soft down of her pillow. Finally it occurred to her that tears would not right the wrong or heal the wounds. Everything seemed to have gone amiss in her life, and neither the sore ankle nor her pregnancy helped her moods of late.

Tamara thought about many things in the long, lonely hours of Falcon's absence. She relived in her mind every moment of their time together. She relived the wonderful days she had spent with Fedora. She even went back so far as to relive the happy moments she had spent with Mason. She realized, sensibly, that she could not allow things to be left as they were. Thus, having a few minutes to herself, she sat at her desk in the corner of her bedchamber and took up pen and paper to write a long letter to Mason Gray. If anyone could provide the answers that she needed, Mason, with his strength and wisdom, surely could. He had never failed her in the past.

351

Several times Tamara began the letter, then wadded it up and threw it to a corner of the desk. Finally, she felt able to compose a letter worthy of sending.

August 20th, 1754,
My dear Mason,

It has been but a little while since I last wrote but, missing you so dearly, I cannot help but spend these few moments renewing my deepest affection for you. So much has happened of late that I simply cannot wait another moment to tell you everything. Too, I pray that, in light of the questions I must ask, you will, in your good time and wisdom, provide answers and relief in my time of trouble.

I have happy news, Mason—our dear Glynnie has married Master Sterling Bain and has moved away from Asher Arms to live with her new husband in Williamsburg, Virginia. I have learned startling news from Glynnie's mother; that she is, in fact, my father's daughter. I am very proud to draw this dear girl to my heart as a sister, and I pray for your happiness as well. Also, jubilantly, I relay to you my firm intentions to wed the man, Falcon, about whom I have written you previously. It is a proud and wonderful confusion to be in love with such a man as Falcon, and I pray you will love him as a son when you meet. I feel confident that you will not be reluctant, Mason, to take him to your heart as you have me.

Tamara started to tell him about her pregnancy, but hesitated. She decided, tactfully and on the spur of the moment, that it would be best to wait. Dipping her quill pen in the inkwell, she carefully continued,

I must tell you that my poor father passed away two months ago. He often spoke fondly of you and I know his respect and esteem for you were high. Falcon and I have managed the estate since father's death and have executed a ten-year contract with Master Bain's estate for the consignment of thoroughbred horses. We both believe it will be a profitable enterprise for Asher Arms.

Mason, as much as I know it pains you, I must ask a question that has troubled me for days now.

Again, Tamara sat back in thoughtful silence. She knew what she had to ask, but not quite how to go about it. It grieved her to think that she might have to lie to Mason, but she knew there was no other way.

Last week, while going through my father's papers, I came upon a letter that must have been written by your beloved Fedora. At this moment, I hesitate to go into its contents in detail, but I ask you to send to me, posthaste, whatever information you have on a Mr. Robert Pickford. Dearest Mason, please be tolerant of my curiosity. I shall, I hope, be able to explain at another time why it is imperative that this information be sent hastily and without delay.

With my deepest affection,
and missing you so much,
Your devoted Tamara

After she had completed her writing and had lain her pen aside, she sat back and read the letter through. It was perfect; she would not have to change a word of it. She did, however, have a pang of conscience that she had not told Mason about the baby she expected.

Strangely, writing the letter had made her feel better. She felt free of the depression for the first time in three days. In fact, she felt almost happy. she folded the letter in thirds, sealed it, affixed her stamp to it, then put it against the candelabra. Tomorrow, she would send one of the servants to the Packard Trading Post, where it would begin the first leg of its three-month journey to Mason. She rose from the desk, then threw herself heavily on the bed.

Through the parted draperies night had fallen. A thin streak of gold parted the timber line from the dark sky, and she lay there silently watching the darkness that had come upon Asher Arms. Sheet lightning sporadically lit the horizon, and faraway rumblings of thunder hinted at the storm heading inland from the Atlantic. It had been dry the past few weeks; a good rain would do them all good, and perhaps wash away a few gloomy dispositions.

Presently she fell asleep. She had deliberately put all thoughts from her mind in those few twilight moments before actual sleep, and when she rose the following morning, she remembered no depressing dreams or thoughts to interrupt her rest. She knew only that she had slept peacefully, and she felt refreshed and vibrant. Even her ankle did not pain her this morning. Thus she rose, walked unsteadily toward her chamber door, and called into the corridor, "Mrs. Upwood, are you about?" Presently she heard the quick footsteps of the smiling servant. "Might I have a bath drawn?" Tamara asked.

"Did you check your bathing alcove, young miss?"

"N—no."

"Do so," she replied cheerfully. "It's ready for you. Why, I can smell the rose water from here."

Tamara shrugged apologetically. "My brain is in a bit of a fog this morning," she said rather sheepishly, pulling back from the doorway.

"How is your ankle?" Mrs. Upwood asked. "Shall I prepare a fresh poultice and bandage?"

"It's better this morning. No need." Mrs. Upwood turned toward the kitchens. "Mrs. Upwood?" She turned back. "Will you let me know if Falcon returns?"

"Certainly, young miss."

Tamara lingered an hour or more in her bath, feeling the satin smoothness of the rose water against her skin. Falcon filled her thoughts. She regretted that she had treated him so badly their last day together, but she felt confident that he would forgive her and return to Asher Arms. They had each other, and they shared the joyous anticipation of their child. Tamara slid down in the cool water, and the golden waves of her hair fell in a silken mass over the side of the tub. She closed her eyes and enjoyed her soothing bath.

Last night's threat of rain had lingered into the morning. The sun slowly slipped away from the window, leaving her chamber in semidarkness. Small droplets of rain became a sudden brutal slash against the windows, and thunder rolled across the skies. A fierce, unexpected crack of lightning made her jump, but she instantly settled back into her bath.

Suddenly, she realized she was no longer alone. Yet she was not alarmed. Rather, she smiled a gentle smile when familiar masculine lips touched her

355

forehead, when familiar masculine hands cupped her face and her mouth was captured in a tender kiss. Without opening her eyes, her arms eased around his shoulders and drew him close.

"Oh, Falcon . . . Falcon, you have returned."

He laughed gently. "My sweetheart, you have gotten soap all over me."

Surprised at his lightheartedness when they had parted on such strained terms, Tamara's eyes slowly opened and met his smiling blue eyes in a dubious gaze. "Do you really mind?" she asked coyly.

"I do not mind," he replied, rising, taking her arms to coax her from the cool bath. "Come . . . you must dry and dress and meet the guest I have brought from Lewes."

"A guest?" she queried. "Mrs. McFurder? Captain Paget?" When he shook his head, she continued curiously, "Who, Falcon? Who might it be?"

"You shall find out," he laughed, "when you come to the parlor." Suddenly the soap slid from her clean flesh, betraying to him her perfect naked form, like a statuesque goddess—the slender hips and legs, her taut, well-rounded breasts and their inviting pink buds, the slight roundness of her abdomen where their child grew. Feeling his physical response to the sensual nearness of her, Falcon averted his gaze and continued in a strained whisper, "I must depart, Tamara, before it is impossible to do so." He picked up the towel from the vanity stool and eased it around her naked form. "You must dress now," he continued with a bit more inflection. "I shall await you in the parlor."

"Falcon?" He had moved toward the door but now turned back. "I acted terribly . . . will you ever forgive me?"

"There is nothing to forgive. You had every right

to be angry. But . . . there are some things I simply will not accept." He approached and tenderly cupped her flushed features. "Dress quickly, and meet the guest I have brought to Asher Arms."

Tamara quickly dried off and found a cream-colored gown in her chifforobe. She dressed hurriedly, pulled her hair into a loose upsweep, and secured it with pearl-studded ivory combs. She lightly pinched her cheeks to add a little color, assayed her final appearance in the cheval mirror, and moved into the corridor. Remembering the letter she had written to Mason, she returned to her bedchamber for it, met Mrs. Upwood in the corridor, and asked that she send one of the servants to Packard's with it. Then she went to the parlor, where Falcon and the mystery guest awaited her.

She entered, limping only slightly, and immediately saw Falcon seated beside the fireplace where a large vase of flowers from the garden hid the sooty blackness of the hearth. A thin, middle-aged man sat on the divan, sipping a goblet of bordeaux. Both men rose when Tamara entered. Tamara thought immediately that the guest seemed pale and sad and vague. But when he spoke, she realized he was merely exhausted from his long journey.

"Miss Fleming." He had set his goblet on a side table and now offered a weak, limp hand which caused Tamara to shudder. "May I say what a pleasure it is to meet you. When do you wish to hold the ceremony?"

"Ceremony?" she questioned. "I—I—"

The gentleman looked surprised. "Your marriage ceremony, Miss Fleming. I am Reverend Hadwin Keefe of the First Lutheran Church of Lewes. I do not journey this far inland to perform a wedding ceremony, but I have made an exception in your case . . . in view of your recent accident.''

Tamara met Falcon's steady gaze. She could not hide her shock and disbelief. All the while she had thought Falcon was gone because he was angry with her. And he had journeyed to Lewes to fetch a minister, so that they could be married! Suddenly, she was both blissful that he cared so much and angered by his egotistical assumption that he could so easily right the wrong. Yet she could not argue with him in the presence of this soft-spoken minister without making him look the fool. She wanted nothing more than to be his wife, but she was still angry that he had found it necessary to plan it this way, without consulting her. Thus, she lowered her eyes and quietly assented.

"Reverend Keefe . . . how long will you be able to stay?" she queried.

"I can stay but a few days," he replied.

"Then the ceremony will take place day after tomorrow. I—I need a day or so to make the preparations." She shot Falcon a secretive, venomous look, then smiled sweetly at the minister. "In the meantime, please make Asher Arms your home. Mrs. Upwood will see to your lodgings. Please . . . excuse me. I must confer in private with my . . . fiancé. Do you have a moment, Falcon?" she continued with sticky sweetness.

Tamara left the house, then moved quickly toward the trail behind the stables. She stopped only when she was several hundred yards from Asher Arms, then turned flashing angry eyes toward Falcon. "How dare you do this without conferring with me?"

His mouth pressed into a thin line. "Do you not wish to marry me?"

Tamara threw up her arms, perplexed. "I want nothing more than to be your wife, Falcon. But—but—oh, what can I say? You do so anger me!"

Falcon approached from behind and tenderly captured her shoulders between his strong hands. His sweet, warm breath whispered against her crimson cheek. "You spoke in anger a few days ago, Tamara. Tell me that you have not regretted your words . . . tell me that you truly want to postpone our wedding. Tell me, if you can do so without lying to me."

She could not, of course, and Falcon knew it. Thus, submitting, Tamara turned into his arms and her cheek rested against his powerful chest, now exposed above the loose rawhide ties of his shirt. "I want to be your wife more than anything in the world, Falcon. However, I had envisioned your dear mother as a witness to our ceremony. But with your vow not to speak to her—"

Instantly, he put her away from him, and he looked rather perplexed. "Then I shall break my hastily spoken vow, Tamara, if that will make you happy. Perhaps I too spoke rashly. I have had several days to think, and I realize that I was too quick to jump to conclusions. My mother did not mean to hurt anyone . . . especially me. I promise, little flower, that I shall send word to the village of our approaching marriage, and make my mother welcome at Asher Arms for whatever length of time you wish her to stay."

Tamara felt happiness bubble within her. "Thank you, Falcon. I—I have been so heavy of heart. You have made me very happy."

Falcon captured her mouth in a tender caress, then drew her to him to feel the warmth of her soft body against his. The hard, brief rain had showered the Delaware forest, and the sun caught the beads of moisture, glazing the trail where they stood in diamond-like rays.

Falcon felt his body respond painfully to the nearness of his beloved . . . his woman. He drew back slightly, then met her smiling eyes, caressing them with a loving gaze. "Now . . . I am very tired. Won't you return to Asher Arms and rest awhile with me?"

She turned and immediately her shoulders were covered by his protective arm. They laughed and joked and held each other as they moved slowly along the trail to Asher Arms and the spacious bedchamber where they would be alone.

# Chapter 24

Tamara had not realized that a simple wedding ceremony could require so much planning. It was too short notice to send news of the marriage to the Bains's Williamsburg estate, but it had been sent by word of mouth throughout the Indian River community, inviting one and all to the celebration of their wedding. Tamara learned that Falcon had gone to the Royal Magistrate in Lewes, had had the required banns waived, and had also secured the license, which would be recorded by Reverend Keefe when he returned to Lewes. Everything seemed to be going perfectly, and the servants combined in a joint effort to prepare the wedding feast that consisted, in part, of thirty pounds of boiled beef tongue and eight roast suckling pigs.

Flaming Bow unwarily happened upon the busy scene the following morning for the purpose of inviting Falcon to join in their late-summer hunt. Falcon, of course, declined, and Flaming Bow offered to take Falcon's written invitation, and apology, back to the village and Falcon's mother before he commenced his month-long hunt deep in the Pocomoke swamp.

Though not on the same grand scale, preparing for her wedding, reminded Tamara of her recent visit to Bain House in Virginia. She suddenly wondered how Glynnie and Sterling were doing, and remembered that they would soon depart for their honeymoon on the European continent. They would not be able to attend her wedding, even if there had been ample time in which to invite them. Tamara did so miss Glynnie and Bridie and Saul and now wished they were at Asher Arms, helping her in these happy preparations.

Late in the afternoon, Mrs. Upwood assisted her in trying on the wedding gown that Mrs. McFurder had sewn some months ago. The ivory satin and crocheted lace seemed heavy as it molded to her slender frame. She wanted to sit a moment, but Mrs. Upwood kept her on her feet, making last-minute tucks to accommodate the roundness of her abdomen.

" 'Tis a good thing, young miss, that you've chosen to be married, what with the wee one growing inside you. The stigma of bastardy is hard to shake in these times. And 'tis the child that suffers—not the parents."

Tamara realized instantly that Mrs. Upwood had not meant to be cruel. Thus she bit her lower lip to keep from responding and patiently allowed the elderly servant to continue tucking and pinning and basting the dress.

That morning, the latest consignment of thoroughbreds had been delivered from Williamsburg. Falcon had already begun working with the horses and was giving his special attentions to a gaited white mare . . . a mare he would present to his new bride as a wedding gift. He had paid for the extra horse prior to leaving Williamsburg and McKenzie Bain had promised an animal "fit for a queen." Falcon was pleased with the choice.

The large iron ovens in the kitchens were kept busy for two days, baking enough food to feed a small militia. Beyond the gardens, the suckling pigs roasted slowly over open fires, emitting an aroma that made Falcon's stomach turn over with hunger. With feigned indignation, the servants kept the bridegroom away from the cooking fires, and he reluctantly settled for the simpler meals prepared for him in the small kitchen at the back of the house.

Falcon dreaded the tense moment that would come when he and his mother saw each other for the first time since their last discussion. She had every right to be annoyed with him, he thought. She should make him suffer for being so stubborn. Many thoughts rushed through his head as he kept himself busy throughout the eve of the wedding, cleaning tack, grooming horses, and reshoeing the sorrel mare Jacob Fleming had given to his daughter.

He was sitting quietly in the lantern-lit stable when he saw the shadow of a woman—Tamara—pass several feet away, heading toward the cemetery just down the hill from Asher Arms. He heard the rustle of her gowns and petticoats and the sudden silencing of crickets as she passed by. His delicate senses detected the sweetness of the lilac perfume she wore. He rose, dropped the hammer to the anvil where he had been working, and approached the stable entrance. As she disappeared beyond the dark timber line, he began to walk slowly in her direction. Even with his eyes closed he could have followed her, for the sweet aroma of her perfume alone would have led the way.

He heard the iron gate of the cemetery creak open and, momentarily, he saw the shadow of her approach her father's grave. Falcon stood in the veil of the dark timber line and watched her drop gracefully to her knees beside the grave. Then he heard gentle weeping, and the shadow of her hand went slowly, caressingly out to touch the recently placed gravestone.

"Oh, Father . . . Father," she whispered. "Tomorrow I shall marry my beloved Falcon . . . and I feel that I have betrayed you. Why couldn't you have understood how much I love him? Why couldn't you have been happy for me and wished me well in my future with him? Oh, why . . . why couldn't you have been more reasonable? Now, I enter my marriage with a sorrowful heart . . ."

Falcon had not felt right eavesdropping on her privacy. But her words startled him, forcing him to make his presence known. "A sorrowful heart, Tamara?" He stealthily come forward and stood in the open gateway. "You will be . . . unhappy in our marriage?"

Tamara rose and hastily moved toward him. Even in the heavy darkness of night, she saw the glimmer of pain in his eyes, as if they had caught a sudden moonbeam. "No, Falcon . . . no," she whispered, taking his hands gently between her fingers. "I could never be happier than I shall be as your wife. It is what I want . . . all I want. Just to be your wife and have your child."

"But you just said. . . ."

She shrugged lightly against him, then dropped her head tenderly to his shoulder. "I was talking to my father . . . wishing that he could have given us his blessing; wishing that he had not been such a stubborn old man. My father has caused the sorrow in my heart, Falcon. Not our love. Oh, please. . . ." Her eyes lifted to meet his dark, hooded gaze. "Be-

364

lieve me when I say that, right now, nothing is more important than us—you and me—and the life we shall make together in this wonderful wilderness. I have been so very happy with you. And tomorrow—'' She smiled a warm, sincere smile. "Tomorrow shall be the first day of our eternal joy and ecstasy, Falcon. I never thought it was possible to be as happy as I am this very minute. I never thought it was possible to love a man . . . any man . . . as much as I love you."

She could tell by the sudden softening of his features that she had pleased him. As his arms slipped around her, she melted into his embrace, molding her body next to his, enjoying the warmth—the desire—that ignored the threads of their clothing and commingled in an aura of misty flame.

"Tell me again that you love me," he whispered, his words caressing the wisps of her golden hair.

"I love you," she responded, nestling against him.

"How beautiful it sounds. Tell me again, Tamara."

Gently, she laughed, "I love you . . . I love you . . . I love you." Then she lifted her smiling eyes to his, unable to restrain her enthusiasm and joy, unable to silence the heavy pounding of her heart that she was sure he could feel against his powerful chest. "I love you, Falcon."

Falcon shrugged playfully against her as his grip tightened. "Well, I knew that—" he responded teasingly, and when, joining in his laughter, she drew back and lightly hit his chest with her fist, he picked her up and swung her around and around until both were dizzy and forced to crumple, together, in a blanket of thick clover. But Falcon immediately regained his footing, then firmly took her hands and pulled her to her feet. "Come . . . let us return to the house and get a good night's sleep before tomorrow comes."

"Oh, I couldn't," she replied happily. "I feel too vibrant and alive to sleep. I think we should . . ." She turned into his arms and her mischievous eyes provoked a smile from him. "Celebrate, Falcon! Let's get everyone from their beds, mother and father and child, and celebrate into the wee hours of the morning!"

"Everyone has been busy," he reminded her, "preparing the feast and making wedding preparations."

She shrugged delicately. "That is true. How thoughtless of me." But she instantly regained her prior good mood. "Then just you and me, Falcon. We shall have . . . a celebration of our own!"

He laughed as he drew her again into his arms. "Very well, love, just you and me, celebrating our happiness. Celebrating a life of eternal togetherness."

Falcon's lips started to meet hers, but just at the moment of touching, a man cleared his throat and stepped from the darkened timberline. It was Meldon Upwood, one of the servants.

"The misses say to return to Asher Arms. The yellow-haired Ind—Falcon's mother has arrived."

It had been many years since Falcon had heard his mother referred to as "the yellow-haired Indian." She had once been widely known as the comely white woman who lived among the trappers and Indians and they had given her the name in a mood of respect and admiration.

Tamara, of course, did not know what Falcon was thinking, or why he remained silent. Thus she replied quietly, "Very well, Mr. Upwood, we'll be right along. Please make Falcon's mother welcome."

When Meldon Upwood had left them alone once again, Tamara turned into Falcon's arms and her hands gently massaged his strong arms. "You are not still angry with your mother, are you, Falcon?"

He looked surprised for a moment. "Angry? Good God, no. I—I was just surprised to hear my mother referred to as Meldon referred to her."

"It is romantic, don't you think? 'Yellow-haired Indian.' Let us make haste. I am anxious to see your lovely mother again. And you—" Tamara laughed a feather-light laugh. "Be nice to her."

Tamara had not meant to scold, but Falcon seemed to take it that way. He held her back when she would have moved toward Asher Arms. "Tamara, Tamara, will you ever forgive me for the tense words I spoke to my mother? You don't know how terrible I feel."

She said nothing, but moved reassuringly close to him. Together they walked toward Asher Arms, enjoying the silence of night and the cool, heady breeze that whipped along the trail.

Fedora had chosen to wait for them on the long porch rather than inside the house. As Falcon and Tamara neared, Tamara broke from Falcon and ran up to meet his mother. She took her hands in a gentle squeeze, then hugged Fedora tightly. "Oh, I am so happy you came," she said quietly. "I was so afraid you wouldn't!"

Fedora smiled at her approaching son across Tamara's shoulder, yet she directed her reply to Tamara. "I wouldn't have missed this for all the world," she replied. "I welcome my new daughter into my heart, and I want nothing more than to witness your exchange of vows with—my son." Falcon approached but said nothing. Then Fedora pulled away from Tamara and met Falcon's gaze. Her face held no expression, and it was evident that she did not plan to commence the conversation. Falcon owed her an apology. Unfortunately, she had left the village before Flaming Bow could deliver her son's brief note.

Falcon looked rather sullen. This man, usually given to command, was suddenly reduced to a quiet state of resignation. He shrugged apologetically. "I gather that you and Flaming Bow have not met today," he said.

"We have not," she replied tonelessly.

"Then how did you know about the wedding?"

"Word travels quickly, Falcon . . . you have lived here long enough to know that."

"And you decided to come to the wedding, despite the words I had spoken?"

"I did," she replied in the same tone. "Your childlike temper will not keep me from my new daughter."

"Childlike temper!" Falcon's hooded eyes narrowed slightly. Yet in the same moment he suppressed his frustration and forced a ragged smile. "You are right, Mother," he said with more inflection. "You know me well enough to know that I spoke rashly and without feeling." Fedora, too, permitted herself to smile. She said nothing, but opened her arms and invited her son into her embrace. "What a woman you are," he whispered, for her ears only.

"So . . ." Tamara now bubbled forth, again taking Fedora's hand. "Did you travel alone?"

"No . . . I was escorted by Kishke's younger son."
Tamara looked around. "And where is he?"

"He went on his way . . . to join Flaming Bow in the hunt."

"Flaming Bow . . ." Falcon interjected, escorting

both women into the parlor, "was supposed to have taken my written apology and invitation to you."

"He may have done so," Fedora offered. "We took a different route in our journey to Asher Arms and may have missed him entirely."

Tamara only now became aware of Fedora's attire—a fashionable dark-blue gown with ecru lace. She was amazed at how easily Fedora led her double life. For a moment, she studied Fedora's features—the sunken cheekbones that had once been round and firm, the slightest discoloration of unlined skin around her sea-green eyes, an unsagging neck. Tamara glanced down, at her slim, firm hands and well-manicured fingernails. It was as if time had stood still for Fedora. She was tall and stately and youthful in her stance. But there was a distinct sadness in her eyes that gave her an aged appearance when her body did not betray it. Falcon did not look anything like his mother. He was the image of his father.

To break her concentration, Tamara bubbled forth, "Well, now that we are together . . . mother, son, and daughter . . . we shall begin our celebration—"

"Perhaps Mother is tired," Falcon offered. Fedora did not respond. Her mind was lost in another time. She looked around a large, well-furnished parlor that had not changed in twenty years. It was exactly the same as she remembered it that night she had fled with her son into a blinding blizzard. "Mother?"

Fedora snapped from her momentary trance. "Oh . . . I do apologize. I was—thinking—the house has not changed at all."

Tamara shrugged apologetically. "I wouldn't know. I've only been here a little over a year."

"Believe me . . . it hasn't," she replied. "Now! What is this about a celebration?"

Suddenly, their moods seemed to commingle into one light, happy one. Falcon poured three goblets of peach brandy, which he passed around. "A toast," he began. "To you, Mother," he said, "and to a happy life. And to you, Tamara—" He smiled as he met her expectant gaze. "whom I order to have a happy life!"

Both women laughed and drank down the brandy. Falcon immediately poured another round. "To you, Fedora," Tamara began in her own toast, "whom I am proud to call mother. And to you, Falcon," she did not smile but held his loving gaze, "the dearest man who has ever lived. How proud I am that you have chosen me as your beloved!"

Falcon's eyes glazed with moisture. But to recover his mood, he quickly drank down the brandy. "Well! How can a marriage go astray with such a toast preceding it?"

Falcon collected the goblets and set them down, but Fedora calmly reminded him, "There are three of us, Falcon . . . I have not offered my toast."

"Ah, more brandy," he laughed, refilling the goblets. "We shall toast ourselves into a state of insensibility!"

Fedora held her goblet gently between her long, slim fingers, swirling the amber liquid as she gazed lovingly into the eyes of her son and his future bride. Then she lifted her glass and quietly began, "To my son, Falcon Gray, who has been a true blessing to me . . . and to my new daughter, Tamara, whom I welcome to my heart." Suddenly, she smiled a smile laced with sadness and regret, "And to my one and only true love. The man I have been unable to forget . . ." she looked directly into Falcon's eyes, "your father . . . Mason Gray."

Without warning, Tamara dropped her goblet to the floor, where it shattered, splashing the peace brandy across the oriental rug. She burst into tears and instantly, Falcon's hands were tenderly caressing her shoulders.

"Oh, Tamara . . . Tamara, I am sorry," Fedora said softly. "I did not mean—"

Tamara, gently squeezing Falcon's hand, turned from him and drew Fedora into the confines of her embrace. "Oh, no . . . no, it's just that you really do love Mason . . . and he's—he's so alone, Fedora. He lost you and Falcon and . . . and me, too. He has no one . . . and it seems so unfair!" She forced a smile, then drew away and her arms eased around Falcon's waist, so that she could enjoy the comfort of his embrace. "Forgive me, I—I've been a bit emotional of late. I don't mean to dampen our celebration. If you'll pour another brandy, Falcon, I wish to seal Fedora's wonderful toast."

The third brandy had been one too many for Tamara. She became lightheaded and giddy and insisted that she would be unable to celebrate further. Falcon summoned Mrs. Upwood, then took Tamara to her bedchamber before returning to the parlor where his mother quietly sat. Falcon absently began picking up the pieces of the goblet that had shattered.

While Tamara slept peacefully on the eve of her wedding, Falcon and his mother spoke well into the night. They reached a mutual decision on a very important matter, but it would be months before Tamara learned of it.

\* \* \*

371

Tamara arose at dawn. She had slept fitfully and felt drugged and tired. She still felt a bit giddy and was disappointed that Falcon had not returned to her in the night. She did, however, enjoy the almost-forgotten habit he had acquired some time ago of placing a single red rose on her window sill. She was drawn toward this renewed sentiment, and toward the refreshing breeze whipping across the garden wall. She looked to the right and beyond the gate, but did not see Falcon at the running pens. He was probably preparing for their wedding that would take place in just over four hours.

An hour later, she met with Reverend Keefe and breakfasted with him. They discussed the wedding ceremony and he was quite surprised when she insisted that the vows be changed to love and honor,'' rather than "love, honor, and obey." It was a request never made of him before. Frankly, he was a little dismayed at Tamara's insurrection against an accepted, and expected, vow of obedience. He departed the breakfast table in a mood of disdain and disapproval.

Soon, Fedora joined Tamara. "Was your chamber comfortable?" Tamara asked.

"Very comfortable," she replied. "I—I've just been walking around the house and the gardens. Many memories have been renewed for me."

"I hope they are not all bad, Fedora."

"Not at all," she replied, smiling. "I had many wonderful moments in this house. I remember your mother, bedridden as she was, her face radiant and youthful, and her eyes so much more alive than her frail body. Oh, Tamara, I remember how much she loved you."

"When things settle down after the wedding, Fedora, won't you stay on for a visit, so that we can talk about Mother? I know so little about her, and there is so much I wish to know."

"I will be happy to, Tamara. In fact," Fedora's hand slid across the table and gently patted Tamara's, "Kishke and I have discussed it at length. If Falcon agrees, I wish to stay on at Asher Arms, to assist you and care for you when your time nears. It will be so wonderful, Tamara, helping you to take care of your baby, as I helped your mother to take care of you."

Tears of happiness moistened Tamara's eyes. "Oh, Fedora, do you mean it? Please, don't jest with me."

Fedora laughed. "I truly mean it, Tamara. It will please me to be with you . . . and Falcon."

"What is this conspiracy?" Suddenly, Falcon's husky voice reverberated from the foyer. He entered the dining room with his thumbs tucked over the waist of his trousers.

Tamara laughed. "No conspiracy, Falcon . . . wonderful news. Fedora is going to stay on and help me until after the baby arrives."

"Good!" he said shortly.

"Of course, son, if you would rather I not—"

Falcon sat, then carelessly lifted his foot to the chair beside him. "I can think of nothing I'd like better," he replied, "than to know Tamara is well cared for by another woman . . . by my mother."

Tamara suddenly realized that it was bad luck to see the bridegroom before the wedding. "Whatever are you doing here, Falcon?" she asked.

"Reverend Keefe just approached me about something you'd requested. You upset the old boy but, frankly, I don't see what the fuss is. I tried to explain that I was taking you as a wife, and not a servant, but I believe I managed to ruffle his feathers a bit more. He walked off, mumbling something about

'What the world is coming to.' " They all laughed together, then Falcon's hands slid across the table and embraced both Tamara's and Fedora's. "How can a man be so lucky—to have a wonderful woman who will soon be my wife, and a mother who has raised me to deserve her. I love you both!"

Fedora gently withdrew her hand. She rose. "Before Tamara can be your wife, we must have a ceremony . . . and we cannot have a ceremony until we have dressed the bride. Now, Falcon . . . you'd best see to your own preparations while Tamara and I retire to the dressing chamber."

Just as she disappeared into the corridor, Tamara turned and blew Falcon a kiss. She just missed his smile, and his hand rising to his lips, to return her sweet sentiment.

Mrs. Upwood's talents as a seamstress left something to be desired. The threads of her tight stitches in Tamara's wedding gown showed in a few places, requiring Fedora to redo some of the work. Her intentions had been good though, and when she appeared just before the ceremony to inquire about her work, Fedora explained that it had been fine.

Tamara could hear the hustle and bustle of guests arriving for the ceremony. She heard children laughing and playing just beyond the gardens, and heard many horses pulling at tethers and nickering among themselves. She heard the occasional clatter of wagon wheels and was delighted that so many from the Indian River community had chosen to attend the celebration. Mrs. Upwood, again not intending to be malicious, was quick to explain that "where there is food to be eaten, the ants will swarm in droves."

Finally, Fedora fastened Tamara's veil in place and secured it with ivory combs decorated with tiny silk flowers. She then removed a delicate white shell bracelet from her wrist and slipped it over Tamara's. "A little gift for you," she said lovingly. "It was all I had."

"Oh, thank you, Fedora . . . it is lovely," Tamara replied, hugging her tightly.

Suddenly, organ music began to play and Tamara looked at Fedora as if her ears were deceiving her. "Fedora, do you hear something? Tell me I have not lost my mind."

Fedora laughed. "Mrs. Upwood had an old organ in her cottage, which she played when she was young. It has been cleaned and tuned and that is what you hear. No, dear girl," Fedora continued, patting her arm reassuringly, "you have not gone mad." The wedding march began to play. "Come . . . it is time that you and Falcon exchanged your sacred vows."

Quickly, Tamara turned and assayed her appearance, the tight-bodiced cream-colored gown with its flowing skirts, the matching veil and silk flowers pressed into the clean masses of her golden hair. She noticed the crimson rising in her cheeks and she realized, suddenly, that she was all aflutter inside. She scarcely felt the bouquet of roses tied with masses of rose-colored silk ribbons that Fedora pressed into her hand.

The wedding would take place in the gardens, which had been decorated with floral-covered trellises and stone pedestals holding urns of red roses and bridal wreath. Tamara felt her knees begin to buckle beneath her, and with the strength of Fedora's presence, she allowed her feet to carry her slowly toward the music of the organ that Mrs. Upwood played, occasionally striking a wrong note. Then she stepped into the bright sunlight and saw the minister and Falcon, who awaited her against the east wall of the garden.

She hadn't seen Falcon look so handsome since the night of Captain Paget's ball. He was wearing tight black breeches and white stockings, and his black patent shoes were adorned by large gold buckles. His ruffled jabot was high and tight at his neckline and his black velvet coat fit snugly across his broad shoulders. His passion seemed to encompass her and draw her hypnotically toward him. She felt her footsteps moving to the rhythm of the organ, and suddenly she felt terribly alone among the many strange faces and expressions.

The path from the house to the makeshift pulpit where Reverend Keefe stood seemed a thousand-mile walk to the trembling Tamara. She felt almost exhausted as she momentarily felt Falcon's hand gently ease out and draw her arm into his own. Then they turned and faced Reverend Keefe, who seemed to have engaged a calmness all his own.

Quietly, he began speaking. "Dearly Beloved: Forasmuch as Marriage is a holy estate, ordained of God, and to be held in honor by all, it becometh those who enter therein to weigh, with reverent minds, what the Word of God reacheth concerning it:

"The Lord God said, It is not good that the man should be alone; I will make him an helpmeet for him.

"Our Lord Jesus Christ said: Have ye not read that He which made them at the beginning, made them male and female, and said, For this cause shall a man leave father and mother, and shall cleave to his wife; and they twain be one flesh? Wherefore, they are no more twain, but one flesh. What therefore God hath joined together, let no man put asunder."

Tamara met Falcon's loving gaze. As they held

each other in a gentle embrace, the words of the soft-spoken minister seemed to drift away. They were lost in their love for each other, and in this moment that would bind them together, for all time, as man and wife . . . a future that they both wanted so very much. And only when Reverend Keefe spoke Falcon's name did they avert their gaze from each other.

"Falcon . . ."

There was no response.

Reverend Keefe gave him a quizzical look. He knew the man only as Falcon and felt the awkwardness of the moment.

"Falcon Gray," Falcon whispered discreetly.

"Falcon Gray," the reverend began again, "wilt thou have this woman to thy wedded wife, to live together after God's ordinance in the holy estate of Matrimony? Wilt thou love her, comfort her, honor and keep her, in sickness and in health, and forsaking all others, keep thee only unto her, so long as ye both shall live?"

Falcon's gaze again met Tamara's. "I will," he said quietly.

"Tamara Fleming, wilt thou have this man to thy wedded husband, to live together after God's ordinance in the holy estate of Matrimony? Wilt thou love, honor and . . ." Reverend Keefe cleared his throat, and just for a moment, his mouth pressed into a disapproving line. "Love and honor him," he began anew, "comfort him, and keep him, in sickness and in health and, forsaking all others, keep thee only unto him, so long as ye both shall live?"

Tamara's eyes had never left Falcon's. "I will," she replied.

Then Falcon took her right hand and repeated after the minister, "I, Falcon Gray, take thee, Tamara

Fleming, to my wedded Wife, and plight thee my troth, till death us do part.''

Tamara then repeated her vows, scarcely recognizing her own voice, which seemed uncustomarily feeble. She had long prided herself on her strength and indomitable courage. "I, Tamara Fleming, take thee, Falcon Gray, to my wedded Husband, and plight thee my troth, till death us do part.''

Then the trembling Falcon took the ring from the pocket of his coat and placed it gently on Tamara's finger. He repeated after the minister, "Receive this ring as a token of wedded love and troth.''

"Forasmuch as Falcon and Tamara," the reverend continued, "have consented together in holy wedlock, and have declared the same before God and in the presence of this company, I pronounce them Man and Wife, In the Name of the Father and of the Son and of the Holy Ghost, Amen.

"What God hath joined together, let no man put asunder.''

Tamara and Falcon were lost in the wonder and ecstasy of their love and adoration. They cared only that they had spoken their vows and that they had been declared legally to be man and wife. They cared only that they were one in God's eyes, and the remainder of Reverend Keefe's service did not matter. A foggy vortex surrounded them, imprisoning them within the confines of each other's loving gazes. Suddenly, the faces of wedding guests were mere blurs, the ground and the forest and the skies became, also, an indistinguishable blur, creating a wonderful state of aloneness for two people whose worlds revolved only around each other. They scarcely realized the service had ended until they were surrounded by loud, boisterous well-wishers, and were being hugged, in turn, by Asher Arms's residents and friends.

Then the celebration, drinking, and feasting began, a merriment that lasted well into the late hours. The exhausted Tamara and Falcon retired to their bedchamber as man and wife. Yet when the door had closed to the bawdy celebrating out-of-doors, their exhaustion was forgotten. They met in a tender embrace and held each other for a long, long while, without speaking, enjoying the loving comfort of each other, and wanting only for their togetherness to go on forever and ever. That it would—could— end was unfathomable, an impossibility, something that could never be. Eternity was theirs to be shared together.

After a moment, Falcon put her gently away from him, then cupped her lovely features tenderly. "I thought it would be different after we were married," he whispered. "But it is not. I thought I would love you more, but I don't. It is impossible, to love you more than I already do."

"I am so happy," she whispered in reply. "And—" She fidgeted with the bodice of the gown she'd been wearing all day. "I want to get out of this gown and be comfortable."

Teasingly, he whispered, "I want you out of it, too."

"Oh, Falcon!" She lightly touched his shoulder, then turned away from him. "Won't you undo the stays, before I smother?"

She dropped her head, then lifted her hair so that he could unfasten the stays of the tight-fitting gown. She felt relief as the weight of the gown fell from her slender form, then she stepped out of it and her massive petticoats as if they were one garment. Momentarily, she dropped her hair, then she felt Falcon's hands rise and tenderly caress her bare shoulders. He eased the shoulder of her camisole down her arms, to be discarded along with her other garments, exposing her well-formed breasts, which he touched gently. Then he stood patiently as she began loosening the jabot at his neckline and did not, at once, meet his alluring gaze. But when she did, shyly, lift her eyes to meet his own, she was immediately surrounded by the piercing warmth of those twin shards of blue fire. And his mouth, blazing like passion's oils, captured her own in a fierce kiss that destroyed any concern she may have had.

The bed, with its covers drawn back, invited them into cool satin sheets. Falcon picked Tamara up in his strong, powerful arms, gently put her on the bed, and adjusted the pillow beneath her head. His eyes did not leave hers as he methodically discarded his clothing to a pile beside her own, then eased into the bed next to her. How lovely she was in her tantalizing state of nudity, which she did not attempt to hide beneath the sheets, her soft, warm body molding against his hard one, safe and secure in his protection and his loving arms. There was almost an urgency in their togetherness this time, and Falcon found the preludes to their lovemaking an encumbrance rather than a pleasure. Her body moved erotically beneath his masterly, commanding caresses, and her heated flesh rose to meet his hands. She drew him near, and invited his mouth to her own. His tongue playfully teased her own and his hand slipped between her thighs, feeling them tighten just for a moment before they fell apart and met his tender entry into that sweet, warm place that begged for him.

"Tamara . . . Tamara . . . I cannot bear this. I must have you—now." Then, without further prelude, knowing that she was as ready for him as he for her, Falcon buried the full, throbbing length of himself deep within her. For moments that seemed like hours they rocked together, in gentle unison . . . on a vast, endless plane, rising, rushing, enveloped within the foggy mist of their inexplicable passion . . . feeling the heat of desire slowly enflame their bodies until there was no turning back. Nothing existed for them as their ecstasy fragmented into the vast universe and they slowly, oh, so slowly drifted back to reality, their ragged breaths slowing in gentle unison as they clung to each other, refusing to unfuse their bodies and become separate and distinct, refusing to allow this earthbound plane to rob them of their unfulfilled hunger and unquenched thirst. As the fire flamed to life again, they began to rock together, imprisoned by urgency, the blinding paroxysm of prowess and passion drawing them together like a magnet. In the warm, welcome nest of each other's arms, they soared far, far away, to a bright, elusive star that existed only for them, and they fused together in wild, frenzied abandon until the earth captured them once again.

*Part Three*

## Chapter 25

*Asher Arms, Seven Months Later*

Tamara resisted the intrusion of the first light of dawn at her bedchamber window. She'd had an uncomfortable night, had been unable to eat anything substantial in two days, and felt clumsy and ugly in her advanced state of pregnancy. And Falcon's frequent compliments that she'd never looked lovelier didn't really help matters much. She merely considered them the basic little untruths—to save feelings—of a doting husband and soon-to-be father.

She pulled herself to a seated position, then fluffed the pillows behind her. Momentarily, Fedora appeared with her breakfast tray and a demure plea that she "try to eat a little this morning." When she adjusted the tray and turned to leave, Tamara took her hand and kept her from walking away.

"Please, won't you stay, Mother? I—I really don't want to be alone."

"You're—upset?" Fedora asked cautiously.

"Not upset . . . just a little hurt."

"Because of Falcon?"

Tamara shrugged delicately. "For the past week,

mother, he has chosen to sleep in another chamber. I do believe he fears he'll roll over in his sleep and hurt the baby—"

Fedora laughed delicately. "He sleeps in another room, Tamara, because you've not been feeling well—"

"I believe it's because I'm fat!" she argued demurely. "And he thinks I'm ugly and disgusting—"

"And I know my son well enough that, fat or not, he will return to your bed when you are feeling better. He loves you very much. Now that your time is near he wants to be with you . . . near you. And nothing, not even a round belly, will keep him from your bed. You must have faith in your husband." Tamara looked a little sheepish but still managed a smile. "Your time is very near." Fedora enveloped Tamara's hand fondly between her own. "This is why Falcon has asked me to take the adjoining chamber, so that I will be close by when your dear little one decides to make its appearance."

"Perhaps you're right," Tamara replied, picking up her fork, immediately stabbing at the lumps of egg on the still-warm plate. "Oh, do I have to eat this?"

"You don't have to . . . but I wish you would."

Tamara eased a tiny bit of the egg into her mouth and began to chew slowly. "Where is Falcon?" she asked, swallowing, discreetly putting down the fork and hoping Fedora wouldn't notice. But she did, and looked sternly at Tamara's hand until she raised it once again.

"He has gone to the trading post, to collect whatever mail has arrived for Asher Arms, and to pick up a few supplies. He will hurry back to be with you."

Tamara dropped the fork and nestled, for a moment, into the soft down of her pillow. Absently, her hand rose to her firm, round abdomen. "Oh, Fedora, why hasn't the baby come yet? Surely it must be just about time."

"I would imagine you've got a week or so to go. Besides . . . babies come when they are ready," she offered, "not when the mother is tired of being fat."

"I wonder if it'll be a girl or a boy."

"Just pray for a healthy baby, Tamara."

"I do . . . yes, I do," Tamara hastily replied, wishing to assure Fedora that either gender was welcome. Suddenly, she thought about her mother's diary, and her delicate hand writing of her father's disappointment that his child had been born a girl. What if Falcon felt that way? Oh, what would she do if he were truly disappointed that she hadn't given him a son?

So deep in thought, Tamara only now realized that Fedora had risen and was moving toward the doorway. Before Tamara could ask for an explanation, Fedora turned and said simply, "Eat, Daughter." Tamara listened to her retreating footsteps in the corridor.

She promptly put the breakfast tray aside and rose from the bed. She could see a heady March wind whistling through the still winter-barren garden and across the wall, to scatter among the firs and the naked branches of the mighty oaks. The winter had not been so bad this year, perhaps, she thought shrugging, because she had stayed indoors most days, safe and secure in front of a blazing fire.

To put herself in a better mood, Tamara chose a bright rose-colored gown—a shift, actually, that Fedora had made for her—brushed her long hair and left it loose down her back, then touched a little color to her pallid cheeks.

387

She was still a bit concerned about Falcon's reaction to the possibility of a girl child. Every time he had spoken of the baby, he had referred to it as "he." Again Tamara's hand fell to her abdomen and she quietly said, "If you're there, little girl, the first thing you must do when you're born is to give your papa a big, big smile to win his heart."

Just before she left her bedchamber, she took the plate from the breakfast tray, went over to the window, and scraped it to the ground, where it was immediately pounced upon by a small dog from the servant's quarters.

Fedora and Mrs. Upwood were dusting in the parlor when Tamara entered. "May I help?" she asked.

"Indeed not!" Mrs. Upwood scowled, clicking her tongue. "You should be in bed."

Tamara turned away. "Oh, poof! I'll get bedsores if I stay another moment in bed! I'm very healthy, you know."

"Nevertheless," Mrs. Upwood continued to argue, "you shouldn't be up and about in your delicate condition."

Tamara said nothing but merely shrugged her shoulders and half-smiled at the silent Fedora.

Then, while the two women busied themselves in the house, Tamara protected her shoulders beneath a thick white shawl and eased out to the porch without detection. It was a little cool, but she was tired of being cooped up in the house and thus found it refreshing. A walk would be welcome right now and would help to ease the boredom she had felt for some days while the women had kept her confined to her bed. She moved quietly toward the trail behind the gardens. She was aware that the boy, Drew, had watched her disappear into the shadows of the timber line.

She'd never before realized how beautiful March could be, with winter hanging on by just a thread, and spring just around the corner, showing itself, first, by the wildflowers lightly scattered throughout the forest. She'd felt ill for days, but now, walking in the cool, refreshing breeze, she felt vibrant and alive once again, and able to face the day, and tomorrow, and all the tomorrows hence. She so looked forward to the wonderful state of motherhood that would soon be upon her. She imagined herself looking down into a cherubic face, and dark eyes that would gradually become like her warm brown ones, or Falcon's startling blue ones. She imagined tiny fingers wrapped around her own, and a tiny button nose, and plump, crimson cheeks. Oh, how happy she was! she thought, lifting her face to the very faint warmth of the sun among the glittering trees.

Suddenly, the wind was like a whispered warning and she had the eerie feeling that someone watched her. With guarded vigilance, she turned on the trail, then stood for a moment unmoving, waiting for that sound—like dry twigs snapping—to break again the silence of morning. Quietly she began to move along the trail, and very soon she saw the rooftop of Asher Arms across the timber line. She did not look behind her, but felt still the piercing eyes and the veil of fear that had so suddenly surrounded her. She was breathing raggedly as she eventually closed the foyer door and stood there for a moment, trying to still the rapid beating of her heart.

"Where have you been, young miss?" Mrs. Upwood's portly frame filled the doorway to the parlor. She had a most annoying habit of drumming her fingernails on her ample hips when Tamara had done something she felt she shouldn't have.

"I—I was taking in the cool air," she replied. "I thought I heard someone . . . out on the trail."

"Well! You shouldn't have been out-of-doors!" Mrs. Upwood scolded. "Serves you right if you had a scare!"

Tamara felt a lump rise in her throat, but coughed delicately to dispel it. She'd been on edge of late and was not in a mood to be scolded like a naughty child. She shrugged her shoulders, caught her shawl as it began to slip, then moved quietly toward the corridor and her bedchamber.

Then everything happened at once. She heard the sudden, frightened cry of one of the servant's children, then the whinny of a horse fast approaching the house. Quickly Tamara moved to the parlor window and saw a child lying on the ground, his mother rushing toward him. But the child sprang to his feet and moved quickly toward the cabin with his mother. Before any of the women in the house could react to the alarm, the door burst open and a large, burly man entered the foyer. He stood there, his feet apart in an arrogant stand, his hand firmly clutching a musket. A rawhide whip was coiled around his thick shoulder.

"Broggard! What are you doing here?" Mrs. Upwood moved toward him, but the whip eased threateningly down from Broggard's shoulder. Sensibly, knowing only too well both Broggard and his penchant for using the ugly coiled serpent that he kept constantly with him out-of-doors, Mrs. Upwood backed away.

Tamara was in a mild state of shock. She stood stiffly against the window, then backed into the draperies, half burying herself in their massive folds. Then Broggard's beady eyes turned full to her, and a wry grin twisted his mouth.

"Wh—what do you want, Broggard?" she asked, her voice trembling with fear.

"Falcon . . . where is Falcon?" he asked in a deep, husky, and probably drunk voice.

"H—he's not here. What do you want with him?" Tamara did not know where her strength came from as she stepped away from the window, then moved into the middle of the parlor and stood there, absently shuffling her foot.

Again, Broggard exhibited his wicked grin. "Falcon and I—have unfinished business."

"What unfinished business?" she asked in a strong voice.

Arrogantly, Broggard moved into the parlor, then threw his huge frame down into one of the delicate Queen Anne chairs beside the hearth. "I had some friends . . . Iroquois warriors. About a year ago, Falcon hunted them down and killed them . . . most of them."

"I—I don't know what you're talking about." Then she remembered Flaming Bow being taken captive by the Iroquois, and Falcon's pursuit to save his friend. "You don't mean . . . the barbarians who took Flaming Bow, do you?"

"They were my friends, missy," he said between clenched teeth.

"Did you come here for revenge?"

Broggard's black, spiked teeth chewed disgustingly on a large wad of tobacco. "Revenge? Hell, no . . . just want to talk to Falcon."

"Why have you waited so long to discuss this with him?"

"Didn't know about it until recently. I ran into a bit of trouble in Pennsylvania, and just got back into these parts. Falcon made a mistake, missy . . . he should have killed the redskins who were drunk when

391

he killed the others still sensible enough to fight. I might never have known about the deaths of my friends.''

''Friends!'' she spat at him. ''What kind of man befriends murdering Indians! What kind of man,'' she continued carefully, ''pulls the lever at hangings, and mutilates naked backs with the cat-o'-nine-tails!''

Broggard ignored her outburst but secretly prided himself in the accomplishments she had thoughtlessly pointed out to him. He waved a long, thick finger at Tamara. ''Looks like, miss, you got yourself into a bit of a mess. Falcon's bastard, eh?''

''Falcon is my husband!'' She did not like the way he looked at her or the way his beady little eyes had settled on her rounded abdomen.

Mrs. Upwood had crept away and now returned with Fedora, who held a knife behind her back. ''What do you want here?'' Fedora asked. ''You have no right to come here.''

Broggard smiled a wicked smile. ''You, Yellow-haired Indian, sit down and shut up.''

''I shan't do—''

''Please!'' Tamara's hand went quickly around Fedora's shoulders. ''Please do as he asks.'' Dear God, she thought, where is Falcon? Why doesn't he return home? What are Broggard's intentions? She could not bear the uncertainty and decided, on the spur of the moment, that it was better to know, so that they could act accordingly. ''Do you intend to kill my husband?'' Tamara quietly asked.

Broggard continued chewing the tobacco, then pulled at his groin. ''Sure do, missy.''

''But why? He has done nothing to you!''

Broggard pulled himself forward in the chair, checked the musket that had been lying parallel to

392

his leg, then repositioned the flint. "Don't forget what he did to my friends, missy. Our feud goes back a long, long time. And I promise you that the moment he shows up through that window there, I'm going to put a hole through him bigger than Delaware Bay. Yup, missy, that's what I'm goin' to do. Besides—" He again settled back. "Your pa's probably turning over in his grave, you bein' big in the belly with Falcon's bastard. We'll put the old man to rest and who knows, you'll probably be better off without 'im."

Through the open window Tamara saw the armed men from the servant's quarters darting about, assuming positions behind barrels and wagons and the corners of buildings. She didn't know what she and the other women inside the house could do, except sit quietly and pray to God that no one got hurt. She was angry and bitter that one man could cause this much fear and wield this much power over so many.

They were forced to sit in the parlor for hours, beneath the close scrutiny of Broggard and the threat of his loaded musket. The fire died down in the hearth and Broggard would not allow Mrs. Upwood to bring fresh logs in. The three women sat together, each devising in her own mind some plan to end this dreaded vigil. Fedora had secretly forced the large kitchen knife into Tamara's hands, with a discreet warning to "protect herself if it became necessary." But no sensible plan to stop Broggard materialized and each, silently, knew she would do nothing to endanger the other.

Twilight had just fallen when the sound of an approaching horse echoed from the trail. Despite her condition, Tamara sprang from her seated position, but Broggard threateningly waved her down with the musket. Then, simultaneously, the women saw Falcon's horse approach the stables where he dismounted, only to be immediately drawn behind a wagon by an alarmed masculine voice. Through tear-filled eyes Tamara saw him look toward the house.

"Oh, please . . . please, Falcon," she whispered, "Stay where you are."

But without a thought to his own safety, Falcon slowly began walking across the clearing. The grinning Broggard arose, then moved confidently toward the foyer.

"Dear God," Tamara cried, "he's going to kill my husband."

Without warning, the agile Fedora sprang past Broggard and pulled open the door. "Falcon . . . he's armed," she screamed, moving quickly across the porch toward him.

Then, like an exploding cannon filling the air, Broggard fired the musket. Fedora screamed, then instinctively flew forward into the shocked and bewildered Falcon's arms. But she was not struck by the bullet. Rather, across Fedora's shoulder, Falcon saw a faceless form crumple dead to the foyer floor, his blood spattered body convulsing in the last throes of life. His musket had backfired.

Slowly, Falcon dropped to his knees, taking the weight of his mother's sobbing form with him. "Dear God . . . where is Tamara?" he whispered harshly.

In that same moment, with confusion running amok and servants resuming positions closer to the house, Tamara quietly stepped over Broggard's dead body, then left the dark interior of the house. She stood there trembling and was held up only by a servant who had seen her stagger and rushed to her side.

Mrs. Upwood was clutching madly at her temples and screaming as her husband rushed into the house.

Tamara did not remember walking past Broggard. She remembered only Falcon's strong arms slowly encircling her, and the still trembling Fedora's soothing words. She felt only the darkness that surrounded her and being pick up in Falcon's arms. Momentarily, she felt the soft fullness of the divan and Mrs. Upwood rushing back from somewhere far away with a cup of cool water.

"I—I am sorry," she whispered, her eyes focusing on the worried faces of Falcon and Fedora. "I don't know what came over me. Is—is everyone all right?"

"Don't speak, Tamara," Falcon spoke soothingly. "It is you we are worried about now." In the background, several of the servants were removing Broggard's body. One of the men had placed a large piece of white cloth over his mutilated face and Tamara turned her head instantly at the sight of so much blood seeping through the fabric. She felt sick to her stomach.

Suddenly, she was seized by an excruciating pain in her midriff. "Falcon . . . Mother," she half sobbed. "I—I feel as though I might die."

Fedora's features darkened with alarm. "Quick, Son, we must take her to her bedchamber. Mrs. Upwood . . . please, gather clean linens."

"Mother, is she—"

Falcon did not finish the statement. His mother had nodded, yet he saw only the deep lines of worry that creased her face. Instantly, he picked Tamara up and moved toward her bedchamber.

* * *

Word of the near disaster as Asher Arms traveled quickly. Kishke, accompanied by Flaming Bow and another brave of the village, arrived at Asher Arms the following morning to escort Fedora back to the village. However, she refused to leave. Right now, she pleaded quietly, her place was with her son and his wife.

The upset that Tamara had suffered had forced her into labor and now, because of the tragedy that had gripped Asher Arms, both she and Falcon's child might die. Falcon was very angry and very bitter, and had not spoken since yesterday evening, when his mother had shut him out of the birthing chamber. "It is not a place for men," she had said. He stood and watched his three Indian friends disappear onto the forest trail and remembered the anguish in Kishke's leathery features as their eyes had met in a silent, undemanding gaze. He remembered Kishke's hand coming up to grip his shoulder for one brief moment, a moment meant to comfort Falcon when Kishke knew that Falcon was like a battlefield inside, wanting only revenge.

Falcon turned and reentered Asher Arms. He went immediately to the corridor outside Tamara's chamber and sat quietly in a chair to await the birth of his child. Fedora and Mrs. Upwood attended Tamara, and Falcon heard not the strong-willed Tamara's cries, but the soothing, worried voices of the two older women. He knew that Tamara would be strong despite her pain. He tried to convince himself, even though he did not feel it inside, that she and their child would survive this ordeal.

So that he himself would survive the long hours he would have to wait, Falcon tried to comfort himself with happy thoughts. He remembered those last few hours of his travels before reaching Asher Arms. He remembered enjoying the crisp March wind, stopping beside a cool creek winding among the hills and dales, and bathing his dusty, travel-weary face. He remembered thinking of his beloved Tamara, and wanting only to return to Asher Arms to be able to rest his head gently upon her abdomen and feel his child fluttering with life. How happy had been these last few months as they had joyfully awaited the arrival of this beloved child together.

And now, just fourteen hours later, she lay in agonizing labor, with her life and the life of their unborn child hanging on by a thread. She and Fedora might have lost their lives, and he silently convinced himself that the whole ordeal might not have happened if he hadn't been away from Asher Arms. He imagined his beloved Tamara lost from him forever. He thought how tragic would have been the death of his mother if Broggard's musket had not backfired. He imagined her sea-green eyes, glazed with love and adoration for them all just hours before, never beholding the firstborn grandchild she had awaited as joyfully as had they. He imagined her arms never being filled with the warm, blanketed bundle whose expected arrival had brightened her eyes.

Distraught, Falcon buried his face in the palms of his hands and closed out all sounds of the morning. He closed out the very delicate cries of his wife just beyond the door. If Tamara died, he would want to die too.

"Falcon?" Quickly, he looked up into Fedora's emotionless eyes. Her arms clutched a small, blanketed form securely to her. "You have a lovely daughter, Falcon." He rose, disbelieving, then approached and looked down into the pink, pinched features of his newborn daughter. Instinctively, his hand rose to touch a tiny hand no larger than his thumb. Then, hearing no sounds from within the birthing chamber, his worried eyes met Fedora's. "Tamara sleeps peacefully, Falcon," she said quietly. "You may go in to her while I see to your daughter."

Mrs. Upwood's proud smile met Falcon when he entered, then she eased past him into the corridor. Falcon approached the bed, then fell to his knees to take Tamara's deathly white hand and draw it to his cheek. He had never seen her looking so exhausted or so pale. Her translucent flesh was like fine porcelain, fragile even to the tenderest touch. He had so greatly feared that she and their child would leave him alone in this land he had once loved above all else not of flesh and blood. Quietly, he dropped his head to the pillow and wept with relief. He had never before realized how much he loved her. Seeing her like this wrenched his heart, like a vicious, lethal hand.

Over the following weeks, matters slowly returned to normal. Their infant daughter, whom they called Rebecca, grew bigger and healthier each day. Just this morning, she had smiled her first smile for her papa, who had cooed adoringly at her before surrendering her to her mother.

Falcon and Tamara, leaving the baby in the care of her grandmother, frequently took long walks along the familiar trails surrounding Asher Arms. On this lovely April morning in the year 1756, with a pre-summer breeze whipping around their slowly moving forms, so close together that not a breath of space existed between them, they envisioned only happiness in the days ahead.

With their six-week-old daughter resting peacefully in her doting grandmother's arms, Tamara and Falcon stole a few intimate moments together off the trail in a quiet little dale where a babbling brook ran peacefully on its journey toward the Indian River.

Only happiness lay ahead for them.

## Chapter 26

The following morning, Flaming Bow and seven other young braves arrived at Asher Arms. A small band of Iroquois renegades had been spotted in the vicinity over the past two weeks, and the Royal Magistrate in Dover had dispersed a company of the Delaware Militia throughout the colony. Flaming Bow, whose heart had too recently been pierced by Iroquois brutality, had formed his own war party. He planned to follow the trail of the savage tribe, which had already left a scattering of dead bodies across Delaware, Maryland, and Pennsylvania.

Falcon, however, declined to join in the manhunt. As he explained to Flaming Bow, he had his own family to think about, and a new consignment of horses from Virginia that needed to be broken in order to meet Asher Arms' commitment to the New York auctions later in the month. He did offer a dozen eighty-caliber pin-fastened muskets from the Asher Arms arsenal, as well as powder horns and shot pouches, which Flaming Bow readily accepted.

The Iroquois were a fierce, fighting lot, as both Falcon and Flaming Bow had learned only too recently. Falcon felt a mountain of guilt as Flaming

Bow disappeared into the forest. He prayed to God that Flaming Bow truly understood his position. A year ago, when he'd readily gone in pursuit of his captured blood brother, he had not been a husband and father. Today, Tamara and his daughter were his most precious treasures. Their safety and well-being took precedence even over his blood brother and his terrible thirst for vengeance against the Iroquois.

Falcon turned from the silent timber line and saw his dear Tamara, her arms wrapped lightly around a support post of the porch. She had gently dropped her head, and her eyes held him in a worried gaze. He smiled, then approached and unwrapped her arms from the post to guide them to his neck. Their foreheads touched ever so lightly.

"And what is my favorite girl doing up so early?" he whispered, touching his lips to her warm cheek.

"Dearly hoping," she answered unhesitatingly, "that you would not leave with Flaming Bow. Did you . . . want to, Falcon?"

"I did not," he replied with her same haste. "I never even thought about leaving my family unprotected. I have set different priorities, Tamara. You and my little Becky . . . you are more important to me than anything," he continued quietly. "Now . . . my love . . . walk with me to the stables. I must single out a couple of horses to keep on the estate. Come, you may help me choose them."

Together they went. It did not take long to select a pair of matching bay mares. Thereafter, Tamara remained at the stables for a few hours, watching Falcon work with the horses. She returned to the house only when Fedora called to her advising that the baby was ready to be fed. Tamara still enjoyed spending this special time with her daughter, although she had not been able to breast-feed and had been forced to resort to goat's milk from a bottle. She had given birth to a healthy baby daughter and so would not hold this oversight against Mother Nature.

She busied herself throughout the afternoon, catching up on neglected financial ledgers, sorting wages for their employees and, on a more domestic note, reorganizing the pot-and-pan cupboard in the kitchens. "Efficiency," she said with a smile, when Mrs. Upwood's arched eyebrow hinted that an explanation was due.

She retired early that evening and spent an hour in a perfumed bath. Then, pulling on her silkiest bed gown as she awaited Falcon, she propped herself against a stack of downy pillows with the ledgers that still required a bit of work. She became discouraged when, through her own carelessness, the ink well tipped over, spilling its contents like black syrup upon the ivory carpet. She abandoned the project for the time being.

She looked around her bedchamber for a moment. It was a bright, happy place, even with the shadows of night flickering across peach-colored walls and clean white ceilings. It was a happy place because Falcon shared it with her. Her happiest moments, aside from being with her new daughter, were the times she spent with Falcon in this room. For a moment she bathed in the glow created by her thoughts of him.

She had closed her eyes for a moment and had lightly drifted off to sleep when she heard the faraway sound of a door being opened. Presently, her chamber door opened, and she saw the tall, familiar form of Falcon entering the dimly lit chamber. She could tell that he was exhausted as he slowly began to remove his clothing.

"Mrs. Upwood has drawn you a bath," she whispered, noticing through the thin veil of darkness how his muscles jumped. "I didn't mean to startle you."

He discarded his shirt, then sat on the edge of the bed to remove his boots. His wide, strong back glowed in the dim light of the lamp. "You didn't startle me," he replied after a moment. "I merely thought you'd be asleep and hadn't expected you to speak."

She touched his muscles, which were moist from his labors. "You're exhausted, Falcon. Bathe quickly, then come to bed and get a good night's sleep."

His eyes, however, turned and gazed at her with a familiar look that intimated anything but sleep. Then he smiled. "Sleep . . . we'll see, Tamara, how exhausted I really am." Then he dropped to his knees beside the bed and roughly drew her to him. "I might be in a mood," he continued, capturing her mouth in a tender kiss, "to make another baby—"

Tamara pulled away with feigned indignation. "And I've got better things to do, husband, than that!"

Laughing, he again drew her close. "What could be better," he gently mocked her, "than making love and making babies?"

Tamara tousled his dark hair. "Perhaps . . ." she teased, her smile changing immediately to a gentle one . . . almost a sad one. "I was so worried today, Falcon, when I first saw you speaking with Flaming Bow. I was so afraid you'd leave me and little Rebecca—"

"You should have more faith in me," he chided. "You must know how precious you are—the two of

403

you—to me." Quickly, he got to his feet, arched his back to relieve the stiffness he felt there, then began slowly discarding his clothing as he moved toward the bathing alcove.

Tamara turned on her side, crooked her arm beneath her head, and watched him in the dim lamplight emitting from the bathing alcove. Suddenly, she realized that in just a few days Falcon would be thirty-three years old. She would do something special for him to celebrate the day of his birth. She watched as he shed his trousers, betraying firm, well-developed muscles and narrow hips. She watched him step into the large tub and sink down into the water, where he let his head fall back, eyes closed, his hands lightly holding the sides of the tub. She didn't know why but suddenly she arose from their bed, stealthily approached, and dropped to her knees beside the tub. Gently folding her hands in her lap, she sat and watched him undetected.

Why hadn't she noticed his strong resemblance to Mason Gray before? How could she have looked into Falcon's dark, hooded eyes from her awkward position in the overturned coach that very first morning they had met and possibly have felt fear? It was incomprehensible that she could have been so blind . . . that she could have seen him as anything but Mason Gray's son.

She studied him for a moment, the masculine profile and full, moist lips that so often possessed hers, the ever so slight cleft in his chin, the dark eyelashes that hardly seemed suitable to a man . . . his silky, black hair . . . oh, how she loved the feel of it beneath her fingers. Suddenly, her hand eased out and touched him, and he jumped as if he'd been shot.

"God, Tamara!" he whispered harshly. "You just

404

scared the hell out of me. I—I must have been half-asleep."

"I've been watching you for a few minutes," she responded. "I must be as stealthy as you, Falcon."

Fully conscious now, he took her arm and tenderly drew her toward him. "I am part of the wilderness, Tamara . . . part of Kishke, although his blood is not my blood. You are my beloved . . . therefore, you are part of me. Of course . . ." he ended, lightly chuckling, "you are stealthy. You must be, to survive in this wilderness. Now—" Falcon's mouth met hers in a whisper-soft kiss, then he sat forward as he released her. "Scrub my back, so that we may retire to a more comfortable place."

Tamara didn't even mind that the bath water splashing over the sides of the tub soaked the bottom half of her gown. Rather than complain, she laughed, quickly rose to her feet, and pulled the gown over her head. She stood beside the tub, her ivory skin golden in the light of the lamp, and enjoyed the caress of Falcon's eyes as he absently rubbed soap on his arms and shoulders. She loved the attention he gave her—almost a blind, virginal look, as if he had never seen her before.

Falcon could not believe how firm and youthful her body had become just six weeks after the birth of their daughter. These past five weeks he had seen her bending and stretching and breathing hard—exercising, she had explained, that Fedora had suggested to her—and he had laughed at her foolishness. But she had been resolute and had stuck with the regimen. It had paid off well.

Their gazes held even as Tamara pulled a towel from the back of the chair and held it out, inviting Falcon from his bath. He rose, stepped from the tub, and allowed Tamara to slowly dry him . . . his broad shoulders, his taut muscles and iron-hard chest, his flat stomach and buttocks, his thighs . . . every part of his body was gently caressed by her soft, patient hands. He could not prevent an involuntary tremor of ecstasy as that most intimate part of him sprang to life beneath the damp towel and her deft fingers. Taking the towel from her and dropping it he cared not where, he picked her up in his arms and moved with her toward the bed.

When he had gently lain her there on the soft sheets and spread the thick golden waves of her hair upon the pillow, he knelt beside her and eased his strong arm beneath her head.

"I love you, Tamara," he whispered, his dark gaze melting into her own. "I love your pretty nose . . . your crimson cheeks . . . your warm, moist lips." He kissed each in turn. "That throbbing little pulse at your throat . . . the pink rosebuds . . . there." He gently touched her breasts, then kneaded each between his teeth. He felt the warmth rush over her naked flesh, felt it move with the tide of his skillful, caressing fingertips . . . he felt her involuntary shudder as his hand lowered . . . lowered, then divided the tight golden curls . . . there . . . blazing the trail for his mouth which left kisses across her gently pulsating chest and the tightness of her abdomen. "How beautiful you are there," he whispered, his warm fingertips easing her thighs apart.

"Where are . . . we going tonight, Falcon?" she asked in a moment of delirious happiness.

"We are journeying, Tamara, to a far place," he replied, easing upwards, covering her body ever so gently beneath his own. "Lovers enchanted . . . we do not want to become strangers to our world of pleasure . . . our world in which we are the only residents. Do we, my beloved Tamara?"

"How romantic you are!" Tamara laughed delicately.

"Romantic . . . hell," he whispered, tousling her gold tresses. "I'm. . . ." He bent and whispered in her ear and they laughed together, their gazes holding . . . warm brown eyes and humored blue ones in a look that went on and on forever. There was suddenly a mutual desperation that, without further prelude, drew Falcon like a powerful magnet. Two separate and distinct entities were now one in their deliriously happy little world as Falcon, with a husky grunt, quickly entered her.

"Falcon, I love it like this." Tamara whispered, teasing his face with brief kisses, "It should always be like this. Always—"

Falcon began to move within her. "And one of us," he gently laughed, "would end up with bedsores. But you . . . God . . . you do something to me . . . something wild and confusing—" Taking her off-guard, Falcon roughly lifted her knees, then eased them across his broad shoulders.

This new and strange experience in their lovemaking drew a delighted moan from Tamara. Never before had she felt such a fullness within her and for a moment, with her head propped up by the pillow, she watched the fusion of their bodies . . . the full length of him easing against her. Digging her fingers madly into the bedcovers, she met the cadence of his pounding hips, his hands roughly pinning down her wrists, then entwining his fingers among hers and tenderly squeezing them.

"Do you like it . . . this way?" Falcon asked.

"It is . . . wonderful," she responded brokenly, scarcely able to catch her breath.

Suddenly, Falcon shrugged his shoulders, allowing her long, lithe legs to slip down the length of his

407

arms. Then, retaining the intimacy, his firm body dropped to her soft one, and his mouth covered the pink bud of her breasts. For a moment, his hips did not move, and his mouth teased and taunted and tormented her breasts, her neck, her earlobes, until she could not bear the pain. And Tamara began to move her hips.

"My wild little vixen!" he teased, nipping her cheeks. "Look at you, all ablush like a naughty schoolgirl wanting to be seduced by the schoolmaster."

"You are my schoolmaster," she laughed. "And yes. . . ." Again, her hips rose and she moaned at the painful, wonderful, erotic fullness of him within her. "Do not disappoint me . . . satisfy . . . this lustful female." She nipped his chin, then entwined her fingers among his damp hair. "Before. . . ."

His mouth covering hers took her words and breathed them into his lungs. Then his hips began to move again, grinding, pounding, slowing to an almost dead stop, then, with a sudden burst of superhuman power, grinding against against her hips, which matched his rhythm and pace.

Afterwards, they lay in each other's arms and watched the shadows of night flicker across the ceilings. Neither could sleep, but seemed to be possessed by some new strength that kept them alert. Sensibly, considering the work he had done today, Falcon knew he should be exhausted. But in the twilight darkness she saw his eyelashes flicker, and a gleam of worry in his crystal blue eyes. They had just made wonderful love and it bothered her that he would allow something to dampen it.

"Something troubles you, my love?" Tamara asked.

He forced the worry from his brow with a brief

smile. "Just a strange feeling . . . in here—" he replied, placing his hand lightly over his chest.

"A feeling of doom? Should I—" Tamara sat forward, "check little Rebecca?"

Falcon's hand caressed her back, then settled for a moment on the slender curve of her hip. "She is just fine. Mother sleeps with one eye open."

Tamara regained her closeness to Falcon. "I cannot sleep. I—I have an urge to walk . . . out on the forest trail where we have spent so many wonderful moments. And there is so much that we have to discuss, Falcon."

"And the Iroquois? What would we do if they were to pounce out at us from some dark place in the forest?"

"Poof!" Tamara shrugged against him. "You have posted ten men around the estate. If there were Iroquois within a league of Asher Arms, we would know it."

"And what must we discuss that we cannot discuss right here?"

"Oh . . . things. Just things. Please, can't we go out-of-doors?" Suddenly, Falcon vaulted lightly to the floor, then stood and began pulling on his trousers. "Where are you going?" Tamara asked.

"What do you mean . . . where am I going?" he asked. "You wanted to walk." Securing the trousers, he turned and put his hand out to her. "I'm a very understanding, open-minded man, Tamara . . . but I will not allow you to walk . . . butt-naked. Now! Up, woman! And put on something comfortable . . . one of those loose shifts you had to wear—" Her hand came to rest in his and he pulled her forward, "when our little Becky was due—"

"Why one of those . . . fat dresses?" she asked

with feigned indignation, deliberately trying not to smile, lest she betray her insincerity.

"Because . . ." Falcon pulled her to him, then eased her arms around his neck. She felt his sweet, whisper-soft breath against her cheek. "They are easy to remove—"

Like a happy child, Tamara danced ahead of him on the trail, scarcely feeling the chill of the late April air. She had made a diversion into the parlor and had brought along a decanter of sherry and two goblets. Falcon walked closely behind her like a protective guardian, his fingers linked at his back. While he had not heeded the warning of one of the guards that they should stay indoors, his eyes suspiciously scrutinized the darkness beyond the trail, where moonlight shone in a brilliant path. Billowing black clouds quickly changed shape above them, occasionally darkening the moon, scattering, gathering strength in the sheet lightning that sporadically lit the night sky. And Falcon's gaze kept drifting to the playful Tamara, and the decanter that shone like crimson glass in the semidarkness.

It was very late, probably after midnight. He had not realized he'd worked so long at the stables. Yet he did not feel tired. Rather, he felt refreshed, and still bathed in the warmth of his and Tamara's lovemaking mere minutes ago.

Soon Tamara took a diversion off the trail and disappeared into a thick underbrush. Falcon, who had been watching the shadows of the forest, watching for alien movements that might detect danger, had not seen her disappear. Suddenly he became alarmed.

"Tamara?" She did not reply. He stood for a moment on the trail, listening, hearing only the crickets and the faraway sounds of the forest and the night. "Tamara!" Still no reply. He began to move hastily along the trail.

Then, when he had moved about thirty feet farther, he heard the clink of glass and immediately, she jumped out at him. "Boo!"

He did not hear the mischief in her voice. He heard only the ceaseless, reverberating pounding of his heart. "Damn it!" he cursed, firmly taking her arms. "Don't do that." Then he saw the pain in her eyes, and the smile fade from her full, pink mouth. He pulled her to him and his firm grip became a caress. "I—I thought something had happened to you. Don't frighten me like that."

Regaining her prior good mood, Tamara pulled back, readjusted the goblet and decanter by pinning them firmly beneath her left arm, and took his hand. "Come . . . let us sit beside the creek . . . over here." They found a comfortable spot where Tamara sat, then put the decanter and goblets on a smooth rock. "How many married couples do you know," she continued, "who make love in the dark confines of their bedchamber, then venture into the forest, to drink sherry and . . . who knows? Perhaps carry on from where they left off?" She cocked her head sweetly to the side and met his gaze. He stood just out of her touching distance, his feet apart, his eyes still moving along the dark timber line. "You're not still angry with me, are you?"

"No," he said shortly, dropping to his knees and meeting her gaze.

"Then erase the blackness from your eyes, Falcon. You're like an angry old bear, waiting to pounce upon an unwary victim. Now, tell me—" She removed the stopper from the decanter, then poured sherry for both of them. "I've been wanting to know for a long time, but just hadn't been able to bring it up—"

"I should have known you had some motive for dragging me out here, Tamara. So . . . don't be mysterious. I have asked you many times to be open with me."

"I want to know, and I didn't want Fedora to overhear." She handed him the sherry and watched as he gently swirled it in the goblet. "What you are going to do about your father?"

"We could have discussed this in our bedchamber, Tamara."

"I would rather discuss it here, with the wind whistling through the trees . . . it reminds me of London, and Gray House, and Mason. I want to know what you plan to do."

Falcon touched the goblet to his lips, took a small drink, then settled against a large rock. "I know you haven't brought it up, Tamara, because of my mother. There is so much to consider. She wants to protect her privacy, and she does not want my father to know about her."

"What is there to consider, Falcon? I truly believe that Fedora wants you to know your father. And . . . her secret is safe . . . safe for all time. Why can't you be your father's son, and allow him to believe that Fedora is gone?"

"It would be a lie," he said softly. "How could I face my father, knowing that my mother—the woman he loves—lives right here? How can I allow him to believe she is dead? I must confess, Tamara . . . there are things that you do not know about. Things that have transpired, in regard to my father."

Such mystery! Tamara thought. It was perhaps part of Falcon's way to approach any matter they discussed with an air of mystery. "What things?" she asked, sipping the sherry.

"Several months ago, Tamara, I wrote to my father."

She was visibly surprised. A moment passed before she was able to reply. "And you told him who you were? Why . . . what made you write to him?"

"Fedora and I had discussed it."

"Fedora changed her mind?" she asked incredulously. "And I was not told?"

"It was something I had to do, Tamara, without an audience. Yes, I wrote to Mason, but I did not tell him who I was. I told him, simply, that I was your new husband and that because of your love and esteem for him, that it was only proper that I personally contact him."

"My new husband. . . ." She took another sip, then quickly drank down the remaining sherry. "May I know, then, what you and Fedora discussed?"

Falcon, too, drank down the sherry, then handed her the goblet to be refilled. "We discussed my future dealings with Mason and how to approach them without Mason feeling betrayed after all these years." Tamara handed him the refilled goblet. "I don't know how you'll feel about what I did, Tamara, but I invited Mason to Asher Arms. When I was at the trading post I picked up his reply."

"I find it odd," she replied, shrugging, "that he would answer your correspondence, when he has not answered my last two." She looked up, her eyes glazed and unreadable. "And shall he journey to Asher Arms? And what of Fedora? Don't you think he would learn about her eventually?"

"Mason stated that business prevented him from making a lengthy trip. He asked that we travel to England instead."

"And shall we?" She knew what he would answer. She knew that nothing would be able to drag him from his beloved Delaware. He had taken every opportunity to tell her so. She felt the deep, painful wrench of homesickness for her England deep within her, compelling her to drop her eyes, lest he see the sadness and disappointment that had suddenly stirred behind them.

"Get that sad look off your pretty face," Falcon said after a moment, taking her hand and holding it between his warm ones. "We shall travel to England, and for a few months, my Delaware will have to get along without her favored son." Tamara squealed with delight as she threw herself heavily against him. "You must remember, though," he continued in a husky whisper, "that Asher Arms is our home, and that we shall return here." He pulled slightly back, then lifted her chin so that their gazes could again connect.

"Oh, Falcon," she responded, flinging herself into his arms. "England . . . my England . . . and Gray House and Mason . . . oh, you will tell him that you're his son, won't you?"

"No," he whispered. "You shall tell him. You've known him as a father, and will know best how to go about it."

"Oh, yes . . . yes, I do know how. But," she pulled back and favored him with a happy smile, "I'm sure he'll know it the moment he looks at you. You're the image of your father. Oh, Falcon, when shall we journey to England?"

"In late July," he replied. "We'll receive a consignment of horses early in the month. I'll get them readied for auction, and I'll have one of the men work with the November consignment. We can remain in England, I would think, until early February."

Tamara was figuring in her head. "But that'll be a good four months aboard ship, Falcon. We'll have only two months. . . ." She shrugged her slim shoulders. Two months were better than none. "But that'll be all right. We can do so much visiting in two months. Do you think Becky will be strong enough to travel? I simply couldn't go without her. Mason will be so pleased with his new granddaughter."

"And I wouldn't think of going without her. She'll make the journey well. She's a fine, healthy child."

Tamara nestled her head against Falcon's shoulder. "Husband, you have made me so happy. So very happy." She closed her eyes for a moment and was content to be held by him. The night wind was cool and pleasant, with the distinct aroma of honeysuckle and woodbine drifting into her senses. She felt Falcon's hands move slowly to her back and hold her in a tender embrace. Yet in the same moment, his grip became firm and alien to the moment.

"My God. . . ." Far across the timber line, toward the Indian River, a misty red ball—appearing calm and peaceful from his distance—glowed on the horizon.

Tamara's eyes flung open and she turned her head in its direction. "What is it, Falcon?"

"Fire . . . God, it must be . . . I can almost see the flames from here." He rose hastily, then pulled her to her feet. Falcon felt a fierce, painful pounding inside his chest that made it almost impossible for him to move. He did not tell Tamara that the direction of the fireball lighting the Delaware sky was almost the exact position of Kishke's village. "With this wind such a fire could be disastrous," he continued, deliberately calm. "I'd better raise the alarm. I can't believe the men have not spotted it."

"Perhaps they have, Falcon." Just then a shot rang out from Asher Arms. "It may be nothing, Falcon," she ended, allowing herself to be dragged along. But she did not believe it was nothing. She had never seen such a sight and was very frightened. She did not want Falcon to leave Asher Arms to take the men with him. She did not want the women and their children to be left alone. Suddenly, she wished that she'd insisted that Falcon teach her to shoot a musket.

"You'll be all right," Falcon said reassuringly, as if he had read her thoughts. "I'll leave several of the men here. Come—we must make haste."

Tamara forgot the decanter of sherry, the goblets; she forgot their happy discussions of England and Mason and Gray House. In the wake of this new disaster, she was unable to be happy.

Somewhere across the Delaware wilderness, below skies that were red as blood, thousands upon thousands of acres of forest and woodland were in danger of being destroyed.

She looked over her shoulder as Falcon continued to drag her back to Asher Arms. She watched the horror of it . . . the beauty of it. And deep inside, she had a very terrible feeling about this new, unexpected peril that had dampened their happiness.

*Chapter 27*

Along the smoke-filled, fiery path toward Kishke's village, Falcon encountered hundreds of men from the surrounding Indian River community who had responded to the alarm. Firebreaks were being dug. Trees, many already pyramids of flame, were being felled, and picks and axes cut into the forest around the fire, contained thus far to a few hundred acres. Falcon's first consideration, though, was to reach the village and see what damage had been done. With Flaming Bow and many of the younger men away on their hunt for the Iroquois, the village had been left in the hands of a few older men and the women and children.

Several of the men of Asher Arms were left along the trail where hands were needed to contain the fire. Falcon, after many diversions off the main trail because of the flames, reached the village with only a handful of men. The villagers had felled the larger trees to the north and had dug a break trench, isolating the village on its peninsula against the Indian River. Except for two destroyed adobes, the village had been spared. Thus, Falcon, his few remaining men, and several of the men from the village moved to the north, where the fire threatened to spread out of control.

Throughout the pre-dawn hours, another two hundred men arrived to fight the fire. But as the morning arrived and the fire continued to spread, the exhausted men drove themselves through sheer force of will. Sweating, iron-hard muscles screamed silently in the pain that wracked their bodies. The homesteads and possessions of hardworking settlers went up in flames. Wildlife and natural resources were destroyed. Then, at midday, when a sudden, unexpected storm drenched the rapidly spreading fire, a body count yielded twenty-seven men killed, among them, Watford and Keeley of Asher Arms.

While the survivors returned to their homes, taking the bodies of those brave men who had died, Falcon returned to Kishke's village. The once familiar trails were now bare black snakes twisting among the even blacker countryside, and the trees, just hours ago green and vibrant in the rebirth of Spring were now bare, broken masts against a smoke-filled sky. And Falcon, too exhausted even to clutch the reins of his horse, dropped his head and allowed the animal to take him where it would.

Soon, the battle-weary Falcon entered the village and was immediately met by Flaming Bow, who had been compelled to return to the village by the fireball on the horizon. The somber-faced Flaming Bow put his hand out and firmly gripped Falcon's shoulder.

"You have survived. Good!"

"I am exhausted," Falcon hesitantly admitted. "I—I must return to my home. But I had to make sure that everything was all right here first."

Flaming Bow smiled sadly. "My father has decided to begin his final journey—"

The exhaustion forgotten, Falcon's head snapped

up in a new burst of energy. He was well aware of the custom of aging Indians to begin a "journey of death" when they felt their usefulness had ended. "Where is he?" Falcon asked.

Flaming Bow dropped his hand from Falcon's shoulder. "He is at his adobe, gathering together the things he needs for the journey. Do not interfere, Falcon. It is his decision."

"And it is my decision to see him," Falcon argued flatly, walking past his blood brother. Falcon entered the adobe and immediately saw the small, bent outline of Kishke kneeling beside his sleeping mat. Falcon approached, then also dropped to his knees. He put his hand on Kishke's shoulder. "What troubles you, Father?"

No expression moved the dark, lined face as his eyes met Falcon's. "I have outlived my purpose, Falcon."

"Why do you think this?"

Kishke dropped his hands, then outstretched them, palms up. They were black and burned. "In these hands I took limbs still red with fire. A sensible young man would not have done this. I took in these hands one of the axes brought by the white men, and I could not lift it to cut the trees. A strong man would have been able to lift it." A thin, bony finger rose and lightly touched the lined skin beside his right eye. "I looked to the flames with these eyes, and I saw only a blur. Good eyes would have been able to see." Defeatedly, his hands dropped to his buckskin-covered thighs. "I tried to run with these old legs, Son, and they shuffled along like a lame old woman's . . . to think with this old head, and my thoughts were like scattering crows. My village needs a young man like Flaming Bow. It is time that I began my journey. I am ready," his gaze held steadfastly to

Falcon's, "to be with my people who have gone before me. Perhaps the Great Spirit shall see fit to give me spiritual strength, and I can protect them . . . there in the happy hunting ground . . . as I was unable to protect my village from his wrath upon this earth. It was an invitation to me to begin my journey, and I must heed it."

"Lightning could strike anywhere, Kishke, even Asher Arms," Falcon argued. "The village was saved."

"The women and the children and the other men saved the village. Not Kishke."

Falcon met the old Indian's unblinking gaze. "And my mother?" he quietly questioned. "Should you not discuss this with her?"

"This once," Kishke replied without a moment's hesitation, "I shall not confer with your mother."

"You are her husband," Falcon reminded him bitterly.

"Your mother—my wife—is a survivor. I do not leave her alone. You will tell her, Son, that my heart is hers. She will understand."

Falcon saw determination in Kishke's gaze, and pride such as he had seen before, but never so intensely. He loved his man who had been a father to him, and it broke his heart that Kishke had lost confidence in himself. Falcon knew that he could say nothing to dissuade him from this suicidal mission he planned to undertake. To even attempt to do so would be an insult. Thus, Falcon's hand fell lightly to Kishke's shoulder.

"Then I shall pray, Father, that you find the peace you seek on this final journey."

A smile so brief as to be nonexistent touched Kishke's craggy features. "You are my true son, Falcon . . . the brother of my son and of my daughter. I pray that you remain a part of their lives."

420

"Always . . . as long as I live . . . I will not forget my family here."

Falcon rose, then offered his hand to Kishke. But Kishke, eyeing it with disapproval, struggled to his feet without Falcon's assistance. Together they walked into the midday sun, where Flaming Bow stood holding the reins of the white stallion that would take Kishke away from them. In the Indian custom, its flanks and shoulders had been painted with the Lenape death symbols.

Just before he mounted, Kishke took the peace pipe he had brought with him and held it out to Flaming Bow. "You are now chief of the Lenapes," he said. "And remember, son, when your thoughts struggle within you, that it is peace that builds nations . . . not arrogance, greed and war." Then Kishke turned, gently cupped his daughter's sad face between his palms, and stepped up to a rock placed beside his horse. With only the slightest exertion, he straddled the fringed buckskin blanket across the stallion's back. The men, with their women and children, created a walled path of respect and farewell through which Kishke turned his horse. They sang the death songs, chanted the death chants. Then it was over and the stallion disappeared over the charred hill east of the Indian River.

Two hours later, Kishke dismounted the stallion at a peninsula far down from the village. He stood for a moment, then dropped the reins of the stallion and spoke aloud a final prayer to the Great Spirit. With a sad smile he slowly moved into the shallow waters of the Indian River and, in a matter of moments, the swift undercurrents carried him on a journey far, far away from the village and the children he had loved.

\* \* \*

Tamara was sick at heart. There was much sadness at Asher Arms as the wives and families of the two men killed by the fire prepared for their burials. Weldon Upwood had assured her that Falcon was all right, but at eight o'clock in the evening he still had not returned to the estate.

Thus, she dawdled around the house, eventually finished updating the ledgers, then went through a stack of invoices that Falcon had brought from the trading post on his last journey. And there, mixed among the accounts of their indebtedness, was a letter from Mason, apparently overlooked by Falcon. Quickly, Tamara broke the Gray family seal, then unfolded the one-page letter.

My dearest Tamara,

My deepest sympathies in the recent death of your dear father.

In other matters, dear girl, you have deeply aroused my curiosity by your questions over the past two years. It leads me to believe that, perhaps, things are not as you would have me think. I believe you to be happy with the young man who is now your husband, yet you seem obsessed with my past. Dear child, I have wished many, many times that I had not told you of Fedora and my son. I treasure my memories of these two dear people. I treasure the things you sent me of Fedora's, but I have put them away, in the special room you once visited, and I am going forward with my life. I pray you shall see fit to do the same.

It was with great happiness that I received correspondence from your husband. New business—I have purchased the Greater Southampton Shipping Company this past year—has kept me deeply engaged and prevents me from journeying to America at this time. I pray your husband accepts the invitation I sent him to journey to England. I have a business proposition that may be of interest to him.

Tamara, you are a daughter to me, and I pray that by year's end you and your new husband shall see fit to be my guests at Gray House for whatever length of time you wish to remain.

Affectionately,
Mason

Postscript: Robert Pickford died under mysterious circumstances in '24. I am surprised that my beloved Fedora even knew his name.

Tears moistened Tamara's eyes. She had hoped beyond all hope that Fedora had been wrong about the death of that vindictive man. When Fedora had told her about Robert's death, it had all seemed a setup contrived to force Fedora and her son away from their homeland. But here it was, in black and white, in Mason's own hand . . . *Robert Pickford died under mysterious circumstances* . . . . Technically and unjustifiably, Fedora was a murderess in her beloved England. Providence had intervened so many years ago. Indeed, had Mason found Fedora and brought her back to England, it might have meant Fedora's death at the hands of an executioner.

In the silence of the parlor, while she sat at the desk and her trembling hands held Mason's latest correspondence, she vowed to put the issue of Robert Pickford to rest. Fedora wanted it that way. She had made Delaware her home for many years and had been happy at Asher Arms these past few months. She had a new granddaughter. Perhaps it was best to forget about reuniting her with Mason. It would probably only further confuse matters. Oh, but she wished Fedora would be more reasonable! Perhaps the true version of Robert Pickford's death had since been learned and Fedora's name had been cleared. Why did she continue to be so skeptical?

So many questions and so few answers. But Tamara knew Fedora well enough by now to know she would remain resolute. Perhaps if Tamara tried very, very hard, she could put the matter to rest once and for all.

At that precise moment, with her thoughts running away with her, the dark-clothed Falcon stealthily entered the parlor. Inctinctively, she smiled for him.

Tamara saw his exhausted face and the smile he barely returned. She was pleased that even though he was very tired he loved her enough to favor her with an adoring look. She hastily arose, crossed the room, and threw herself heavily into his arms. "I was so afraid for you," she whispered, disregarding the sooty blackness that dirtied her cream-colored gown. "We lost two men, but I'm sure that you're aware of it."

"Yes," he replied shortly.

Tamara drew back, then coaxed him to the comfortable chair beside the hearth, where a large vase of roses had been placed. But he was hesitant to sit, in view of his dirty clothing. "It's all right," she coaxed. "The chair needs to be cleaned anyway." Tamara dropped to her knees beside him. "There were other casualties, I understand?" she questioned grimly.

"A few," Falcon replied, enfolding the hand she rested gently on his chest. "It is expected in such a disaster that a few good men will be lost." Falcon smiled a very brief, sad smile. "Kishke died." He added no detail, but simply left it at that.

"I am so sorry," she replied. "I know how much he meant to you."

"Yes . . . Flaming Bow is now chief. Yet he remains determined to track the Iroquois war party reported to be in the area. I wish to disperse some of our men to the village until Flaming Bow returns. Several have volunteered. And I must tell Mother about Kishke."

"I heard you, Son." Slowly, Fedora entered the room, her hands tucked into the large paniers of her dress. Strangely, she showed no emotion. "He had lived a good life. And he was happy."

Falcon rose, then put his hand out to her. "Do you wish to know how he died?"

"I will assume that he died as a result of the fire, Falcon. I wish to hear no other version. If there is another, then simply do not tell me." When for a moment his silent gaze met hers, she knew what Kishke had done. He had mentioned it once, just before they had parted. Thus Fedora turned and soon disappeared into the corridor.

Falcon's gentle gaze met Tamara's. "She is very brave," he said.

"The bravest," she agreed. "She will be all right, Falcon. Don't worry about her."

Falcon gently squeezed Tamara's hand. "I don't know what I would do without you," he said fondly. "Without you and little Becky, I wouldn't want to go on. Tamara . . ." He had a strange look in his eyes—a look that bewildered her and made her wonder what was on his mind. "I know I had told you last evening that we would journey to England in the autumn—"

Tamara drew a trembling hand to her throat. "Oh,

Falcon," she whispered. "You haven't changed your mind, have you?"

Falcon took her hand and held it in a gentle embrace against his chest. "Good God no, Tamara. I am suddenly confronted by a desperation to know my true father . . . to know Mason Gray. I have talked to Hawley at the stables, and he is agreeable to completing the training of the horses. What would you say if we departed, say, by the end of May?"

"A month . . . oh, Falcon!" She drew close, to feel the tenderness of his fingers entwined among her golden tresses. "That means we could see Mason in three or four months. I—I just can't believe it. I am going home to England!"

"*We* are going home" he softly amended, "to our father—yours and mine. And you," he continued, forcing a gentle laugh, "must figure a way to tell Mason Gray who I am. I do want him to know. I will not live a lie in the face of my father. Except for you and my daughter, and of course, Fedora, he is the most important person in the world to me."

"I will . . . yes, I know exactly how to go about it. It's like a mad, scheming plan inside my head, and I cannot wait for it to reach fruition. I can't wait to see Mason's face. Oh, I do wish that Fedora would accompany us!"

"That is impossible," Falcon replied.

"Yes, I know. I still wish there was a way."


Mason Gray had been all aglow for the past two and-a-half months, digesting the possibility that Tamara and her new husband might journey to London to be with him. Anticipating their visit, he had made plans and had gone about making arrangements for his various business for the next year so that whenever Tamara and her husband arrived, he would be able to spend a day or two each week enjoying their company.

He had also gathered together Tamara's various correspondence over the past two years and had made written notes of her questions and subjects of inquiry insofar as Fedora and his child were concerned. True, he had stated in his last letter that he would allow them to rest peacefully in his memories. But he could not help thinking that Tamara had another motive for keeping this area of interest alive. He had quietly adopted the silent law that what she didn't know wouldn't hurt her.

The morning he made the decision to look further into the matter of Robert Pickford, he spent an hour or two in the locked room on the third floor. He sat among the easels, dried paints, and canvases stacked against the wall, reminiscing on the days before his need to have this room when Fedora had always been within calling distance. He remembered her smiling green eyes and silken waves of waist-length hair. He remembered following her like a love-struck puppy, and always finding a reason to summon her to him. He remembered her gentle indignation and the smiles that always followed it.

Fedora, being the most sensible of the two, had tried at first to dissuade his amorous attentions, pleading the wide gap in their social classes. But Mason, a smooth talker desperately in love with this gentle serving girl, always managed to bring her around to his way of thinking. He remembered the time that she had quit her service to Mason's father in an effort to avoid the frequent confrontations with Mason and had briefly taken a domestic position on the north side of London. But Mason had found her and she had reluctantly returned to Gray House. Just a week thereafter they had journeyed to Scotland to be married in a secret ceremony. If it hadn't been for Robert Pickford, Mason's father may never have found out about them.

Oh, the reminiscences! Would he ever be able to roust her lovely features from his memories? Slowly, Mason rose, relocked his secret room and, when summoned to his noonday meal, sat and absently picked at it until it scarcely resembled the meticulous plate that had been set before him. Tamara had asked about Robert Pickford. He was obsessed with knowing why.

Thus, in the afternoon Mason made a surprise visit to the home of Robert Pickford's widow, Julia. Julia, who had never remarried, had not been treated fairly by the passage of time. She was fifty-four, but old beyond her years, with loose hanging jowls and pepperings of gray hair protruding from a bright red, tightly curled wig. She looked something like a caricature of ancient royalty, with many strands of jewels dangling from her neck and wrists. Nevertheless she was hospitable and directed her maid to make a fresh pot of tea.

"To what do I owe this honor?" Julia Pickford greeted.

"It has been a very long time," Mason replied. "It is time to rebuild the burned bridges and renew old acquaintances."

"It has been over thirty years," Julia reminded him with only the slightest hint of mockery in her voice. "Tell me," she settled back and, for a moment, her silence compelled his gaze to meet hers. "You have some special reason for visiting me, eh? What with your many enterprises, a new one, I understand, in Southampton, and your activities in the

Parliament, I would hardly expect you to have time to visit a ghost from your past."

She was right, of course. He had been much too busy and could not sensibly account for his visit this morning. And he could tell by the narrowing of her eyes that she saw right through him. Thus he felt he should come right to the point. "I would like to know about Robert, Julia, in the days after we ceased to be on speaking terms."

"May I ask why?"

"It is important to me," Mason replied, standing. "If you do not wish to talk to me about this, I shall certainly understand."

A plump, lily-white hand fluttered at Mason. "Sit, Mason, I shall tell you anything you want to know about Robert." The maid brought a silver tray and set it on the table between them. Silently, Julia poured two cups of cinnamon tea, sweetened them, and handed one to Mason. "I really am not sure what you want to know," she began in a husky voice. "I do know that the abandonment of your friendship was a lethal blow to Robert. He never quite got over it."

"He betrayed me," Mason replied unhesitatingly. "I confided in him—my closest friend—and he betrayed me to my father."

For a moment, Julia looked around the well-furnished but gaudily adorned parlor of her London home. She thought about her brother, and what would have happened in the family if he had taken a serving girl as a wife. It would have been as disasterous, perhaps, as the ousting of Fedora Hartley by Mason Gray's father. Then, she quietly looked back to Mason. "Robert was not the traitor, Mason. You betrayed your social class and your father. You rebelled against taking a wife suitable to your station, and Robert did the only thing he could do. You had made a mistake, and Robert wanted only to help you out of it.''

Mason dropped his head. "He accomplished only breaking my heart, Julia. My wife and son were more precious to me than anything.''

"Your wife," Julia replied, sitting forward, her dark gaze boring into Mason's, "murdered Robert. How could you forget that?''

Mason could not prevent his shocked look. He felt himself begin to shake so violently that he was forced to return the teacup to the table. "I—I never knew anything about this," he mumbled. "And I certainly do not believe it.''

"It is true. When Robert journeyed to Northampton to see your wife—''

"Why would Robert want to bother? He had accomplished his purpose and had torn us apart. Why couldn't he have left well enough alone? And how did this . . . this alleged act of murder take place?''

"I had only the information contained in a letter from Master Walworth in Northampton—''

"May I see this letter?''

Julia shrugged her shoulders. "The letter burned when the east wing of this house burned . . . .'' Julia Pickford again settled back, then linked her fingers and let them fall to the thick folds of her gown. "I understood many years ago that your wife and child had died in America. What good can come of dragging all this from the gutters now, Mason?''

"We are not dragging anything from gutters!'' Mason immediately retorted. "I knew nothing—absolutely nothing—of this alleged act of murder.''

Julia was now the one to look surprised. "Then I am very sorry. I had no idea.''

"Tell me, Julia, what you remember of the letter you received."

Drawing a crooked index finger to her chin, she sat for a moment in silence. "It was from Master Stephen Walworth," she eventually began, "and stated only that Robert had died following a fall at his home in Northampton. It stated that the woman responsible—your wife—had been properly dealt with and that in view of the extenuating circumstances surrounding Robert's death, she had been indentured to an American for the remainder of her life. The letter stated that justice would better be served in that manner than by having the woman hanged. My confidence was solicited and I did not argue," she continued, dropping her eyes, "because Robert was dead and you had been his closest friend. I could see no purpose being served in your wife being hanged for Robert's death."

Mason sadly shook his head. "I just can't believe this, Julia. With your permission—as Robert's widow and sole survivor—I wish to look further into this matter."

"Then you must see the new master of Park House, Master Shelley Walworth."

"He was but a child when all this transpired. What could he possibly tell me?"

"That I cannot tell you," Julia replied, arising. "All I can suggest is that he will have control of his late father's personal papers. Perhaps some new information will come to light. I cannot see, Mason, why you drag this up after thirty long years."

"I have my reasons." Mason, too, arose, then gently took Julia Pickford's hand. How sad and lonely she must have been all these years! While she had not been blessed with feminine beauty, she was a gentle, kind woman who now controlled the Pickford wealth. He wondered why she had never remarried. "Thank you for seeing me, Julia."

He left the stately house near Piccadilly Circus, knowing that he would never again see Julia Pickford.

He had begun this quest because he thought perhaps Tamara knew something about Fedora that he did not. Now it had become an obsession with him to clear Fedora's good name. It did not matter that she had been dead these many years. He knew only that the gentlehearted Fedora could never have been responsible for the death of another human being. And, by God, if it was his last mortal act, he would prove it.

Thus, the following week he made arrangements to visit Master Shelley Walworth of Park House in Northampton where Fedora had served his father prior to being sent to America. Mason had not visited Park House in almost thirty years. He was surprised to be received so hospitably and equally surprised that Shelley Walworth remembered him.

Shelley had been nine years old when Mason had last visited the elder Walworth. He remembered a rather plump, obnoxious, runny-nosed boy who'd spent the better part of his days pulling pranks on his father's house guests and shooting peas through a tube at the serving girls. He recalled a rather amusing story that Fedora had told him of how she'd taken him up by the ear and walloped the devil out of him. But now, this same person stood before him, a tall, slender man of forty years, with wide graying side whiskers gracing a youthfully handsome face.

Shelley Walworth outstretched his hand and gave Mason a hearty handshake. "Master Gray, I am surprised that you remember me after all these years. I haven't seen you since I was a child."

432

"Yes . . . I am sorry I didn't make it to your father's funeral some years back."

"Nor I to yours," Shelley replied. "Come, we shall sit out on the terrace and talk. My wife is cutting roses for the house. I'd like you to meet her."

In the following moments Mason met a very gracious lady carrying a basket of roses who immediately excused herself, pleading weakness from the heat. Then he and Shelley sat and chatted about the old days, and Mason, anxious to return to London on the eight o'clock coach, brought up the reason for his visit.

"Sir, I do not know if you are aware that my first wife was employed for better than a year in the domestic service of your father—"

"Yes, I am aware of it. In fact, I remember her. Who could forget such a pleasing face!"

Mason smiled sadly. Yes, indeed, who could? "I have learned rather distressing news just recently. It has come to my attention that Fedora was accused of a murder—"

"Murder?" Shelley laughed. "That dear, sweet thing. Preposterous! When was this vile act supposed to have taken place?"

"During her service here, at Park House."

"I don't believe it!"

"Neither do I," Mason replied. "In going through your father's papers, have you found anything that might substantiate such an incident?"

"No, I haven't," Shelley Walworth admitted. "But there are several boxes of my father's personal papers that I have not touched since his death. Tell me, is the alleged victim known?"

"Master Robert Pickford of London."

"Damn!" Shelley Walworth lurched forward. "I

433

thought the drunken fool had been found dead some distance from here . . . from unknown causes."

"I—I have no facts, sir. About your father's papers, do you think that perhaps you could go through the boxes?"

Shelley sat forward and gave the older man's arm a reassuring pat. "I must journey to Wales for a few weeks, but I shall leave the papers with my solicitors—who will be discreet—with instructions to send any documents to you that contain the name of Fedora Gray."

"Or Fedora Hartley. You can absolutely assure the confidentiality of your solicitors?"

"Absolutely, Sir Mason . . . meanwhile, I would suggest that you check with the Northampton constable's office for any reports of such a murder. There may still be some papers concerning this lying about in a dusty old cellar somewhere."

"I shall do that prior to leaving for London."

Shelley Walworth suddenly remembered something he had overheard—a conversation between his father and another man some years after Fedora's departure from Northampton. "Didn't your wife die in America, Sir Mason?"

"She did," Mason replied.

"Then why this urgency at this late date?"

"I loved Fedora very much. If this black crime crowds her memory, then I wish to clear it. She was a good woman . . . a proud woman—"

"And a pretty one," Shelley replied, cutting him short. "I was madly in love with her myself, at the age of nine years. Even after she cuffed my ears, I remained resolutely in love with her. I think, in a way, that I still am."

Mason took the younger man's hand and held it for a moment. "And so am I, young man. So am I.

Now!" He withdrew his hand, took his cape that had been retrieved from a closet by the butler and turned toward the door. "I can expect those documents soon?"

"If there are any documents, yes, in the next few weeks, sir."

"Make it two weeks, young man."

Shelley Walworth laughed. "Very well . . . two weeks. And sir—" Mason met his unblinking gaze, "I hope you find what you are looking for."

Shelley walked out-of-doors with the departing Mason. Soon Mason's hired coach was brought around and in a matter of moments, Master Shelley Walworth became a blurred figure against a massive brownstone house . . . a house where his beloved Fedora had once lived.

## Chapter 28

Throughout the day, Tamara hummed happy tunes and smiled genuinely happy smiles. She packed for the trip, made arrangements for the management of Asher Arms, and generally secured all matters that could possibly arise while they were away. She conferred with both the solicitor, Mr. Inness, and their accountant, Mr. Marland, both of whom were apprised of the trip and the need for their more dedicated services during their absence. Falcon had journeyed to Lewes and had secured passage for them, the baby, and a nanny aboard one of Captain Paget's ships as far as Norfolk, Virginia, then aboard *HMS Wythe* which would depart Norfolk on May 27th for Southampton.

As the days quickly passed and the time for departure neared, Tamara began to feel all aflutter inside. She closed her eyes and imagined disembarking at Southampton. She imagined feeling cool English soil beneath her feet and drawing crisp English air deeply into her lungs. It had been so long since she'd walked along the Thames or through Covent Garden with Mason. It had been so long since she'd attended an opera or a royal ball, as she and Mason had once done almost weekly. It had been so long since they'd sat on the veranda throughout a cool summer afternoon and discussed everything from good horses to foul weather.

"Oh, Mason . . . Mason . . . soon," she reflected, propping her chin lazily on her palm as she stared out the parlor window.

"Daydreaming again, eh?" She turned at the brisk sound of Falcon's voice and her soft brown eyes solicited a retraction, which was not to be forthcoming. "No need for denials," he continued lightly, "I saw you, standing there . . . I heard your thoughts . . . you're three thousand miles away, in England, I'd imagine."

Coyly, Tamara's fingers linked at her back and she sauntered slowly and deliberately toward him. "Why, sir, I do believe I've been unjustly accused!"

"Have you?" he replied, arching a dark, humored eyebrow. "And don't you employ that drawling Virginia accent on me, dear wife!"

"Why, suh . . . whatever are you talkin' about?" She smiled, then flung her arms around Falcon's waiting neck. "Oh, Falcon . . . I was daydreaming, and enjoying every shameless moment of it. I am so happy. I can't believe that in just over two weeks, we'll leave for England. My sweet England!"

"Yes, and we have only two weeks to attend business," he reminded her, slowly removing her arms from his neck with a hint of gentle chastisement. "Have you made a list of things that still need to be done?"

"We are so prepared," she replied, defiantly returning her arms, "that we could depart on the morrow and leave nothing undone. I believe Mr. and Mrs. Upwood will manage Asher Arms just fine during our absence. We could stay gone a year and everything would go perfectly.''

"But we will not be gone a year, Tamara.''

She slumped for a moment, pulled away, then again linked her fingers behind her. She had tried several times to talk him into a longer stay in England, but he had fought it at every turn. "I know, Falcon, though it won't be me who hurries our return home. And who knows? Once you've met with your father, you may also wish to stay longer.''

Falcon's hands rose to Tamara's shoulders in a gentle caress. "I won't deny that possibility," he said, touching his mouth lightly to her cheek. "Have you found a nurse to care for our daughter on the trip?''

"I thought I'd ask Cassie, Mrs. Upwood's daughter . . . .''

"That won't be necessary, Tamara.'' Fedora quietly entered, carrying a basket of freshly cut flowers and a pair of garden shears.

Falcon, again raising a dark eyebrow, went to the liquor cabinet and poured a sherry. Tamara's eyes followed Fedora as she placed the basket of roses on a small table. "Whatever do you mean, Mother? We must have a nanny for Rebecca so that Falcon and I can enjoy a little time to ourselves on the journey, and once we arrive in England. I really shouldn't expect Mason to employ a nanny. It would be rather presumptuous.''

Fedora gave her a gentle look. "There is no need of a nanny, Tamara,'' she met Tamara's bewildered gaze, "when I shall accompany the two of you to England.''

Tamara could not prevent her surprised look. "But, Mother—we've—you and I—we've discussed the . . . the Robert Pickford affair several times. I

438

can't have you endanger your life like this. I would rather you stayed at Asher Arms, where you are safe."

"Poof!" Fedora approached Tamara, and her arm tenderly circled Tamara's shoulders. "Thirty years ago, I was a pretty young thing with a round, cherubic face—unlined, I might add, and without this—" Her hand lifted to her thick hair with only the slightest glimmerings of silver. "Today, I am a thin, fifty-year-old woman who can go unrecognized among old aquaintances—if I assume another identity."

Fedora was serious! Tamara could tell by the firm set of her mouth as she awaited a reply. She looked to Falcon, who had silently turned away, his thoughts known only to God. "Falcon? What do you think of Mother's proposal?"

She had expected him to be sensible, to adamantly refuse to allow her to return to England. But, unsmiling, he replied, "I think it's a damned good idea. We've been away much too long."

Tamara was shocked, and a little annoyed that he did not agree with her on this very delicate matter. He was not being sensible.

"You see, Tamara?" Fedora said, squeezing her shoulder "My son thinks it's a good idea. Besides, who will know? I shall remain in the nursery with Rebecca, and no one will know who I am except you and Falcon."

"And what about Mason?"

Fedora laughed softly. "Men do not customarily visit nurseries," she replied. "The baby is brought to the man. It shall be so at Gray House. Now, let's see . . . ." Fedora again laughed, yet there was some unreadable emotion behind her humor, akin to fear and dread, but not quite. "What identity shall I assume? Ummm, what do you think of . . . Jane Stafford? I had a friend by that name when I was a wee bit of a girl.''

"Fedora . . . I just don't know. I am so afraid for you.'' Tamara gently pulled away, then fell heavily to the divan. She sat there, unmoving, refusing to meet Fedora's gaze, refusing to look toward the liquor cabinet, where Falcon was pouring another sherry. She did not see his pinched, worried frown.

"Nonsense! I will not spend six months or a year separated from my granddaughter! She wouldn't know me when she returned, and I couldn't bear to have her afraid of me. I shall go to England, even if I must arrange my own travel . . . .''

"Very well.'' Falcon, who had been so quiet, startled both women when he spoke. He then approached and wrapped his mother within the confines of his arms for a moment. "Jane Stafford . . . I like that.'' Just then, Rebecca began to cry. Tamara started to arise, but Fedora raised her hand.

"I shall see to Rebecca. You and Falcon, I suppose, shall need time to discuss matters. Let me say, though, that I shan't be talked out of this. It is something I dearly want—just to be with my granddaughter, and near Mason, even if he does not know I am there.''

Fedora had scarcely disappeared into the semi-darkness of the corridor before Falcon sat on the divan beside Tamara. "I'm afraid I'm responsible for this,'' he said. "I wanted the best possible nanny for our daughter, and I am the one who suggested the trip to Mother. I am the one who asked her to reconsider the stand she has taken.''

"How could you endanger her like this, Falcon?'' Tamara asked woefully. "She is safe here at Asher Arms. What will happen to her in England? Oh,

440

Falcon!" Tamara lightly rested her head against Falcon's shoulder. "We could have taken Cassie as nursemaid for Rebecca."

"But would she have been a better nursemaid than an adoring grandmother?" Tamara had suggested Cassie, Mrs. Upwood's daughter, once before, but Falcon knew that the girl could be somewhat careless at times. And he was overly protective of his little daughter. She and her mother were very precious to him. He met Tamara's silent gaze, a gaze that did not at the moment indicate disappointment. He knew that his paternal vigilance very much pleased her and that she really wanted Fedora to accompany them.

"Oh, but I am worried about Fedora," she continued to argue. "What if something should go amiss?"

"What could go amiss?"

Tamara shrugged. "Someone might recognize her."

"As she said, Tamara, time changes a person. She is my mother, and I feel good about her going. This trip will not only open many doors for us, I hope, but provide the rest and relaxation we both need after everything that has happened. Mother wants to care for our daughter. Be happy about it . . . and stop worrying so."

Again, Tamara lightly shrugged her shoulders. "She is so dear to me, Falcon. If anything happened to her, I don't know what I'd do."

Falcon pulled her to him and tenderly held her for a long, long while.

In the days to follow Tamara learned that Falcon could be irritatingly disagreeable. She was well aware that each passing day that brought them closer to their departure made Falcon's nerves tighter, like the mechanical coil in a music box. Regardless of what he'd said, he was worried about Fedora . . . worried tht someone might learn who she was and tie her to a thirty-year-old crime. These thoughts kept him in constant turmoil as he tried to stay busy around the estate. What would he tell Mason about Fedora? Surely he would tell him that Fedora had died. And Mason would want explanations, to know precisely—the day, month, and year that it happened. Tamara wondered herself what Falcon would tell his father. Would he be able to keep the secret that Fedora—Mason's beloved wife—was hidden behind the title of nanny in the makeshift nursery of Gray House?

As she muddled through the days of last minute preparations and through Falcon's troubles, Tamara characteristically created troubles of her own. Mason believed that Fedora and Falcon had died thirty years ago. After all these years, she planned to thrust at him a son lost to him by time and distance, a son believed dead and beyond the reach of mortal man, a son Mason had never forgotten. Suppose he was reluctant to accept Falcon as his son? Only now, with their trip just three days away, did this possibility even enter her mind. Logically Mason should reject such an idea. Perhaps in one of her frequent letters to him she should have dropped a subtle hint. Tamara smiled to herself. Subtle hint, indeed! She recalled one of the principles she had strictly lived by . . . something Mason had instilled in her as a very young child. "Come right out with it, girl . . . never beat around the bush! If it's important enough to say, then say it!"

Finally, the eve of their departure was upon them. Tamara busied herself throughout the morning with last-minute instructions, packing the baby's things in a new canvas bag, checking and double-checking on the schedule for the horses—the day they would arrive at Asher Arms and the day they were expected at auction. She had made long schedules of things to be done, and now, she went over the lists to make sure she had omitted nothing. She went over the kitchen inventory with Mrs. Upwood, added to and deleted from it, and by noon was confident that everything that needed to be done had been done. All they had to do now was wait for morning light, at which time they would depart for Lewes—she and Falcon, Fedora, Baby Rebecca, and Mr. Upwood, who would return the pack horses to Asher Arms. Once in Lewes they would await the departure of Captain Paget's ship for Norfolk in three days time. They planned to spend two evenings as the captain's guests—evenings the captain would customarily fill with some type of quickly thrown together entertainment. Tamara hoped he would not engage them in one of his boring dances.

Falcon and Tamara retired early that evening, hoping to get a good night's sleep and arise very early, so that they would reach Lewes by the following morning. Normally, it was a good two days' journey, but they were hoping to make good time.

The village of Lewes, nestled peacefully against the Delaware Bay, appeared just over the rise of the hill. The four travelers were exhausted. The only one well rested was Rebecca, who slept peacefully in her grandmother's arms. They entered the village, went first to Bethel McFurder's shop for a short visit, and within an hour a carriage was taking them to Captain Paget's large house on the bay. The dour Mrs. Tweed met them at the foyer and explained that Captain Paget was away for the day. However, their rooms had been prepared and were awaiting them. Tamara was glad that she had not been assigned the gaudy little room with its stenciled furniture.

The following two days were relaxing. The only entertainment Captain Paget had arranged was a croquet game the first afternoon of their visit, to which he invited an old friend and his wife. Otherwise, they enjoyed the lazy days and relaxing nights. Early on a Friday morning, Captain Paget arranged their transportation to the bay, where they boarded a small schooner bound for Norfolk, Virginia.

Falcon had said very little the last three days, but seemed content to be with Tamara and simply hold her close to him. While Fedora succumbed to a bout of seasickness, Tamara and Falcon stood at the rail of the schooner *Starr* and watched the eastern coastline through a misty veil. Falcon held the three-month-old Rebecca, and she cooed happily snuggled there in her father's protective arms.

Tamara, too, was very happy. By tomorrow morning they would be well on their way across the Atlantic Ocean, toward her beloved England and Mason and Gray House, with its drafty old corners and niches, and its prim and proper servants. She thought of dear old Martha, who would rather pull teeth than smile. How she'd missed that dear soul, with her pouting mouth and pinched brows, always immaculate in her blue-and-white serving dress, a crinkled little hat pinned firmly to her thin, graying hair.

Late Thursday evening they disembarked at Norfolk and, despite the fact that most passengers would board the following morning, were granted permission to board the *HMS Wyeth* and settle into their quarters. They had started up the gangplank when Tamara heard her name called. She turned just in time to see Glynnie running toward her, lifting the satin skirts of her gown up to her knees as she moved swiftly along. The ties of her lavender bonnet had come untied and she was trying desperately to hold it to her head as she moved happily along the pier.

"Tamara—Tamara"

"It is Glynnie," Tamara said gleefully. "I must see her!" She half-ran down the gangplank and met Glynnie in a warm embrace. As they hugged each other, Tamara watched the slow approach of Sterling Bain, who eyed them amusedly. "How did you know I'd be here?" Tamara asked, pulling slightly back.

"You had mentioned the *Wyeth* in your last letter, and I had Sterling check the sailing schedule. I just had to see you, Tamara, to tell you . . . ."

Tamara had never seen her half-sister looking so pretty. Her cheeks were flushed in the cool Atlantic breeze, and happiness glazed her lavender eyes such as she had never seen before. "To tell me what, Glynnie?" Falcon and Fedora approached. "Glynnie, Sterling, please meet my mother-in-law, Fedora Gray, and this," she took Rebecca from Falcon's arms, "this is our little Rebecca."

Introductions went around, Glynnie and Sterling admired the baby, an then the quiet Fedora, taking charge of Rebecca, went aboard the *Wyeth* while Tamara and Falcon enjoyed a short reunion with their friends.

Momentarily, the smiling Tamara reminded Glynnie, "You still have not told me . . . whatever it was you were going to tell me."

Glynnie smiled widely, then again hugged Tamara. "I am going to have a baby," she whispered. She pulled back to gaze at Tamara through tear-mois-

445

tened eyes. "Mother told me . . . and I am so happy to be your sister."

"Oh, Glynnie. . . ." Tamara embraced her warmly. "I'm glad—I'm so glad. I have dearly wanted you to know."

While Tamara and Glynnie found a comfortable place to sit and commenced to discuss everything they had not covered in their quarterly correspondences, Falcon and Sterling walked a little way down the pier and talked about business. Several seamen loading goods onto one of the ships watched the two women, and one was so bold as to whistle at them in the presence of their husbands. Falcon gave the man a threatening look. The seaman then turned back to his work and the jeering of the other dockloaders.

Soon, though, the heat began to affect Glynnie, and she and Sterling were required to depart sooner than they had planned. Tamara and Falcon stood on the pier and watched until their carriage was well out of sight.

"Who would believe someone could change so much?" Falcon reflected quietly.

"Glynnie, you mean?"

"Of course, Glynnie . . . she is no longer that spoiled, selfish little girl who used to spy on me from the cover of bushes . . . who looked for ways to intimidate you and generally make our lives miserable."

"That girl is gone, Falcon . . . a lady just rode away with her husband. And, just think, by the time we return to Asher Arms, she will have a dear little one of her own. It doesn't seem possible."

They turned toward the gangplank, then waved to Fedora, who stood at the ship's rail, watching them. She had that adoring, motherly look in her eyes.

They were assigned to comfortable cabins beneath the quarter deck, and after sharing a meal with the captain, they retired to their beds. Exhausted by the past few days of traveling, they slept through the boarding of passengers the following morning. By the time they left their cabins at half past one in the afternoon, the American coastline had disappeared from sight. All they saw were the gentle lapping waves of the Atlantic, and a scattering of gulls against the blinding blue sky.

Over the next few weeks, they met and befriended other passengers and spent long hours engaged in games of chess and backgammon to relieve the boredom of travel. Fedora, however, was content to spend her time with Rebecca, with whom she shared a cabin. She was reluctant to accept Tamara's invitation to join the activities of the other passengers, and Tamara just as reluctantly allowed her to isolate herself. She did, however, spend time with Fedora and Rebecca in Fedora's cabin in the hours after the evening meal.

Falcon had befriended the captain of the *Wyeth*, a tall, broad-shouldered Frenchman his own age, who instructed him in the workings of a ship. Falcon learned about halyard lines and spritsails and mizzen topsails, and Tamara, laughing at her own ignorance, merely hugged him tightly when he so enthusiastically tried to pass on to her what he'd learned each day.

Fedora continued to suffer her moments of seasickness, though not as frequently as when they'd first set sail. While Rebecca slept in her bassinet, and Fedora on her comfortable cot beside her, Falcon and Tamara walked on the deck on a late June evening. The clean, fresh, salty aroma of the Atlantic filled their senses, and a gentle breeze rustled among

447

the satin folds of Tamara's gown. They listened to the calls and commands of the seamen breaking the silence of the midnight hour and heard the laughter of the male passengers below deck engaging in games of skill and chance.

They had been aboard ship for five weeks, and their legs were getting a little sea-weary. Captain LeSeur had said they'd dock at Southampton in three weeks time, and they were eager to feel solid earth beneath their feet once again.

Falcon and Tamara had spent long hours in their cabin, holding each other in the aftermath of love, discussing Mason and the best way to go about introducing father and son. They planned to take it one step at a time and were confident that everything would work out. Falcon, however, was worried about Fedora and her adamant refusal to face Mason Gray. She had vowed to remain the anonymous figure tucked away with Rebecca in the nursery, and Falcon reluctantly had to accept it. Perhaps it was just as well.

Tamara began to spend long hours with Fedora in her cabin. While she knew they meant no harm, the amorous attentions of the seamen aboard the *Wyeth* had begun to fray her nerves. Falcon shrugged it off as "the idiosyncrasies of men guided by the law below their beltlines," and Tamara, although she did not expect Falcon to cause a fuss with the crew, was enraged by the nonchalant stand he had taken. She suspected, though, that Falcon would rather die than admit he was jealous.

Still a little annoyed, she had brought it up again in their cabin while she changed into her sleeping gown and prepared for bed. Falcon had already retired and was lying on his back with his open palms tucked beneath his head, waiting for her to join him.

"You shouldn't let it upset you," he said for the hundredth time.

"I'm not upset," she explained. "It's just terribly uncomfortable spending time on deck with an undisciplined gang of men whistling and jeering at me like I was the madame of a brothel or something. I feel like a—a freak in a traveling show!"

Falcon laughed. "Come here," he gently coaxed. She had just tied the bow of her gown and turned toward him, reluctant to answer his call. She linked her fingers at her back and allowed her gaze to wander over the shadows of the low-hanging ceiling in a deliberate attempt to ignore him. "Come here," he repeated with more firmness.

Tamara sighed aloofly, refusing to look at him, refusing to meet his humored gaze. "You'll just laugh at me," she replied, lifting her pert nose. "Frankly, dear husband, I'm in no mood for it." He turned to his side, supported himself on his elbow, and held his hand out to her. Slowly she moved toward the wide, spacious bed and sat beside him. Instantly, she was wrestled into his arms and she fought him with feigned indignation. "Falcon . . . let me go, you—you brute!" He was unusually playful this evening, and held her tightly, ignoring her protests, and her struggles to free herself of his steadfast grip. "You can be such a brute, Falcon!"

He lightly nipped her shoulder, which had been bared in her struggles to free herself. "Brute . . . yes, perhaps . . . but right now—" His grip became a gentle caress. "Right now, Tamara," he whispered, "I want to be gentle, to feel you against me, to love you—"

Only now did she smile. She lightly flicked her nose

against his own, then touched her mouth to his in a gentle caress. "And suppose I do not want to make love?" she teased.

Instantly, he pulled her across his body, eliciting a tiny, surprised cry from her. "Of course you do," he replied seriously. "I'm the man of your dreams. Isn't it fun," he continued, capturing her mouth in brief kisses, "to feel the rushing waves of the sea beneath us as we soar to those hights? Enjoined, entwined, rocking together?"

"Oh! How crude you can be!" But she had spoken without feeling. Just the mention of those special moments surfaced the desire in her, and she felt the warm rush of bold passion across her bared flesh. Falcon was slowly untying the bow holding the bodice of her gown together, and as it slowly slipped from her arms, he waited for her soft, full breast to fall into his waiting mouth. His masterly hands inched over the curves of her body, lowering, gripping the hems of her gown to draw it upwards, away from her smooth, round buttocks and perfectly-shaped thighs. Her knee fell between his legs, easing them apart, and she lowered herself to him, to allow him to capture her mouth in a long, volcano-hot kiss.

"Falcon . . . wouldn't it . . . be interesting . . ." she whispered brokenly, accepting his ravenous kisses, "to make love . . . with me on top?"

He pulled away, startled for a moment, then he gently laughed. "Sounds wonderful. Tell me more."

Meeting his humored gaze, she lightly slapped his cheek. "Oh, you . . . I should . . . grab you . . . and make you wince from the pain." Her hand lowered, across his flat belly, and her long, slim fingers closed around him. He could not prevent his involuntary shudder of exquisite pleasure . . . of her hand confidently caressing him. His trembling hands cupped her face and pulled it down to his own, to seize her mouth in a fervent kiss. Then, without a moment's hesitation, he roughly pulled her gown over her head and dropped it to the floor.

She had straddled him and her hands moved assuringly over his iron-hard chest, gently raking her fingernails through the thick dark hair there. He started to take her shoulders, to pull her down to him, but she gently shrugged away from his hands. "I am the master this time," she whispered provocatively, "and you are my prisoner. I shall—" She bent and touched her cheek to his, "be the dominator, and you my willing subject."

"Indeed?" he whispered, taking her shoulders. "Break my hold if you can." Instantly, her hand again lowered, to gently caress his aroused flesh. "God, woman," he groaned. "What are you trying to do to me?"

Rather than respond, Tamara lowered her breast to his waiting mouth. When he had teased and tantalized it to peaked perfection, she offered him the other. Her fingers slid through his thick dark hair, caressing his temples, his neckline, while her mouth teased his features with spellbinding kisses. And every time he tried to take over, to be the dominating master, her hand lowered to his throbbing maleness. Then, when she was sure her own caresses had made him her willing prisoner, she moved slightly and slowly lowered herself onto him.

Instinctively, his hips rose from the bed so that he could bury himself full inside her. She moaned and did not prevent his arms from capturing her and pulling her hot, moist mouth down to his. Then, momentarily, she sat erect and began to move up and

451

down on him, arching her back so that she could feel the ultimate fullness of him.

Falcon was delirious with passion and want, and saw her ivory torso through the blur of his sheened eyes and the semidarkness of the midnight hour. He watched her rock back and forth on him, back and forth, lowering herself to him with the driving passion of total abandon. He had never seen her like this. And he loved it.

Then, when he could no longer bear the pain, his arms rose and firmly gripped her passion-filled body. He eased to his side, taking the weight of her with him, just for a moment, breaking the physical bond. With only the slightest adjustment, he was between her thighs, regaining the intimacy and driving himself with full force deep within her. He pounded and grinded and drank in the moans of her erotic kisses, then eased his hands beneath her buttocks to pull her ever so close as he exploded deep inside her like a thousand volcanoes erupting, simultaneous to her own wildly pulsating fulfillment. They did not feel the thick, soft covers beneath their bodies . . . they felt only the misty cloud that lifted them to familiar heights . . . and it seemed like hours, instead of seconds, before they came down again.

Their bodies entwined, their breathing slowed in gentle unison, and a few minutes passed before either could speak.

"I like that," Falcon whispered huskily, "you on the top, like a goddess towering over me."

Tamara said nothing, not even to remind him that he had swiftly assumed the superior position, but nestled against him, feeling his body against her soft, erratically breathing one. Every session of lovemaking was a new experience for her. She knew she would never grow weary of her one and only love.

And she hoped, in the silence and stillness of the midnight hour, that he would never grow weary of her either.

Soon they fell asleep in the warmth and comfort of each other's loving arms.

## Chapter 29

The *Wyeth* dropped anchor thirty miles off the English coast to repair damage to a topmast and backstays. The intensity of the storm the night before had flooded cabins and galleys, and one crew member was missing and presumed swept overboard. Many passengers had huddled together, fearing for their lives.

While Falcon and other young male passengers went topside to assist in the repairs, Tamara stayed with Fedora, bailing buckets of water out of her cabin. Rebecca slept peacefully in her bassinet, unaffected by the noise and the hoisting of new masts among the threadbare canvas sails that had been wipped by the savage storm winds.

The dark, overcast sky threatened another storm. Moments ago, while gathering enough buckets for the women to use in their cabins, Tamara had noticed the pinched, worried features of Captain LeSeur as he'd looked toward the red horizon. Several weeks ago, while dining with them in his quarters, Captain LeSeur had told them a rather horrid tale of losing a ship seven years before; he and eight other men had drifted for four weeks in a longboat before being picked up by another ship. He had lost his ship a mere forty miles from the American coastline, yet the tide had carried him out to sea, toward the Virgin Islands to the south. Perhaps the captain had a reason to be worried, Tamara thought. Surely he wouldn't want to go through that experience again!

What was she thinking? Tamara berated herself. The loss of the ship would mean the loss of the passengers as well. She hadn't pictured herself and her family victims of the sea. Yet her thoughts and fears seemed to focus on Captain LeSeur. She should worry about their own lives, too.

"Look!" Tamara turned at the humored tone of Fedora's voice. She wearily dropped her bucket, then wiped the beads of perspiration from her forehead. "Look, Tamara, I can see the cabin floor."

"Wonderful," Tamara replied with biting sarcasm. "Only a hundred or more buckets of water to be bailed!"

Silence. Tamara met Fedora's gaze only when she saw that she, too, had stopped bailing water. She was surprised to see a tiny smile light Fedora's thin features. "We are bailing water," Fedora gently chastised. "Be thankful we are not condemning our dear ones to watery graves. With the intensity of the storm last might, I am surprised we are not doing just that this very minute."

Tamara felt ashamed. She dried her hands among the folds of her gown, then approached Fedora and put her arms tenderly around her. "Forgive me. I am just so terribly tired. I didn't sleep a wink last night, even before the storm began. Did you?" She drew back and favored Fedora with a smile of her own. "If there was a dry bed anywhere aboard ship, I'd lie down and go to sleep and . . . and to the devil with all this water!"

Together they laughed, then with mute understanding they returned to their exhausting chore.

An hour later, Rebecca awakened, pulled herself
to a sitting position and chewed on the sides of her
bassinet as she watched her mother and grandmother
mopping up the last of the storm waters. She laughed
happily when her mother turned toward her, drew
her hands to her hips, and tapped her toes in mock
annoyance.

"You little dickens," Tamara laughed, picking
Rebecca up when she raised her hands to her, "you
sit there and laugh at your mama and grandmama as
they struggle with this terrible work." Rebecca joined
in her mother's laughter, then buried her fingers gently in Tamara's damp hair.

Fedora had found a damp corner of a chair and
sat down to enjoy a few moments' rest. She was the
first to see Falcon's tall frame fill the doorway. She
smiled.

"What have we here?" Falcon asked. He approached, disentangled Becky's fingers from Tamara's hair, then took her in his arms. "Don't tell
your papa, Becky, that these two lazy women made
you do all the work!" Rebecca held her father's gaze
in a moment of wonder before shyly returning his
smile. Then she dropped her head of short, tight
brown curls to his firm chest. "I thought so," Falcon continued, laughing, "Becky is exhausted by all
her labors."

Tamara sat beside Fedora on the chair, then
dropped her arm across Fedora's shoulder. Their
heads touched. "Is the damage repaired, Falcon?"

He was totally wrapped up in his little daughter.
"Hmmm?"

"The damage . . . is it repaired?"

"Oh, yes, we'll raise anchor in less than an hour

456

and be underway. Captain LeSeur believes we can dock before the next storm."

Tamara thought of the age old warning, *Red sky at night, sailor's delight—Red sky in the morning, sailors take warning*. "I don't know," she replied shakily, "the sky looks pretty bleak."

Falcon, holding his daughter close to him, looked at the two women. "So . . . you have bailed out this cabin . . . what about the other?"

The two women slumped against each other, moaning simultaneously. "I—I couldn't carry another bucket of water," Tamara sighed, "How about you, Mother?"

"Nor I," Fedora replied, gently laughing. "I'm exhausted."

" 'Tis a good thing, then, that I put a couple of the crew on the job," Falcon replied, fighting the hint of a smile. "Lazy women, Becky," he teased, kissing his daughter's plump, round cheek.

In these hours of trouble, Tamara thought, it was good that they could laugh about something. She could see that Falcon, too, was exhausted. Within an hour, as the ship was once again underway, mattresses were brought up from cots and beds and placed on deck for drying out. Bed linens and blankets hung from every guide line and stay. Passengers and off-shift crews found dry flooring throughout the quarter and below decks for light snoozing. And, despairingly, throughout the evening and morning hours, the sky continued to darken and rumble across the watery horizon.

Thus there was much cheering and jubilation as the English coast came into view shortly before seven o'clock the following evening. They rounded the Isle of Wight and briefly dropped anchor at Portsmouth, where a wealthy passenger was picked up in a longboat, then sailed in a northwest direction into the bay at Southampton.

Falcon and Tamara stood by the ship's rail as they docked, and Tamara tried not to notice how violently Falcon was trembling. He was in England, the home of his birth, about to meet a father who had no idea he was even alive. He would have to hide his mother beneath the guise of nursemaid and pretend she was dead, and he could see no sense in it. He didn't believe the poppycock about his mother being responsible for a man's death. She was a kind, gentle woman . . . a woman very much in love with a man she had not seen in thirty-three years, a man who thought she was dead. Through no fault of her own, she was forced to hide behind the assumed identity of Jane Stafford and the title of nursemaid for her own granddaughter. It seemed terribly unjust and Falcon silently became very angry. He had a nasty habit of brooding when things didn't go the way he wanted.

"Falcon?" Tamara gently spoke his name. Startled, his nerves jumped. "The passengers are disembarking. Shall I fetch Mother?"

Slowly, hesitantly, he released her. "Yes. In the meantime, I shall bid farewell to Captain LeSeur."

Tamara went first to Fedora's cabin, where she was changing the baby into clean, fresh clothes, then checked on their trunks and baggage, which miraculously had been stored above the storm waters and had not gotten wet. Then, when Fedora was ready, Tamara summoned a seaman to take their baggage down the gangplank and to find a boy to hire a carriage and load their baggage. When these last-minute preparations made, she knocked timidly at Captain LeSeur's cabin door.

The young cabin boy answered her knock.

"Is Mr. Gray still with the captain?" she asked.

"He is, miss," the bright-eyed boy replied. "Shall I fetch him?"

Falcon, however, had heard her voice and, affectionately tousling the boy's dark hair, stepped past him into the cool English breeze whipping across the bay. Fedora, carrying the baby, had traversed the gangplank and stood on the dock beside the trunks and baggage. She fondly watched Falcon, his arm resting across Tamara's shoulder, coax her along the narrow gangplank.

The Southampton dock was like a beehive, workers darting here and there, loading and unloading goods, chasing off illegal dock barters and mischievous boys who would steal produce out of crates being loaded for shipment.

Tamara had not realized how Falcon really felt inside until he approached his mother and said, "How can you be so calm and indifferent, Mother?"

"Why . . . whatever do you mean, Son?"

"By this afternoon, we shall enter the house of my father where you will hide in the nursery and not even let him know you are alive. And you stand here, silent and unaffected by it all."

"Falcon!" Tamara pulled away from the embrace of his arm and looked at him as if he'd just lost his reasoning. "How can you speak to Mother like that? We have been away from Asher Arms for more than two months, and all this time you have let Mother believe that you wanted her to accompany us."

"He is right, Tamara." Fedora's voice was a sad whisper. "Perhaps I should remain here in Southampton while you visit the home of your father."

"No!" Tamara spoke harshly, sitting on one of the small trunks. "We'll get this out right now, and either we'll all journey to London, or none of us will!''

Falcon wasn't sure what had driven him to attack his mother like that. He was ashamed; it showed in his crystal-blue eyes. "Mother, I am sorry . . . I thought I could accept this farce, you being merely the nursemaid of our daughter. In my heart, I want you to be who you are . . . Fedora Gray, my mother and Mason's wife. I am just so very proud of you. I can't bear the thought of my father thinking you are a mere servant.''

Fedora took her son's hand and gave it a gentle squeeze. A reassuring smile touched her lips. "I was a servant when I met your father, Falcon, and he loved me nonetheless. I was an indentured servant when I journeyed to America with you at my bosom, and I see nothing wrong with being a servant now. It is what I want. Mason must never know who I am. It would endanger both his reputation and—'' She hesitated to add, "and my life.''

Falcon touched his lips to her cheek in a fond kiss. "Forgive me for being such a lout.''

Fedora laughed quietly. "You are forgiven, Son.'' Then she whispered, "And I understand.''

Tamara arose, then smoothed down the wrinkles of her gown. "Then I forgive you too, you—you lout!'' But her harsh words were insincere. She smiled, then threw herself into Falcon's waiting arms. "Now,'' she continued quietly, "there is a young fellow there that I have paid a farthing to carry our bags and summon a hired carriage. Shall we be underway?''

"Thank you,'' he whispered, "for overlooking my abominable temper.''

* * *

They did not arrive at Gray House until well after the midnight hour. Fedora remained in the carriage while Tamara approached the large front door of Gray House and firmly knocked. Minutes went by. She knocked again. Soon she saw a lamp being lit in a first floor window off to the right—Martha's room—then the light moving from room to room toward the foyer. A small viewing door was opened and Martha, seeing only the dark form of a young woman, called crossly, "Who are you and what do you want this time of night?"

"Martha, it is me . . . Tamara."

Instantly Martha cried out, then slammed the viewing door. Within seconds the main door opened and Martha, taking Tamara's wrist, pulled her into her embrace. "Child, what are you doing here? None of us knew you'd be arriving. Dear child!"

Tamara returned her embrace, laughing, greeting the other servants who responded to the sudden commotion. "Is Mason here?" she finally got around to asking.

"No . . . he's in Southampton, possibly until Wednesday."

"We were just in Southampton," Tamara responded with disappointment.

"Come . . . bring your family in," Martha invited, looking past Tamara toward the dark figure of a man standing beside the carriage.

Falcon and Fedora were invited into the foyer, introductions went around, and the servants passed around the now bright-eyed, cooing Rebecca, who enjoyed the attention she was getting.

While bedchambers were being prepared, Fedora strolled through the large parlor off to the right. Tamara saw the sadness of reminiscence in her sea-green eyes. Fedora's fingers caressed furniture that had

461

stood in the same place when she was a servant at this house . . . they touched the mantel over the cold hearth where a brass-framed miniature portrait of Mason sat beside one of Mary Rhee Portland. She had once met the sad-faced Mary. Fedora had never pictured her as Mason's wife, yet they had spent twenty years together.

Her gaze returned lovingly to the portrait of Mason. She had never before realized how much Falcon favored him. That alone would shock the unwary Mason.

So little had changed in the house that Fedora felt a sudden chill cross her shoulders, as if the ghosts of yesterday flew back to her. How sad and lonely Mason must have been in this drafty old house. Fedora felt tears moisten her eyes, yet they dried instantly when she spied a large portrait of Mason's father tucked around a dark corner of the parlor. Her mouth pressed into a thin, angry line as her eyes swept over the stern, immovable, evil features of the man who had forced her away from the only man she had ever loved.

"Fedora?" Tamara quietly spoke her name. "The bedchambers are prepared. Rebecca may sleep in her bassinet tonight. In the morning, Jacobs will bring down Ryan's old crib from the attic and polish it up."

"Jacobs?" Alarm lit Fedora's eyes. "Ezra Jacobs?"

"Why . . . yes. What is wrong, Fedora? You look als if you've seen a ghost."

"No" she replied, "he may see the ghost. Jacobs and I served this house together when I was young. He may recognize me."

Tamara laughed hesitantly. "Jacobs wouldn't recognize a hen from a horse," she countered politely. "He's blind as a bat!"

Fedora patted her hand, then both women moved toward the stairs. "Just show me to my bedchamber. I am anxious to tuck myself in for the duration of my stay. But, please—" Fedora halted, then turned and took Tamara's hands gently between her own. "I want to see you every day, Tamara. I want you to tell me everything about Mason . . . what he is doing, where you will be going with him . . . how he looks and feels."

Tamara, smiling, lightly touched her cheek to Fedora's. "Everything, yes, I will tell you everything, Mother. You can be assured of that."

Everyone retired to bed and slept peacefully except for Falcon. He lay in the wide bed, his palms tucked behind his head, his eyes watching every shadow flicker across the twelve-foot-high ceilings. The chamber was large and well furnished, and the massive furnishings struck him as monsters waiting to pounce upon an unwary victim in the darkness. Falcon felt like such a victim. He almost wished he'd remained in Delaware. His nerves tingled as if there crawled through him a million vicious ants.

In the silent darkness, with Tamara curled up beside him and peacefully sleeping, Falcon put himself in Mason's shoes. Mason believed he had lost a wife and child to an injustice, had thus remarried a woman of his father's choosing, had lived an unhappy life with the woman he had never really loved, and had raised another son. Over the course of the years he had lost his second wife to some mysterious malady, and he had lost his second son to a tavern brawl. The only light in his life had been Tamara, and she had been taken from him by the loyal call of a gravely injured father. For the past three years

Mason Gray had been alone in this drafty old house. He had accepted the loss of his loved ones, and had somehow managed to continue with his life, sad and lonely as it might be. He had buried himself in various business enterprises; had corresponded, as his only happy pastime, with Tamara, who had been a daughter to him; and had pushed all the dark memories to the back of his mind. In just three days' time, he would return to Gray House and would suddenly be confronted by a man who was his miraculously resurrected firstborn son, and would be under the same roof with the woman who had been his beloved first wife. And this he would never know . . . not if Fedora had her way.

"Falcon?" Tamara's fingers slid gently across Falcon's bare chest. His hand closed over them. "Can't you sleep?"

"I—I was just thinking."

"About what?" she asked sleepily, nestling against him.

"Lots of things," he replied. "Nothing really important."

Then, to satisfy Tamara and to keep from having to answer questions, he closed his eyes and forced himself to sleep.

The following morning, he arose early, dressed, and took a few moments before the servants arose to familiarize himself with his father's house. He looked in on Rebecca and Fedora, who still slept, then went down to the library and chose a book from the many Mason kept on three walls of shelves. Soon he heard the rattling of pots and pans and dishes in the kitchens to the rear of the house, and thirty minutes later Martha, who had seen him sitting quietly there, brought him a tray of breakfast.

"Thank you, Martha."

"You're welcome, young master," she replied, unsmiling in her usual way. "What will be your desire for the noon meal?"

"Whatever you prepare," he replied, "shall suit me just fine."

Martha shuffled away, mumbling something about Master Gray not being quite so easy to please.

Tamara still had not made an appearance at noon. Falcon looked in on her and found her still sleeping. He had not realized how exhausted she was. He also looked in on Fedora, who had been brought both a breakfast and lunch tray, and who now sat beside a well-lighted window, engaged in an intricate work of needlepoint. Jacobs, Mason's manservant, had brought down a crib which had been polished to a high gleam, and Rebecca sat on clean white linen, playing with an assortment of toys that had also been brought from the attic.

Falcon was about to pick up his daughter when Martha appeared at the doorway. "Young master, there is a gentleman to see you. He awaits you in the parlor."

Falcon was visibly surprised, as was Fedora. He saw her fingers close tightly over her needlepoint. "No need for alarm, Mother," Falcon said as soon as Martha's footsteps had faded down the corridor. "Martha is old and may be confused. It is probably someone for my father."

Falcon started toward the doorway, then turned back. He started to say something but changed his mind. Then he gently closed the door and moved in the direction of the stairs and the parlor where this mysterious visitor awaited.

Falcon was quite surprised to meet Captain André LeSeur and, relieved, offered his hand. "Up from Southampton, eh?" Falcon greeted warmly.

"Sooner than I expected," he replied. "I'll not sail out until the last week of August, so thought I'd stay in London throughout the month. I thought perhaps you'd enjoy spending the afternoon at the Sporting Club with me. It'll be quite enjoyable, and there are no nagging women allowed."

Falcon, bored of both his reading and the quietness of the house, gratefully accepted his invitation. He returned to his bedchamber, donned a jacket suitable to the sporting club, then lightly kissed the sleeping Tamara's cheek. Giving Martha his afternoon curriculum, to be given, in turn, to Tamara when she awakened, he departed with Andre LeSeur, anxious to see more of London than he'd been able to see in last evening's midnight darkness.

An hour later, Tamara was coaxed from her bed only by Martha's scolding tone. She sat forward, outstretched her arms and groaned lazily. "What time of morning is it, Martha?"

The poker-faced Martha, who had been dusting the furniture, suddenly halted. "It's three in the afternoon, young miss. Disgraceful to be abed this time of day!"

"Where is Falcon?" she asked, ignoring Martha's biting tone.

"He's gone to the Sporting Club with a Captain LeSeur."

"Indeed? And Moth—the nursemaid, Miss Stafford?"

"Doing her needlepoint in the nursery. A quiet one she is, eh, young miss?"

"Y—yes." Tamara's arms circled her drawn up knees. "That's what we like about her. She's quiet and uncomplaining. And she's so good with Rebecca."

" 'Tis a sweet little girl you have there, young miss.

466

Coos and laughs and never cries . . . a noncomplainer, like her nursemaid.''

Tamara smiled. "You see? That's what we like about Miss Stafford. She's a good influence on our little Becky.''

Martha set her dustrag and a small bottle of oil on the dresser. She clapped her hands, briefly linked her fingers, then went to the chifforobe, where Tamara's freshly pressed dresses had been hung. "Let's see, miss, what do you wish to wear today?''

"Oh, Martha." Tamara fell back to her pillow. "Must I rise? It just feels so good to stay in bed and be lazy, and have nothing in the world to care about.''

"You've got plenty to care about," Martha scolded. "A message arrived this morning. Master Gray, it seems, has picked up information that has him all agog with senseless good humor, and he will be home at Gray House this afternoon, his intention to relax before getting back to business. He's been rushing here and there, to Northampton, back to London, to Plymouth and Southampton, and back home again. I can hardly keep pace with him these days.''

Tamara was confused. "Is he engaged in business, do you think?''

"Not that I'm aware of. It's some personal quest he engaged in some months ago. He's been quite secretive about it. Doesn't talk much. I do believe—'' Martha picked a rose satin gown from the chifforobe, "how about this one, missy?''

"That'll be fine," Tamara replied hastily. "You were saying?''

"Hmmm?''

"About Mason. You do believe—''

"Oh, yes, I was about to say that I believe Master

Mason is getting a little befuddled in his advancing age."

Tamara laughed as she swung her bare feet to the floor. "Why, Martha! Mason is a good twenty years younger than you. And you! You're a spry old thing, aren't you?"

Tamara was sure she noticed a hint of a smile on the craggy old face. "Spry, indeed!" Martha replied. "I'll keep pace with you two-legged pups any day!"

Colleen, the upstairs maid, appeared. "Shall I draw a bath for you, miss?" she asked quietly.

"Thank you . . . yes," Tamara replied.

Half an hour later, Tamara lingered lazily in her bath, fighting the need to dry off and dress. She felt she could sleep for a thousand years, yet she wanted to be fresh and clean and pretty when Mason arrived. She was a little annoyed with Falcon. His first day in London, and he was off seeing the sights with his new friend, Captain LeSeur.

When she had dressed and brushed back her long loose hair, adorning it with a small bouquet of silk rosebuds, Tamara left her bedchamber and went to the nursery. Fedora was napping in the rocking chair, her unfinished needlepoint resting in the folds of her tan dress. Rebecca, too, was sleeping, so Tamara stealthily closed the door and traversed the stairs to the main floor of Gray House. She was famished and immediately drawn to the kitchens by the aroma of beef pudding and peasecod.

Martha enter the dining room and set a place at the head of the table. When she saw Tamara, she waved her wrist, ushering Tamara into the dining room. "Come, missy . . . I've prepared you a meal. What with you sleeping so late, you should be made to wait for dinner."

Tamara sat before the steaming plate of food, only

now realizing how famished she really was. Martha had poured her a glass of white wine to enjoy with her meal. She checked on Tamara a few minutes later and, seeing that she had almost finished her meal, brought her a small bowl of rum-poached peaches.

"You eat like that, missy," she mumbled, turning to leave, "you'll soon have the girth of a cow . . . worse yet, of old Martha."

"Martha?" Tamara's voice halted the elderly servant's retreat. "Have I told you how happy I am to be back at Gray House?"

"Harrumph!" Martha drew her hands to her hips in mild annoyance, yet Tamara could not help but notice the tiny smile of approval. "It's about time, too! You've been away much too long!"

Martha returned to the kitchen and Tamara quickly ate the dessert that had been brought to her. Only when she was as stuffed as a Christmas goose did she rise, walk out to the veranda where the roses were in bloom, and stand there, admiring the sweet fragrance of Mason's immaculately cultured gardens. She heard the faraway chants of the street barters—they were as commonplace in London as waves on the Atlantic—the birds chittering, and the mad whirring of hummingbirds diving for the bowls of sugar-sweetened water Mason frequently placed throughout the gardens.

She was so happy to be home at Gray House. She was anxious to see Mason and enjoy those special moments with him, to attend the opera and walk through Covent Garden with her arm linked through both his and Falcon's. She was so eager for Mason to see little Rebecca and to be able to inform him that she was his firstborn grandchild.

She was so eager for him to learn that his son was alive.

So deep in her thoughts, she did not hear the veranda doors squeak open, nor the silent footsteps approach from behind her.

Suddenly, she caught the sweet, familiar aroma of tobacco and turned, her eyes immediately lifting to smiling blue ones.

With a happy cry, she threw herself into Mason Gray's arms.

## Chapter 30

Tamara held Mason tightly for a few long, wonderful moments, then drew back to gaze lovingly over his thin features. How resplendent he looked in his fashionable black breeches and matching waistcoat! Yet he looked tired and had allowed his side whiskers to grow a trifle full. Otherwise, he appeared the same as when she had last seen him. His eyes twinkled with that old familiar warmth and friendliness and instinctively, unable to restrain her glee, she again hugged him tightly.

"What a surprise for these weary old eyes," Mason said huskily. "I had no idea you'd be here so soon."

"But you did expect us, didn't you?" Tamara questioned, drawing back to favor him with her best smile.

"I had thought perhaps at the first of the new year." Gently, Mason touched his fingertips to her smooth cheek. "How I have missed you!"

"I just couldn't wait to see you again, Mason," she replied happily, taking his hand as she sat in one of the sturdy iron chairs on the veranda. She patted another chair, inviting him to sit beside her.

"I was terribly disappointed when I arrived last evening and you were not at home. Tell me about your new shipping company. Oh, Mason, tell me everything. I have so many, many things to tell you!" Tamara laughed gaily. "Perhaps we should take turns telling each other our news!"

Mason gently patted her hand. "Martha tells me that you have brought your family . . . your little one—"

"Yes, she is asleep upstairs. Do you wish to see her?" Tamara started to arise, but Mason held her back.

"In a moment, Tamara. First we must talk."

Tamara cocked her head to the side and studied his suddenly set features. He had something on his mind. She could tell by the way his brows pinched. It was one of those looks she had seen before . . . a look that always worried her. "Is there something wrong, Mason?"

"Perhaps, child, it's the first time in many years that nothing has been wrong. I must admit that things couldn't be better. Do you remember—" Tenderly, he imprisoned Tamara's hands between his. Silence fell between them, and he had a look in his eyes that hinted he might be carefully composing something in his mind. "Do you remember asking me about a man named Robert Pickford?"

Tamara felt her heart beat suddenly cease. "I—I do," she replied. "But we don't really have to discuss that right now, do we?" Oh, but she wanted to think happy thoughts . . . not this gloomy happening of many years past. . . .

At the moment, Mason wanted nothing more than to see Tamara's young daughter. He summoned a world of restraint from within himself, keeping him from rising from the chair and quickly traversing the short distance that kept him from that dear child. But right now other things took precedence. "Yes . . . we must talk about it. If you'll indulge a weary old man, I promise you, child, you'll never again have to hear the name of Robert Pickford."

"Very well, Mason," she replied hesitantly. "You have my ear, but only for a few minutes."

"A few minutes is all it will take." Again, Mason smiled. In a moment of silence, he couldn't help but notice how lovely Tamara looked, and to remember how very much he had missed her these past three years. This old house had been lonely without the sweet call of her voice and the vibrant patter of her footsteps through the gloomy halls. "Over the past two-and-a-half years," he began quietly, "you have constantly kept Fedora and my son alive through your correspondence and your questions. I overlooked your questioning . . . rather, I accepted it as you meant it, with the curiosity of a dear daughter. When you asked about Robert Pickford, I became very curious myself. My past seemed to have become an obsession to you, and I was very troubled that you allowed it to hold you so firmly, and possibly to affect your own life." For a moment Mason grew quiet, and in that time he studied the pretty woman who sat beside him . . . no longer the naive young girl he had reluctantly put aboard ship at Southampton. How pretty she looked in her satin gown and the tiny spray of silk roses in her hair! How soft and inviting were the golden tresses the lay gently upon her ivory shoulders! He hoped to God that her new husband was good to her and appreciated the treasure he had won. She deserved no less.

"Do go on, Mason. About Mr. Pickford—"

"Well, I know this should wait until we have all

become acquainted, but it is not something that would interest your new husband. Therefore, while he is away, it is best to put this matter behind us so that he will not be burdened by our problems, yours and mine. This matter from years past is, after all, out little secret.''

*It is not something that would interest your new husband*. The words Mason had just uttered trickled like a slow moving brook through Tamara's head. If only he knew . . . if only Mason knew how very much Falcon was a part of this past that was *our little secret*. ''Do go on, Mason,'' she coaxed, drawing herself to the edge of her chair. ''Then we can go on to happier matters.'' She could not deny that she was more than a little curious.

''After I received your letter asking about Robert Pickford, I began looking into his sudden death. I learned, first from his widow, Julia, then from Shelley Walworth, the present master of Park House in Northampton where Fedora had last been employed, that Fedora was supposed to have been responsible for Robert's death. I found it preposterous, and I requested that Master Shelley Walworth look into his late father's papers for substantiating evidence.''

''And did he find anything?''

''Not personally,'' Mason continued. ''The only document containing Fedora's name was a bit of tattered paper bearing the initials 'R.P.' and a Plymouth address. The item was sent to me by Shelley's solicitor in Northampton. Thereafter, I made a journey to Plymouth and to this mysterious address. It turned out to be a disgraceful, vermin-infested boarding house. The landlady—quite a coarse and common shrew—informed me that the tenant named Roger Parr had recently moved from the apartment and to new quarters at Newgate Prison, where he awaited execution for the murder of a fellow tenant.''

"Who is this Roger Parr, Mason? And what does he have to do with the late Mr. Pickford?''

"Everything, girl . . . everything in the world. This afternoon, upon arriving back in London, I journeyed to Newgate Prison and I visited the mysterious Mr. Parr to find out what he knew about my Fedora. Imagine my surprise,'' Mason cleared his throat, "to find that Mr. Parr was, in fact, my dear old friend, Robert Pickford.''

"What?'' Tamara withdrew her hand from Mason's and, shocked, fumbled with a fine gold chain at her neck. "Robert Pickford isn't dead?''

"Oh, yes . . . yes, he is now. He was on his way to the gallows when I paid a guard the sum of five pounds to be admitted to see him. But thirty-three years ago he wasn't dead. He merely wished to be believed dead by a nagging wife. He gave up the Pickford fortune and was well compensated by the late Master Walworth to assume a new identity. But he squandered the money on cheap women and cheaper wine, and fell to a life of squalor. He spent several years in debtor's prison, and was rescued by the resources of the late Master Walworth. Don't you see, dear Tamara, my Fedora was forced away from England by a vicious hoax between Walworth and my father. She did not die a murderess, and I have spent six very happy months proving it!''

"Then, she—had she not died in America, she could have returned to England and your arms, and she'd have been safe?''

"Yes,'' Mason replied quietly. "And, by God, if I die tomorrow, Tamara, I'll die content that my Fedora's good name is untainted. Bless her—she shall never be dead as long as I live. And now, we need never discuss this again. Agreed?''

Even as she nodded her head in assent, tears moistened Tamara's eyes. She thought of all the years Fedora had spent away from England, fearful of the hangman and of spoiling Mason's unblemished reputation. She thought of all the hard years Fedora had spent as the wife of the brutal trapper, and the years she had hidden away in the village as the wife of a good-hearted Indian chief twenty years her senior. And she thought of Falcon, denied the past thirty-three years with his father, all because of a vicious deception. She scarcely felt Mason patting her hand like a concerned father.

''Come, Tamara . . . we must go upstairs to see that pretty child.''

Tamara heard him speak, but did not actually hear his words. Her thoughts were far away, across a scattering of oriental carpets, beyond a wide mahogany staircase. Her thoughts were with the unwary Fedora, free of the bonds, at last! She could live again as Fedora Gray, without fear of being unmasked as a murderess or harming the reputation of the man she had always loved. Tamara had not realized her thoughts had made a blank, oval void of her features until Mason's hand lightly fell to her arm. She jumped as if she'd suddenly been struck.

''Let us visit your little Rebecca,'' Mason repeated.

''No . . . you go on alone, Mason. Tell the . . . the nursemaid to allow you as much time as you want with her.''

''You will not accompany me?''

Tamara smiled hesitantly. ''It is getting on into the afternoon. My husband should be back at any moment and I wish to greet him when he arrives.''

Mason did not want to leave her alone with a world of confusing thoughts pinching her pretty oval features. Yet he simply had to see the child he considered to be his granddaughter. Thus, tenderly embracing Tamara once again, he reentered the house and was soon traversing the staircase to the nursery that had been set up in the west corridor.

Fedora had just fed Rebecca a formula of molasses-sweetened milk and a bowl of strained peas. She had then changed the baby's nappy and gown and had sung a song that had lulled her peacefully to sleep. Fedora felt a little sad this evening. She wished things had been different. She wished that she could have come to England without the deceptive cover. She wished she could meet her beloved Mason face-to-face and say simply, "I have always loved you." Yet she knew she could never do that. She would have to accept Tamara's daily visits, and enjoy hearing about Mason and his activities. She would have to be content to see Mason through Tamara's eyes. Oh, how unfair life had been! But she had known when she had made the decision to accompany Falcon and Tamara to England that it would have to be like this. Thus she pulled her chair into the darkness of the window, where evening twilight had dropped its veil upon Gray House. Then she sat, gently rested her hands among the folds of her gown, and lay her head back against the rocker in a moment of fond reminiscence.

She remembered her beloved Mason . . . tall and dark-haired and broad-shouldered, his gentle voice always reassuring, speaking those sweet words of adoration that had made her love him so. She remembered how much he had loved their baby son.

She remembered the light that had shone in his eyes as he had held him gently to him and promised him all the greatness of the world.

The door opened. Thinking it was Tamara, Fedora turned, preparing to speak and make her presence known. But the dark form entering the room was a man, and not the familiar form of her son. For a moment, her breathing ceased. Surely, she thought, it cannot be Mason. Tamara would prevent this from happening.

Fedora remained deathly still, her eyes wide yet curious when she saw the man approach, then bend over Rebecca's crib. She had thought Rebecca slept, but now heard her coo at this new face perched above her. Then the friendly child raised her arms and the man—her beloved Mason—picked her up and held her to him.

"What have we here?" he whispered adoringly. "A bright-eyed little girl who wishes to come to her grandpapa?" Fedora watched in a mixture of awe and fascination and fear of discovery as Mason turned and began to pace back and forth, speaking endearingly to the baby. "You know, I raised your mama as my own daughter, therefore I am your grandpapa. And you can't ask for a better one," he gently laughed. "I can spoil you so badly that your mama wouldn't be able to live with you. But—" Mason continued to pace, "I wouldn't do that . . . no, not for a moment." Mason released a sudden humored laugh, then held Rebecca slightly away from him. "Oops, little girl. I think it is time for your nanny to change your nappy. Where might you have hidden her?" Instantly, he saw the seated form of the woman against the darkness of the window. "Pardon me, miss . . . but your young charge is as wet as a London storm." The shocked Fedora did not move, but continued to sit. "Come," Mason gently chastised, "I shan't bite you. This child must be changed before she floats away."

"Yes, I'll change her." Fedora attempted to disguise her voice in a harsh whisper. "If you'll send Tamara to me, I'll have her bring the child down with her, so that you may spend whatever time together that you wish."

"Nonsense! I'll wait right here while she is changed." Something familiar captured Mason's eye . . . a strand of golden hair caught by a sudden moonbeam . . . a smooth crimson cheek that may once have been youthfully round. Slowly, he returned Rebecca to her crib, then tried to see the seated woman through the veil of darkness that surrounded her. But he could see nothing of her but a thin, dark outline. "Please, approach me," he ordered huskily.

Slowly Fedora arose. She stood for a moment, silently trying to coax her heart to resume its gentle pace, for it seemed it had suddenly ceased beating.

"Sir, I beg your grace in departing," she again whispered harshly. "I'd prefer not to change the child in your presence."

"Poppycock! Come forward, madame . . . please."

Fedora was at odds, not knowing what to do. How could Tamara have allowed this to happen? She could have remained in the darkness for ten thousand years, but the man standing just out of her reach would not have departed. Thus, remembering only too well how persistent Mason had been as a young man, and knowing he would not leave until she had obeyed his wishes, she stepped into the light of the single lamp and her gaze lifted to his.

"Mason," she quietly whispered. "This was not supposed to happen."

That voice . . . those eyes, like polished emeralds . . . her golden hair, like wheat shimmering beneath an autumn sun . . . it could not be. He had lost all reasoning. Perhaps he had died and had yet to realize it. Perhaps this was heaven, as he had always hoped it would be.

"Tell me," he whispered in reply, lightly touching his fingertips to her cheek that unconsciously moved to meet his touch, "that this is really not happening . . . that I am dreaming." Tears sheened Mason Gray's eyes, and he saw nothing of his ghost but a wonderful blur . . . an aura of light magnified, breaking his vision into a million tiny fragments. Then, tenderly, he drew the vision of her into his arms and felt a warm, solid form—a familiar form that had once lain with him in the gentlest of raptures, the sweetest of dreams. And he knew, beyond a shadow of a doubt, that this lovely vision was his beloved Fedora, and that Tamara had brought her home to him. "How . . . can this be?" he whispered brokenly.

The emotional Fedora could not speak, but gently returned Mason's embrace. She had imagined this warmth, this gentleness, a million times in the past thirty years, but it was still a new and wonderful experience. And she knew, no matter the legal ramifications—no matter if she died tomorrow for a crime she did not commit—that she wanted to spend these moments with Mason, her first and only true love. She could not imagine being any happier than she was this very minute.

"I had to return," she whispered quietly, feeling the tears burn her cheeks, "to take back my personal things . . . you do have them, don't you?"

"My letters . . . yes." Mason did not relax his embrace, but tenderly caressed her back through the thick fabric of her garment. "But you do not need them, Fedora. You have me now."


Mason had been upstairs only a few minutes when Tamara heard a carriage approach the front entrance and stop. Immediately, she heard the voices of men, one of which was Falcon's. Before he entered the house, Tamara quickly sought out Martha in the kitchens, where she was putting last-minute garnishes on their evening meal. Martha was visibly surprised by Tamara's request that she be given the keys to the house. Hesitantly, Martha handed them to her, and Tamara sought out the familiar key to Mason's sanctuary.

"Martha, send Jacobs to the room on the second floor posthaste, will you?"

"Martha had seen the key she'd selected from the ring. "I wouldn't invade the master's privacy, young miss," she scolded. "He won't like it a bit!"

"Please, just send Jacobs there. I'll await him." She favored the elderly servant with a brief, yet warm smile, "I'll explain everything later. Promise."

Falcon entered. Tamara quickly told him what had transpired—information that drained Falcon's face a deathly white and pinched his brows into a confused frown. "He is with Mother . . . now?" he asked incredulously.

"Yes, this very minute. . ."

"Does he know about me?"

"Not yet . . . please await me in the parlor."

"Tamara, what are—"

"I'll explain in a bit, husband. Oh, please—" Ta-

481

mara pleaded desperately, scarcely able to restrain her elated tone. "Allow me this fancy!"

Falcon merely shrugged, bewildered by the urgency in her voice and the fact that his mother was, even now, with Mason. It was all so incredible. Suddenly, the guilt of many months was gone. He would not have to deceive his father when they met. He would not have to fabricate lies and look his father in the eyes when he spoke them. A great burden was lifted from his shoulders.

In a matter of moments Tamara returned, followed closely by Jacobs, the elderly manservant to Mason Gray. He was carrying an easel and Tamara carried a large canvas covered by a piece of aged linen. Tamara chose a place in the parlor with favorable light and directed Jacobs to put the easel there. She then carefully removed the linen from the canvas and placed it on the easel where it had sat hidden in Mason's private sanctuary for the past seventeen years.

"Tamara, what on earth—"

"No! Stay there, Falcon," Tamara said, halting his approach. "This is a very important moment."

Then he remembered a night many months ago, when Tamara had told him of the unfinished painting . . . the blank, oval void that should have been the face of Mason's son. He only now realized what Tamara intended to do.

Tamara positioned, then repositioned the easel, standing it in the best possible light. With a bubbling enthusiasm that could scarcely be contained, she clasped her hands like a happy child, then, unclasping them, turned and fled up the stairway to the nursery.

She was just about to enter when the door opened. Mason, holding Rebecca, and Fedora left the nursery. Her gaze moved rapidly between them, then she said to Mason, "Are you surprised?"

"Surprised!" he echoed. "I think I've died and gone to heaven. I—I just can't believe it." His gaze averted to Fedora and held, transfixed.

"Come . . . come, Mason—" Tamara coaxed him on ahead, then asked Fedora in a whisper, "Did you tell him about—"

"Falcon?" she replied, cutting Tamara short. "No. I believe he's afraid to ask, lest he receive bad news."

"Wonderful!" she replied, then whispered, for Fedora's ears only, "Did he tell you about Robert Pickford?"

"He did," she replied.

"And are you happy?"

Mason had just begun his descent of the stairs when Fedora halted, then took Tamara in her arms. "Thank you, Daughter. You have given me the greatest gift of all."

"But, I've given you nothing, Mother."

"You have given me happiness. You have given me back my life. Had it not been for your persistence, keeping the past alive for both Mason and me, he and I may never again have seen each other."

Tamara was quite pleased. "I am so happy for you, Mother. Come . . . I have another surprise for Mason. And you know what it is!"

Fedora laughed, then watched Tamara bound ahead and quickly descend the stairs. Martha appeared, and without explanation, Tamara took Rebecca from Mason's arms and handed her to the elderly servant. She then took Mason's hand and coaxed him toward the parlor.

Falcon stood silently against the mantel. Hearing Tamara's happy voice, he started to speak some endearment to her, but at that moment his gaze met his father's. There was no expression there, only a perplexed look that instantly became shock and disbelief. Mason held the fixed gaze of a man who might have been himself thirty years ago. He had no doubt who this man was.

Tamara coaxed Mason to the easel, then handed him his tray of paint tins and a brush. Slowly, Mason averted his gaze to the canvas . . . to the unfinished portrait of his beloved son, a portrait he had begun when the boy, whom he had refused to believe was dead, would have been eighteen years old.

Emotion choked in his throat. He felt a weakness in his legs that threatened to bring him down. And just when he may have succumbed to the physical affliction, Falcon said in a lighthearted voice, "Let's get on with it, Father. I'm already fidgeting like an ant-bitten puppy." He spoke as if they'd seen each other just yesterday.

In a broken, emotion-filled voice, Mason replied, "Be still, Son . . . I've waited a long, long time. . . ." He lightly coughed, regaining his momentarily lost composure. Then he quietly repeated, "I've waited a long, long time for this."

Tears moistened his eyes. Quietly, he put down the brush and paint tray Tamara had handed him and slowly approached his son. Their eyes met for a moment that felt like a thousand hours to the elder Gray. Tenderly, he drew his son into his embrace, then opened his arms to both Fedora and Tamara. They hugged each other tightly, forgetting all the past pains and worldly hurts.

They were a family, together again, and that was all that mattered from this moment on.

*Part Four*

*Chapter 31*

*Asher Arms, Four Years Later*

Tamara wasn't quite sure where the years had gone. She knew only that she'd been deliriously happy, and there was nowhere else on earth she would rather be than in the arms of her doting husband. They had two beautiful children who enjoyed scampering along the trails of the Delaware forest where they'd been born, who made distant friends with the four-legged creatures that quickly darted out of their paths, giving each an endearing name. At four-and-a-half years, their daughter, Rebecca, was slender and pale and quiet-spoken. She enjoyed spending time alone, writing her alphabet on her slate board, or arranging wild flowers in tiny vases for presentation to her loved ones. Little Jonah, at three years, was the image of his papa, with dark, curly hair and clear blue eyes that narrowed mischievously as he hid among the flora, waiting to pounce upon his unwary sister who was content simply to gather the flowers that grew profusely along the trail.

Tamara and Falcon walked along slowly, holding hands, watching the exasperated Fedora attempting to gather the children to her so that she could keep a closer eye on them. They'd brought a picnic lunch, which would be enjoyed later in the day. The hot July morning was perfect for swimming, and Tamara, knowing it would be impossible to keep the children out of the water, had brought a fresh change of clothing for each.

They had only a few more days together before Falcon journeyed back to Lewes, to resume the business of running the American end of his father's shipping company. Fedora would not return to England just yet, but would remain at Asher Arms to birth Flaming Bow's first child, which was due in the early fall. It was a special request Flaming Bow had made of her, and she had accepted the request as an honor. After the birth, Falcon would escort Fedora to Norfolk, where she would board ship to return to Gray House in London. This trip to the colonies was Mason and Fedora's second since they'd remarried almost four years ago. Tamara remembered the simple wedding ceremony in the parlor of Gray House, watching the reunited lovers renew their vows of eternal togetherness . . . a togetherness divided by thirty-three years of deceptions and misunderstandings. Nothing save death would part them again. Three days ago, Tamara had heard Mason speak just those words.

Very soon, they moved onto the trail that led down to the creek where Tamara often brought the children. Sunlight trickled through the spring-green foliage of the forest, scattering silver threads upon the thick, cushioned ground where Falcon spread the picnic blanket. Fedora went in pursuit of the giggling Jonah, then returned with him playfully fighting in her arms for "Becka to wun wif' me." Soon, their energies exhausted for the moment, the children sat beside the creek and began tossing small pebbles at the quickly darting minnows. Then Jonah jumped into the shallow water and, giggling, tried to catch the fast moving creatures with his little hands. They all laughed and Jonah, throwing up his hands in feigned despair, allowed his grandmother to retrieve him from the water.

So many things had changed in the past four years. Since Falcon had taken over the management of his father's business in Lewes, a branch of his Southampton Shipping Company, the family frequently traveled back and forth between Asher Arms and the recently remodeled fisherman's cottage beside the Delaware Bay. Tamara remained at Asher Arms without him only when a consignment of horses was expected from Virginia. She enjoyed jaunting back and forth between Asher Arms and Lewes. Rather than viewing it as an inconvenience, Tamara felt that maintaining two households kept her busy and on her toes. And the children did so enjoy the long journey along the Indian River and the frequent visits to Flaming Bow's village.

Falcon reclined against a century-old oak, coaxing Tamara to lie back against him. He absently chewed a bit of straw, closed his eyes, and caressed Tamara's summer-warmed shoulder through her thin blouse.

Sterling and Glynnie were due for a visit at the end of August, scarcely a month away. It had been a year since they'd visited. Their twins would now be two years old. The arrival of the babies had done what two years of Glynnie's living at Bain House had not. The feelings of snobbish family members had warmed somewhat toward Glynnie, and she was now an accepted member of the household. Glynnie had held no bitter feelings, but had graciously accepted the attention of those vindictive family members who had once introduced her in their social circles as "that scullery maid their Sterling had married."

"What are you thinking, Tamara?"

For a moment, Tamara was startled from her fond reminiscences. She smiled for her husband, then allowed her gaze to drift across the clearing where the children quietly played. "I was thinking about Glynnie and Sterling. It'll be so wonderful to see them again, and to see how the babies have grown!"

"You know, Tamara, she was very happy to learn you were her sister."

"No happier than I," Tamara replied. "It was a shame dear Saul died so suddenly, yet it was probably his death that motivated poor Bridie to tell Glynnie about us." Tamara nestled back against her husband. "Thank God she is mature and understanding." Tamara sighed reminiscently. "Not to change the subject, but . . . do you know what I wish, Falcon?"

"What is that?"

"I wish Mason would sell that gloomy old house in London and move to the colonies. Wouldn't it be wonderful to know that we could see those two dear souls anytime we wished?"

"I would like nothing better . . . but it's not practical. Father has various and sundry businesses to manage, and the bulk of the management must be done in England."

"He should retire," Tamara quietly reflected.

"And he would wither and die," Falcon quickly chastised. "Keeping busy keeps him alive. Don't let Mother hear you speak of Father as if he's a decrepit old man ready for the grave!"

Tamara gently laughed. "I suppose I shouldn't. I think Mother has given Mason a good bit of her own energy. Yet, that which she retains . . . look at her!"

she continued, her hand resting on Falcon's strong chest. "Scampering among the trees and underbrush after those children! How does she do it? The children exhaust me in a minute!"

"That's because," he tenderly whispered in her ear, "I keep you so busy . . . at night. . . ."

Tamara felt a crimson flush rise in her cheeks. "That you do!" she whispered in reply, again snuggling against him. "But that revitalizes me . . . not exhausts me!"

Slowly, Falcon's arms eased around her slim waist and rested there. He enjoyed the sweet, clean aroma of her loose hair, lying on her shoulders like puffs of golden clouds.

Throughout the morning, Fedora watched the children with a careful eye. She waded in the stream with them, dismally hoping to prevent Jonah from submerging his head and holding his breath, to worry her. Afterwards, when they'd shared their picnic meal, Fedora took the children for a walk along the forest trails, where Rebecca picked a bouquet of wild flowers and Jonah chased every scampering sound he heard.

In the silence created by their absence, Tamara took the blanket nearer to the water, spread it over a thick patch of clover, and invited Falcon to sit beside her. A warm, golden ray of light touched their tenderly entwined bodies. The forest muffled the voices and the laughter of Fedora and the children as they scampered ahead of her. Falcon's arm, resting lightly across Tamara's shoulder, tightened as he drew her very close. Their lips met in a tender kiss.

"I have been so happy," he quietly confessed. "I grew up with a bitter heart and a chip on my shoulder the size of a mountain . . . I once believed that

I didn't deserve this happiness . . . but I do!" he ended in a lighthearted laugh. "I deserve you, by George! I worked hard enough to win your love."

She smiled but said nothing and gently enfolded his hand within her own. Did he truly realize how very much she loved him? Oh, yes—yes, he did! They sat beside the brook that babbled over smooth white rocks, gazed through the thick foliage of the Delaware forest, and watched the sun slowly sink upon the horizon.

The far away laughter of Fedora and the children drifted away for one brief moment as their eyes met and held each other's in a loving gaze. A sudden summer breeze, carrying the sweet aroma of honeysuckle and fresh pine, whipped gently around them.

Life was perfect for them. They had their family, their dear, sweet children, and each other . . . for as long as forever lasted.